Trickin'

Trickin'

Brandi Johnson

www.urbanbooks.net

Urban Books, LLC
78 East Industry Court
Deer Park, NY 11729

ISBN 13: 978-1-60162-512-0
ISBN 10: 1-60162-512-X

First Printing July 2012
Printed in the United States of America

10 9 8 7 6 5 4 3

Distributed by Kensington Publishing Corp.
Submit Wholesale Orders to:
Kensington Publishing Corp.
C/O Penguin Group (USA) Inc.
Attention: Order Processing
405 Murray Hill Parkway
East Rutherford, NJ 07073-2316
Phone: 1-800-526-0275
Fax: 1-800-227-9604

Chapter One

"Ra'Keeyah, get yo' butt up and fix yo' brother somethin' to eat," her mother yelled from the comfort of her own bed.

Ra'Keeyah tried her best not to wake up from the dream she was having.

"Girl, did you hear me?" her mother yelled again, right before Ra'Keeyah's lips met with Usher's.

"Yeah, I heard you, dang," Ra'Keeyah huffed as she rolled from one side of her full-sized bed to the other. "She get on my damn nerves," she fumed as she grabbed her pink, shabby robe from off the foot of her bed.

"Oooh, I'm tellin' Momma what you said," Ra'Keeyah's nine-year-old brother, Jaylen, said, as he stood in the hallway outside her bedroom door.

"Shut up, dummy, and come on," Ra'Keeyah huffed as she walked out of her bedroom.

"You a dummy," he retorted following his big sister.

"I don't know why she couldn't get her lazy ass up and fix you somethin' to eat; shit, you ain't none of my son," she fussed at her little brother on the way down the stairs.

"I'm tellin' Momma you said that too," Jaylen said, as they entered the kitchen.

"Shut up and sit down, snitch!" Ra'Keeyah demanded, and Jaylen complied. "And if you tell Momma anything, I'ma beat you up when she goes to work," she warned.

Ra'Keeyah grabbed a box of Frosted Flakes out of the cabinet and slammed it down in front of her brother and did the same with a bowl and the gallon of milk.

"Momma said you 'pose to make me somethin' to eat," Jaylen looked up at his sister and said.

Ra'Keeyah smacked her lips and grabbed the box of cereal and filled up the bowl with cereal and milk before walking over and turning on the thirteen-inch television that sat on top of the kitchen counter. She hopped up on the bar stool and turned the channel to BET.

"Spoon, please," Jaylen said as soon as his sister got comfortable.

Ra'Keeyah turned around and looked at her brother like he was crazy. "Look, li'l nigga, I'm sicka' you," she said, hopping off the bar stool and walking over to the silverware drawer. Ra'Keeyah grabbed a spoon out of the drawer. "Huh," she said, shoving it into his face.

"You betta' hadda' got me one," Jaylen said, quickly snatching the spoon from his sister's hand.

"Oooh, I can't stand you," she said, walking back over to the bar stool and taking a seat. Ra'Keeyah picked up a *Us Weekly* magazine and began flipping through the pages. "Dang, these jeans are nice," she stated aloud, referring to the ones that Christina Aguilera was wearing. "Available at Macy's," she said, reading the bottom of the ad. "I gots to have these."

"The only way that's gon' happen is if you go out and get a job," her mother said, walking into the kitchen looking like she had been out drinking all night from all the overtime she had been working.

"That ain't gon' happen," Jaylen laughed, before sticking a spoon full of cereal into his mouth.

Ra'Keeyah shot her brother a dirty look. "Shut up, nigga!" she grimaced.

"You shut up," he shot back.

"Make me," Ra'Keeyah challenged.

"All right, already, y'all. I ain't tryin'a hear that shit!" their mother yelled. "And what I tell you about sayin' *nigga?*" she looked at Ra'Keeyah and asked.

"You said don't say it in yo' house," Ra'Keeyah replied, throwing the magazine on top of the counter.

"Don't get jazzy, hefah," her mother said as she maneuvered around the kitchen, making herself a cup of instant coffee. "Now you know I'm gon' need you to keep yo' brother tonight, 'cuz I'm doin' another double shift."

"Dang, Momma, I wanted to stay all night at Shayna's house tonight," Ra'Keeyah whined. "How come Aunt Nancy can't keep him?"

"Look, girl, stop all that damn whinin'. Now, tonight is Nancy's bingo night. She can't keep him," her mother explained. "And plus, I done told you that you not gon' be doin' all that spendin' the night over at Shayna's house. They got a little too much goin' on over there for me."

Ra'Keeyah knew her mother was right about all the different types of activities going on over at Shayna's. Her house was definitely the party house.

"Dang," Ra'Keeyah huffed and jumped down off the bar stool. "I'm tired of babysittin' him," she said walking past the table where her brother sat smiling. "What you smilin' for? I should slap that smile right off yo' face," Ra'Keeyah stated angrily.

"And if you slap him, I'ma slap yo' ass," her mother said, before taking a sip from her coffee cup.

Ra'Keeyah didn't pay her mother any attention. She just continued staring down at her brother. "I can't stand livin' here," she mumbled on her way out of the kitchen.

"I didn't hear you," her mother yelled out. Ra'Keeyah didn't say anything; she just kept it moving to her bedroom.

She walked into her bedroom and slammed the door behind her. "Damn, she act like he my son. Why I always gotta watch that li'l nigga?" Ra'Keeyah was fuming. Her cell phone rang as she looked for something to wear. She snatched it off of her nightstand and quickly answered it. "Hello?"

"What's up, bitch? We goin' to the mall today or what?" her best friend, Shayna, started in.

"Good morning to you too, ho," Ra'Keeyah answered.

"Oh, good morning," Shayna laughed. "Are we goin' to the mall today or what?"

"And you know it!" Ra'Keeyah exclaimed. "I just seen these jeans in a magazine at Macy's that I want to wear to the game next Friday," Ra'Keeyah said. "You know they cost an arm and a leg 'cuz they got Christina Aguilera's ass modelin' in them."

"I bet they do. Shit, if you want 'em, get 'em," Shayna said.

"I am," Ra'Keeyah beamed as she rambled through her closet.

"You still spendin' the night tonight?" Shayna asked as she rolled a blunt for later on.

"Naw, I can't. I gotta babysit Jaylen," Ra'Keeyah said, disappointed.

"Damn, you always babysittin' his ass. Yo' mom act like he yo' son," Shayna replied, shaking her head.

"Who you tellin'?"

"You gon' miss out. We gon' kick it tonight," Shayna said excitedly

"What's new? Y'all always kickin' it. That's another reason why I can't stay," Ra'Keeyah laughed.

Shayna started laughing too. "Anyways, hefah, I'm about to jump in the shower and get dressed. Me and Quiana will meet you at the bus stop at 12:00 P.M. And don't be late!"

"I'm not. And don't forget the big purse this time. You know last time we couldn't hardly get nothin'."

"I got you," Shayna assured her.

"All right, talk to you in a few." Ra'Keeyah hung up the phone and continued searching through her closet. She decided on a pair of black Apple Bottom jeans, a red Apple Bottom shirt, and a pair of red, retro-chic platforms before jumping into the shower. After she got out, she opened up the bathroom door to let some of the steam out so the mirror would clear. She then put on her clothes and started brushing her hair as her mother walked past and stopped. "Where you get that outfit from?" she asked skeptically.

"You bought it, Mom, when we went to Citi Trends," Ra'Keeyah said, keeping her cool, because she knew her mother was not going to let up that easy.

Her mother looked the outfit over once more. "I don't remember buyin' that."

"You did, about three months ago," Ra'Keeyah said, trying to convince her mother of her lie.

"Okay, maybe I did. But if I didn't, I'ma tell you now, you and them friends of yours better not be out there at that mall up to no good, 'cuz if you are, and get caught, you bet' not call me to come and get you outta jail," her mother warned.

"Mom, ain't nobody out at the mall doin' nothin' but window-shoppin'. We don't steal," Ra'Keeyah said defensively.

"I'm just lettin' you know don't call me if you are, 'cuz I ain't comin' to get you!"

"Okay, Mommy, dang, I just told you we don't be out there doin' nothin' but window-shoppin'," Ra'Keeyah said as her mother walked away.

Ra'Keeyah finished doing her hair and applying her makeup before spraying on a few squirts of her sample bottle of Love Chloe perfume that she'd snatched off the counter at Nordstroms. She turned around to check out her backside before walking out of the bathroom.

Ra'Keeyah quickly walked past her mother's room, hoping she wouldn't get stopped. No such luck.

"Hey, Key-Key," her mother called.

Ra'Keeyah rolled her eyes and stomped her foot quietly. "Yes, Mom," she huffed.

"Don't 'yes, Mom' me. Bring yo' butt here." Ra'Keeyah turned around and walked into her mother's room. "Are those my gold hoops in your ears?" she asked.

Now I know she didn't call me in here to ask me about these earrings, Ra'Keeyah thought. "Yes, Mom, they are."

"Stay outta my jewelry box. You got your own jewelry." Ra'Keeyah's mom looked her lovely daughter up and down from head to toe. It seemed like only yesterday when she'd held her beautiful baby girl in her arms. Now she was sixteen with a shape like a Coke bottle.

"What, Mommy?" Ra'Keeyah asked. "What you lookin' at me like that for?"

Ra'Keeyah's mom smiled. "I'm just lookin' at how much you've grown up, that's all. I can remember when you were a chubby little girl runnin' around here eatin' up everything in sight," her mother laughed.

"I ain't chubby no more," Ra'Keeyah said, putting her hands on her hips.

Her mother's demeanor became serious. "Ra'Keeyah, let me ask you a question."

Here we go again, Ra'Keeyah thought. "No, Mommy, I'm not sexually active, if that's what you gon' ask me," she lied again. Even though Ra'Keeyah had only been with two people, she didn't have the heart to tell her mother, because she wouldn't have understood.

"Well, I wonder how you got all them hips and ass, and I didn't get no ass until I started havin' sex," her mother remarked.

"I was blessed with all this," Ra'Keeyah said, turning around, striking a pose.

"Okay, blessed," her mother laughed, throwing a pillow at her.

Ra'Keeyah dodged the pillow and laughed. Then she looked at her watch. "Okay, Mommy, I gotta go. I gotta meet Shayna and Quiana at the bus stop in fifteen minutes."

"All right, but be back here by seven."

Ra'Keeyah turned around and rolled her eyes as she walked out of her mother's room.

"Aha, that's why you gotta babysit me tonight," Jaylen said, while walking toward his bedroom.

"That's why I'ma beat yo' ass when Mommy leave, now, aha *that,*" Ra'Keeyah whispered before walking down the stairs.

Jaylen made a U-turn and ran into his mother's room. "Mommy, Key-Key said she gon' beat me up when you leave."

Ra'Keeyah smiled, shook her head, and continued down the stairs. She walked into the kitchen and grabbed the *Us Weekly* magazine and quickly flipped through the pages. Once she found the Macy's ad, she ripped it out, folded it up, and stuck it in her back pocket as she walked out of the kitchen.

"Shit, I'm gettin' these damn jeans," Ra'Keeyah said, grabbing her red Coach bag off the sofa and heading out the front door.

Chapter Two

"Damn, what's takin' the bus so long to get here?" Shayna asked, looking up and down the street as they waited on the bus to arrive.

Ra'Keeyah looked at her loud and impatient friend and shook her head. Shayna was Ra'Keeyah's best friend and had been ever since second grade. Shayna was five feet five, and 144 pounds of pure feistiness. She sported a short haircut and had pretty almond-shaped eyes with a smooth mocha-colored skin complexion. She'd been told on numerous occasions she resembled Nia Long, but had an attitude like Naomi Campbell.

"I don't know, but I wish it would hurry up," Quiana added, putting her hands on her small waist. Quiana was the most laid-back of the three, but if anything jumped off, she didn't mind getting down and dirty. Quiana was light-skinned with hazel eyes. She was an inch taller than Shayna, with long, silky hair that came to the middle of her back. Rumor had it her father was a Puerto Rican trick, and by the way Quiana acted and looked, the rumor could have been true.

The three girls stood at the bus stop chitchatting as a pack of motorcycles came riding down the street.

"Damn, look at all them niggas on motorcycles!" Shayna announced as if no one else could see them.

"Dang," Ra'Keeyah said, shocked.

"Oh, that's the Road Runners," Quiana said, as if it was no big deal. "Them niggas get money and lots of it!" she stated. "They runnin' the dope game around here."

"Oh yea, I heard about them. That nigga, Brick, from New York, is the president or something," Shayna said.

"I done heard about him, but I don't know him," Ra'Keeyah said. "I heard his money is longer than the George Washington Bridge."

"I heard that ain't the only thing he got long," Quiana laughed.

"You nasty, hefah," Shayna laughed too.

"That black-ass nigga is fine as hell," Quiana smiled. "He got all these hood rats chasin' after him."

"Look at the pot callin' the kettle black," Ra'Keeyah smirked.

"Anyway," Quiana cut her eyes and continued talking, "I would love to have that nigga in between these thighs."

"You would love to have anybody in between them thighs," Shayna joked.

"Ha-ha. If you wasn't my cousin I would punch you in the eye," Quiana joked back.

"Y'all crazy," Ra'Keeyah laughed.

The three girls looked across the street as the pack of men and women parked their bikes in front of Mr. Wilson's corner store. The store was the hangout for all the big-time ballas, depending on what side of town they were from. Mr. Wilson sold liquor, soul food, drugs, weave, and anything else you could think of in his store. Ra'Keeyah watched as some light-skinned girl with a butt much bigger than hers got off the back of a black and red bike that she adored.

"That bike is nice as hell!" Ra'Keeyah exclaimed. A rush of excitement swept over her because she had always been fascinated with motorcycles ever since she was a little girl. Her father used to always ride her on the back of his until he'd sold it for a few packs of smack. Ra'Keeyah wanted to know who the owner of that motorcycle was, because whoever it was had taste—good taste at that.

"It is," Shayna and Quiana agreed.

"That's the brand-new BMW S100RR," Ra'Keeyah stated, knowing her brand of bikes.

Shayna and Quiana both shot her a crazy look. "I have never met a chick that loves old-school music and motorcycles more than you," Shayna laughed.

The mystery man waited for his pick of the week to get off the back of his bike before he got off himself. He pulled his helmet off, attempting to press the wrinkles out of his Red Monkey jeans before looking over at the three girls standing at the bus stop and smiled.

"Damn," the three girls said in unison.

"That's him, y'all," Quiana said happily.

"Him who?" Shayna asked, still mesmerized by the sexy dark chocolate hunk that shot a smile their way.

"Brick. The nigga we was just talkin' about," Quiana said, excited.

"Oh, that's the nigga that got these bitches going buck-wild over him. Shit, I see why. Homey is fine as hell!" Shayna replied with a smile.

"He sure is," Ra'Keeyah added as the bus pulled up. The three girls boarded, put their money in the change collector, and walked to the back of the bus. The entire ride to the mall Shayna and Quiana rambled on about what they wanted to wear to the basketball game the following Friday, while thoughts of riding on the back of Brick's motorcycle danced around in Ra'Keeyah's head.

***

"Okay, now we all know what we want," Quiana said as they sat in the food court preparing for what was about to go down. "So we need two size nines and a size seven."

"I wear a five, now," Ra'Keeyah corrected her.

"Dang, you still on a diet, LisaRaye," Shayna joked.

"I'm not on no damn diet. I've just been watchin' what I eat," Ra'Keeyah laughed. "And would you stop callin' me LisaRaye, 'cuz I don't look nothin' like her."

"She sure don't," Quiana said, rolling her eyes.

"Yes, she do," Shayna disagreed with them both.

"Jealousy is not a good look for you," Ra'Keeyah replied to Quiana.

"Anyway, you know I gotta keep my bedroom body together," Ra'Keeyah laughed.

"I don't know what for. It ain't like you gon' let nobody see it," Shayna laughed.

Ra'Keeyah laughed as well. "That's okay. Just know when I do decide to let a nigga see all this again," she said pointing to her body, "they will be pleased with what they see."

Quiana rolled her eyes again. "And again, anyway. So we gon' need two size nines, a size five, two large shirts and a small shirt," Quiana stated.

A strange feeling swept over Ra'Keeyah. "Y'all know what? I don't think we should do this today. I just got this funny feelin' all of a sudden."

"Aww, man, stop actin' like a scary bitch," Quiana spat angrily.

"They was watchin' us kinda' tough when we was in there pickin' the shit out," Shayna added. She'd felt the same as Ra'Keeyah but had kept her thoughts to herself. "So maybe we shouldn't get nothin' today."

"Damn, man, you lettin' Ra'Keeyah's scary ass rub off on you. We going in there and get them clothes. I need somethin' to wear to the game Friday and that's that," Quiana stated angrily.

"I'll tell you what. Y'all gon' and get y'all shit. I'm not goin'," Ra'Keeyah stated firmly.

"Come on, girl, you know we gotta be fly for the game Friday. This is the biggest game of the year," Quiana said, trying to persuade Ra'Keeyah.

"That is true," Shayna agreed.

Just as Ra'Keeyah was about to give in to the pressure her friends were putting on her, she recalled the conversation she'd held with her mom right before she'd left the house. If Ra'Keeyah didn't know anything else, she knew her mother wasn't playing about not coming to get her out of jail.

"I'm cool, y'all. I'll just wear somethin' outta my closet or come back tomorrow. I just got a bad feelin' about today. Me and my mom just had a conversation about me stealin' right before I left the house," Ra'Keeyah said.

"Suit yourself then," Quiana said as she stood up from the table. "And don't think I'm gettin' yo' scary ass nothin' either." Quiana threw the big purse on her shoulder and waited for Shayna to follow suit.

"I didn't ask you to get me nothin', Quiana. I'm straight," Ra'Keeyah said, irritated with the entire conversation.

Shayna looked at Ra'Keeyah with begging eyes. Ra'Keeyah shrugged her shoulders at her best friend. "I'm sorry, but I can't," she said to Shayna. "I gotta follow my gut on this one."

"Come on, Shayna," Quiana said. "I got a couple of other stores I wanna go in too."

Shayna looked at Ra'Keeyah again before getting up from the table and following her cousin. She looked back at her best friend one last time, hoping she would change her mind before disappearing into the crowd.

Ra'Keeyah looked at her watch and waited a few minutes before getting up from the table. She had half an hour before the next bus would arrive so she decided to walk around the mall and do a little more wishful window-shopping.

Ra'Keeyah walked into Lady Foot Locker and picked up a pair of a hundred-and-twenty-dollar sneakers. She wanted them bad, but knew she couldn't afford them, and she knew good and well her mother wouldn't dare spend that type of money on one pair of shoes. "Maybe I can have Shayna get 'em for me next time she takes us on a shoppin' spree," she said as she placed them back on the rack.

As Ra'Keeyah made her way to the bus stop, she pulled out her cell phone wanting to call and check on Shayna. She could have cared less about Quiana. They really weren't friends in the first place. She tolerated her because she was Shayna's cousin.

Ra'Keeyah called Shayna's cell phone two times back to back and each time it went to voice mail. She started to worry, but then it dawned on her that every time they were out stealing, Shayna would turn her phone off. She didn't want any type of distractions while they were doing their thing.

"Oh well, I'll call her later," Ra'Keeyah said as the number five pulled up.

Ra'Keeyah boarded the bus and took a seat in the back. She shut her eyes and said a quick prayer for Shayna. Even though Quiana got on her last nerve, she asked for protection for her as well.

Once the bus stopped, Ra'Keeyah got off and looked over at Mr. Wilson's corner store wishing she was the one getting off the back of Brick's bike, instead of the other chick. She smiled and continued on her way home. Ra'Keeyah knew that even if Brick had any speck of interest in her, they would never work. Her mother wouldn't dare approve of her dating an older man, especially one that sold drugs. She walked up on the porch, and her mother snatched the door open. The look on her face told Ra'Keeyah that it wasn't anything good.

"Where the hell have you been?" her mother snapped.

Ra'Keeyah walked in and looked at the clock on the wall that read 6:22 P.M. "What? You told me to be back before seven so I'm thirty-eight minutes early," she said, confused.

"I gotta call from Shayna's mom, and she told me she was on her way out to the mall 'cuz her and Quiana got caught stealin'! And didn't you tell me you was goin' to the mall with them?"

Oh shit, I told them bitches today was not a good day, Ra'Keeyah thought. "I did go to the mall with them, Momma, but I wasn't stealin' nothin'. I left them and came home early 'cuz you told me to be home by seven," Ra'Keeyah lied.

"So you mean to tell me that you didn't know what they were out there doin'?" her mother asked skeptically.

"No, Momma, I told you I left. I didn't know they were stealin'," she lied again, while walking past her mother to go into the kitchen to get herself something to drink. Ra'Keeyah opened up the refrigerator and grabbed a bottle of water.

"Well, you better be glad you wasn't out there stealin', 'cuz I just told yo' ass before you left this house that I wasn't comin' to get you outta jail," her mother said, following her into the kitchen.

"I don't steal." Ra'Keeyah was on a roll with the lies that were coming out of her mouth. "And I told you that earlier," she said, walking out of the kitchen and heading up the stairs.

"I done told you before I didn't want you to hang with them fast-ass girls. Somethin' told me y'all be out to that mall up to no good," her mother fussed as she followed her up the stairs.

Ra'Keeyah walked into her bedroom and sat on her bed while her mother stood in her doorway and continued to fuss. "I don't be out to the mall doin' nothin'. If I was, don't you think I woulda' been with them when they got caught stealin'?" Ra'Keeyah asked, before taking a sip of her water.

Her mother thought for a brief moment. "I'm not lettin' yo' ass off the hook. I don't care what you say, you knew they was out there stealin'!"

Ohhh, she gets on my nerves, Ra'Keeyah thought. *Why don't she just gon' and get ready for work?* "All right, Momma," Ra'Keeyah said, blowing her off.

"All right, my ass. Now you might not be out there stealin', but yo' ass can go to jail too for bein' with them while they're doin' it."

"All right, Momma," Ra'Keeyah said again, not in any mood to argue with her mother. Her thoughts were on what was going to happen to Shayna.

"I refuse to let you turn out like them, Ra'Keeyah," her mother said as she turned to walk into her own bedroom. "*All we do is window-shop*," her mother said, mocking Ra'Keeyah's words.

If you only knew that I'm already like them, she wanted to say but didn't have enough nerve. Ra'Keeyah waited a few seconds before slamming her bedroom door shut.

"Don't be slammin' no damn doors up in here. You don't pay no bills," her mother yelled.

"Shut up!" Ra'Keeyah said quietly. She walked over to her dresser and grabbed a T-shirt and a pair of sweats and changed into them. She could still hear her mother fussing as she got ready for work. "Damn, I can't wait until she leaves!"

"Did you hear me, Key-Key?" her mother yelled.

"No, what you say?" Ra'Keeyah grimaced.

Ra'Keeyah's mother opened up her room door and stuck her head in. "I said dinner is in the oven. Make sure Jay-Jay eat!"

"All right," she responded before her mother turned to walk away. Ra'Keeyah grabbed her iPod Touch off the nightstand and put her headphones on not wanting to hear anything else her mother had to say. She turned to one of her favorite old-school songs by Kwamé. "*Only yoooooou can make me feel the way that I dooooo*," Ra'Keeyah sang loudly, as her mother walked into her bedroom.

"I'm leavin'," she looked at her daughter and said.

"Huh?" Ra'Keeyah answered, never taking the headphones off.

"If you take them damn headphones off you can hear me!" her mother yelled.

Ra'Keeyah still didn't know what her mother had said, but in order to keep her from slapping the headphones off her head, Ra'Keeyah took them off voluntarily. "I couldn't hear you."

"I said, I'm leavin'. Go downstairs and fix your brother a plate."

"All right," Ra'Keeyah answered.

Her mother walked over and gave her a kiss on the cheek. "See you in the mornin'."

"See ya," Ra'Keeyah replied and hurried past her mother and went downstairs to fix her brother a plate of food. "Jay-Jay, come and eat," Ra'Keeyah hollered upstairs to her brother.

"Bye, Mommy," Ra'Keeyah heard her brother say. Ra'Keeyah turned the television to SpongeBob, poured her brother a glass of Kool-Aid, and rushed back up to her room. She knew that the cartoons would keep her brother busy while she relaxed her mind. She waited a few minutes after she heard her mother's car start up before pulling her weed stash from under her bed.

She tore the wrapper off the Swisher Sweet and put it up to her nose. "Ummmm," she said, as she picked up the razor and cut it down the middle. She quickly ran to the bathroom and poured its contents down the toilet and flushed it. She waited a few seconds to make sure she didn't leave any evidence behind.

"Are you finished eatin', Jaylen?" she yelled down to her brother.

"Nooooo," he replied.

Ra'Keeyah knew her brother's plate was probably still full, so she had plenty of time to smoke her blunt. She went back into her room and shut the door. She picked up the nickel bag that Shayna had swiped from her mom's boyfriend and put it up to her nose. "This some fire!" she said excited. She then opened up the little bag and poured the weed into the Swisher. She licked the Swisher and wrapped it to perfection.

As soon as Ra'Keeyah was about to light the blunt, her cell phone rang. "Shit," she snapped before laying the blunt down on her bed. She calmed down when she saw that it was Shayna.

"Hello?" she quickly answered.

"Bitch, I shoulda' listened to you," she said as soon as Ra'Keeyah answered the phone. "But nooo, I had to listen to my dumb-ass cousin. I see why you don't care too much for her. She just stupid, and I was stupid for followin' her stupid ass," Shayna fussed.

"I don't wanna say it but—" Ra'Keeyah started.

"Well, don't," Shayna said, cutting her best friend off.

Ra'Keeyah laughed. "Well, what did they do to y'all?" she asked while pressing the wrinkles out of one of her many motorcycle posters that she had hanging on her bedroom wall as Shayna continued to ramble on.

"Bitch, that is not funny. They called the police and my ignorant-ass mom. She came out there yellin' and cussin' like a damn fool! I wanted to ask her when did she start carin' about what I do, but I didn't, because I didn't want her to let them take me to jail," Shayna laughed. "Thank God they didn't press charges."

"Yea, that's good."

"But they said we can't ever come back into their store."

"Ever?"

"Never, ever," Shayna responded with a laugh.

"Damn, well, I guess you won't be gettin' *that* outfit for the game Friday," Ra'Keeyah teased.

"Shit, bitch, I gotta have *that* outfit. I'ma 'bout to put one of my Diana Ross wigs on and go back up in there Wednesday and get my outfit. Them bitches don't stop no show. I'm one of the coldest boosters in town," Shayna bragged.

"If you was so cold, you wouldna' got caught," Ra'Kee-yah laughed.

"Shut up, and what you bouta' do?"

Ra'Keeyah couldn't wait any longer. She picked up the blunt and the lighter and lit it.

"Bouta' sit here and blow one," she said, taking a pull. "You wanna come blow?"

"Damn, I wish I could, but Moms is trippin'. The broad talkin' 'bout I'm on punishment for a month. You know better than that."

"Where all these rules comin' from all of a sudden?" Ra'Keeyah asked.

"I know, right?"

"You know I will be out and about tomorrow. I just ain't in the mood to listen to her mouth tonight. Ya' feel me?"

"I feel you," Ra'Keeyah said laughing.

"All right, girly, enjoy your blunt and take a toke for me," Shayna said.

"I got chu'," Ra'Keeyah said before hanging up.

Ra'Keeyah sat back on her bed and continued getting blowed. She lay there thinking about how Shayna's mom could even try to punish her for something she'd taught her to do. Shayna, her mother, her mother's boyfriend at the time, and her aunt Deesha would all go out boosting together when they needed money for crack. They'd made it a family affair. Shayna wasn't on drugs, but she had addictions. Boosting, credit cards, and check scams, as well as tricking niggas, young and old, out of their money. Her mother had tried to clean her life up somewhat over the years and also had tried to warn her daughter about her conniving ways catching up to her time and time again, but Shayna never listened. She always told her mother that everyone was in charge of their own destiny. Shayna's mother didn't want to see her only daughter traveling down the same road to destruction that she herself had traveled. But it seemed like the more she tried to keep Shayna from turning out like her, the more she realized Shayna would have to find out for herself.

Chapter Three

Ra'Keeyah hurried home from the bus stop. It was finally Friday, and tonight was the most anticipated basketball game of the year. Senior high versus Madison was the highlight of the season. Everybody who had a name was going to be there, and even people who didn't have one were going to be there trying to get one. Everybody was going to be dressed in their best. No one really watched the game. It was like one big fashion show. That's why Ra'Keeyah had to bring it with the outfit she was going to put on tonight.

She walked in the house, threw her book bag down by the front door, and headed straight to the kitchen. "Hey, Momma," she said, as she opened up the refrigerator and searched for something to eat.

"Hey, baby," her mother replied as she chopped up a green onion for her spaghetti sauce. "What you lookin' for in there?"

"I'm starvin'," Ra'Keeyah said, as she continued looking for something to snack on, but came out empty-handed. She slammed the refrigerator door and began raiding the cabinets.

"Don't you see me cookin'?" stated her mom.

"Well, that's gon' take a long time. I'm hungry now," Ra'Keeyah said, as she continued rambling through the cabinets until she found an oatmeal cream pie.

"Didn't you eat lunch at school?" her mother asked as she chopped up the bell pepper.

"No, 'cuz I don't eat the meat loaf at school," she replied, taking a bite of the cream pie. "Ugggh, this mess is old," Ra'Keeyah said before tossing it in the trash can.

Ra'Keeyah's mother stopped chopping her vegetables and put her hands on her hips. "Now what the hell you throw that pie away for? You don't buy no damn food around here," her mother fussed.

"It tasted old, Momma. Dang," Ra'Keeyah grimaced.

"I just bought them about two weeks ago. That damn thing wasn't old," her mother continued to fuss. "You and your brother get on my nerves actin' like money grow on damn trees around here." Her mother continued chopping her vegetables.

"Mom, it didn't taste right," Ra'Keeyah stated. "If it makes you feel better, I'll buy you another box."

Ra'Keeyah's mother stopped dead in her tracks. "That's not the point I'm tryin'a make. Yo' aunt Nancy done lost her damn mind, tryin'a sell me a hundred dollars' worth of food stamps for sixty-five dollars. When did the price go up?" her mother asked rhetorically. "Shit, I been givin' her fifty dollars for a hundred for the longest! So I'm gon' hafta' try to find someone else to buy stamps from, or we gon' starve around here."

"I ain't gon' starve," Ra'Keeyah replied.

"Well, I don't know how yo' narrow ass gon' eat. Look, Ra'Keeyah, I can't afford to pay the rent, all the bills, includin' *your* cell phone bill, my car note, and put food on the table. You're sixteen now. You old enough to get a job and help out around here," her mother ranted.

"All because I threw away an oatmeal cream pie I gotta get a job?" Ra'Keeyah asked, confused.

"You damn right!" her mother yelled. "Shit, McDonald's and Burger King is hirin' kids your age every day!"

"Me, Ra'Keeyah Jaz'Mire Jackson, work at McDonald's?" she said, pointing to herself. "Puhleeze, not me."

"I don't know where you got that bourgeois-ass attitude from, Ms. Thang," her mother snapped, "but take a look around. We a long way from Beverly Hills. Whether you know it or not, we one step away from havin' to move to a homeless shelter."

Ra'Keeyah sighed heavily, looked at the clock, and walked out of the kitchen.

"I'll tell you what," her mother yelled at her back. "I was gon' wait until the summer to make you get a job, but you got three weeks to come in here with somethin' or I'm turnin' your cell phone off. That'll save me some money."

Ra'Keeyah never thought in a million years she'd have to find a job. She'd always had this crazy idea of finding a good man to take care of her every need. But if she didn't find a good one in the next three weeks, she knew she had no other choice but to go out and find a job. Her mother was serious about cutting her phone off, and her cell was like air to her; it was something she couldn't live without.

"Mommy said you gotta babysit me tonight," Jaylen ran into his sister's room and said.

Ra'Keeyah stopped rambling through her closet and turned to face her brother. "I bet you I don't. I'm goin' to the game tonight!" Ra'Keeyah snapped. "Yo' li'l nappy-headed ass will be right here by yourself." Ra'Keeyah's heart beat fast as she hurried out of her room in search of her mother. "Mom," she called out as she hurried down the stairs.

"Yea," her mother answered from the kitchen.

Ra'Keeyah walked in the kitchen where her mother stood washing the dishes. "Mom, did you say I had to watch Jaylen tonight?" she asked and waited impatiently for her mother to answer.

Her mother gave her a look of confusion. "What are you talkin' about?"

Jaylen ran into the kitchen and pushed his sister from behind. "Siiiiiike," he giggled and ran back out of the kitchen and upstairs to his room.

"I can't stand him," Ra'Keeyah laughed, feeling relieved, because there was no way in the world she was going to miss this game.

Her mother laughed and shook her head. "Y'all two are somethin' else," she said and continued washing the dishes.

Ra'Keeyah ran up the stairs and back into her room. She had less than two hours to get dressed for the game, and she had no idea what she was going to wear. She still had a couple of new outfits that she was saving for a time like tonight. After about twenty minutes of debating on what to wear, she finally made up her mind. Ra'Keeyah knew she'd have to wait on her mother to leave for work before she got dressed, because she didn't feel like answering the hundred-and-one questions her mother was going to ask about where and how she got her clothes.

Ra'Keeyah plugged in her blow dryer and CHI flat-irons that she'd stolen from JCPenney's before jumping in the shower. The hot water abused her body for a few seconds before she adjusted the temperature. She grabbed the Motions shampoo out of the shower caddy and lathered her growing hair. She then quickly rinsed it and added some conditioner. Ra'Keeyah began humming and dancing in the shower until her mother stuck her head into the bathroom door.

"I'm gone," her mother yelled, nearly scaring her half to death.

"Okay, Momma," Ra'Keeyah responded and began rinsing the conditioner out of her hair.

"Now, I want you home by eleven, and I don't want nobody in my house while I'm at work!" her mother said.

"All right, Momma," Ra'Keeyah said nonchalantly.

"And you know I'ma call the house phone to make sure you're here," her mother stated, clearly.

"I know, Momma," Ra'Keeyah sighed. She knew that her mother would call the house phone at 11:01 P.M., and she would be there to answer it like always. But if they had anything planned as soon as she hung up with her mother, back out the door Ra'Keeyah would go until her mother's next break at 4:30 A.M.

Ra'Keeyah thought her mother had left the bathroom, but she knew it was too good to be true. Her mother wouldn't dare leave without giving her famous speech. "Now don't get into no trouble tonight, because I'm not gettin' off work early to come get you outta jail," she said, while Ra'Keeyah mimicked her.

"I won't, Momma," Ra'Keeyah replied, while rolling her eyes.

"Come on, Momma," Jaylen yelled from downstairs. "Darius waitin' on me so we can play the Xbox."

"I'm comin', boy, don't rush me," their mother said, closing the bathroom door and heading down the stairs.

Ra'Keeyah turned off the water and stepped out of the shower. "Good, they gone," she said, when she heard the front door slam. She grabbed her towel off the hook on the back of the bathroom door, wrapped it around her, and rushed out of the bathroom. She went into her room and hooked her iPod up to her boom box and turned it up as loud as it would go. Waka Flocka Flame bumped out of the speakers as she pulled her outfit from out of the back of her closet. She looked at it like she'd never seen it before. She laid it across her bed, walked over to her drawer, and pulled out a matching panty and bra set and put it on.

She grabbed the Johnson's baby lotion off her dresser and rubbed it all over her body. She then walked over to her bed and picked up her black House of Dereon jeans with the pink designs on the back pockets and slipped into them. She then put on her pink House of Dereon shirt before walking back over to the closet, pulling her black and pink Nike Air Max out. Shayna had gotten these for her with a married man's credit card. Shayna had taken Ra'Keeyah and Quiana on a shopping spree with the credit card. The three girls had put on wigs and went in and out of stores and shopped till they nearly dropped. They'd spent nearly five thousand dollars in one day. They each had about seven outfits a piece, numerous pairs of shoes and boots, perfumes, panties and bra sets, jewelry, makeup, and anything else they could think of buying.

"*I go hard in the mutha'fuckin' paint, nigga,*" Ra'Keeyah rapped as she walked out of her bedroom and into the bathroom. She picked up her blow dryer and began drying her hair. Once she finished, she laid the blow dryer down and began looking in the mirror. She opened up her brown eyes as wide as she could while running her hand across her high cheekbones, the ones she'd inherited from her grandmother. Her smooth caramel complexion was flawless, except for the mole on her bottom lip. She turned her head from left to right, inspecting her entire face as her bone-straight hair that hung a little past her shoulders swung freely.

"Damn, I look good," she said, and continued doing her hair. Half an hour later, Ra'Keeyah had straightened out all of her hair. She had it looking like she'd just left the salon. It was long and silky looking, which, according to Shayna, really had her resembling Lisa-Raye. Ra'Keeyah put on some pink eye shadow to accentuate her outfit and Lip Smacker lip gloss before walking back into her bedroom. She shut her door and gave herself a complete once-over in the mirror that hung on the back of the door. She checked to make sure her backside looked good in her jeans. Pleased with what she saw, she walked over to her dresser and sprayed on a few squirts of Baby Phat Luv Me. She then grabbed her pink Coach bag off the bed and headed downstairs.

Ra'Keeyah turned the television in the living room to the Weather Channel to make sure she didn't need a jacket before calling Shayna.

"What's up, chick?" Shayna answered with her lungs full of smoke from the blunt she was enjoying.

"Bitch, I know you ain't over there gettin' ya' wig blew back without me?" Ra'Keeyah snapped.

Shayna blew the smoke out before speaking. "Don't worry, chick. There's plenty weed to go around. I just needed somethin' to calm my nerves real quick. My moms over here trippin', talkin' 'bout I'm still on punishment and can't go to the game." Shayna took another pull from the blunt and held it in until she started to snicker.

"Imagine that," Ra'Keeyah replied. "Anyway, how we gettin' to the game?"

"My mom's boyfriend is gon' drop us off, and you know we'll find a way home." Shayna took one last pull from her blunt and put it out. She blew the smoke out before continuing on with her conversation. "You ready?"

"Bitch, I was born ready," Ra'Keeyah laughed before sitting down on the sofa.

"Okay, well, we bouta' go pick up Quiana, and then we gon' swing by and get you."

"Okay, cool. I'll be waitin'." Ra'Keeyah hung up the phone and turned the television to the throwback Jamz station and listened as Bell Biv DeVoe sang "Poison." She stood up and paced the floor, then looked in the mirror that hung on the living-room wall over and over, making sure that her hair and makeup were still intact. Twenty minutes later her ride came and Ra'Keeyah turned off the television, all the lights, and headed out the door, hoping for a fun-filled night with no problems. Ra'Keeyah knew better though, because any night out with Shayna, there was sure to be some type of drama.

Chapter Four

Shayna's mom's boyfriend, Joe, dropped them off on the side of the school; they wouldn't dare be seen getting out of an old, beat-up minivan. Joe had money and plenty of it. He supplied the hood, along with some big-time businessmen with the best grown weed straight out of Cuba, but he still lived and dressed as if he was broke. Joe didn't want to bring no heat to himself or anyone he hung around, so he kept the beat-up van and had been rocking the same pair of Chuck Taylors for the past two years. At first, Shayna had to get used to her mother dating a white man, but Joe talked and acted blacker than anybody else in their hood.

"See y'all later," Joe said, stopping to let the girls out. "What time you want me to pick y'all up?" he asked Shayna.

"We cool. We'll get a ride from somebody," she replied, while opening up the door.

"All right then, but if you can't find nobody to take y'all to the crib, call me," he said with a crooked smile.

Ra'Keeyah thought Joe was kind of creepy. He reminded her of an old pedophile. She frowned and slid the back door open, got out, and Quiana got out behind her.

"Let me hold twenty, Joe, till later on," Shayna said, leaning into the passenger-side window.

"Damn, girl, you sho' know how to milk a brotha," he said, digging into his pocket, pulling out a wad of money. "I just gave you two twenty sacks of my best." Joe handed the money to her.

"Appreciate it," Shayna said, taking the money and walking away from the van.

"Hey," Joe called out, "call me later."

Shayna nodded and continued walking with Ra'Keeyah and Quiana following behind her.

"He creeps me out," Ra'Keeyah said as they walked toward the entrance of the school. "Why your mom datin' that pilgrim?"

"Who, Joe?" Shayna asked, knowing who she was talking about. "He cool, and plus, he treats her better than any black man she ever had."

Ra'Keeyah rolled her eyes while pulling her ticket out of her pocket. "To each his own." She gave the man standing at the door her ticket and brushed past him.

The three girls were standing in the middle of what looked like thousands of people trying to get into the gymnasium. They were being pushed and shoved in every direction.

"Dang, it's packed in here," Ra'Keeyah said, leaning up against the wall, trying to avoid getting run over by the die-hard fans trying to find themselves a good seat. "I'm goin' to the bathroom. I gotta pee."

"Me too," Shayna said. "You comin' to the bathroom with us, or do you wanna go find us some seats?" she asked Quiana.

"I'ma go find somewhere to sit."

"All right," Shayna said as she and Ra'Keeyah turned to walk away.

"These people is rude as hell," Shayna snapped as some lady bumped into her and didn't say excuse me. "Now, they gon' think I'm dead wrong if I start goin' ham on 'em," she said, as her cell phone started to ring.

Ra'Keeyah smiled and continued maneuvering through the crowd. As they walked down the busy hallway, she looked over and saw Brick leaned up against the wall laughing and talking to a few dudes. She quickly turned her head and followed Shayna into the bathroom.

Once inside the bathroom, the lines were long. Shayna hung up her cell phone as they waited on a stall. Two stalls became available at once, and Ra'Keeyah went into one and Shayna the other.

Ra'Keeyah could hear some girls walking into the bathroom giggling and talking about how fine Brick was and how bad they wanted to get with him. As she wiped herself, she heard the toilet flush next to hers and the stall door open.

"Sorry, boo-boo, but he's already taken," Ra'Keeyah heard someone say. "But it's cute that you little girls got a crush on *my* man." Ra'Keeyah flushed the toilet, buttoned her jeans, and walked out of the stall the same time as Shayna. Ra'Keeyah recognized the girl as the one getting off the back of Brick's bike at Mr. Wilson's store.

Ra'Keeyah and Shayna walked over to the sink to wash their hands. The entire time they listened as Brick's chick checked the two young girls about her man. The crazy thing was, they stood there and took it.

"Ummmp, couldn't be me," Shayna said loudly, while grabbing a paper towel out of the dispenser and drying her hands.

Ra'Keeyah looked over at Shayna with her mouth open. She should have known her best friend couldn't keep her mouth shut just until they got out of the bathroom. "Excuse me?" Brick's girl stopped talking to the first two girls and asked Shayna.

Shayna threw the balled up paper towel in the trash and stood her ground. "You heard me, I said it couldn't be me. You wouldn't be talkin' to me all crazy and shit over no nigga!" Shayna snapped.

Brick's chick sized Shayna up. "I wasn't even talkin' to you, so mind yo' mutha'fuckin' business!" she snapped. The other two girls were relieved the heat was off of them and aimed at Shayna; they broke camp as fast as they could.

"Come on, Shayna, let's go," Ra'Keeyah said, lightly grabbing her shoulder. "This shit crazy."

"Yeah, you need to listen to yo' girl, before things get real ugly up in this bathroom."

Shayna had a sinister grin on her face as she spoke. "You right, I'ma leave, 'cuz this shit don't have nothin' to do with me, but just remember what I said. You could never talk to me like you just talked to them two dumb hoes." With that being said, Shayna and Ra'Keeyah walked out of the bathroom.

"Bitch, it never fails. Every time we go somewhere you get into it with somebody!" Ra'Keeyah huffed. "Dang, that shit didn't even have nothin' to do with you."

"I don't give a flyin' fuck! She was in there reprimandin' them two scary bitches like they were her kids or somethin'!" Shayna grimaced. "Who the fuck she think she is? Okay, them girls think Brick is fine. Big fuckin' deal! What she gon' do, go around checkin' every bitch that think Brick is cute?"

"Ugggh, you just don't get it do you?" Ra'Keeyah asked before Shayna's cell phone started ringing.

"Hang on." Shayna answered her phone and talked as they walked back toward the gymnasium. Ra'Keeyah looked over at Brick and his friends who were still in the same spot.

"Psssst," Ra'Keeyah heard someone say as she tried to keep up with Shayna, but it was useless. She ignored the catcall and kept it moving. "Hey, shorty," the voice called out again.

Ra'Keeyah turned around with a mug on her face. "What?" she snapped, but eased up just a little once she realized Brick was the one trying to get her attention.

"Damn, baby, calm down," Brick smiled. "I just wanted to let you know that you got toilet paper stuck on the bottom of your shoe." Brick and his friends started laughing.

"Oh, thank you," Ra'Keeyah stammered. She was so embarrassed; she wanted to die right then and there. She knew her face had to be as red as a fire engine. She looked down at her shoe and lifted it up. Quickly, she pulled the piece of toilet paper off and threw it on the floor. Ra'Keeyah could still hear them laughing as she walked away.

"What happened to you? I turned around and yo' ass was gone," Shayna asked, once Ra'Keeyah made it over to their seats.

"I don't even wanna talk about it," Ra'Keeyah said, still embarrassed.

"Why is your face so flushed? What happened?"

Ra'Keeyah broke down and told her about what had just happened. Shayna didn't want to laugh, but it was way too funny not to. Quiana didn't care; she busted out laughing.

"That shit ain't funny," Ra'Keeyah pouted. "How would y'all like it if a fine-ass nigga told y'all that y'all had toilet paper stuck on the bottom of your shoe?"

Shayna wiped the tears away that were forming in her eyelids. "At least he told you. I'm quite sure he wasn't the first person to spot the toilet paper at the bottom of yo' shoe." Shayna couldn't help herself; she started laughing again, which started Quiana back up.

"Fuck y'all, hoes!" Ra'Keeyah thought about how silly she must have looked dragging the piece of toilet paper and to make it so bad, turning around with an attitude when he tried to tell her about it. Finally, she busted out laughing herself.

After the third quarter, the three girls walked up to McDonald's where everybody gathered after all of the games. They left early not wanting anyone to see them walking, but to their surprise the parking lot was jam-packed. Music was blaring from different cars; people were standing around laughing, talking; some were even dancing, while others were trying to get boo'd up for the night.

Shayna, Ra'Keeyah, and Quiana quickly mixed in with the crowd, hoping no one had spotted them walking into the parking lot.

"I'ma hafta' get me a car," Shayna said, shaking her head.

"Now how do you plan on doin' that with no job?" Ra'Keeyah inquired.

"I don't know just yet, but I bet you, I'll have me a load by the summertime."

"All them old-ass men you be fuckin', you shoulda' been had a car," Quiana stated.

Quiana must have struck a nerve because Shayna went ham on her cousin. "Mind your fuckin' business, hater, and worry about all them niggas you fuckin' for free," she snapped.

"You don't know what I'm gettin'," Quiana argued.

"A wet ass," Shayna retorted. "Truth be told, I coulda' been had a car!"

"Whatever," Quiana said, waving her cousin off.

"How many diamonds, shoppin' sprees, pounds of weed, money, or anything else, for that matter, have you ever got from a nigga?" Shayna pointed her finger in her cousin's face as she spoke. "None!" Shayna answered for her. "Bitch, I done took you on numerous shoppin' sprees with the money I get from them old-ass men."

"Come on, y'all, cut all that out," Ra'Keeyah intervened. "See, I told you, you always gettin' into it with somebody!" All Ra'Keeyah could do was shake her head.

"And you sayin' *that* to say *what?*" Quiana grimaced.

"I'm sayin', stop fuckin' for free, bitch! It cost to get this pussy here," Shayna yelled, causing other people to look over at them.

"Come on, y'all, mutha'fuckas lookin' over here and shit," Ra'Keeyah pleaded.

"You right, I'm cool," Shayna said, calming down just a little. "I still love you," she said to Quiana. Quiana was so mad at the truth she didn't even respond. "I don't give a fuck if you don't acknowledge my apology. I'm hungry; let's go get somethin' to eat with this twenty dollas Joe gave me."

"Shit, you know I'm game for a free meal," Ra'Keeyah laughed as she and Quiana followed Shayna into McDonald's. The girls stood in line for what seemed like forever.

"May I take your order?" the girl behind the counter asked with a slight attitude.

Shayna turned around, looked at Quiana and Ra'Keeyah, and said, "Whatever happened to service with a smile?"

"Here we go again," Ra'Keeyah said before placing her order.

"I want the number ten with an orange drink, no salt on my fries, and I want extra tartar sauce and add lettuce, please," Shayna replied with a fake smile. Then she looked over at Quiana and waited for her to tell the cashier what she wanted.

"I'm straight," Quiana said.

"I ain't gon' beg you to eat," Shayna said turning back around.

"Y'all need salt and ketchup?" the chick behind the counter asked, while scratching her messed up weave job.

"Naw, and I hope you wash your hands before you get to handlin' our food," Shayna frowned.

The girl rolled her eyes and smacked her lips. "Anything else?" Shayna shook her head no. "Your total is $8.95."

"I got this," a male's voice said.

Shayna and Ra'Keeyah turned to see who was being so generous.

Brick shot both of the ladies a smile before handing the cashier a twenty-dollar bill.

Ra'Keeyah felt embarrassed about the toilet paper incident all over again. "Thank you," both girls said.

"Shit, if I woulda' known you was payin', I woulda' ordered me a sandwich for later on, after I smoked my L," Shayna said in a joking manner, but in reality was serious as a heart attack. Any time she got the chance to spend someone else's money, she was on it!

Brick smiled again. "You wanna order somethin' for later on?" he offered Shayna.

"No, thank you," she responded while taking her order from the lady behind the counter.

"What about you?" he looked at Ra'Keeyah and asked while collecting his change from the cashier.

"No, I'm fine," she said coyly.

"That you are," he winked and walked away.

"Oh my goodness, girl," Shayna squealed with excitement. "He is super-duper fine! And he got hellava game. You see how he just paid for our food and walked away all suave and shit?"

Ra'Keeyah turned and looked behind them. "You better not say that too loud. His chick gon' fuck you up," Ra'Keeyah joked.

"Shiiiit, I'll slap that bitch to sleep, wake her ass up, and slap her to sleep again," Shayna said with a dead serious look on her face.

Ra'Keeyah laughed. "He is cute, but you know I'm not messin' with no more drug dealers. They bad news."

Shayna rolled her eyes. "Just 'cuz you got caught up with one thug don't mean they all bad," she laughed. "What would you consider Marshall?"

"He's not a thug. Marshall is sweet and kind. And plus, I don't have to keep him hidden from my momma 'cuz he don't sell dope," Ra'Keeyah said.

"Yeah, he is kinda' square," Shayna laughed. "Ol' Farnsworth Bentley-ass type of nigga." Shayna continued laughing.

Ra'Keeyah laughed too. "Don't be talkin' about my friend like that! I told you them the type of men I will be messin' with from now on. No more bad boys for me," she stated adamantly.

Shayna turned up her lips, knowing her best friend couldn't stand going out with a square for too long. If Shayna didn't know anything else, she knew Ra'Keeyah would get bored real quick dating the preppy type and for sure put an APB out for the next thug that crossed her path.

The three girls were getting bored, watching the same old tired females trying to hook up with anyone they could. Shayna couldn't find them a ride with anyone decent. They had a few offers, but declined them all. The dudes either weren't on their level or just too broke for them to ride in their beat-up cars. Shayna decided to call Joe to come and pick them up.

"You sure you don't wanna hang out with us a little longer?" Shayna asked Ra'Keeyah as they pulled up in front of her house.

"Naw, I'm cool." Ra'Keeyah had had enough of her best friend's drama for one night. All she wanted to do was go in the house, smoke a blunt, and go to bed.

"All right, call me tomorrow, LisaRaye," Shayna joked.

Ra'Keeyah playfully pushed Shayna in the back of the head before sliding the door open to the minivan. "I will," she said, as she stepped out. She said good-bye to Quiana and Joe before closing the door.

Shayna made Joe wait until Ra'Keeyah got into the house safely before letting him pull off. Ra'Keeyah stuck her key in the door and walked in the house. She turned the porch light on and waved, letting them know that she made it in. Joe blew the horn twice before speeding off.

Ra'Keeyah locked the door behind her and headed up to her room. She instantly lifted up her mattress and grabbed the half-smoked blunt, the ashtray, and the lighter. She kicked her shoes off, sat back on her bed, and lit it. As she took a long pull, Brick invaded her thoughts. She tried desperately to shake his pearly white smile out of her memory bank but couldn't. She took a few more pulls and put the blunt out. Ra'Keeyah smiled before standing up and walking over to her dresser to get the air freshener. She sprayed her room, and then began taking off her clothes. All she kept thinking about as she got undressed was Brick and wishing he was there to keep her company.

Chapter Five

Brick lay in his king-sized bed knocked out and was awakened by his ringing cell phone. He reached over and grabbed it off the nightstand.

"Hello?" he answered with his face still half-buried in his pillow.

"Good mornin', baby," Pauline said in her usual cheerful tone.

"What's up, Ma?" Brick said, rolling over onto his back.

"Brice, I got somethin' to tell you, but I don't want you to get upset."

Brick quickly sat straight up, alarming Piper with his sudden movement. "What's wrong, Ma?" he asked suddenly.

"Now, I don't want you to do anything stupid when I tell you this. I'm just tellin' you 'cuz I think you should know."

"Ma, what is it?" he asked again in a somewhat raised tone.

"When I went outside this mornin' to leave for work, I noticed somebody had thrown a brick through the back window on my car."

"What?" he snapped loudly. "Your alarm didn't go off?" Piper was wide awake now; she couldn't go back to sleep even if she wanted to, loud as Brick was talking.

"Son, I was so tired when I got off work last night, I musta' forgot to set the alarm."

"Ma, what I tell you? I told you to keep your alarm set at all times, on the house and the car."

"I know, son, I know," Pauline said, sounding as if she was a nervous wreck.

"I'ma find out who did it, and when I do, they gon' have a lot of explainin' to do." Brick was upset. He could handle someone messing with him, but when it came to his mother, biological or not, he had no under-standing. "All right, Ma, call your insurance company. I'm about to get dressed, and I'll be over."

"Okay, baby."

Brick hung up the phone, stood up, and walked over to his closet. He was mumbling as he searched for something to wear.

"What's wrong with Pauline now?" Piper asked, sit-ting up.

Brick continued rambling through his closet as he spoke. "Somebody threw a brick threw her car window. I'ma find out who did it, and when I do, its gon' be on and poppin'!" he said angrily, pulling out a pair Ed Hardy jeans with a shirt to match.

Piper rolled her eyes. "Why she gotta call you every time somethin' happens?" she fussed. Piper couldn't stand Pauline because she felt she depended on Brick way too much. And deep down, she thought Pauline was the reason why Brick hadn't settled down and married her, or given her the baby she'd been dying to have.

Here we go again, Brick thought. He turned to face Piper. "Who else she gon' call?" he asked, irritated.

"The damn police, that's who!" she stated firmly. Piper was fed up. Every time Pauline called Brick, he dropped whatever he was doing to go to her aid.

Brick turned up his face as if something smelled. "The police? Only snitches deal with the police where I'm from!"

Piper grabbed her pack of cigarettes off the nightstand and shook one out. "I'm from the same damn place you're from," she said, before picking up her lighter. "So that's bullshit!" She lit her cigarette before slamming the lighter back down on the nightstand.

"Broad, I'm from the Bronx, and your bourgeois ass is from Syracuse. You come from money, and I come from the gutta'. Yo' ass grew up with maids and shit, and I grew up where my mutha was a maid. So tell me how we come from the same place?" Brick was tired as hell of arguing with Piper about what he did for Pauline. Pauline and Brick's relationship ran deeper than anyone could ever understand. She was there for him when his own mother had left him for dead. Pauline was the reason he wasn't doing life in the penitentiary. He'd never trusted anyone enough to tell them his story. It was something he'd always kept to himself.

"You can't solve everybody's problems, Brick. You're not Superman, and you need to start tellin' mutha'fuckas that!"

"You act like I'm goin' to see about any old chick. I'm goin' to check on my mutha!" Brick snapped.

"She ain't even yo' mutha!" Piper snapped back. "You do more for Pauline than you do for the woman that had you! I don't understand that."

"It ain't for you to understand," Brick said, heading toward the bathroom.

Piper threw the covers back and got out of bed yelling, "Every fuckin' time she call you, you go runnin'." She smashed the half-smoked cigarette in the ashtray before putting on her clothes. "Why? Because she cooked yo' dope, held your money and guns, and gave you a place to stay? You act like you owe her yo' life!"

"I do," Brick said, turning on the shower and stepping in, ignoring his bitching girlfriend.

He got out of the shower and quickly dressed. Piper was sitting on the edge of the bed still pouting while he groomed himself. Brick brushed his teeth, and then ran some pink moisturizing lotion through his tight curls. He looked closely at his dark skin, checking for blemishes, before squirting on some Kenneth Cole Black. Then he walked out of the bathroom, looked over at Piper, and shook his head. He called a couple of his boys and told them to question the neighbors about Pauline's window. He even went as far as telling them to offer cash to the first person who gave them information.

After that, he walked over to Piper and leaned down to give her a kiss. She moved away, letting him know she still had an attitude.

Brick shook his head. "What's your problem for real, girl?"

Piper looked up at him. "I don't have no problem, Brick. I'm just gettin' sick and tired of certain shit, that's all."

"Yeah, me too," he said grabbing his cell and his truck keys and heading out of the bedroom, leaving Piper and her attitude to keep each other company.

Brick got in his truck and reached under the seat to make sure his 9 mm was still in place. After confirming that it was, he buckled his seat belt, started up the truck, and pulled off. Special Ed's "I Got It Made" bumped out of the speakers as he drove. He still couldn't believe somebody had the audacity to break out his mother's car window. Anyone that knew of him knew he didn't play about his three M's: his money, his mother, or his main bitch.

Brick pulled up in front of Pauline's house, jumped out of his new Explorer, and hit the alarm. He looked back and admired his truck before walking on the porch. Pauline opened the door as he was about to stick the key in the lock.

"Hey, son," she said, greeting him with a hug.

"Hey, Ma," he said, hugging her back. "You called the insurance company yet?" he asked, closing the door behind him and heading to the living room.

Pauline followed behind him. "Yes, I called and made the claim already. They said they were gon' send Safelite out to fix it later this afternoon," she replied.

"Okay, that's what's up." Brick put his cell phone and keys on the coffee table before taking a seat. He grabbed the remote, turned the TV on, and got comfortable.

"You hungry?"

"I'm starvin'. What you cook?" he asked, looking up from the news he was watching.

"I cooked some sausage, eggs, and biscuits. I cooked extra 'cuz I knew you was comin' over."

"Heck, yeah," he smiled. Pauline smiled back before going to fix Brick a plate.

Five minutes later, Pauline walked back into the living room with Brick's plate in one hand and a big glass of orange juice in the other. She set it down in front of him before taking a seat next to him.

Brick picked up the plate and began devouring his meal.

"Dang, boy, slow down," Pauline laughed. "You act like you ain't ate in years."

"I feel like it, Ma. I'm tired of fast food," he said, and continued smashing his food.

"You need to get you a woman that can cook and leave Piper alone."

Brick laughed before picking up his orange juice. "She can cook a little bit."

"I'm not talkin' 'bout hot dogs and Ramen noodles," Pauline stated.

Brick laughed again. "Are y'all gon' ever get along?"

"Nope," Pauline replied quickly. "For one, she too jealous hearted for me, and two, she's the one that got the problem with me. I tried to be nice to the girl on account of you, but she too damn simpleminded for me."

"Who you tellin'? I be tryin'a tell her that shit," Brick said, finishing off his juice. "She think you be coverin' for me when I be stayin' out all night." Brick placed his plate and his glass on the coffee table.

"I don't uphold your wrongdoin', unless it's a matter of life or death. And frankly, my dear, she don't matter," Pauline laughed. "Shit, when she used to call me and ask me had I seen you, I'd tell her no, and she'd act like I was lyin' to her."

Brick shook his head. "I tried to tell her, but she don't be wantin' to hear it."

"You shoulda' left that dingy-ass broad in Syracuse where you found her."

Brick couldn't help but laugh. He lay his head back on the sofa and closed his eyes.

"You tired?" Pauline looked over at him and asked.

"Just tired of these streets, that's all."

"Well, when you gon' settle down with a good girl and give me some grandbabies?"

"Shit, Ma, you know I'm not stickin' my shit in nobody without protection, so that might never happen," Brick opened his eyes and said.

The house phone began to ring and Safelite popped up on the TV screen. "You just ain't found the right one, that's all. But eventually, you'll find that chick that'll make you wanna settle down and have kids," Pauline said as she got up to go retrieve the phone.

Brick closed his eyes again. "I don't know. She gon' have to be pretty damn special for me to hit her raw," he said to himself, because Pauline was already in the dining room on the phone talking to the Safelite man.

Just as Brick was about to drift off to sleep his cell phone rang. He picked it up checking the number. He answered it when he saw Bob T's name.

"What's up, nigga?" he answered. "Tell me what you know."

"Hey, man, I just got word that some li'l niggas on the north end broke out your mom's window. It was an accident, though," Bob T said. "I guess they was throwin' a brick at a dog that was chasin' them. They missed the dog and hit your mom's car window."

"That ain't no excuse!" Brick snapped. They coulda' came and knocked on her door and told her what happened. Find them niggas and run they pockets. They gon' pay for my mom's shit!"

"I'm on it," Bob T said before hanging up.

Relieved that his crew was on top of their game, Brick lay his phone back down on the coffee table and closed his eyes again. He could sleep easy knowing it was kids who broke out his mom's window and not someone trying to get him out of his hookup. Mistake or not, Brick refused to let it slide. If he let this go, niggas would surely continue to try him.

Chapter Six

It had been two-and-a-half weeks since Ra'Keeyah's mom had threatened her to get a job or get her cell phone turned off. Even though Ra'Keeyah was kind of nervous about her mother going through with it, she had yet to go and fill out one application. She had hoped that something miraculous would happen where she wouldn't have to work. Little did she know, today was her lucky day.

Ra'Keeyah walked out of her fifth-period class and headed toward the lunchroom. She was starving, but she was not hungry enough to eat the slop they were serving.

"What's up, momma?" Shayna asked as Ra'Keeyah approached their lunch table.

"What's up?" Ra'Keeyah asked before setting her books down and taking a seat across from her. "Where Quiana?" she asked, looking around.

"Her goofy ass up there gettin' some salt for these cold-ass french fries," Shayna said, pointing toward the condiment table.

Ra'Keeyah shook her head. "I don't see how y'all be eatin' this nasty-ass food they be servin' up in here."

"It's better than starvin' like yo' ass be doin'," Shayna said before taking a sip of her chocolate milk. "That's why yo' ass been losin' all that damn weight; hell, you don't eat," Shayna laughed.

Quiana walked back over to the table and took a seat. "What's up?" she asked Ra'Keeyah.

"'Sup?" Ra'Keeyah replied before responding to Shayna's smart remark. "For your information, I do eat. I'm just picky about what I put in my mouth. Too bad I can't speak for everybody at this table," she looked over at Quiana and smirked.

Shayna looked over at Quiana and started cracking up. It took Quiana a few minutes to catch on to Ra'Keeyah insinuations. "Bitch, don't start," Quiana frowned. "You kill me. You act like you ain't never sucked a nigga's dick before," she griped as she dipped a fry into some ketchup.

"Like I said, I'm picky about what I put in *my* mouth," Ra'Keeyah stated.

"Whatever." Quiana rolled her eyes.

"You can roll 'em, you can stroll 'em, but you betta' control 'em," Ra'Keeyah laughed, hitting Quiana with an old-school saying.

Shayna began cracking up again. "Aww, man, you went way back with that one," she said, wiping the moisture away from her eyes. "And as far as me suckin' a nigga's dick, you betta' believe I'ma get paid for it," Shayna snapped. "Speakin' of gettin' paid," she said checking her vibrating cell phone. Shayna smiled widely before speaking. "See, *this* what I'm talkin' about!" she said, showing her girls the text message from one of the married men she was messing around with.

"How about a shoppin' spree?" Ra'Keeyah said, reading the text aloud. "Damn, you lucky," she exclaimed.

"You gon' get enough of fuckin' them old men," Quiana laughed.

"For your information, I have never slept with this one," Shayna stated firmly. "All I ever had to do for him was shake my ass a little and let him eat it from time to time."

"That's it?" Ra'Keeyah asked, surprised. "Shit, do he got a brother?" she joked.

"Right!" Quiana agreed.

Shayna stared at her friends for a brief moment before speaking. "Are y'all serious?"

"About what?" Ra'Keeyah asked confused.

"About him having a brother," Shayna replied.

"I don't know about her, but I am," Quiana replied quickly.

"I was just jokin'," Ra'Keeyah stated.

"I wasn't," Quiana assured.

"I thought you couldn't see yourself fuckin' an old man?" Ra'Keeyah said to Quiana.

"Shit, I'll fuck an old woman if she gon' take me on a shoppin' spree!" Quiana laughed.

Shayna and Ra'Keeyah laughed as well. "You a nut," Shayna said. "Anyways, I was gon' wait until later to ask y'all this, but what better time than now." Ra'Keeyah and Quiana waited impatiently for Shayna to talk. "Well, Calvin asked me if I had any friends that look like me that would be willin' to dance for some of his buddies."

"What you mean, 'look like you'?" Ra'Keeyah inquired.

"You know, black with a lotta ass," Shayna explained proudly.

"So what you tryin'a tell us is these men are white?" Quiana asked.

"Yea, they are," Shayna answered. "But their money is green!"

The thought of dancing for a bunch of old white men, let alone them touching all over her body, made Ra'Keeyah's skin crawl. "I don't know about that," she grimaced.

"Do these old men got a lotta money?" Quiana inquired, not focusing on the color of their skin but the amount of green in their wallets.

"These men I'm talkin' about own their own business; a couple of them are big-time attorneys, one of them owns a BMW car lot," Shayna said excitedly. "Now you know I wouldn't have y'all fuckin' around wit' no broke niggas."

"I thought you said we didn't have to fuck 'em?" Ra'Keeyah said.

"Just a figure of speech," Shayna smiled. "And plus, all these men I'm talkin' about is men that goes to counselin' with Calvin."

"Counselin'?" Ra'Keeyah and Quiana asked simultaneously.

Shayna laughed. "Yes, counselin'. Calvin and his friends have problems with their libido, so they have to go to counselin' for it."

Quiana had a confused look on her face.

"They got a problem with they dick!" Ra'Keeyah explained to Quiana in laymen's terms.

"Oh, wow," Quiana laughed. "What more could we ask for? A bunch of old white men with sick dicks," she laughed even harder.

Shayna and Ra'Keeyah laughed as well. "Right," Ra'Keeyah agreed.

"Don't think of it like that," Shayna said. "At least we don't have to sleep with 'em and still get paid."

"But what if one day their dick starts workin' and they wanna fuck?" Ra'Keeyah asked seriously.

"Key-Key," Shayna squealed.

"What? I'm serious," Ra'Keeyah responded.

"Then give 'em what they want," Shayna answered. "But make sure you charge 'em. And make sure y'all use *protection*," she said, emphasizing protection more for Quiana's well-being than Ra'Keeyah's.

"You don't see nothin' wrong with a bunch of old white men with money wanting three high school girls dancin' for them? Ain't that illegal?"

Shayna laughed. "Yea, it would be illegal if they *knew* that they were high school girls and not three beautiful, black, nineteen-year-old women."

"Nineteen?" Ra'Keeyah asked. "Girl, you a fool."

"How much we gon' get paid?" Quiana inquired. The amount of money they were going to receive piqued Ra'Keeyah's curiosity as well.

"Altogether, it's six men. We chargin' each of 'em two-fifty to dance for 'em, and that's not including what they gon' be throwin' at us while we up there shakin' our ass," Shayna said.

"So that's fifteen hundred off top," Ra'Keeyah interjected.

"Right," Shayna agreed. "So that's five hundred a piece, but I get fifty dollars from each of you for my finder's fee."

"What?" Quiana grimaced. "What you mean finder's fee? You actin' like you pimpin' us or somethin'!"

"Bitch, this is a business. And I'm a businesswoman. Either you pay me my fifty dollars, or you don't dance!" Shayna snapped. "It's as simple as that. 'Cuz, bitch, if it wasn't for me, you wouldn't even be gettin' the four-fifty that you gon' be gettin'."

Ra'Keeyah respected the fact that Shayna was about business and didn't knock her hustle on wanting fifty dollars for setting everything up. But Ra'Keeyah wasn't sure if she was down for dancing, even if the money was good. There were just certain levels she wasn't willing to stoop to, and shaking her ass for cash was one of them. She had to really think on this.

Quiana waved her cousin off. "Whatever."

"I mean, damn, Quiana, you act like I'm takin' all y'all money!" Shayna said. "Y'all get to keep anything y'all make extra. All I'm askin' for is fifty punk-ass dollars. Y'all still makin' out like a fat rat."

Quiana thought for a brief moment. "I guess you right," she agreed.

"I know I'm right," Shayna laughed. "So, are y'all down or what?"

"I am," Quiana answered without hesitation. The thought of finally making her own money and not having to depend on Shayna had her smiling from ear to ear.

"I got another question," Ra'Keeyah said to Shayna.

Shayna smiled. "What now?"

"Where you know Calvin from? How you know he ain't the police?"

Quiana was fed up with all Ra'Keeyah's questions. "Are you gon' do it or not, damn!" she snapped. "What difference does it make where she know the mutha'fucka from?"

Ra'Keeyah looked at Quiana like she had just lost her mind, and then turned her attention back to Shayna. "Anyways, like I was sayin', where do you know Calvin from?"

"I met Calvin through Joe," Shayna explained. "Joe be sellin' Calvin and all his buddies weed. So one day I rode with Joe to Calvin's office, and he asked Joe if I belonged to him, and when Joe told him no, he asked me if he could get my number, and it's been on and poppin' since then."

"Wow." Ra'Keeyah was surprised. "And here it is people think that only black folks be buyin' and smokin' bud."

"You'd be surprised. 'Cuz when Calvin and his friends be buyin' bud from Joe, they spend big doe! They be buyin' pounds at a time."

"I bet they do," Ra'Keeyah said.

"So, back to business. Are you dancin' with us or what?" Shayna asked, changing the subject back to the question at hand.

"I still don't know," Ra'Keeyah said.

Quiana smacked her lips. "You had Shayna go through all that shit, and you still don't know?"

"That's what I said," Ra'Keeyah answered as the bell rang. "I'll holla' at y'all," she said grabbing her books off the lunch table and heading to her sixth-period class. Shayna shook her head and smiled as she watched her best friend disappear up the lunchroom stairs.

Chapter Seven

Ra'Keeyah lay in her bed attempting to study for her history test, when all she really wanted to do was smoke a blunt and relax. But she knew the way her grades were slipping, she had to at least get a C on her test to keep from failing the class. Ra'Keeyah's mother had warned her time and time again that she'd better bring her grades up or she'd be babysitting her little brother the entire summer. No matter what it took, Ra'Keeyah refused to spend her summer sitting in the house with her annoying brother.

"What you doin'?" Ra'Keeyah's mother stuck her head in her bedroom door and asked.

What it look like I'm doin? Ra'Keeyah wanted to say. "Studyin'," Ra'Keeyah looked up from her notes and answered.

Her mom pushed the door all the way open and walked in. "That's good." She looked around her room as if she'd never been in there before.

What yo' nosy ass lookin' for? Ra'Keeyah thought. "You need somethin' from outta here?" she sat up and asked her mother.

"No. I'm just lookin' around, that's all," her mother said as she continued looking. "You got somethin' to hide?"

"No, I don't have nothin' to hide. I was just wonderin' why you was all up in here lookin' around, that's all."

"I'm not allowed to look around in a room in my house where I pay rent?" her mother asked as she walked over to Ra'Keeyah's dresser and began rambling through stuff.

"Ma, what is you lookin' for?" Ra'Keeyah frowned. "Don't nothin' on my dresser belong to you!"

"Correction," her mother snapped. "*Everything* on this dresser belongs to me."

"Dang, Ma, why you come up in my room trippin'?" Ra'Keeyah grimaced.

"'Cuz I can," her mother replied. "This my damn house, and I do what I want!"

"Here we go, Johnny Gill with this 'My, My, My,'" Ra'Keeyah huffed.

"You damn right," her mother said. "I'm the one with the job and payin' all the damn bills so you right, everything is mines!" Ra'Keeyah shook her head as her mother continued to fuss. "Have you found a job yet?"

"Not yet," Ra'Keeyah answered while rolling her eyes.

"Have you even attempted to go out and fill out some applications?"

"Yeah, I filled out some applications," Ra'Keeyah lied. "Shoot, I can't make these people hire me."

"Like I said before, McDonald's is hirin' folks your age every day!" her mother snapped. "Yo' lazy, lyin' ass ain't been nowhere to fill out nothin'."

"Whatever, Mom," Ra'Keeyah said, standing up from her bed.

"Whatever my ass!" Ra'Keeyah's mother yelled while pointing her finger in her daughter's face. "I told you, you had three weeks. Your time is up! Your phone will be off tomorrow."

The thought of her phone being disconnected hit Ra'Keeyah like a ton of bricks. She didn't want her mother to know that she was affected by it. So Ra'Keeyah played it cool. "Do you," she said nonchalantly.

"I am," her mother replied while walking past her and out into the hallway. "I'm gon' do me, and you gon' do you. 'Cuz your ass is still gon' work while livin' under this roof."

"Whoooa," Ra'Keeyah said. "So you mean to tell me you gon' get my phone turned off and I still gotta get a job?"

"You damn right, Ra'Keeyah," her mother answered. "You sixteen. You old enough to be helpin' me out with the bills and shit."

"That's foul!" Ra'Keeyah argued.

"No. What's foul is I got a broad livin' up in my house thinkin' she gon' be up in here livin' and eatin' for free!" her mother yelled. "Ra'Keeyah, I'm tired of gettin' paid on Friday mornin' and broke Friday night. It ain't right, Ra'Keeyah, and you know it!"

"Well, I don't want you to do nothin' else for me, since every time you do, you throw it up in my face!" Ra'Keeyah spat angrily.

"You don't have to worry about me doing shit else for you!" Her mother fussed as she stood in the hallway outside Ra'Keeyah's bedroom door. "Your mouth done got too mutha'fuckin' smart for me! You betta' watch it before I go up in it!"

Ra'Keeyah closed her eyes and shook her head. "All right, Mom," she said, uncaringly.

"You wanna talk and act grown? Yo' ass about to see what it feels like to be grown! Next time you ask me for somethin', I'ma remind you that you don't want me to do nothin' else for you!"

"That's fine," Ra'Keeyah responded. "I'ma get a job."

"You better," her mother said as she turned to walk away. "And I ain't playin'!" Ra'Keeyah's mother walked into her room and slammed the door behind her.

Ra'Keeyah was fed up. Every time her mother came home from having a bad day she took it out on her. It wasn't Ra'Keeyah's fault her father had died from a drug overdose and wasn't around to help out. Nor was it her fault that she'd had Jaylen by a married man and was stupid enough to believe his promises to leave his wife! In Ra'Keeyah's mind, her mother had taken all of her problems out on her for as long as she could remember. Ra'Keeyah was done; she would no longer be the target for all her mother's misery.

She lifted up her mattress and grabbed the last of her half-smoked blunt and the lighter. She needed to calm her nerves and fast before she said something to her mother she'd later regret. She then grabbed her jacket and cell phone off the foot of her bed and walked out into the hallway. She looked over at her mother's bedroom door and contemplated going in her room and giving her a piece of her mind but decided against it. She put on her jacket as she walked down the stairs heading toward the front door.

"Where you goin'?" Jaylen asked.

Ra'Keeyah scowled down at her little brother who was kneeled down in front of the television watching cartoons. "Mind yo' business," she said and continued out the door. She called Shayna as she walked off the porch.

"What's up?" Shayna answered while rambling through her closet.

"On my way over there so I can calm my nerves," Ra'Keeyah answered as her feet quickly beat the pavement.

"What's the matter wit' you?" Shayna quit rambling and asked.

"Me and my mom just got into it," Ra'Keeyah said heated.

"About what?"

"The same ol' shit, me gettin' a job and helpin' her around the house. But you know it's more to it than that. She just usin' that as an excuse," Ra'Keeyah said. "Anyways, what you doin'?"

"Lookin' for somethin' to wear tonight."

"Where you goin' tonight?"

"Me and Quiana is dancin' for Calvin and his friends tonight at the Holiday Inn. You sure you don't wanna make some of that money?" Shayna asked. "It's plenty to go around."

As bad as Ra'Keeyah wanted to say no, she knew dancing would be the only way she'd make her own money and get her mom off her back. Working at McDonald's wasn't going to cut it! Stooping that low just to make a dollar was something she really didn't want to do, but Ra'Keeyah had to do the inevitable and had her mother to thank for it.

"Count me in, bitch! I'ma bouta' get paid," Ra'Keeyah said, hanging up the phone and hurrying to Shayna's house.

Chapter Eight

Ra'Keeyah was a nervous wreck as she, Quiana, and Shayna got dressed in the hotel bedroom. All that kept going through her mind was what she had gotten herself into it. More than a few times she wanted to call her mom and tell her to come pick her up, but she'd ask too many questions, giving her something else to bitch about. So she put her big girl panties on and stuck it out.

"I can't wait to go out here and make this money," Quiana said as she rubbed glitter all over her body.

"I know that's right," Shayna agreed as she sipped on her favorite St. Claire Green Tea Vodka.

Ra'Keeyah couldn't believe how calm Quiana and Shayna were. They laughed and joked with ease. They acted like they'd been doing this type of mess for years.

"You all right?" Shayna looked over at Ra'Keeyah and asked.

"Yeah, I'm cool," she responded as she reluctantly slid into her one-piece, G-string bathing suit.

"Damn, girl, where you get all this ass from?" Shayna laughed while slapping Ra'Keeyah on her round backside and watching as it jiggled. "You look like LisaRaye for real now!" she laughed harder.

Ra'Keeyah swung at Shayna's hand. "Bitch, you betta' gon'. I don't get down like that," Ra'Keeyah laughed too, easing some of her anxiety.

"Here, let me help you." Shayna grabbed Ra'Keeyah's strings and tied them around her neck. "Why you shakin'?"

"I ain't gon' lie, I'm a little nervous," Ra'Keeyah admitted.

Shayna walked over to the dresser and poured a shot of St. Claire Green Tea Vodka in a shot glass. "Here, drink this," she said shoving it in Ra'Keeyah's face. "This'll calm your nerves."

"I'm cool. You know I don't drink," Ra'Keeyah said, moving the shot glass out of her face. "You remember what happened the last time I drank some liquor."

Both Quiana and Shayna began to laugh. "Yeah, we had to carry your ass all the way home," Quiana said, taking the shot from Shayna's hand and taking it to the head.

"You was sick for days," Shayna laughed.

The thought of how she'd felt that night got Ra'Keeyah lightweight queasy. "I know, man. I was sick as a dog."

"You haven't drank nothin' since then, have you?" Shayna asked, as she buckled up her three-inch stilettos.

"Nope, and don't plan on it," Ra'Keeyah said, before applying lip gloss to her lips.

"I wonder how many gon' show up," Quiana said. "I'm tryin'a make some doe tonight."

"I don't know, but I'm ready to do this and get it over with," Ra'Keeyah said while rubbing glitter on her breasts.

Shayna peeked out the door and smiled. "Okay, ladies, y'all ready? Calvin just nodded his head, giving us the okay to come on out."

"*That's* what's up!" Quiana said, excited.

Ra'Keeyah's heart raced as they walked out of the bedroom and out to the sitting quarters.

"Have mercy," a couple of the men said simultaneously.

"What I tell you?" Calvin boasted. "I told you they'd
be gorgeous," he said with a huge smile.

"My goodness, you didn't lie," one of the men replied.

"Okay, fellows, calm down," Shayna announced to
the six men in the room. "Me and my lovely friends are
about to put on a show that will definitely get yo' dicks
hard," she said with laughter.

Laughter rang throughout the room. "Bring it *on*
then," someone shouted.

Shayna walked over to the boom box and pushed
PLAY. Plies "Put It On Ya" came blaring out of the speakers. They were bumping and grinding to the beat. The
way they moved, anyone that didn't know them would
have thought dancing was their profession. Money
was flying from every direction. The more money that
landed on the floor, the harder the girls gyrated.

The plan was once the first song went off, Beyoncé's
"Ego" would come on; then they would separate and
gyrate all over the men for extra cash. Things didn't
go as planned, at least not for Ra'Keeyah. Once Plies
went off, she was stuck in one spot. She couldn't bring
herself to let them old men fondle her. One of the men
stood from his chair and grabbed her by the wrist, pulling her over to him. She looked down at the light blue
veins on the back of his hands and instantly got freaked
out.

Shayna tried to discreetly mean-mug Ra'Keeyah
while making her money all at the same time. Quiana
was so engrossed in making her own money, she didn't
even notice what was going on.

Ra'Keeyah quickly snatched away from the man and
ran back into the bedroom. She wiped at her skin as
she sat on the bed. A few seconds later, Shayna walked
into the room.

"You okay?" she asked her best friend.

"Yeah, I'm fine. I just need a few minutes to pull myself together, that's all," Ra'Keeyah replied.

"Okay, well, bitch, it's rainin' twenties out there. I'm bouta' go get paid," Shayna smiled.

Ra'Keeyah smiled back. "I ain't mad at you."

Ra'Keeyah stood up from the bed and paced back and forth. As bad as she didn't want to go back out there, she knew she had to. Too much money was being made out there; money that she most definitely needed. She looked over at the St. Claire Green Tea Vodka that sat on the dresser, walked over, poured herself a shot and took it to the head. A few seconds later, she took another to the face. Not feeling the effects quick enough, she put the bottle up to her lips and took a long drink before slamming the bottle back down on top of the dresser.

Ra'Keeyah wiped her mouth, applied more lip gloss, and headed back out to the party. Shayna looked over at her best friend and smiled. Beyoncé's "Video Phone" was playing. She started dancing and getting back into the groove of things. The three ladies walked back into the middle of the floor. Cali Swag "Teach Me How To Dougie" came on, and they broke out into another routine that required them rubbing on each other's breasts, which sent the old men over the edge.

Ra'Keeyah turned around and bent over and made her ass clap like hands. If that didn't get the old men's desert bones hard, they didn't know what else would. Ra'Keeyah made it rain with that move. Money started flying like fireworks on the Fourth of July. Shayna didn't know what caused the sudden change in Ra'Keeyah, but whatever it was, she definitely wasn't mad at her! Chris Brown's "Deuces" was the last song on the CD. When that came on, the girls knew the party was almost over, which made them step their game up.

Ra'Keeyah gyrated all over the men's laps, literally dry fucking each one she danced on. She decided if she was going to belittle herself by dancing for these old men, her pockets would most definitely be on swole when she got finished.

At the end of the night the girls were pleased with the outcome. Once Quiana had counted her money, she didn't mind giving Shayna her fifty-dollar finder's fee. She still had over eight hundred dollars to herself. The men loved the ladies so much that they set up another party for the following Saturday. Quiana was ecstatic. If left up to her, she'd dance for them every night of the week. Shayna was happy as well.

"Well, 'cuz, you came through with this one," Quiana said to Shayna.

Shayna smiled. "Thanks. You know I wouldn't steer you and Ra'Keeyah wrong. All I ask y'all to do is trust me."

Quiana looked at her stack of bills again before speaking. "I won't ever doubt you again."

Shayna looked over at Ra'Keeyah who was sprawled out on the California king-sized bed knocked out. A little after the men had left she lay across the bed and started counting her money and before long, she was snoring. Shayna gathered her best friend's money and put it in her purse before throwing the comforter over her body.

"We ain't leavin'?" Quiana asked.

Shayna looked at Quiana like she'd just asked one of the dumbest questions in the world. "Bitch, this suite is paid for tonight, so why would we leave?"

"I feel you," Quiana smiled widely and lay down next to Ra'Keeyah and drifted off to sleep with her money still in her hand.

Shayna looked down at her two sleeping friends before going into the bathroom to remove her makeup. As she stared at herself in the mirror, her horrible past began to haunt her all over again. Thoughts of the abuse she'd endured as a child popped up in her mind. As hard as she tried to forget and move on with her life, something wouldn't let her. She burst into tears as she thought about all the horrible things her mother had let happen to her. She tried to stop the tears, but it was useless; they continued to flow. Shayna stuck her head out the bathroom door to make sure Ra'Keeyah and Quiana were still asleep. She wiped the tears away the best she could and walked out of the bathroom. She walked past the girls out to the sitting area, balled up on the sofa, and cried herself to sleep.

Chapter Nine

For the next two months, Ra'Keeyah, Shayna, and Quiana danced for the men every Saturday. What started out as them dancing for six men quickly turned into ten men. They didn't complain because the more men they danced for meant more money in their pockets. For the first time in her life, Ra'Keeyah had money of her own. She'd started paying her own cell phone bill, buying her own clothes, and even kicking her mother out a few ends to pay some bills. She'd even gone as far as buying her little brother the latest Jordans and a couple of summer outfits.

Ra'Keeyah's mother was finally proud of her because she was really stepping up and showing responsibility. But she also threatened to put her out if she found out that she was messing around with any drug dealers. Ra'Keeyah assured her mother that she wasn't and had lied and told her that she had a job at Mr. Wilson's corner store. At first, her mother wasn't too pleased with the place her daughter chose to work, knowing Mr. Wilson had a thing for young girls, but ended up giving her credit for even finding a job. Still skeptical because of all the money Ra'Keeyah was spending, her mother asked her if she was sleeping with Mr. Wilson for money. The look Ra'Keeyah shot her mother told her she definitely wasn't.

It was Sunday morning and Ra'Keeyah was determined to sleep in. She would have if it wasn't for her mother laughing out loud while she talked on the phone. Ra'Keeyah's body was sore from all the dancing she'd done the night before. Shayna and Quiana were amazed when she started doing splits. Actually, Ra'Keeyah had amazed herself, because she hadn't done splits since she was a cheerleader in middle school.

Ra'Keeyah heard her mother walking toward her bedroom and closed her eyes, pretending she was still asleep. That just let Ra'Keeyah know that she was about to talk about something that she didn't want Ra'Keeyah to hear. Her mother stuck her head in the door, waited a few seconds, and shut the door back.

Ra'Keeyah waited a few minutes and climbed out of the bed when she heard her mother's bedroom door close. She slowly opened her bedroom door, snuck into the hallway, eased up to her mother's door, and put her ear up against it. She overheard her mother telling the person on the phone that she was going to Mr. Wilson's store before heading to work and ask him if she really worked for him. Ra'Keeyah thought she'd convinced her mother how she made her money, but she'd thought wrong.

Ain't that about a bitch! Ra'Keeyah thought as she snuck back into her bedroom and eased the door closed. "I gotta trick for her connivin' ass," she said, lying back down in her bed trying to come up with a plan. Before long, Ra'Keeyah had drifted off to sleep for some much-needed rest.

She woke up to her little brother staring down into her face. Her heart nearly jumped out of her chest. "Move, li'l nigga," Ra'Keeyah yelled while pushing Jaylen out of her face.

"I'm hungry, Ra'Keeyah," he said.

"What you tellin' me for? I ain't none of yo' momma," she said, throwing the covers back and sitting up. "Where Momma at anyways?"

"She went to work."

Ra'Keeyah climbed out of bed and stretched her arms. "She didn't feed you before she left?"

"No, she was runnin' late," Jaylen answered. "She told me to wake you up and have you fix me somethin'."

"I guess you'll be starvin' till she bring her black ass home," Ra'Keeyah laughed as she walked out of her room and into the bathroom.

"Key-Key," her brother whined.

"Shut up, crybaby, and go down to the kitchen and wait on me. I'll be down there," she said before closing the door in his face.

Ra'Keeyah washed her face and brushed her teeth before going down to the kitchen and fixing her brother something to eat. After she washed up the few dishes she'd messed up, she made Jaylen get in the tub and get dressed.

"Shit," she said as she brushed her little brother's hair, hoping her mother didn't go to Mr. Wilson's store.

"What's wrong?" he asked.

"Did Mommy say she was goin' to Mr. Wilson's store before she went to work?"

"No, I told you she was runnin' late," Jaylen said.

"Oh yeah, that's right. Well, go downstairs and watch TV or play your Xbox until I get dressed. And if you be good, I'll take you to the store and buy you some candy."

"Okay," Jaylen said and ran down the stairs to watch SpongeBob.

Ra'Keeyah was relieved that her mom hadn't had time to stop at Mr. Wilson's store to give him the third degree yet. She knew she had to beat her mother to the punch. She ran into her room and found one of the shortest miniskirts she had and a shirt that showed off the belly ring that she'd kept hidden from her mother. Mr. Wilson liked young girls so Ra'Keeyah knew if she dressed the part, she could get him to do anything she wanted him to do. She dug in her drawer finding a pair of thongs and ran into the bathroom and jumped in the shower.

Once Ra'Keeyah got dressed, she brushed her hair into a side ponytail, applied some lip gloss to her lips, and looked at her reflection in the mirror. She turned around to check out her backside before pulling her thongs up so you could see the top of them. Pleased with what she saw, Ra'Keeyah hurried down the stairs.

"Come on, boy," she said to Jaylen who was glued to the television.

Jaylen looked away from the television and asked, "We goin' to get my candy?"

"Yep."

Jaylen hit the PAUSE button on the remote so he could pick back up where he'd left off when they returned from the store. "Key-Key, why you got them clothes on?" Jaylen asked as they walked out the door.

Ra'Keeyah looked down at her outfit and asked, "What's wrong wit' my clothes?" she asked defensively.

"They look too little," he answered innocently. "Key-Key, what's that stickin' outta yo' stomach?"

Ra'Keeyah quickly covered her navel. "It's a belly button ring," she answered as they walked down the street.

"Do Mommy got a belly button ring?"

"No, Jaylen," Ra'Keeyah rolled her eyes.

"Well, I'ma tell her to get one 'cuz it looks cool," Jaylen smiled.

"No, Jaylen, you can't tell Mommy I got a belly button ring," Ra'Keeyah said quickly. "She would kill me if she found out!"

"Why?"

"Mommy don't like piercings or tattoos," Ra'Keeyah explained. "So she would be real mad at me if she found out that I got a piercing. It's gon' be our little secret, okay?"

"Okay, Key-Key, I won't tell her, I promise," Jaylen said as they stood at the busy intersection waiting to cross the street.

Ra'Keeyah grabbed her brother's hand before walking across the street. "Okay, you better not," she warned.

"I won't," he reassured her before opening up the door to Mr. Wilson's corner store.

Ra'Keeyah took her hand and smoothed down her hair. "Pick you out some candy. I'm about to go talk to Mr. Wilson," she said to Jaylen.

"Okay."

Ra'Keeyah sashayed up to the counter with a huge smile on her face. Mr. Wilson was so busy counting his packs of cigarettes he didn't even notice Ra'Keeyah standing at the counter. She cleared her throat, catching his attention. He turned around and once he laid eyes on her, a huge smile crept across his face.

"Hey, Mr. Wilson," Ra'Keeyah smiled back. "What you doin'?"

"Countin' my cigarettes; what it look like, gal?" he said.

Don't get smart you old watered-down pimp, she wanted to say and would have if she didn't need him to lie to her mother for her. "I need a favor," Ra'Keeyah said.

Mr. Wilson leaned over the counter with a huge smile on his face. He was close enough Ra'Keeyah could smell the stale liquor coming out of his pores. "What you need me to do, pretty gal?" he asked as he eyeballed her from head to toe.

Ra'Keeyah wanted to throw up all over the counter and then slap him across the face for eye-fuckin' her without her consent. "I told my mom I work for you, and she said she was gon' come ask you," Ra'Keeyah said.

"Yo' mommy don't even come in here. She act like she too good to come in ol' Petey Wilson's store," he said, sucking his teeth. "And if she did come in here and ask me, what you want me to do? Lie to her?"

Well, duh? Ra'Keeyah thought. "Could you do that for me?" she asked, before squinting her eyes and biting down on her bottom lip as a form of seduction. Ra'Keeyah's eyes went straight to Mr. Wilson's package and like she knew it would be, it was standing at attention.

"What you gon' do for me?" he asked in a slight whisper.

Give you a toothbrush for that one tooth you got danglin' in yo' mouth. Ra'Keeyah laughed at the thought. "What you want me to do?"

"How old are you, gal?"

Normally Ra'Keeyah would have lied about her age in a heartbeat, but in a situation like this, she had no choice but to tell the truth. Especially if Mr. Wilson wanted what she thought he did. "Sixteen," she answered without hesitation, hoping that would keep him from asking her for sex. But even if he did, him lying to her mother was not worth her letting him climb his old, decrepit tail on top of her.

"Aww, man, you jailbait. I'll go to jail for fuckin' wit' you," he said, disappointed.

Ra'Keeyah was more than relieved. "Yea, you would," she said, acting as if she was disappointed as well.

"You sho' gotta body like a grown woman," Mr. Wilson said. "Well, since I can't stick it, let me lick it."

Nigga, are you crazy! "You can go to jail for that too, Mr. Wilson," Ra'Keeyah said.

"Well, you gotta let me do somethin' for lyin' to yo' momma. Shit, I ain't gon' do it for free," he stated. "At least let me touch it."

This nigga is a straight perv, lookin' just like Jerome off of Martin! "Okay," Ra'Keeyah agreed, thinking, how bad could that be? And he was right; nothing in this world is free!

"I'm about to go look at these shoes Mr. Wilson got in the back of the store," Ra'Keeyah hollered over at Jaylen who was busy watching the TV that hung on the wall.

"Hurry up, while ain't no customers in here," Mr. Wilson said, sounding like a sneaky freak. Ra'Keeyah quickly followed him to the back of the store. He led her into the storeroom and closed the door behind them. Ra'Keeyah wasted no time lifting up her short mini, trying to get this over with. She then held her panties to the side, revealing her freshly waxed pouch. Mr. Wilson's mouth began to moisten at the sight.

Ra'Keeyah almost backed out when Mr. Wilson lifted his hand toward her chocolate cave. As many times as she'd been inside of Mr. Wilson's store, she'd never once paid any attention to his long, skinny fingers with his bitchlike fingernails. Only thing was going through Ra'Keeyah's mind while he fingered her was *I hope he don't cut me.*

Mr. Wilson sucked the finger he took out of Ra'Keeyah's dripping wet box. "Come on, let me lick it," he said, quickly getting down on both knees.

Ra'Keeyah took a sudden step back. "You got some money?" she asked, sounding like Shayna.

"Yea, how much you want?" he asked, surprising Ra'Keeyah.

"Gimme a hundred dollars," she said just throwing out an amount.

"That's all? Shit, I can give you that outta my cash register."

Damn, if I woulda' known that, I woulda' asked for more! Ra'Keeyah thought as she threw her leg up on a stack of boxes, exposing all of her business.

"My goodness, that's one of the prettiest pussies I've ever seen," Mr. Wilson said, leaning in for the kill. Just as his tongue was about to explore the unknown, he heard his chimes over his front door ring. "Damn," he snapped as he struggled to get off his knees. "Get yourself together and come back when I close," he said, wiping the beads of sweat from his forehead and walking out the door, leaving Ra'Keeyah standing in the middle of the floor.

Ra'Keeyah waited a few seconds and walked out the door. "I like them shoes," she said, playing it off for whoever had just walked in the store. She surely didn't want anyone to know what she and Mr. Wilson were in the back doing.

Ra'Keeyah's heart nearly jumped out of her throat when she saw who Mr. Wilson was talking to. Of all the people in the world to walk in the store while she was in the back with Mr. Wilson getting her freak on—Brick! Ra'Keeyah felt dirty and embarrassed. She quickly walked over to her little brother whose eyes were still glued to the television set, hoping she didn't look guilty.

"You got your candy?" she asked.

"Yea, it's right here," he said, showing her.

"Let's go," she said and hurried him out the door.

"You didn't pay for the candy," he whispered.

"Trust me, I paid a lot more than what it was worth."

"We goin' down," Jaylen said.

"Shut up, boy, and come on," she replied and hurried home.

"That's you?" Brick asked Mr. Wilson as soon as Ra'Keeyah walked out of the store.

"Naw, man, that ain't me," he replied with a sly grin. "She just some young gal that lives in the neighborhood, that's all."

"Ummm-huh," Brick laughed. "You know yo' old ass be havin' all them young girls in the back of your storeroom blowin' their backs out." Brick laughed even harder.

Mr. Wilson held his head back and let out a hearty laugh. "What can I say? I can't help these young gals like ol' Petey Wilson."

Brick's demeanor became serious. "All right, man, I'm outta here. I just came in here to check on you," Brick glanced up at the football game that was playing on TV. "Let me know when you run out of packs and I'll drop some more off."

"All right, man, will do," Mr. Wilson said. "Gimme two days and I'll have the rest of your money."

"If you stop trickin' off wit' all these young hoes, you'd have my money on time," Brick laughed.

"Naw, man, it ain't even like that, young Blood. I had to pay my sister's rent and shit. You know how that is," Mr. Wilson said.

"Naw, man, I don't," Brick said as he turned to walk away. "I'll be back in two days," he called out over his shoulder.

"Cool and thanks, man, for bein' so understandin'," Mr. Wilson said gratefully.

"This one's on me; the next one's on you." If it was anyone else that didn't have his money on time, Brick would have made them pay dearly. But because Mr. Wilson was never late paying up, Brick cut him some slack. Old man or not, when it came to his money, Brick showed no remorse.

Brick walked out of the store, jumped in his truck, and started it up. He checked his rearview mirror to make sure no police were in sight before pulling off. Mc Breed's "Ain't No Future In Yo' Frontin'" was blaring out of the speakers. He bobbed his head as he drove down the busy intersection. He looked over and noticed the same chick that he'd just seen minutes earlier in Mr. Wilson's store. She was standing on the sidewalk talking on her cell phone. He slowed down thinking about stopping, but it was too late; he'd already passed her.

Brick looked at his watch. "I got a li'l time to kill," he said, busting a U-turn.

Ra'Keeyah didn't recognize the SUV so she started easing her way up the sidewalk as the black Explorer started to slow down. "Come on, Jay-Jay," she called out to her little brother who was playing in the yard. "I don't know who the hell this is." Ra'Keeyah and her little brother walked up on the porch and opened the screen door.

"Where you goin', li'l mama?" somebody yelled out the passenger-side window.

Ra'Keeyah stopped and turned around. "Who that?" she asked with a slight attitude and walked to the end of the porch to see if she could recognize the person.

"Come and see," he toyed. "I don't bite."

"I'm straight. Anyways," Ra'Keeyah said and continued her conversation on the phone. "I told you I don't know who it is. They drivin' a nice-ass truck though." Ra'Keeyah was still trying to figure out who this strange person was that called out to her.

Brick turned the engine off, opened the door, and got out. He had a huge smile on his face as he walked around the front of the truck.

Ra'Keeyah nearly went into cardiac arrest when she saw Brick walking up her sidewalk. "Let me call you back," she said to the person on the other end of the phone. "I said let me call you back, dang," she huffed before hanging up. Ra'Keeyah attempted to pull her skirt down to look more presentable, but it was so short it wouldn't budge.

"What's up?" Brick asked, as he walked up and stood on the bottom step of the porch.

"What's up?" Ra'Keeyah asked, confused, not knowing what Brick wanted. It was weird because they'd never even spoken except one time, and here he was pulling up at her house like they'd been longtime friends.

"Nothin', just chillin'," he responded with a smile.

There was an awkward silence as Ra'Keeyah looked Brick over from the top of his naturally curly hair to the bottom of the Air Maxs he wore. Brick was doing the same; he couldn't help but be pleased with the sight before him.

"How'd you know where I live?" Ra'Keeyah finally asked, breaking the silence.

"I didn't know. I just seen you standin' out there on the sidewalk," he said. "So I stopped. Is that okay?"

"Oh. Well, um, what you want?" she asked, trying to sound more concerned than rude.

"Oh, I came to get my money for that food I bought you and yo' girl at McDonald's," Brick teased.

"Yeah, right!" Ra'Keeyah laughed.

Brick laughed too. "Naw, I'm just playin', but fa' real, Mr. Wilson told me to come get his money for the candy you and your son stole from his store."

"What?" Ra'Keeyah asked, surprised. "We ain't stole no candy!"

"See, I told you we was goin' down," Jaylen said.

Ra'Keeyah turned around and scowled at her brother. "Be quiet, Jaylen."

"I'm just jokin'," Brick busted out laughing. "You got a cute son."

"Son? That ain't my son; he my little brother," she responded. "I don't have any kids," she said, setting the record straight and answering Brick's next question.

"Oh, okay," Brick said, pleased with the answer.

"You got an accent," Ra'Keeyah said, loving his New York dialect.

"That's only 'cuz I'm from New York. Y'all talk country as hell down here," he laughed.

Ra'Keeyah laughed too. "Whatever, nigga. You wanna sit down?" she asked, hoping he would say yes.

"I was wonderin' if you was gon' wait until my legs fell off before you asked me," he joked. Brick walked up on the porch and took a seat on the swing and began swinging.

"Lord, you worse than my brother when it comes to that swing," Ra'Keeyah laughed, taking a seat in one of her mother's patio chairs. "How come y'all just can't sit on the swing without movin' it?"

"The whole purpose when you sit on it is to swing. That's why it's called a swing, ain't that right, li'l man?" he asked Jaylen.

"That's right," Jaylen laughed, before walking in the house.

"He somethin' else," Ra'Keeyah shook her head and laughed. "You got kids?"

"Naw, I don't have none."

"What?" Ra'Keeyah asked, shocked. "I'm surprised a big playa like you don't have kids all over the place."

Brick shook his head. "Naw, not me. I don't get down like that."

"That's good to know." Ra'Keeyah made a mental note of that.

Brick stared at Ra'Keeyah as he rocked back and forth on the swing.

"What you starin' at me for?" she asked, feeling a little uneasy.

"You know who you look like?"

Ra'Keeyah rolled her eyes into the top of her head. "Don't tell me. LisaRaye," she replied with a cocky attitude.

"I was gon' say Cicely Tyson, but if you say LisaRaye, then who am I to argue with you?" Brick laughed.

Ra'Keeyah laughed as well. "No, you didn't say Cicely Tyson."

Brick continued laughing. "I'm just playin'. I was gon' say LisaRaye."

"Whatever," Ra'Keeyah rolled her eyes playfully.

Brick looked at his ringing cell phone before answering the call. "Hang on, li'l mama. 'Sup?" he answered. "That's what I'm talkin' about. I'll be there in about ten minutes."

Ra'Keeyah's heart sank. She really didn't want Brick to leave, but looking at the clock on her cell phone, she knew it was almost time for her mother to get off work. So the timing was actually right. Ra'Keeyah knew if her mom pulled up and saw Brick sitting on her porch, she'd flip out. The truck he drove down to the clothes on his back personified a drug dealer. Even though there was nothing going on between her and Brick, her mother would have no understanding.

Brick stood up from the swing and pressed out his pants with his hands. "Okay, li'l mama, I gotta make a run," he said.

"Okay. Well, thanks for stoppin' by," she said, not knowing if those were the proper words to use.

Brick must have seen the disappointing look in Ra'Keeyah's eyes. "I woulda' stayed a li'l longer, but I have to go get this money."

"Okay, I understand," Ra'Keeyah said, hoping she didn't seem desperate.

"Can I get your number?" he asked.

"You gon' use it?" she joked.

"I wouldna' asked for it if I wasn't gon' use it," he smiled. "Yo' man ain't gon' get mad about me callin' you, is he?"

"I don't know. I don't have one," she replied. "But the question is, is yo' crazy chick gon' get mad when you call me."

Brick smiled and started walking off the porch. "Let me handle that. All right, li'l man?" he yelled into the house at Jaylen.

"Bye," Jaylen replied and continued playing his Xbox.

Ra'Keeyah rambled off her number as she and Brick walked down the sidewalk to his truck. "Now you know this was kinda' awkward, right?"

"What was?" Brick asked, walking around to the driver's side of the truck.

"You stoppin' over my house for no apparent reason."

Brick shot Ra'Keeyah one of his million-dollar smiles. "I'm a spur-of-the-moment typa' nigga," he winked.

Ra'Keeyah smiled. "Whatever."

Brick got in and started up the truck. His loud music made Ra'Keeyah jump, making him laugh. "I'ma hit you up later on, aiiiight?" he said, after he turned the music down.

"Okay," she replied, sounding love struck.

Ra'Keeyah turned and walked away as Brick pulled off. She stopped and watched as he disappeared around the corner. Then she quickly ran back up the walk and into the house. She flew up the stairs to change her clothes before her mother got home. She couldn't wait to call Shayna to tell her who had just left her house. Ra'Keeyah was floating on cloud nine as she dialed her best friend's phone number.

"What it do?"

"Girrrrl, let me tell you!"

Chapter Ten

It had been three weeks since Brick's unexpected visit and Ra'Keeyah hadn't heard from him since. Deep down, she was hurt and still wanted him to call, but she knew eventually she'd get over it just like she did everything else. It was the end of May and summer vacation was right around the corner. Ra'Keeyah had done what she'd set out to do; she passed all her classes with Cs. Her mother thought of her grades as being average, but if she knew what measures Ra'Keeyah went through to get those Cs, she'd be happy for her daughter.

Staying up until two or three in the morning studying while drinking Monster Energy Drinks, and drinking a Grande Cappuccino from Starbucks every morning became habit for Ra'Keeyah in order to keep up in school. She knew that would be the only way she'd be able to pass because on the weekends she had to work and wouldn't have been able to study at all. Dancing for Calvin and his friends was really paying off. Ra'Keeyah had stacked her money and planned on buying a car. She was tired of depending on Marshall to take her everywhere she needed to go and riding the bus was definitely cramping her style.

Ra'Keeyah's mother tapped lightly on her bedroom door and waited to be invited in. "Come in," Ra'Keeyah yelled.

Ra'Keeyah's mom walked in with a huge smile on her face. "You really look nice. Marshall ain't gon' be able to keep his hands off of you," she laughed.

Ra'Keeyah was wearing a pair of red Capris, a red and white top with a plunging neck, and some red and gold stack sandals. She accentuated her outfit with gold hoop earrings, gold bangles, and the gold ring with matching necklace Shayna had bought her for her birthday the previous year.

"Mom, me and Marshall are just friends," Ra'Keeyah said. "So he better keep his hands to himself if he don't want me to cut him," she joked.

Her mother laughed. "Where is he takin' you to-night? You know he's a nice guy. You really should consider makin' him your boyfriend."

"We goin' out to eat and to see that new movie *The Help*," Ra'Keeyah answered, ignoring her mother's last statement.

"I heard it was a good movie. Let me know how it turns out."

"I will," Ra'Keeyah smiled before checking herself out in the mirror from every angle.

"I've always liked your hair like that," her mother said, running her hand down Ra'Keeyah's freshly flat-ironed hair. "And it's growin' too."

"Thanks."

"Okay, well, I'ma let you finish gettin' ready for your date," her mother said walking toward the door. She stopped and turned around. "Ra'Keeyah," she called out.

"Yea, Momma?"

"I really want us to start talkin' more, you know, like we used to when you were little. You'll be grown in a few more years, and I feel like I've missed out on a lot workin' all the time." Ra'Keeyah listened as her mother poured out her heart. "I want you to be able to come and talk to me about anything and trust me to be understandin', okay?"

Ra'Keeyah was shocked but grateful to finally hear those words coming from her mother. She'd longed to have a loving relationship and be able to sit and talk with her mom when she was having problems and have her mom put her arms around her and tell her everything would be okay. Ra'Keeyah wished she could have told her mother about her first crush, her first kiss, and even when she'd lost her virginity. But she was happy that her mother wanted to work on their relationship. Ra'Keeyah figured that it was better late than never.

She smiled at her mom and spoke with sincerity. "I'd like that."

Ra'Keeyah's mother kissed her on the cheek before walking out of her bedroom. Ra'Keeyah was making a few last-minute touch-ups when her cell phone rang. She picked up the phone and checked the number.

"I don't know who this is," she said before answering. "Hello?"

"What's happenin', li'l mama?" Brick asked.

Ra'Keeyah was so excited to hear his voice she didn't know what to do. "What's up?" she answered quickly.

"What you gon' get into tonight? You feel like some company?" Brick needed a break away from everybody, including the streets. He was tired of being around people that only cared about his street status or how much money he had in his pockets. The little time he'd spent over at Ra'Keeyah's house a couple of weeks ago had made him remember what normalcy felt like.

Ra'Keeyah wanted to say yes so bad, she could taste it. Of all the times her mother worked double shifts, how come tonight couldn't have been one of them! She would have loved for Brick to come over and sit on the porch with her so she could watch him rock back and forth on the swing until the wee hours of the morning.

"Or you wanna go for a ride instead?" he asked.

Ra'Keeyah was glad that Brick had come up with another plan. She would have been too embarrassed telling him that he wasn't allowed over.

"What we ridin' in?" She was hoping he'd say on his motorcycle, but for real, she didn't care if he picked her up in a 1980 Pinto, just as long as she was with him.

"In style," Brick said.

Ra'Keeyah smiled. "That's how I like to ride." She was so lost in her phone call with Brick she'd forgotten that quick that she had a date with Marshall. "Damn," she said.

"What's the matter?" Brick asked.

"Nothin'. I forgot I had to do somethin', but it can wait," she said.

"You sure?"

"Yea, I'm sure." Ra'Keeyah had to come up with a plan and quick. Marshall would be there in less than half an hour to get her, and he was always on time. "What time you comin' to get me?"

"I'll be there in about twenty minutes. Is that cool?"

"Yea, that's perfect," she said happily.

"Talk to you then, li'l mama," Brick said.

"Okay," Ra'Keeyah said before pushing the end button on her cell phone. Her mind was working overtime as she dialed Marshall's phone number. She didn't know what excuse she was going to come up with, but she knew she wasn't passing up a chance to spend time with Brick.

"Hello?" Marshall answered.

"Marshall, I'm not gon' be able to go to the movies tonight." Ra'Keeyah moaned as if she was in some kind of pain. "I just came on my period, and I got the cramps really bad," she lied.

"Oh, wow," he said sympathetically. "Well, do you need me to bring you something for the pain?"

"No, thank you. My mom just gave me some Midol," Ra'Keeyah moaned again.

"Well, take care of yourself and I hope you feel better," Marshall said. "And maybe we can catch the movie next weekend."

"Oooooh," she wailed. "Yeah, maybe. Okay, Marshall, I'm about to lie down and put a heatin' pad on my back."

"Okay, call me later."

"I will," she said and quickly ended the call. Ra'Keeyah couldn't help but laugh at the performance she'd just given. She deserved an Oscar. Now it was time for her to put on that same award-winning performance for her mother. Ra'Keeyah put on a sad face, walked out into the hallway, and knocked on her mother's bedroom door.

"Come in," her mother yelled. Ra'Keeyah opened the door and walked in. "What's the matter with you?" she asked when she saw the look on her daughter's face.

"Marshall can't go to the movies. He called and said he got a toothache."

"Oh, wow, that's too bad," her mother said.

"I know, right?" Ra'Keeyah agreed. "And I'm all dressed up with nowhere to go."

"Well, don't be sad, Key-Key. Can't you call Shayna and see what she's doin' tonight? You know she *always* doin' somethin'."

Ra'Keeyah sighed heavily. "I guess. I really wanted to go see that movie though," Ra'Keeyah was on a roll.

"I know, baby. Maybe y'all can go next weekend."

"Yea, maybe," Ra'Keeyah replied and turned to walk out of her mother's bedroom. "I'm about to go call Shayna to see what she's gon' do tonight."

"Okay, let me know before you leave," her mom said.

"I will." Ra'Keeyah walked out of her mother's room and closed the door behind her. She hurried to her room hearing her cell phone ringing. "Damn, I'm good!" she said before answering it. "Hello?"

"I'm on my way," Brick said.

"Okay, I'll be ready." Ra'Keeyah ran to the mirror to make sure she still looked okay. She applied some chocolate lip gloss on her lips, ran her fingers through her hair, and threw her phone into her purse. "Mom, I'm leavin'," she ran into the hallway and yelled.

"Okay, be back by curfew," her mother called out.

Whatever! "Okay," she yelled and hurried down the stairs and out the front door. Ra'Keeyah knew it didn't matter what time she came home, as long as she was there before her mother woke up. With her being with Brick and Jaylen being over at their Aunt Nancy's, her mother would be getting some much-needed rest without any interruptions.

Ra'Keeyah had a huge smile on her face as she walked down the front walk and spotted Brick's black BMW motorcycle coming down the street. The sound of the engine purring brought back a lot of old childhood memories of her father.

Brick pulled up to the curb and shut the engine off. Ra'Keeyah looked up at her mother's bedroom window and hoped she wasn't looking out being nosy. Brick took off his glasses, got off the bike, and walked around to the sidewalk.

He smiled at the astounding sight before him. "You look good," he said, pleased.

"Thank you," she replied bashfully. "And so do you." Brick sported a pair of dark blue Coogie jeans, a white and dark blue Coogie button-down shirt, and a pair of crispy white and blue Campus Suede Adidas.

"You ever been on the back of one of these before?" he asked.

"Not nothin' like this. I used to ride on the back of my daddy's Harley," she answered, quietly.

"So you know the basics about riding on the back? You know when I lean you lean too," Brick said.

"Yeah, yeah. I just told you I'm not new to this," Ra'Keeyah said with an attitude.

Brick took the helmet off the back of the seat. "If I woulda' known you were gon' be lookin' this good, I woulda' drove the Lex," Brick smiled. "Unless you wanna go in the house and change."

There was no way Ra'Keeyah was going back in the house. With her luck, her mother would be up. "No, I'm fine. I can ride in this."

"Okay, suit yourself." Brick put the helmet on Ra'Kee-yah's head and adjusted the strap. "Now, I don't wanna hear you bitchin' about your hair bein' messed up," he laughed as he walked back around the motorcycle and got on.

"I'm still gon' look good, even with my hair messed up," she said as she climbed on the back of the bike.

"You hope," he laughed, starting up the motorcycle.

Ra'Keeyah wrapped her arms around Brick's waist. "Hold on tight," he said before taking off.

The sound of the wind tunneling through the helmet was like music to Ra'Keeyah's ears. It had been a long time since she'd been on the back of a motorcycle, and man, it felt good. She closed her eyes and for a split second imagined she was riding with her father. Ra'Keeyah missed him so much. She would have given anything just to be able to talk to him.

"You okay?" Brick asked, rolling. He handled the powerful motorcycle like a true champion as he sped down the open road.

"I'm good," she replied as they rode down dark, back roads that she had never been on before. Under any other circumstance, Ra'Keeyah would have been afraid traveling without knowing her destination, but for some reason, she felt safe with Brick. Ra'Keeyah held on to Brick like he belonged to her. She could smell the scent of his cologne Guilty blowing in the breeze. *He smells so good*, she thought, and then rested her head on his back and enjoyed the ride.

Chapter Eleven

Forty-five minutes later, Brick pulled up at a diner that sat in the middle of nowhere. There were several other motorcycles parked outside. He shut the engine off and waited for Ra'Keeyah to get off the bike before getting off himself.

Ra'Keeyah took off the helmet and strapped it on the back of the bike. "What we doin' way out here?" she asked while looking around.

"I don't know about you, but I come to eat," Brick said, smiling.

"Has anyone ever told you that your mouth is somewhat smart?" she smiled back.

"Nope, you're the first," he smiled again.

"What my hair look like?" she asked, while attempting to smooth it down with her hands.

"It look all right. Here, let me help you," Brick said, smoothing it down real hard.

Ra'Keeyah moved her head away from him. "Damn, nigga, you tryin'a break my neck?" she laughed.

"I was just tryin'a help a sista out, that's all," he winked before walking over and opening up the door. "After you."

"These white folks gon' kill our black asses," she mumbled as she walked into the diner. Ra'Keeyah was shocked when she saw that all the customers were black except maybe three.

"Now what was you sayin' as we were walkin' in?" Brick asked, smiling.

"Nothin'."

"Hey, Brick," the waitress walked over and greeted him with a huge smile. Her smile slowly faded when she looked over at Ra'Keeyah, who she promptly checked out up and down, and then turned her attention back to Brick.

"What's up, Davinette?" he replied while scanning the half-crowded restaurant.

"Long time no see," she said. "Where you been?"

"I been busy," he answered, spotting the person he was looking for.

"I made your favorite lasagna last week. You missed it. Maybe next time I make it, I'll call you and you can come over and get you some," Davinette smirked.

Brick laughed, catching on to what Davinette was insinuating. "We'll see."

If it was left up to Davinette, lasagna wasn't going to be the only thing on the menu. "Aren't you gon' introduce me to your little friend?" Davinette asked snottily.

Brick looked at Ra'Keeyah, and then back at Davinette. "Sit her by the window," Brick said, avoiding the question. Even if he would have known Ra'Keeyah's name, he still wouldn't have told her. "I need to go over here and handle some business. I'll be right back," he said to Ra'Keeyah.

"All right," Ra'Keeyah replied and followed the nosy waitress to her table and took a seat.

"My name is Davinette, and I'll be your waitress for the evenin'," she said with a fake smile before shoving a menu in Ra'Keeyah's face. "What you want to drink?"

"I mean, I haven't even had time to open the menu," Ra'Keeyah said calmly.

"We have what every other restaurant has," Davinette shot back.

"You know what? I'm not even thirsty," Ra'Keeyah said, laying the menu down on the table. She wasn't going to take any chances on having this rude chick spitting in her drink.

Davinette stood over the table staring down at Ra'Keeyah while cracking her chewing gum. "So, um, you his pick for the night?" she finally said.

No, this bold bitch did not just ask me that! Ra'Keeyah thought. She didn't know if she should answer her question calmly or do one of Shayna's numbers and go ham on her.

Ra'Keeyah looked up at Davinette with a smile on her face. "Where did that come from?" she asked, taking the civil way out, only because she was too far out to call for backup in case she needed it.

"Oh, I was jus' askin'," Davinette replied, innocently.

"Well, if you really must know, me and Brick are just friends," Ra'Keeyah stated, slightly annoyed.

"Oh, don't get me wrong. I wasn't bein' nosy or nuttin' like that. I was just askin'," Davinette lied.

"Well, no, you don't have to worry about me gettin' in your way, if that's what you worried about. Have at him," Ra'Keeyah said.

Davinette laughed. "No, it ain't even like that, honey. I been knowin' Brick for a long time. And if I wanted him I don't think I would need permission from you or nobody else."

"Oh, okay. Well, don't you have some other tables to wait on?" Ra'Keeyah asked, wanting this crazy broad as far away from her as possible.

"What's up, li'l mama, you miss me?" Brick walked over to the table and asked, taking a seat across from Ra'Keeyah.

Ra'Keeyah was relieved to see him before things got out of hand. Davinette rolled her eyes and stormed away from the table. Ra'Keeyah shook her head and smiled. "You really got these hoes goin' crazy over you, don't you?"

"Let me guess, Davinette?"

"Yeah, man. Her crazy ass over here askin' me if I was your pick for the night," Ra'Keeyah grimaced. She was ready to go before things got out of hand. "That broad don't know me. I'll fuck her ass up!" Ra'Keeyah snapped.

Brick laughed. He loved himself a feisty woman. "Calm down, li'l mama, she do that to everybody I bring up in here. She be trippin'," Brick laughed some more.

"Ummph, just how many females do you bring up in here?" Ra'Keeyah asked, feeling somewhat jealous.

Brick smiled. "It ain't even like that. I handle a lot of business out here."

"Well, maybe you need to give that nut, what she want, and then maybe she'll stop trippin', 'cuz I ain't the one."

"Naw, I'm straight. She been tryin'a get at me since I moved down here," Brick said picking up his menu, checking to see what the special was. "Plus, I don't like women who force themselves on men. That's worse than a woman shakin' her ass for cash."

"I feel you on that." Ra'Keeyah's heart sank because shaking her ass was just how she made her money. But until she found someone to take care of her every need, she'd continue doing what she did to get hers.

"What you wanna eat?" Brick asked, steering the conversation away from Davinette. "The meat loaf is good," he suggested.

"I'm straight. I ain't even hungry."

"Why not? The food here is excellent," Brick said.

"I don't trust that broad," Ra'Keeyah replied. "Shit, she might do somethin' to my food!"

"I'll tell you what. I'll go in the back and order our food, and have the owner bring it out to us," Brick said. "How does that sound?"

"Yeah, right. You don't got it like that!" Ra'Keeyah laughed.

"You wanna bet?"

"What you wanna bet?" Ra'Keeyah asked, knowing that Brick had pull, but not enough to have the owner of the restaurant serve them their food.

"If I win, I get to kiss you," he smirked.

"And if you lose what do I get?" Ra'Keeyah questioned.

"And if I lose, you get to kiss me," he smiled, showing off his snow-white teeth.

"Well, what's in it for me?" Ra'Keeyah laughed. "Who said I wanna kiss you?"

"Trust me, you do," he winked. "Now, what you want to eat?"

Ra'Keeyah felt herself getting all warm inside as the thought of kissing Brick ran through her mind. She picked up the menu and began scanning it to keep her mind occupied with something other than lip-locking with Brick. After a few minutes she decided on the meat loaf.

"Good choice," he said, standing up. "I'll be right back. I'm goin' to place our orders."

Ra'Keeyah watched as Brick disappeared through the double doors that lead to the kitchen. She shook her head and smiled. Then she looked around at the décor in the diner and thought it reminded her of the

TV show *Happy Days*. It had the big, old-fashioned juke box in the corner and pictures of old-fashioned cars hanging everywhere. License plates from every state hung neatly around the diner, along with autographed pictures of movie stars. Looking from the outside of the building, no one would have ever thought it was so cozy on the inside.

Brick walked back toward the table with a smile on his face. "Our order should be out in a few," he said, sitting down.

"I can't wait; I'm starvin'," Ra'Keeyah said.

"Me too," Brick agreed. He looked over at Ra'Keeyah and just stared at her. He stared so long, she started feeling uncomfortable.

"What you lookin' at?" she finally asked.

"I was jus' checkin' you out, li'l mama," he said with a smile.

"Can I ask you a question?" Ra'Keeyah said. Brick nodded his head. "Do you even know my name?"

"Yea, li'l mama," he joked. "Naw, but for real, I don't," he admitted.

"That's a shame," Ra'Keeyah said, shaking her head. "I could be a deranged serial killer and you wouldn't even know it."

"You too pretty to be a deranged serial killer," Brick smiled. He thought for a brief moment and said, "You gon' tell me yo' name? Just in case I heard it on *Unsolved Mysteries* or *America's Most Wanted*," he joked. Ra'Keeyah shook her head no. "What yo' name is?" Brick said, sounding like Li'l Jon.

Ra'Keeyah busted out laughing. "You so silly, boy." A dude that could make her laugh was a big plus in her book. "Are you always this crazy?"

Brick smiled. "I love to laugh. But I rarely ever have time to have fun. I be so busy in them streets. People that don't know me think I'm real serious. Don't too many people know I have a silly side."

"I don't know why people think you so serious, 'cuz all you do is smile," Ra'Keeyah said.

"I smile 'cuz I'm wit' you," he winked.

Ra'Keeyah rolled her eyes. "Whatever," she laughed while looking over his shoulder. "I think that's our food comin'."

Brick turned around to see if it was. He smiled when he saw the owner coming toward them with their plates.

The owner put their meals down in front of them. She looked over at Ra'Keeyah and smiled. "How you doin' tonight? I'm Pauline, the owner of the Road Runner's Diner," she said, sticking out her hand for Ra'Keeyah to shake.

Ra'Keeyah was shocked. Impressed was her exact feeling. She smiled back and shook her hand. "Ra'Keeyah," she introduced herself, and then looked over at Brick and playfully rolled her eyes.

"Ra'Keeyah," Pauline repeated. "That's a pretty name."

"Thank you."

"Okay, well, enjoy," Pauline said before walking away from the table.

Brick bowed his head and prayed over his food, and Ra'Keeyah followed suit.

"So, you want your kiss now or later on?" he asked after blessing his food.

"We might as well get the torture over with," Ra'Keeyah joked. She closed her eyes and puckered her lips.

"Might as well." Brick leaned over the table and planted a kiss on her cheek. Ra'Keeyah's eyes shot open. "There," he said, sitting back in his seat. She turned up her face. "What? You expected more than that? I don't know you like that," he joked.

Ra'Keeyah started laughing. "You silly," she said, and began eating her deliciously prepared meal.

"What do you do for a livin'?" Brick looked at Ra'Keeyah and asked before sticking a fork full of mashed potatoes into his mouth. Ra'Keeyah nearly choked on her green beans. "You okay? Can we get some water over here," Brick summoned to Davinette and asked.

Davinette brought a half glass of water and slammed it down on the table before walking away.

"Yeah, I'm okay," Ra'Keeyah answered once her airways were cleared. "My food went down the wrong pipe."

"Well, slow down. You over there eatin' like the food gon' jump off the table and run away," he laughed.

Ra'Keeyah laughed too. "Shut up, nigga."

"Now back to what I was sayin'," Brick said. "What do you do for a livin'?"

Damn, he's persistent, Ra'Keeyah thought. "I'm in between jobs," she responded quickly, hoping that would answer his question.

"Okay, I see you avoidin' my question," Brick said, finishing off his meal.

"I answered you, dang. I told you I'm between jobs," Ra'Keeyah said smartly. "What more do you want me to say?"

"Calm down, li'l mama. I didn't mean to offend you," Brick smiled. "I don't care what you do for a livin', as long as you ain't no stripper."

"And what if I was?" she asked, needing to know.

"Just know, Brick don't fuck wit' no strippers."

"And why not?"

"'Cuz I don't want my woman havin' no job that consist of men rubbin' all over her body. If anybody gon' be touchin' all on her, its gon' be me!" he stated adamantly.

"You must be one of them jealous typa' niggas."

"I ain't jealous. I can get any woman I want," Brick said. "I'm just not gon' stand for my woman bein' no damn stripper, point-blank period!"

Ra'Keeyah could tell by the way Brick spoke that he was very adamant about not having a stripper as his woman. She knew if things went any further between her and Brick, eventually she would have to tell him the truth. But right now, all she wanted to do was bask in the ambiance.

After laughing and talking for another hour, and Brick receiving numerous text messages, he decided it was time to go. Ra'Keeyah really did not want to leave; she would have stayed at the diner all night if Brick wanted to, but she knew he had business to tend to.

"Bye, Brick," Davinette sang as he and Ra'Keeyah made their way to the exit.

Brick smiled. "Bye, Davinette."

"Silly, bitch," Ra'Keeyah said, before walking out the door.

Brick came outside as Ra'Keeyah put the helmet on. He could tell by her body language that she had a slight attitude.

"What you mad about, li'l mama?" Brick asked.

"I ain't mad," she said snottily.

Brick walked over to her and lifted her chin up with his finger. "Don't let that broad get up under your skin," he smiled, put his glasses on, and climbed on the bike. Ra'Keeyah was touched by his remark. It kind of gave her a sense of peace, as if he was saying to her that no one can come between them. With that being said, Ra'Keeyah climbed on the back of the motorcycle, wrapped her arms around Brick's waist, and held on for the ride.

Chapter Twelve

Brick woke up to the smell of bacon cooking. He had to be dreaming because Piper definitely couldn't cook. He looked over at the light blue paint on the walls and smiled, realizing he was in Pauline's guest bedroom. Brick rolled out of bed and noticed he was still fully dressed, shoes and all. He shook his head in disbelief. "I need to quit drinkin'," he said as he made his way out of the bedroom and across the hall to the bathroom.

"I see you finally got up," Pauline yelled out from the kitchen.

"I know," he said, closing the door behind him, rushing to get his pants unzipped to release the urine that he'd been holding all night.

"Breakfast is ready."

"Ahhhhh, okay," Brick moaned as he stood at the toilet pissing for what seemed like ten minutes. After washing his hands, he grabbed a new toothbrush and washcloth out of the linen closet.

"Your food's gettin' cold," Pauline called out.

"I'm comin', Ma," Brick said after he rinsed his mouth out with warm water. He looked at his teeth in the mirror to make sure they were sparkling before walking out of the bathroom.

"Good mornin', son," Pauline said when Brick walked into the kitchen.

"Good mornin'," he replied as he sat down at the kitchen table. He waited patiently as Pauline fixed his plate and set it down in front of him. Then he bowed his head in prayer before he started eating. Seeing Brick still prayed over his food made Pauline proud. She was always glad to see some of the lessons she'd tried to instill in Brick still stuck with him.

Pauline stared at her son for a brief moment before speaking. "So, what brought you over here last night?" she asked.

Brick swallowed the food he had in his mouth before replying. "Me and Piper got into it last night," he said and continued eating.

Pauline waited for Brick to go into detail, but he didn't. "About what?" she finally asked before sipping on her morning cup of coffee.

"About the same shit we always arguin' about," he said, getting angry all over again. "Me bein' in the streets. I told her she don't be complainin' about me bein' in the streets when I'm lacin' her ass with Coogie, Ed Hardy, and all that other expensive shit she be rockin'!" he ranted.

Pauline nodded her head in agreement. "True. But you still have to look at it from her point of view too, son." Pauline didn't just look at it through her son's eyes; she also felt where Piper was coming from as well. "You do run the streets a lot more now, and you ain't only out there makin' money. So how do you expect her to feel?"

"Whose side are you on?" Brick grimaced. "I thought you didn't like Piper."

"I'm not on anyone's side, Brice. I'm just tellin' it like I see it," Pauline replied. "And I don't care for her. It's just that everyone deserves a fightin' chance."

"Ma, I try to spend time with Piper. But I got so much money wrapped up in several different places, and I need to stay on top of it or niggas will try to play me," Brick explained. "And if one of these niggas fuck over me, I'm goin' to the pen for the rest of my life for killin' one of these lame-ass niggas."

"I thought that's what you had Bob T, Ricco, and the rest of them dudes for," Pauline said.

"Ma, them my boys and all, but you know I don't trust no one when it comes to my money or my broad," Brick responded, feeling like he was stuck between a rock and a hard place when it came to his money and his relationship with Piper.

"Do you love her?" Pauline asked out of nowhere. "'Cuz if you do, you can make it work, but if not, then let her go so she can find someone who does."

Brick thought a quick second before answering. "I don't know, Ma. I thought I was in love with her at one time. I mean, don't get me wrong; she a good girl and all, but here lately, I been wishin' she would just gon' and move back to Syracuse wit' her parents," Brick stated, confused. "I mean, she got a lot of good qualities. She's down for me, I can trust her with my money, and she put up with all the bullshit I put her through with all these other bitches I be fuckin' wit', 'cuz she know at the end of the day that I'm comin' home to her." Pauline listened as her son poured out his feelings.

"So you want her to go home so you can be laid up wit' all these gold-diggin' hoes that only see dollar signs instead of the color brown when they look into your eyes?" Pauline spat.

"It ain't even like that, Ma. I can do that wit' her here," Brick argued. "It just seems like me and Piper's lives are headin' in two totally different directions. She wants to live in a house wit' a white picket fence, have kids and a dog. And I don't want that."

"Why not, Brice? You're nineteen years old. You not gettin' any younger, you know?"

"I know that, Ma. And I probably will feel like that too one day, but right now, I don't. The lifestyle I live ain't tailored for no babies," Brick explained. "Hopefully, Piper will find someone to give her that fairy-tale lifestyle she's lookin' for, and trust me, I will be more than happy for her when she does."

Pauline stood up from the table and gathered the empty plates. "Well, what about that Ra'Keeyah chick? You seem to be spendin' a lot of time wit' her."

Brick smiled widely. "I ain't gon' lie, Ma. I like Ra'Keeyah a lot. She keeps a smile on my face, and she makes me laugh," he said. "I feel so stress free when I'm around her, and she's feisty, just like I like 'em. We're just friends, though. I never even tried to fuck her. Not sayin' that I wouldn't; I just haven't."

Pauline had never heard her son express his feelings about a woman like he had just done about Ra'Keeyah. "Well, maybe you should make it official wit' her," she suggested.

"I don't know, Ma. She the kind of girl that ain't gon' stand for no shit," Brick said, smiling.

"Well, maybe that's the kind of chick that you need in yo' life. One that's gon' keep you grounded and out them streets. And jus' maybe, I can get a grandbaby or two," Pauline said, sliding that in.

Brick shook his head. "I don't know what I want for real."

"Well, I think it's time for you to find that special someone," she said, placing the dishes inside of the dishwasher.

"Ma, I don't just want a woman that I can live with," he said. "I want one that I can't live without! And when I find her, I will know she's the one."

Pauline placed her hands on her hips and asked, "How you gon' know she's the one, boy?"

Brick smiled. "Trust me, I'll know."

"Well, when you find her, will you let me know too?" Pauline smiled back.

"I got chu'." Brick stood up from the table and kissed Pauline on the cheek. "I'm about to go home and talk to Piper."

"Yea, you do that, and let me know how everything turns out, okay?" Pauline shook her head, wishing she had the solution to her son's problem.

"I will, Ma."

"I love you," Pauline said as Brick turned to walk out of the kitchen.

Brick turned around to face his mother. "I love you too," he smiled and made his way out the door.

Pauline closed her eyes and said a quick prayer for her son and thanked God in advance for whatever was about to happen.

Brick walked through the front door and called out Piper's name.

"I'm up here," she yelled from the bedroom.

Brick picked up the mail and sorted through it before making his way up the stairs. "What you doin'?" he walked into the master bedroom and asked.

"Packin'," Piper said, as she filled her Louis Vuitton suitcases with as much of her belongings as she could.

"Where you goin'?" he asked, shocked.

"I'm movin' back to Syracuse wit' my parents," she said and continued packing.

Brick had just told Pauline he wished Piper would move back to Syracuse, but now that it was actually happening, he had mixed feelings about it. On one hand, he wanted her to stay, knowing things still weren't going to change, and on the other, he wanted her to go back to New York because he was fed up with all her nagging and accusing him of cheating, even though he was.

"For what?" Brick asked, as his heart beat quickly.

Piper stopped packing her bags and looked over at him. "Because I'm tired of your shit, that's why," she shouted. "How long did you think I was gon' continue to put up with you fuckin' all these tired-ass broads around here?" Brick didn't answer. He just stared at Piper. "Answer me, dammit!" she screamed as tears formed in the lids of her eyes. "I was a fool to believe things would be any different here." She shook her head as the tears began to steadily flow down her cheeks.

Brick hated to see Piper cry. In fact, he hated to see any woman shed a tear, especially when he was the cause of it. It stemmed from watching all the tears his biological mother had shed for whatever reasons.

"Come on, Piper, don't cry," Brick begged, feeling sorry for all the pain he'd caused her. "Don't do this to me, baby," he said, sympathetically.

"Do *what* to you, Brick?" Piper questioned as the tears flowed. "I haven't done anything to you but loved your black ass like you deserved to be! And what did you give in return?" she asked, rhetorically. "Not a mutha'fuckin' thing!"

Brick walked over to Piper and grabbed her wrists. "Come on, baby, let's sit down and talk."

Piper snatched away from Brick. "What's to talk about, Brick? You wanna talk about how you lied to me and told me how things would be different if I moved to Ohio with you? Or how you promised me that you'd never cheat on me again?" Piper was fed up. "There's nothin' to talk about, Brick; I'm done!" she snapped.

Brick sat on the edge of the bed and watched as Piper toted all of her things downstairs and out to her car. He wanted to beg her to stay, but his pride and his need to be with other women just wouldn't let him.

Once Piper had her brand-new Acadia that her parents bought packed to capacity, she entered the bedroom one last time and looked around to make sure she had all her stuff. "If I forgot anything, just throw it away or give it to one of your bitches," she said.

"Come on, Piper. I don't have no bitches," Brick lied.

"Whatever you say," Piper replied with an uncaring attitude, even though the thought of Brick being with anyone else tore her up on the inside.

"So this is it, huh?" he asked.

Piper avoided making eye contact with Brick, because she knew if she did, he would sucker her right back in with his long, beautiful eyelashes. "This is it," she said, looking over at a picture of a black Jesus hanging on the bedroom wall.

"Well, what you gon' do when you get back home, moneywise?"

"Did you forget I have my pharmaceutical degree?" she asked. Brick shook his head no. "And if that don't pan out, did you forget that both of my parents are doctors?" Brick shook his head no again. "I had money before I started fuckin' wit' you, Brick."

"I know," he stated. "I just wanted to make sure you was gon' be cool, that's all."

"Well, if you really must know, my father already has a job lined up for me. So I'll be okay, and if not, I'll manage."

"This is crazy, Piper, and you know it," Brick said.

Piper threw her hands up in the air because there was nothing else left for her to say. "You right; it is crazy, Brick. Tell me how long did you want me to sit around and be a dummy? I did it for too long, and now I'm tired and fed up."

"You ain't right, Piper. I took good care of you," he said, hoping to make her feel guilty.

"Brick, me and you want two totally different things out of life. I wanna go back to the life I was livin' before I met you. I had an honest-payin' job. I wanna get married and have children, you don't. I want all the things that you are afraid of achieving in life."

Piper struck a nerve when she used the word "honest."

"Get the fuck outta here," Brick spat! "Did *you* forget how I met yo' ass?" Brick asked, fed up with the Ms. Goody Two-shoe persona Piper was putting on. "Did you forget that when you worked as a pharmaceutical rep before, that you was the one supplyin' me with all the Oxys I needed? And if it wasn't for me keepin' you on your toes, yo' knuckle-head ass woulda' got caught and been doin' a bid in the pen! So don't throw that *honest* shit my way!" Brick was heated and decided he was glad she was leaving because he would have to be bothered with all the bitching and the arguing otherwise.

"Whatever, Brick," Piper said waving him off. "What you want, a thank-you? Thank you, Brick, for havin' my back, like I've always had yours since day one!"

"You always gotta be sarcastic," he said angrily. His cell phone began to vibrate. He took it out and checked the number.

"Which one of yo' bitches is that?" she said with an attitude.

Brick didn't answer her. He just put his phone back in the holder.

It was no use. They weren't getting anywhere by talking so Piper decided it was time for her to leave. "Okay, well, it's gettin' late, and I need to get on the road."

Just knowing Piper was really getting ready to leave for good did something to Brick all over again. It was like his feelings were flip-flopping. "You sure you wanna leave?" Brick asked one last time, just to make sure.

Piper nodded her head yes. "Even if I didn't want to, I need to," she said, turning to walk away.

"Why?" he asked, not knowing if he really wanted to know the answer or not.

Piper turned around, walked back over to Brick, and planted a soft kiss on his lips. "Call me when you grow up. You know how to reach me." With that being said, Piper winked before walking out of Brick's life.

Brick walked over and looked out the bedroom window, watching as Piper pulled off. A feeling of loneliness swept over him as he walked over and lay across his comfortable bed. He couldn't believe she was finally gone. He didn't know whether to shed a couple of tears or do a couple of backflips. Whatever he decided, it would have to wait until after he woke up from his nap.

Chapter Thirteen

Shayna and Ra'Keeyah were at the mall getting their hands and feet done. They hadn't been spending nearly as much time with each other since Shayna had become so heavily involved with Calvin.

"So fill me in on what's been goin' on with you and Calvin," Ra'Keeyah looked over at Shayna who was sitting in a nice big comfortable chair next to her.

Shayna smiled. "Girl, he is so romantic. He been takin' me to Columbus and Cincinnati to these nice, expensive-ass restaurants," Shayna said. "He even be lettin' me drive his Benz and everything."

"Wow, *that's* what's up," Ra'Keeyah smiled, happy for her friend. "Why he gotta take you so far just to eat?"

"He do gotta wife and family here, Ra'Keeyah. And girl, he got a nice-ass crib too," Shayna bragged.

Ra'Keeyah looked at her best friend like she was crazy. "Bitch, you done lost your mind. You been inside the man's house?" Shayna nodded her head yes. "Well, where was his wife?"

"He said she was out of town visitin' her sick mother," Shayna said like it was no big deal.

"Girl, you be takin' some hell-a-fied chances," Ra'Keeyah said shaking her head.

Shayna shrugged her shoulders. "Oh well. I didn't force myself in his house. He invited me. Damn, bitch, can you scrub the bottom of my foot any harder!" Shayna looked down at the Chinese lady and snapped.

Ra'Keeyah threw her head back and started cracking up laughing. "Bitch, you a fool," she said and continued laughing. "You gon' make that broad karate chop you in the throat."

Shayna frowned down at the Chinese lady who was going off in her native language. "Yeah, whatever, and Hong Kong fuey to you too," she said, rolling her eyes. "Anyways, what was I sayin'?'" she asked, losing her train of thought.

Ra'Keeyah shook her head. "We was talkin' about you goin' all up in that man's house."

"Oh yeah. Well, like I said, he invited me in, so I went," Shayna said.

"I don't know what I'ma do wit' you," Ra'Keeyah smiled at her best friend.

Shayna laughed. "I don't know either. So, what we gon' do this summer?"

"I don't know. Shit, you all boo'd up. You ain't gon' have time for me," Ra'Keeyah said. "You done fell in love wit' a white man."

"Whatever," Shayna protested. "Only white man I ever been in love wit' is Benjamin Franklin," she said. "Hefah, I always got time for you. Calvin and his wife is goin' to Europe for a month, so I'ma have all the free time in the world."

"Dang, a month in Europe?" Ra'Keeyah asked, astounded. "We still gon' be dancin' for everybody else, right?"

"Hell, yeah! Calvin already set everything up for us," Shayna said. "He told me him and his wife go away every summer for at least a month. Hell, last year he took her to Bora Bora."

"I wish I had a man to take me on extravagant getaways like that," Ra'Keeyah said wishfully.

"I told him I don't give a damn how long they gone. He better leave me some damn money!" Shayna snapped. "Shit, Brick got money! Have his black, sexy ass take you on a trip."

"Girl, me and Brick are just friends. He got a woman, remember?" Ra'Keeyah asked, wishing it was her instead of Piper.

"Oh, girl, I knew I was gon' tell you some—," Shayna balked and frowned down at the Chinese lady for digging under her toe too hard. "Girl, you put some shoes on these folks and they don't know how to act! Anyways, I called you the other day to tell you that Brick and Piper broke up!" Shayna said, excited. "But you didn't answer your phone."

"You lyin'?" Ra'Keeyah asked, surprised. "I haven't talked to him in a few days, so I really don't know."

"Well, I do. 'Cuz my cousin Tabitha's baby daddy, brother-in-law, or somethin' like that, be doin' a lot of business wit' Brick and his boys. And I guess Bob T, Brick's right-hand man, told somebody that Brick and Piper broke up and she moved back to New York wit' her parents," Shayna said.

Ra'Keeyah tried to digest the information that Shayna had just relayed, but it was kind of difficult to put it all together. "So in other words, you sayin' Brick's right-hand man, Bob T, told somebody that him and Piper broke up and she moved back to New York?" Ra'Keeyah asked, trying to figure it all out.

"I just said the exact same thing," Shayna laughed. "I just made a short story long, that's all."

Ra'Keeyah laughed. "Wow, that's crazy."

"I know, right? So maybe you can get your chance to be wit' him."

Ra'Keeyah thought for a brief second. "Girl, please. Do you know how many bitches gon' be lined up at his front door?"

"Yea, I can only imagine. Shit, girl, you better pitch you a tent and stand in line wit' them hoes, and may the best bitch win!" Shayna laughed and threw up her hand, giving Ra'Keeyah a high five.

Ra'Keeyah laughed too. "I don't know about all that. Plus, you know Elaine ain't havin' that!"

"Tell yo' moms to loosen up. Shit, you can't help who you like, drug dealer or not!"

"I wish it was that easy wit' her," Ra'Keeyah sighed. "Ever since my dad overdosed, my mom has hated all drug dealers. She holds them all responsible for that bag of bad smack."

"Wow, that's crazy," Shayna said, getting out of the chair.

"Who you tellin'?" Ra'Keeyah agreed, and done the same.

The two friends walked up to the register to pay for their services.

"You wanna leave a tip?" the Chinese guy behind the register asked.

Shayna looked at him like he'd just called her out her name. "I gotta tip for you, all right. Tell that broad over there," she said pointing, "to go back to school and learn how to do pedicures," she snapped.

"Huh? I don't understand?" the guy replied.

"You need to go back too," Shayna said, taking her change from the man's hand.

"Oh my gosh, you are so rude," Ra'Keeyah mumbled as she handed the man her money.

"Shit, it's the truth," Shayna said while she waited for the man to hand Ra'Keeyah her change.

"Let's get outta here before we get beat up," Ra'Keeyah joked.

"Girl, I ain't thinkin' about these fools," Shayna laughed as they walked out the door.

***

"What you doin'?" Jaylen walked into his sister's room and asked.

"Tryin'a take a nap. What it look like?" she asked jokingly.

Jaylen climbed up on Ra'Keeyah's bed and lay next to her. "Mommy said I have to go to Aunt Nancy's the whole summer since you gotta work and can't babysit me."

"Ahhh, well, you'll have fun over there, playin' with Darius, Dayvonn, and the rest of the clan, won't you?" Ra'Keeyah said, feeling kind of bad for her brother.

"I guess. But sometimes Day-Day be mean to me and won't let me play his game," Jaylen said.

"I'll tell you what. Next time Day-Day don't let you play his game, I'ma come over Aunt Nancy's house and kick his ass, okay?" Ra'Keeyah smiled.

Jaylen smiled back. "Okay," he squealed laughing.

"Jaylen, come on," their mother yelled out. She stuck her head in Ra'Keeyah's room and smiled. "What y'all two characters in here doin'?"

"Nothin', just talkin'," Ra'Keeyah answered.

"Come on, Jaylen, it's time to go. Go get your bag."

Jaylen climbed out of Ra'Keeyah's bed. She sat up and grabbed him by the arm. "Don't forget what I said, okay?"

"Okay." Ra'Keeyah pulled her brother close and gave him a big, sloppy kiss on the cheek. "Uhhhh, you nasty," he laughed, wiped the kiss away, and ran out of her room.

Their mother laughed too. "Y'all silly. Okay, well, I will see you in the mornin', and you already know."

"Don't be havin' nobody in my house," Ra'Keeyah said, finishing her mother's sentence. Her mother shook her head and walked away. When Ra'Keeyah heard the front door close, she lay back across her bed and thought about calling Brick to see if he was okay after his breakup with Piper. She wanted him to know that she was there if he needed to talk, but was too scared to. She'd rather wait until he called her first, like he always did.

Ra'Keeyah was bored out of her mind. She tried calling Shayna several times, only for it to go straight to her voice mail. She even called Quiana to see what was on her agenda for the night, but no luck; she didn't answer either. Ra'Keeyah picked up the remote, turned on the television, and began channel surfing.

"Awww, man, this my movie," she said tossing down the remote and stopping at the old cowboy movie with the black actors. "*Thomasine and Bushrod,*" Ra'Keeyah said aloud and began watching the movie. Halfway through the movie, Ra'Keeyah had drifted off to sleep, only to be awakened by her ringing cell phone. She rolled over, grabbed her phone, and checked the number. A huge smile crept across her face. "Hello?" she answered, her voice sounding as if she'd just woke up.

"Hey, li'l mama, did I wake you?" Brick asked.

Ra'Keeyah sat straight up. "Naw, I was just lyin' here," she lied. "What's up?"

"Nothin' really. I just went and rented these movies and wanted to see if you wanted to come over and check 'em out wit' me," Brick said.

"You want me to come over to your house?" Ra'Keeyah acted surprised because she didn't want Brick to know that she already knew about his breakup.

Brick laughed. "Yeah, girl."

"What you rent?" Ra'Keeyah inquired.

"I rented some classics," Brick replied. "I got *Above the Rim, Menace II Society,* and *Love Jones.*"

"Love Jones?"

"Yea, nigga, *Love Jones*," Brick answered. "That's one of my favorite movies," he admitted.

"Ahhh, Brick gotta soft side to him," Ra'Keeyah teased.

"Ain't nothin' soft about me but my lips," Brick said. "So are you comin' or what?"

Ra'Keeyah glanced at the clock. She had exactly fourteen hours, three minutes, and twenty-two seconds to spend with Brick before her mother got off work. "Yeah, I'm comin'. You gon' come get me?"

"Yeah, I'll be there in about thirty minutes," Brick said.

Ra'Keeyah jumped out of bed. "Okay, I'll be ready."

"One," he said before hanging up the phone.

Ra'Keeyah ran around her room like a crazed lunatic, looking for something to wear. Since it was hot as hell outside, she decided to put on a denim, strapless, Rocawear romper, with the words Rocawear written in glitter across the front and a pair of silver flat sandals. Thankfully, she'd just gotten a pedicure or else she would have had to settle for tennis shoes. She laid out her silver Rocawear earrings, necklace, and purse before going to take a quick shower. Once out of the shower, she rubbed Johnson's baby lotion all over her body before getting dressed. Ra'Keeyah then slicked her hair back into a ponytail, grabbed her purse, and went downstairs to wait for Brick to arrive.

Ra'Keeyah was anxious. She acted like this was the first time she'd ever spent time with Brick. Actually, it was the first time he'd ever invited her over to his place. She paced back and forth, looking out the window every time a car rode by. Ra'Keeyah stuck a piece of Doublemint in her mouth because she had read somewhere that chewing gum calms the nerves. It wasn't working because she was still a nervous wreck. Five minutes later, Brick pulled up and started getting out of his car. Ra'Keeyah turned out the lights and hurried out the door, meeting him on the walkway.

"Y'all females don't want a nigga to be a gentleman no more, do y'all? If it ain't rough it ain't right, huh, man?" he laughed.

Ra'Keeyah laughed too. "I mean, I seen you comin' so I just saved you a trip to the door."

"Whateva'," Brick said playfully. "I bet if I woulda' pulled up and just blew the horn, you woulda' flipped out on me."

"You right," Ra'Keeyah smiled as they made their way to the car. "Damn, how many cars do you own?" she asked as Brick opened the door to a brand-new inferno-orange Camaro Coupe, with the black Rally stripes going up the hood.

Brick smiled. "Not enough." He closed the door and walked around to the driver's side.

Ra'Keeyah was amazed to see the orange interior trim kit. She ran her hand across the dashboard before sitting back. "This bitch is nice," she said, buckling up her seat belt.

"You think so?" Brick smiled.

"Hell, yeah," Ra'Keeyah replied, ecstatic.

Brick buckled his seat belt as well before pulling off. "It's all right. I've seen better." Ra'Keeyah had never seen a car like it, let alone been inside of one. "I just ordered a pizza. I ordered half meat lovers and half veggie 'cuz I don't know what you like and don't like," he said, heading to pick up his order.

"That's cool," she responded.

Brick reached over and hit PLAY on the CD player. George Howard's "No No" came blaring out of the speakers. Brick was jamming to the music. Ra'Keeyah looked over at him. The way he moved to the music turned her on big time. He looked over at her and smiled and continued grooving to the music.

Ra'Keeyah smiled back. *Damn, this nigga is fine*, she thought. *I can really get used to this. If I play my cards right, I'll be the bitch that replaces Piper.* Ra'Keeyah got comfortable in her seat and bobbed her head to the music for the rest of the ride.

Chapter Fourteen

Brick pulled up in the driveway of his single-family home and parked right next to his black Lexus. He shut the engine off, grabbed the pizza box off of Ra'Keeyah's lap, and got out. Ra'Keeyah opened up the car door and got out as well. She looked around at the well manicured houses as they made their way up the walkway and thought how nice the neighborhood was. Brick put the key in the lock and opened up the door. He held the screen door open for Ra'Keeyah to walk in first.

When Ra'Keeyah walked in her eyes went directly to the sixty-inch Samsung TV that hung neatly over the fireplace. She had seen some big televisions, but not quite this big.

"Make yourself at home," Brick said, handing Ra'Keeyah the pizza box. "I'm about to go get us somethin' to drink."

Ra'Keeyah took the pizza and walked over toward the big white leather sectional. She removed her shoes, not wanting to step on the white shaggy rug that lay in front of the sofa. She moved the white, teal, and silver throw pillows to the side before sitting back. She was amazed at how beautifully decorated the area was. The color scheme went so well together. The whites, silvers, and teals splashed throughout the entire room in artwork, pictures, statues, and even the stone surrounding the fireplace. She held the box on her lap, not wanting to set it on top of the coffee table because everything on the table looked too expensive to touch.

"What type of wine you drink?" Brick yelled out from the kitchen. "White or red?"

"White," Ra'Keeyah replied, not really liking either, but needing something to calm the butterflies she had in her stomach.

"Sweet or dry?" he yelled out again.

"Sweet," Ra'Keeyah replied, still checking out the well-put-together décor.

Brick walked back into the living room carrying two wineglasses, two plates, a bottle of wine, and some napkins. "Why you still holdin' that pizza on your lap?" he laughed, setting the plates, glasses, wine, and napkins on the coffee table.

"I was scared to move the stuff on the table. Everything looks so expensive," Ra'Keeyah admitted.

"Girl, you can't hurt none of this stuff," Brick said, rearranging the contents on the table, making room for the pizza box. He then sat next to Ra'Keeyah, grabbed the remote, and turned the television on. He opened the wine, filled both of their glasses, and opened the pizza box. "This looks good as hell," he said, reaching in, throwing two pieces on his plate.

Ra'Keeyah was shy at first and watched as Brick devoured his pizza.

"You ain't gon' eat?" he asked, picking up his glass and drinking the wine straight down before reaching back into the box for two more slices of pizza.

Ra'Keeyah shook her head. "You greedy," she said, picking up her plate and carefully putting a piece of pizza on it, not wanting to drop anything on the white rug.

"What you wanna watch first?" Brick asked, finishing off his plate of food.

"I don't care," Ra'Keeyah replied.

Brick stood from the sofa and walked into a small office that adjoined the living room. "We'll watch *Menace II Society* first," he said while putting the movie in.

Ra'Keeyah set her plate back down on the coffee table, wiped her mouth with a napkin, and then sat back. "That's fine," she said, before finishing off her glass of wine.

Brick walked out of the room with a smile on his face and took a seat next to her. Within seconds the movie started to play. The loud music coming from the surround sound made Ra'Keeyah jump.

"You all right?" Brick laughed.

"Damn, it sounds like we in a movie theater," she stated.

"My bad. Me and my niggas was watchin' the game with the volume up loud." Brick walked back into the adjoining office and adjusted the volume on the surround sound. "Is that better?" he asked, walking back over and taking a seat on the sofa.

Ra'Keeyah nodded her head yes before filling up her glass again and taking a sip. After twenty minutes of watching the movie and sipping on wine in complete silence, she needed to use the bathroom. "Can you show me where the bathroom is, please?" she looked over at Brick and asked.

"You would have to pee durin' the best part of the movie," he joked, while standing up.

Ra'Keeyah stood up from the sofa and her head started spinning. "Sorry, my bladder has poor timin'," she said following Brick down a short hallway, hoping she didn't stumble.

"First door on your left," he said, pointing. "That's my half bath. If you wanna get a little more comfortable, I got a full bath upstairs, with a TV in it," he smiled.

Ra'Keeyah laughed. "The half bath will do. All I have to do is pee."

"I was jus' makin' sure. Wash yo' hands," Brick joked before walking back into the living room and taking a seat.

After Ra'Keeyah used the bathroom she walked back in the living room and took a seat on the sofa. Brick looked over at her and smiled. "You are so pretty."

"Thanks," Ra'Keeyah blushed and poured herself another glass of wine. After about her fourth glass of wine, Ra'Keeyah had started feeling a little tipsy. "Who decorated your place?" she asked, feeling a little more at ease now that she'd almost finished off the entire bottle of wine by herself.

"My mutha decorated it for me," he said, looking around at all the hard work she'd put into it.

"She sure did a nice job," Ra'Keeyah said. "You better not have no kids wit' this white furniture."

"Who you tellin'?" Brick agreed.

Ra'Keeyah lay her head back on the sofa and closed her eyes. "You okay?" Brick asked.

"Yeah, just a little tipsy, that's all. The room was startin' to spin," she chuckled.

"You was killin' that wine like a true champ, and you didn't eat nothin' but one slice of pizza."

"I'm not a real big eater," Ra'Keeyah opened her eyes and said.

"You scared you might get fat?" Brick asked while laughing.

"Been there, done that," she replied seriously, and left it at that.

"What you mean by that?" Brick questioned, not getting the reaction he expected to get.

Ra'Keeyah debated about whether she should tell Brick about how fat she used to be or how the kids used to tease her in school because of it. She didn't want him to throw it up in her face later on so she decided not to.

"I don't wanna talk about it," Ra'Keeyah replied.

"Look, li'l mama, I hope you don't think that I would ever hold nothin' against you or judge you about your past," Brick said sincerely. "Unless you were a stripper, of course; other than that, you can trust me."

Every time Brick mentioned he had something against strippers it literally made Ra'Keeyah sick to her stomach. It made her feel like she was less of a woman because she shook her ass for cash. She wondered how he'd react if and when she came clean about how she made her money. Ra'Keeyah needed to know why Brick had such harsh feelings toward strippers. Maybe his reasons would help her to want to do something different.

"Okay, I'll tell you what. If you tell me why you have so much animosity toward strippers, I'll tell you about my childhood," Ra'Keeyah said.

"Okay," Brick agreed, gathering his thoughts before speaking. "I don't like strippers because my biological mother was one."

Ra'Keeyah's eyes widened. She was surprised he would share something so personal with her, and he barely even knew her. "Wow, that's deep," were the only words she could find to describe how Brick must have been feeling.

"Who you tellin'?" Brick said. Ra'Keeyah was speechless and didn't know what else to say. "I can remember when I was like five years old, sittin' in the dressin' room of the strip club my mom worked at playin' with my Hot Wheels for hours at a time," Brick continued. "I didn't know what my mom was out there doin'. All I know is she told me that I wasn't allowed to come out there while she was workin'."

Ra'Keeyah hung on to every word that came out of Brick's mouth. "I got bored one day and snuck outta the dressin' room and was peekin' out in the bar area and saw my mom half-naked. Men was feelin' all over her, smackin' her on the ass, and she was enjoyin' it," Brick said shaking his head in disgust.

Ra'Keeyah could hear the hurt in Brick's voice as he revisited his childhood.

"I couldn't stand watchin' them men touch all over her body like they was doin'. So I ran out there and swung on one of the men that was rubbin' on my mom's ass, tellin' him to get off of her," Brick chuckled.

"I know that's right," Ra'Keeyah said, intrigued by his heroism at such a young age.

"My mom grabbed me up, apologized to the nigga, and drug my ass back into the dressin' room," Brick said. "I thought she was gon' hug me and thank me for tryin'a protect her; instead, she beat my ass and told me I better not bring my narrow black ass back out there."

"What?" Ra'Keeyah asked, surprised.

Brick nodded his head. "Yeah, man. I remember tellin' her that I didn't want them men touchin' her like they was. I felt it was my job to protect her since my dad was in and out of the penitentiary," Brick said. "She told me to mind my own damn business 'cuz that's how she made her money and was gon' continue to make it whether I liked it or not."

"Dang, she told her five-year-old son that?" Ra'Keeyah asked, stunned.

"Yep," Brick replied. "For that reason, and a few others I'd rather not talk about, I lost all respect for my mom and any other woman that strips. To me, it's degrading for a woman to get undressed in front of a bunch of strange men for money."

"So you don't go to strip clubs?" Ra'Keeyah asked.

"Hell, naw!" Brick replied. "You wouldn't catch me up in there givin' them tired-ass hoes my hard earned money."

Ra'Keeyah didn't agree with Brick's way of thinking. "Don't you think some of them women have to be up in them clubs to make a livin' for themselves and their children?" Ra'Keeyah asked.

"Naw. Them hoes up in the club 'cuz they wanna be. My mom was up in the club 'cuz she wanted to be. She made that perfectly clear to me at five years old. It's plenty of jobs out here," Brick said. "So you can miss me wit' that shit!"

"Well, a lot of women ain't qualified enough to get a job that will take care of them and their family," Ra'Keeyah said, trying to get Brick to see that every woman doesn't strip because she wants to but because she has to.

Brick was determined not to give strippers an inch of respect, no matter what Ra'Keeyah said. "That's fuckin' bullshit, and you know it!" he said getting angry. "I don't wanna talk about strippin' no more," he said.

"You know when you get angry your accent gets thicker," Ra'Keeyah smiled.

"Do it?" Brick smiled as well. Ra'Keeyah nodded her head yes. "Do it turn you on?" Brick joked. It surprised him when Ra'Keeyah nodded her head yes again. "Down boy," Brick said, feeling his manhood starting to rise.

"You nasty," Ra'Keeyah said, laughing.

Brick laughed as well. "Okay, now it's your turn to talk about some of your childhood memories."

"My shit don't even compare to yours," Ra'Keeyah said.

"That's okay. I still wanna hear it," he responded.

"Okay," Ra'Keeyah started. "Well, from the time I was three until I was ten, I was real fat." Brick looked at Ra'Keeyah like he didn't believe her. "It's true. I was way overweight. My cousins and the kids at school used to make fun of me all the time. Even my mom started talkin' about me, hoping that would help me to stop eatin' so much, but it didn't; it only made me wanna eat more." Ra'Keeyah stopped talking for a brief moment to keep herself from breaking down into tears. "Only person that would never say anything about my weight was my daddy. He used to tell me he didn't care how big I got; I would always be his little angel." Tears formed in Ra'Keeyah's eyes as she talked about her father.

Brick grabbed a napkin off the coffee table and handed it to Ra'Keeyah.

"Thank you," she said, taking it and dabbing at her eyes. "Sorry."

"It's okay."

"Anyway, my weight got so out of control, my mom started takin' me to all kinds of specialists, a dietician, but nothin' was workin'. I just couldn't stop eatin'. I even started peeing in the bed." Ra'Keeyah looked over at Brick and dared him to laugh.

"What?" Brick asked, trying to keep from laughing.

"I'm done talkin'!" she huffed.

"What I do?" Brick laughed.

"You laughin' at me," she pouted.

"Okay, okay, I'm sorry. I won't laugh no more," Brick promised. Ra'Keeyah gave him the evil eye. "I promise."

"Anyways. After my dad died I stopped eatin' and lost sixty pounds in less than two months. Once the weight was gone, I vowed to never gain another pound.

That's why to this day I watch what I eat 'cuz I don't ever wanna go through what I went through as a child ever again," Ra'Keeyah said. "Kids can be real cruel."

"I agree. I can't believe you lost all that weight at ten years old," Brick said, amazed.

Ra'Keeyah nodded her head yes. "It scared the hell outta my mom, but I was so depressed because the only person that didn't care about the way I looked was gone." Ra'Keeyah couldn't stop the tears from flowing this time.

"Sorry to hear that," Brick said sincerely. "Can I ask what happened to him?"

"He overdosed on heroin," she answered as the tears steadily flowed. "I'm so embarrassed." Ra'Keeyah continued wiping her tears away.

"Don't be," Brick said, using his finger to help dab away a tear.

"Now you probably think I'm a big crybaby," Ra'Kee-yah laughed, still crying.

"Naw, li'l mama, I don't think that. Death of a loved one is hard to deal wit'," Brick said, feeling her pain. "I lost my pops from a drug overdose too."

"Wow," Ra'Keeyah said, surprised that they had something so heartwrenching in common.

"Come on, let's talk about somethin' else," Brick said, wanting to change the subject before his emotions started showing.

"Okay," Ra'Keeyah agreed. "But just to let you know while we're on the subject, my mom hate drug dealers and would never allow me to be friends with one, let alone fuck around wit' one." Ra'Keeyah was glad she could finally clear the air and tell Brick the reason why he could only come over and visit when her mother was at work.

"Oh, so that's why I never met yo' moms and you only let me come over when she at work," he said.

"Yep, that's why," Ra'Keeyah admitted. "I can't change her way of thinkin', just like I can't change the way you feel about strippers," she teased.

"I guess I won't be comin' over for Thanksgivin' dinner," Brick replied, before his cell phone began vibrating. He took his phone out of the holster and checked the number. "Excuse me, I gotta take this call." Brick stood up and walked toward the kitchen before answering his phone. Five minutes later, he walked back into the living room where Ra'Keeyah sat watching the end of the movie.

"Is everything okay?" she asked, concerned.

Brick was hesitant at first. "I need to make a quick run. It won't take long, I promise."

"Do you wanna just drop me off at home?" she asked, not wanting to get in the way of his business.

"No, no, I don't want you to leave yet," he said. "I won't be gone long."

"Okay," Ra'Keeyah replied.

Brick bent down and kissed her on the forehead. "I'll be right back. Make yourself at home," he said, grabbing his car keys and hurrying out the door.

"Make myself at home, huh?" Ra'Keeyah said aloud. She grabbed the wineglasses, the empty bottle, and the pizza box and headed to the kitchen. She couldn't believe her eyes when she walked in. There were dirty dishes on the counter, in the sink, and on top of the stove. Ra'Keeyah shook her head. "I can't believe he let this kitchen get like this." She looked under the sink and found some Cascade before filling the dishwasher with dishes. She wiped off the stove, the granite countertops, and swept the floor. Then she took the full trash bag out and replaced it with a new one and found the Swiffer dust mop and ran it across the hardwood floors to remove the stuck-on stains.

After the dishwasher stopped, she removed the dishes and put them away. "There," she said, wiping the sweat from her brow. "Now this is what a kitchen is supposed to look like." Ra'Keeyah turned out the kitchen light, walked back into the living room, and took a seat on the sofa. "Dang, this nigga been gone for about an hour," she said, looking at the clock. Ra'Keeyah walked into the office and put *Love Jones* in the DVD player before getting comfortable on the sofa.

After another hour had passed, Ra'Keeyah became furious. "This nigga is gon' take me home as soon as he gets here!" she fumed. "How in the fuck you gon' invite me over, then leave me here? This nigga got me fucked up!" Ra'Keeyah lay on the sofa and tried to watch the ending of the movie, but she was so upset she couldn't even get into it. "I should go in there and fuck his kitchen back up," Ra'Keeyah complained while yawning, and before long, she drifted off to sleep.

Chapter Fifteen

Brick walked in and noticed Ra'Keeyah asleep on the sofa. He quietly lay his keys down before walking into the kitchen to get himself something to drink. He was surprised when he walked in and found everything so nice and clean. He'd been meaning to clean the kitchen but had been too busy to do so. Brick couldn't stand clutter or filth so eventually he would have gotten around to doing it himself. He was glad that Ra'Keeyah had taken it upon herself to help a brotha out. He grabbed a bottle of water from the refrigerator and drank it straight down before walking back into the living room.

He stood over Ra'Keeyah and smiled down at her. He then grabbed the remote and turned the television off before tapping her on the shoulder. "Get up, li'l mama," he whispered.

Ra'Keeyah barely opened her eyes. "Huh?" she asked.

"Come on so you can go get in the bed," Brick said, helping her up. "I can't have you slobbin' all over my white furniture," he joked.

"Shut up," Ra'Keeyah said, still half-asleep. She grabbed her purse and followed Brick up the stairs to his bedroom.

Brick turned on the light, closed the door behind him, and threw back the goose down comforter for Ra'Keeyah, before walking over to his dresser to get some fresh clothes. Ra'Keeyah set her purse down on the nightstand and stood next to the bed watching as Brick removed his shirt.

My God, where did you get a body like that from? Ra'Keeyah thought as her eyes wandered over every inch of his washboard abs. Brick had tattoos all over his chest, back, stomach, and arms, which made Ra'Keeyah even more attracted to him.

"Aren't you gon' get into bed?" he asked smiling, fully aware of her checking him out.

"Yeah, I'm about to," she stammered. "Are these sheets clean?" she asked, before climbing into bed.

"What you mean by that?" Brick replied.

"I mean have any other female been layin' on 'em," Ra'Keeyah stated seriously.

Brick started laughing. "Naw, li'l mama. I just changed my sheets this mornin'. I ain't no nasty-ass nigga. Yea, my kitchen was fucked up, but I do clean up."

"I was just makin' sure," Ra'Keeyah said, climbing into the big, comfortable bed and throwing the comforter over herself.

"So you just gon' sleep cowboy style in my bed?" Brick asked smiling.

Ra'Keeyah sat up with a confused look on her face. "Wit' all ya' clothes on," he explained.

"Oh," Ra'Keeyah started laughing. "You act like I got some pajamas over here. What else am I gon' sleep in?"

Brick tossed Ra'Keeyah one of his oversized DGK T-shirts. "Put this on. I'm goin' to take a shower," he said, before walking into the master bathroom.

Ra'Keeyah climbed back out of bed and waited until she heard the shower come on before taking off her romper. She slid into the T-shirt that fit like a dress and climbed back into the bed. "Damn, I need to call

Shayna to cover for me," she said, reaching over and getting her cell out of her purse. She had six missed calls, two from Shayna, one from her mother, and three from Marshall. She quickly dialed Shayna's number.

"Hello?" Shayna answered, still half-asleep.

"Are you asleep?" Ra'Keeyah quickly asked.

"Naw, bitch, I was practicin' to be dead," Shayna said smartly. "Hell, yeah, I was asleep. It's three o'clock in the mornin'.'"

"Anyways, hefah, I need you to cover for me," Ra'Kee-yah said.

"Where you at, Ms. Thang?" Shayna pried.

"Don't worry about all that. Are you gon' do it or what?" Ra'Keeyah asked quickly because she heard the shower cut off.

"Haven't we always covered for each other?" Shayna asked.

"Yeah," Ra'Keeyah whispered.

"Well then, you know I got chu'."

"All right, I'll be over in the mornin'.'"

"Okay, call before you come so I can be up waitin' on you," Shayna said.

"All right."

"Hey," Shayna called out.

"Yeah?"

"Don't do nothin' I wouldn't do," she laughed.

"Bye, bitch," Ra'Keeyah laughed too before hanging up. She heard the bathroom door opening, so she quickly threw her cell phone back into her purse and acted like she was asleep.

"You asleep?" Brick looked out the bathroom door and asked.

"Almost," Ra'Keeyah lied.

"How was you almost asleep and I heard you out here on the phone?" Brick asked.

Ra'Keeyah sat up in the bed. She was instantly turned on by the sight before her. Brick walked out of the bathroom with a towel wrapped around his neck wearing a pair of boxers. His hair and chest were both still wet from the shower.

He walked over and sat on the edge of the bed. "Dry my back off for me, please." Ra'Keeyah didn't hesitate. She grabbed the towel from around his neck and did what he asked her to do. "You bet' not of been talkin' to yo' nigga," Brick said, standing up and walking around to the other side of the bed, grabbing his pillow.

Ra'Keeyah was turned on even more by his jealousy. "Nigga, like I told you before, I don't got no man. I have friends. Just like I'm sure you do," Ra'Keeyah said. "And furthermore, I wouldn't play you by talkin' to none of 'em in your house. I got way more polish than that."

"That's good to know," he said relieved before walking back around the bed with his pillow.

"Where you goin' wit' that pillow?" she asked.

"To the guest bedroom across the hall," Brick said, opening the bedroom door. "You got a problem wit' that?"

"You can have your bed. I can go into the guest bedroom," she offered.

"Naw, that's okay. This bed is much more comfortable than the one in there. I don't want you to wake up in the mornin' wit' ya back all fucked up."

"You don't have to go in there. You can sleep in here wit' me," Ra'Keeyah suggested. "Plus, I don't wanna be in here by myself."

"You just want me to sleep wit' you," Brick joked, before turning the light off and making his way back around to the other side of the bed.

"Nigga, please," Ra'Keeyah laughed and lay back to get comfortable.

Brick climbed into bed and scooted over toward the middle. "Damn, li'l mama, you can scoot over this way some. Yo' ass on the edge of bed," he laughed. "Don't say nothin' when you be on the floor in the mornin'.'"

Ra'Keeyah laughed, realizing how close to the edge she really was and scooted back. She was quite shocked when the back of her body met up with the front of Brick's. She didn't know whether to move or stay where she was. She went with her instinct and didn't budge.

"Now *that's* what I'm talkin' about," Brick said, scooping Ra'Keeyah around the waist, pulling her in as close as he could.

Ra'Keeyah could feel the bulkiness of Brick's manhood against her backside as they both lay still. After fifteen minutes of complete silence, she heard Brick snoring. She couldn't believe he had the audacity to fall asleep with all the fineness he had laying next to him. Ra'Keeyah kept moving, hoping it would wake him, but to no avail. Brick was out for the count. Ra'Keeyah rubbed her backside up against him, trying to get some type of reaction out of him. She felt it jump a couple times, but that was about it. After several unsuccessful attempts to get Brick aroused, Ra'Keeyah tried her hardest to go to sleep, but the intense throbbing sensation between her legs wouldn't let her.

"Oh my goodness," Ra'Keeyah huffed. She snatched the pillow from under Brick's head and got even madder because it didn't faze him. She placed it between her legs and finally drifted off to sleep, frustrated as hell!

"Good mornin', sleepyhead," Brick said, walking into the bedroom.

Ra'Keeyah opened one eye and looked at him. He was fully dressed and looked as if he had been up all morning. "Mornin'," she said, reaching over and grabbing her cell phone, checking the time. "Nigga, it's seven thirty-three!" Ra'Keeyah snapped.

"Haven't you ever heard the sayin', 'The early bird gets the worm'?" he asked.

"Whatever," she said, waving him off.

"I went to Bob Evans and grabbed us some breakfast. There's a towel and new toothbrush on the bathroom sink; use it," he smiled and winked. "I'll be downstairs waitin' on you." Brick walked back out of the room and headed down to the kitchen.

"Thanks," Ra'Keeyah said but Brick was already gone. She rested a few more seconds before climbing out of bed. Then she took Brick's T-shirt off and laid it across his bed, grabbed her romper off the floor, and shuffled into the bathroom. "Dang, I look crazy," she said looking at her wild hair in the mirror. Ra'Keeyah turned on the water, washed her face, between her legs, and brushed her teeth. She changed back into her own clothes and used Brick's brush to brush her hair back into a neat ponytail before making her way downstairs.

Brick was sitting at the kitchen table reading the newspaper when Ra'Keeyah walked in. "I hope you like omelets," he said, taking the lid off of her food.

"I do." Ra'Keeyah sat down across from him. She bowed her head in prayer and started eating.

"Did you sleep good?" Brick asked, making general conversation before taking a sip from his orange juice. Ra'Keeyah nodded her head yes and continued eating. "That's good. What you gon' get into tonight?"

Ra'Keeyah wanted to say nothing, but she knew she had standing obligations. She had to make her money and wasn't going to let anyone get in the way of that, not even Brick.

"Umm, I gotta babysit my little brother and his friend tonight," she lied. "But just until my mom gets off work though."

"Oh, so you won't be busy all night then?" Ra'Keeyah shook her head no. "So you wanna come back over here and spend some time wit' me again?"

"Are you gon' leave me in the house again by myself for anotha' three or four hours?" Ra'Keeyah asked sarcastically.

"Man, I got caught up. My niggas was holdin' a dice game, and once I start gamblin', it's hard for me to stop," Brick said, laughing.

"Yeah, whatever. You probably was caught up between some bitch's legs, if anything," Ra'Keeyah replied, getting slightly jealous at the thought.

"Now what sense would it make for me to leave the house to go get some pussy when I had some right here?" Brick asked.

"Who said you had some right here?" Ra'Keeyah snapped back, knowing she would have given it up to him in a heartbeat if he hadn't fallen asleep.

"I just know," he winked and finished off his orange juice.

"Whatever," Ra'Keeyah smiled. "You think you got it like that, huh?"

"I might not, but *he* does," Brick said, pointing down to his manhood.

Ra'Keeyah laughed. "He who?"

"Rufus," Brick answered.

"Rufus?" Ra'Keeyah said, laughing even harder. "What typa' down South, backwoods, country-ass name is that?"

"My mom gave it that name when I was about fifteen," Brick answered.

"Your mom?" Ra'Keeyah asked, confused. "That also sounds like some down South, backwoods shit to me too."

"Not like that," Brick said, giving his story some clarity. "This nasty broad burnt me when I was fifteen. When my mom took me to the doctor she started singin' 'the roof, the roof, the roof is on fire, we don't need no water; let the mutha'fucka burn'." Brick started laughing. "It's funny to me now, but it damn sure wasn't back then. So that's how *he* got the name Rufus."

"Oh, I get it," Ra'Keeyah laughed. "The roof is on fire."

Brick looked at his G-Shock Hyper Color watch. "It's eight-fifteen. I gotta be somewhere at nine. You ready?" he asked Ra'Keeyah, not really wanting her to leave.

"Yeah," she said, getting up from the table. "I left my purse upstairs. I'm about to go get it."

Ra'Keeyah went upstairs to retrieve her purse. She took her phone out and looked at the caller ID. She saw where her mom had called her three more times, Marshall called twice, and Shayna had called twice. "Damn, I know my mom is gon' be trippin'." Ra'Keeyah quickly dialed Shayna's number to see if her mother had called her.

"What it do?" Shayna answered.

"Did my mom call you?"

"Yep, but I didn't answer," Shayna replied.

"We gon' have to come up wit' somethin', 'cuz I know she gon' be trippin'," Ra'Keeyah worried. "I just hope she don't try to put me on punishment or some dumb shit like that for me spendin' the night without askin'. I got plans tonight."

"Don't worry. By time you get over here, I'll have a whole story conjured up for you," Shayna assured her friend.

"Thanks, girl," Ra'Keeyah said gratefully.

"That's what I'm here for. I'll see you in a bit." Shayna hung up the phone, lit a blunt, and lay back on her bed. She knew Ra'Keeyah's mom was far from a fool, so whatever story she came up with had to be good!

The entire ride to Shayna's was a quiet one, only because Brick's cell phone kept ringing nonstop. Ra'Keeyah didn't mind because she was too busy trying to come up with a story of her own to tell her mom. She decided whichever story was the most believable between hers and Shayna's would be the one she told.

"Right there," Ra'Keeyah pointed, showing Brick which house Shayna lived in.

Brick pulled up to the curb and stopped the car. "Hang on," he said to the person on the other end of the phone. "So I'm gon' see you later on, right?" he asked Ra'Keeyah before she got out.

Ra'Keeyah smiled and nodded her head yes. "I'll call you when I'm ready to be picked up."

"Okay, do that." Brick leaned over and gave her a quick peck on the lips before continuing his conversation.

"Damn, that's all I get?" Ra'Keeyah asked, while opening the car door.

"I got you later on," Brick replied. "Naw, I ain't talkin' to you," he said to the caller.

"Whatever, talk to you later." Ra'Keeyah got out and closed the door behind her. Brick was still running his mouth on the phone as he pulled away. "Damn, he got some soft lips. I can't wait until tonight," she said excited, as she made her way up Shayna's walk.

Chapter Sixteen

"What the fuck you mean, somebody stole your purse from a party that you didn't even have permission to go to?" Ra'Keeyah's mother screamed. "Then on top of that, your phone and Shayna's phone was in the purse! How irresponsible can you be, Ra'Keeyah?" her mother fussed. "A two-hundred dollar phone is just gone!"

Dang if my phone really was gone, you cussin' me out like you paid for the mutha'fucka," Ra'Keeyah thought as she stood in the middle of her mother's bedroom getting cussed out. "Dang, Ma, you act like I asked somebody to steal my purse," she huffed. "I set it by Quiana before I got up and went to the bathroom. And when I came back, my purse was gone," Ra'Keeyah lied with a straight face.

"It doesn't matter, Ra'Keeyah. You will be seventeen years old next week, but sometimes you have the sense of a ten year old!" Ra'Keeyah's mother shook her head; she was disgusted by her daughter's carelessness.

No, this bitch did not just say I have the sense of a ten year old! She is really buggin' out!

"Just go on to your room, Ra'Keeyah! I don't even wanna look at you right now. You just throw money away like it grows on trees!" her mother fumed.

Ra'Keeyah turned to walk away. She was just glad that her mother didn't say anything about her being on punishment. *Maybe I shoulda' stuck wit' my own story and told her ass I got abducted by aliens, then maybe*

she woulda' been more understandin'. Ra'Keeyah was
about halfway out the door when her mother dropped
the bomb on her. "And don't ask to go nowhere tonight,
'cuz the answer is no!"

Ra'Keeyah stopped and turned around. There was
no way she was staying in the house on a Saturday
night. For one, she had money to make, and two, she
had already made plans to stay all night with Brick.

"Mom, that ain't fair!" she huffed. "I'ma be seventeen next week, and you still treatin' me like a child!"

"You act like a child, you gon' get treated like one!"
she said nonchalantly.

"So I'm just s'pose to sit in the house all night by myself?" Ra'Keeyah questioned.

Ra'Keeyah's mom lay across her bed to try to take a
nap. "I don't care what you do. All I know is you betta'
not leave this house," her mother warned.

You got me fucked up, Ra'Keeyah thought before
turning to walk out of her mother's room. *If you think
I'm about to sit up in this bitch, you got another thing
comin'!*

"And don't think I'm not gon' call the house to check
to see if you here."

"I don't give a fuck what you do," Ra'Keeyah mumbled before slamming her mother's bedroom door shut.

"And stop slammin' my damn door!" her mother
screamed.

Ra'Keeyah was furious. She walked into her own
bedroom and slammed the door behind her. Then she
picked the cordless phone up off the nightstand and
called Shayna to tell her what had just gone down.

"Well, at least she bought your story about both of us
gettin' our phones stolen," Shayna said, as she looked
for a sexy outfit to wear tonight.

"Yeah," Ra'Keeyah agreed.

"So what you gon' do about tonight?"

"I'ma dance, and then I'm goin' to spend some time wit' Brick," Ra'Keeyah stated. "I'm not gon' let her stop me from doin' what I wanna do. Shit, I'm almost grown!" Ra'Keeyah was fuming.

"Yeah, you will be an old lady next Saturday," Shayna joked, trying to cheer her best friend up.

"You got a lot of nerves," Ra'Keeyah laughed. "'Cuz yo' ass will be seventeen twelve days after me."

Shayna laughed too. "I know, right?" Shayna's demeanor became serious. "So what you gon' tell yo' mom? 'Cuz you know she gon' be callin' the house every chance she gets."

Ra'Keeyah took a deep breath. "I don't know, but I'ma come up wit' somethin'."

"Well, let me know. And if I can think of somethin' I'll call you back," Shayna said.

"Don't forget to call me on the house phone," Ra'Keeyah reminded her friend.

"Oh yeah, your cell phone is over here," Shayna chuckled.

"I know," Ra'Keeyah whined. "I'm startin' to have withdrawals. I need my cell phone!"

"You a nut, girl," Shayna laughed.

"I'm serious," Ra'Keeyah admitted.

"I know you are. I be feelin' the same way when I don't have my phone."

"All right, girl, I'm about to take a nap. I got a long night ahead of me," Ra'Keeyah said, lying across her bed.

"Okay, talk to you later," Shayna replied before hanging up.

Ra'Keeyah lay in her bed trying to think of any excuse she could feed her mom on why she couldn't stay home on a Saturday night. She thought until her head began to hurt and still came up with nothing. Tired of thinking, Ra'Keeyah drifted off to sleep for a much-needed rest.

Two-and-a-half hours later, Ra'Keeyah woke up feeling refreshed. She still needed a plan to get out of the house tonight. Hell, if push came to shove, she'd just leave and suffer the consequences later on.

"Key-Key," Jaylen knocked on his sister's door and yelled.

"What, Jaylen?" she answered.

"Can I come in?" he asked loudly.

"What you want, boy?" Ra'Keeyah asked, not feeling like being bothered. Jaylen opened his sister's door and stuck his head in. "I didn't tell you to come in here, nigga."

"I got somethin' to tell you, but I don't know if you want mommy to hear it," Jaylen whispered loudly.

Ra'Keeyah laughed at her brother's failed attempt to whisper. "Come in and close the door behind you." Jaylen walked into Ra'Keeyah's room and shut the door before climbing in her bed. "Now what you got to tell me?"

Jaylen jumped back out of his sister's bed and looked out in the hallway to make sure the coast was clear before climbing back into bed with her. "Me and mommy just left Mr. Wilson's corner store."

"So?" Ra'Keeyah grimaced. "What you tellin' me for?"

"Guess who I saw?" he asked shyly.

"Jaylen, I don't got time to be playin' no guessin' games wit' you!" Ra'Keeyah said slightly annoyed. "Who did you see?"

"Bricks."

"Brick," Ra'Keeyah corrected before laughing. "No s at the end." Ra'Keeyah was now interested in what her brother had to tell her. "And what was he doin' there?" she questioned.

"He was talkin'," Jaylen answered.

"To who? He wasn't talkin' to no girl, was he?" Ra'Keeyah asked, anticipating the answer.

"No, he was talkin' to Mr. Wilson," Jaylen said.

"Oh, okay," Ra'Keeyah replied, relieved. "Well, did he speak to you?"

Jaylen nodded his head yes. "He winked and waved at me. I told Mommy I knew him, but she didn't believe me."

"Well, next time you see him, don't tell Mommy you know him, okay?"

"Okay, so this another one of our secrets?" Jaylen wondered out loud.

"Yep, Brick is gon' be another one of our little secrets, okay?" Ra'Keeyah said.

"Like the belly button ring?"

"Yep, just like the belly button ring," she said.

"Okay," Jaylen agreed before climbing out of the bed. "Hey, Key-Key?"

"Yes, Jaylen," Ra'Keeyah answered.

"Can you take me over Brick's house one day?" he asked out of nowhere.

"I sure will," she answered with a smile.

"Yesssss," Jaylen replied happily before walking out of the room.

"I love that boy," Ra'Keeyah said laughing before getting out of bed. She walked over to her closet to try to find something to wear. She had new outfits with tags still on them, so she had a lot to choose from. "I gotta look extra sexy tonight," she said as the house phone began to ring. She looked over at it and ignored it.

"Ra'Keeyah, telephone," her mother yelled.

"Who is it?" Ra'Keeyah asked smartly.

"Pick it up and see," her mother snapped.

"Hello?" Ra'Keeyah asked, with a slight attitude.

"Hey, how come you haven't been answering your cell phone?" Marshall asked.

"I lost it," Ra'Keeyah snapped, feeling he was out of place for questioning her.

"Oh, okay. Well, I was just wondering if you were up for dinner and a movie tonight."

Nigga, please, Ra'Keeyah wanted to say. "I'm on punishment," she answered in a hurry. "My mom said I can't go anywhere tonight."

"What did you do, if you don't mind me asking?" Marshall asked sounding proper.

I do mind, nosy-ass nigga! "I stayed over at Shayna's last night without askin'."

"Well, okay, call me when you get off punishment."

"I will," Ra'Keeyah said in a rush before ending her call. She heard her mother walk into the hallway and stand outside her door and a light quickly went off in her head. She turned the volume all the way down on the phone before speaking. "I can't go to the movies tonight, Marshall. My mom said I'm not allowed to leave the house." She paused before continuing. "I know it's the last night for it, but what you want me to do? Ignore what my mom said?"

Ra'Keeyah's mom stood in the hallway listening to her daughter's conversation. She felt kind of bad because she knew how much Ra'Keeyah wanted to see that new movie. But she also remembered Ra'Keeyah had disobeyed her by staying out all night without asking. She liked Marshall and wanted her daughter to be with a young, working, respectable guy like him, so bending her own rules wasn't going to hurt anything.

"Yeah, I'll see if she'll let me go to the library wit' you tomorrow," Ra'Keeyah said to the dial tone. "Okay, I'll talk to you later." Ra'Keeyah hung up the phone, hoping that her plan would work. She started counting backward from ten. As soon as she got to one, her mother walked into her room and looked down at her daughter. Ra'Keeyah sat on her bed, pretending to be occupied with her nails. "What you in here doin'?" her mother asked.

"Oh, nothin'," Ra'Keeyah answered nonchalantly.

"Was that Marshall on the phone?" her mother asked, already knowing because she was the one who answered the call.

"Yea," she answered happily. "You know what, Mom? I'm really startin' to like Marshall a lot," Ra'Keeyah lied with a huge smile on her face.

That was the best news Ra'Keeyah's mom had heard in a long time. She could finally sleep easy knowing her daughter was interested in someone like Marshall and not some drug-dealing thug that wears his pants sagging down to his knees.

"That's nice," her mother smiled. "I didn't mean to be dippin' in your conversation, but I overheard you sayin' he wants to take you out tonight."

"Mom, you was listenin' in on my conversation?" Ra'Keeyah asked, pretending to be upset.

"No, no, baby, it wasn't like that," her mother explained. "I was comin' in here to see what you were doin', and I heard you talkin' on the phone, that's all," she said, stretching the truth.

"Oh, okay," Ra'Keeyah responded, knowing better.

"Now, you know I normally don't go back on my word, but this time I will make an exception."

"What you talkin' about, Mom?" Ra'Keeyah asked, already knowing.

"I'm gon' let you go out with Marshall tonight," her mother smiled.

Ra'Keeyah smiled too. "For real, Mommy?" she asked, pretending to be surprised.

"Yep," her mom answered happily.

Ra'Keeyah stood up from her bed and gave her mother a tight hug. "Thanks, Ma!"

"You're welcome, baby," her mother said, hugging her back. "Let me know when Marshall gets here. I want to say hello to him."

Shit! Ra'Keeyah thought. Ra'Keeyah had to think quickly. "Oh, he at work right now and don't get off till seven so we're goin' to the last show, if that's okay," Ra'Keeyah lied, knowing her mother had to be at work at seven so she would be long gone by the time Marshall was supposed to arrive.

"Oh, damn," her mother said, a little disappointed. "Well, be sure to tell him I said hello," she said walking out of her daughter's room.

"I will," Ra'Keeyah said, closing her bedroom door behind her mother. She waited a few minutes, jumped on her bed, and started kicking and waving her arms. She was ecstatic that her plan had worked. Ra'Keeyah couldn't wait to call Shayna and tell her the good news. She pulled herself together and got up off the bed. Then she walked back over to the closet to find herself something to wear.

Ra'Keeyah shook her head as she rambled through her closet. A huge smile crept across her face before saying her three famous words: "Damn, I'm good!"

Chapter Seventeen

Ra'Keeyah waited for her mother to leave before packing her overnight bag. She planned on being back before her mother's shift was over the next morning, but wasn't leaving the house without all the much-needed necessities. She threw an outfit, clean pair of underwear, soap, deodorant, feminine wipes, tooth-brush, toothpaste, perfume, and a pack of Doublemint gum and some condoms she had for a while in her bag before calling Shayna to tell her that she was ready to be picked up. Ra'Keeyah was so excited about what the night could bring she could barely contain herself.

"Money and a much-needed orgasm. What more could a girl ask for?" Ra'Keeyah said on her way down the stairs to wait for her ride.

Twenty minutes later, Shayna, Joe, and Quiana pulled up in front of Ra'Keeyah's house. Ra'Keeyah turned off all the lights and locked the door behind her. She hurried down the walk and jumped in the old, beat-up minivan.

"What's up, LisaRaye?" Shayna said once Ra'Keeyah got in the van.

"Don't start," Ra'Keeyah laughed. "What's up, every-body?" she spoke.

"What's up?" Joe looked in the rearview mirror and smiled, giving Ra'Keeyah the creeps.

"What's up?" Quiana spoke back.

"You got everything?" Shayna asked, making sure.

"Yea, but I don't understand why you told me not to bring an outfit to dance in tonight," Ra'Keeyah said, confused.

"'Cuz I got everything covered," Shayna replied. "Everything we need is in the trunk."

Ra'Keeyah felt uncomfortable on the drive to the Holiday Inn. Joe continuously gawked at her through the mirror. Ra'Keeyah thought when she bucked her eyes at him he would catch the drift, but he didn't and continued staring.

"You need to be watchin' the road instead of watchin' me," Ra'Keeyah finally got fed up and snapped. All Joe did was laugh and continued driving.

"Joe don't give you the creeps?" she leaned over and whispered asking Quiana.

Quiana laughed and shook her head no. "Naw, he don't bother me," she whispered back.

Damn, her and Shayna fucked up, 'cuz that cracker is weird as hell! Ra'Keeyah thought. She was relieved when they finally pulled up in front of the hotel.

"All right, Joe, I'll call you later," Shayna said, opening the door and getting out.

"All right. Y'all shake it, but don't break it," he said laughing as Quiana and Ra'Keeyah got out. Shayna and Quiana laughed as well.

"That was so corny," Ra'Keeyah grimaced and threw her bag over her shoulder, making her way to the hotel's entrance with Quiana in tow.

"You don't like Joe, do you?" Quiana asked Ra'Keeyah as they walked into the hotel lobby.

"Not at all," Ra'Keeyah replied and left it at that.

Shayna walked around to the back of the minivan and pulled her big duffle bag of goodies out before joining the girls in the hotel lobby. She walked over to the front desk, gave the guy the room number, and waited on him to hand her the key. She smiled as they headed to the elevator.

"I got a feelin' we gon' make some money tonight," Shayna beamed with excitement, pushing the arrow that pointed upward.

"I hope so," Quiana added. "I seen these sharp-ass Christian Louboutins that I gots to have."

Ra'Keeyah shook her head as the elevator doors opened. "So you gon' spend all that damn money on one pair of shoes?"

"Yeah, why not?" Quiana asked, not seeing anything wrong with it.

"Wow, you really are a dumb broad," Ra'Keeyah spat.

"I tried to tell you," Shayna laughed.

"What's so dumb about me buyin' a pair of shoes I want?" Quiana asked. "You act like I'm askin' one of y'all to buy 'em."

"You can go right to DSW or somewhere and get a nice pair of shoes that's gon' look better, cost less, and leave you wit' some extra money to buy a matchin' outfit," Ra'Keeyah said, sounding like her mother.

"But they won't be Louboutins," Quiana explained.

"The only difference gon' be is the name and the color on the bottom of the shoe," Shayna said. "Shit, bitch, gimme a hundred dollars and I'll paint all the bottoms of your shoes red!"

"And I'll help you," Ra'Keeyah laughed.

"Whatever," Quiana said, rolling her eyes, not wanting to admit her girls were right.

Ra'Keeyah, Shayna, and Quiana stepped off the elevator at the top floor and walked over to the door. Shayna unlocked the door, and they all walked in.

"What's up, my brown sugar?" Calvin greeted them with a smile when they entered the sitting area of the suite.

"Hey," Shayna cooed as she walked in and set the duffle bag down on the floor.

"Hey," both Ra'Keeyah and Quiana said and continued walking to the bedroom to get dressed.

"What's in the bag?" Calvin inquired.

"We got a li'l surprise for you and the fellas tonight," Shayna smiled.

"I hope you don't mind, but I invited a couple more of my buddies," Calvin said, putting his arms around Shayna and giving her a kiss on the lips.

"But I thought we agreed to leave it at ten," she said, stepping back from him.

"We did," he stepped toward Shayna and wrapped his hands around her waist. "Look at it like this; you and your girls will be makin' a lot more money tonight because these guys aren't a part of my counseling group either."

Shayna thought for a quick second. "Yea, I guess you right. But after tonight, you can't keep invitin' all these people. My girls ain't comfortable wit' dancin' for all these strange-lookin' men you be bringin' up in here," Shayna said, picking the duffle bag up off the floor.

"Strange?" Calvin laughed. "My friends aren't strange, but if it makes you feel any better, I won't invite anyone else," he promised before kissing Shayna on the neck. "Now go on in there and get ready. The boys will be here any minute." Calvin patted Shayna on her rear end and sent her on her way. "Hey," he called out.

Shayna turned around. "Yeah?" she answered.

"I think he might be ready for some loving tonight," Calvin said, groping himself.

"You got your wallet?" Shayna asked with a smile.

Calvin reached around and pulled his wallet out of his back pocket. "Does this answer your question?" he asked, opening the wallet, revealing a wad of money.

"It sure does," Shayna beamed with excitement before walking into the room with her girls to get dressed. She dropped the duffle bag down on the bed and began unzipping it.

"What's in the bag?" Quiana asked.

"Just hold your horses, you'll see," Shayna said, pulling out a bottle of her favorite St. Claire Green Tea Vodka and some plastic cups. "Here, set that on the dresser," she handed it to Quiana. Quiana rolled her eyes, grabbed the bottle and the cups, and placed them on the dresser. Shayna reached back in the bag. "Here," she said, handing Ra'Keeyah an outfit to put on.

"What's this?" Ra'Keeyah asked, looking at the electric blue string that Shayna had just handed her.

"Y'all go put 'em on," Shayna said, and handed Quiana the same outfit but in magenta.

"Uhhh-oh," Quiana smiled on her way to the bathroom to put on her sexy outfit.

"What's wrong wit' the stuff we normally wear?" Ra'Keeyah asked.

"It was all right, but these," Shayna held up her black outfit, "are bound to get us more money."

Ra'Keeyah and Shayna both got undressed and slid into their new bodysuits. Ra'Keeyah was so used to wearing a regular bathing suit to dance in, putting this on had her feeling completely naked in her triangle top bodysuit that barely covered her nipples. It had a thong bottom with a multistrap halter bodice and a choker silhouette that went around her neck.

"Look at you," Shayna smiled. "You look good in that outfit!"

"I feel like a fuckin' stripper for real," Ra'Keeyah pouted.

"What do you think you are?" Quiana walked out of the bathroom and asked. "We look hot," she smiled.

"Where you get these outfits from anyway, Strippers 'R' Us?" Ra'Keeyah joked.

"Naw, fool," Shayna laughed. "I ordered 'em from DiscountStrippers.com," Shayna answered.

"Oh, Lawd." Ra'Keeyah shook her head.

"Y'all ready?" Calvin tapped lightly on the door and asked.

"Give us a few minutes," Shayna said before checking her backside in the mirror. "How do I look?"

"Hot!" Quiana replied with a huge smile.

"You look a'iiiight!" Ra'Keeyah joked.

"Whatever," Shayna joked back. She walked over to the dresser and popped the top on the bottle of vodka. "Y'all want some?" she filled her cup halfway up.

"You know I do," Quiana said, walking over to the dresser and pouring herself a double shot.

"I might as well. Shit, I'ma need somethin' to keep my mind off of this outfit I got on." Ra'Keeyah poured herself a double shot as well, taking it to the head. "Oooooh, that burns," she said, setting her cup back down on top of the dresser.

"Let's go, y'all." Shayna finished off half of her drink, saving the rest for later.

"I'm ready," Quiana said, amped.

"We're ready," Shayna yelled out to Calvin. Calvin pushed PLAY on the boom box. When R. Kelly's "Bangin' the Headboard" came on, the girls sashayed out of the room like professionals. The room full of men went wild. It was always loud when they came out, but this time it must have been the outfits that had the men acting like caged animals. Cheers, whistles, and hand clapping rang throughout the room as the three girls began to dance.

Ra'Keeyah instantly noticed that there were more new faces in the room. She looked over at Shayna and rolled her eyes, but continued dancing. Shayna knew she had a royal cussing out coming. Hopefully they'd make enough money to make Ra'Keeyah give her a pass.

After about forty-five minutes of dancing, rubbing on hard and limp dicks, and being touched on, Ra'Keeyah had had enough. She was ready to go. She gathered all of her money and looked over at the clock that read a quarter to nine. She wanted to spend as much time with Brick as she could before it was time for her to go home. She walked over to Shayna who was grinding on one of the men's laps and tapped her on the shoulder.

Shayna looked back. "What's up?" she asked.

"I'm about to go."

Shayna stood up from the man's lap. "I'll be right back." She then turned her attention to Ra'Keeyah. "Why you leavin' so early, girl? It's rainin' money up in here!"

"I know," Ra'Keeyah agreed, looking over at Quiana who was getting money stuffed in her straps left and right. "I'm goin' over to Brick's. If I stay here, I won't have that much time to spend wit' him 'cuz you know I gotta be home before my mom get there."

"I feel you," Shayna said.

"Okay, then, get back to what you were doin'. I'm about to go shower and change my clothes. And you know I got a bone to pick wit' you," Ra'Keeyah said.

"I know. We'll talk later." Shayna gave Ra'Keeyah a hug before walking back over to entertain the men.

Ra'Keeyah turned and walked toward the bedroom. The entrance was blocked off by one of the men who couldn't keep his hands off her all night. "How much?" he boldly asked.

"How much for what?" Ra'Keeyah asked, confused and pressed for time.

"Sex," he replied.

"What?" Ra'Keeyah snapped, shocked and offended. *This mutha'fucka must be mistakin' me for some type of trick or somethin'!* Ra'Keeyah thought.

"Oh, I'm sorry if I offended you," the man apologized. "I just thought, oh, never mind," he said and turned to walk away.

Ra'Keeyah thought for a quick second. She could definitely used the extra money. She wondered how much she could actually make by sleeping with this guy. "Wait a minute," Ra'Keeyah said, stopping him. He turned back around. "How much you willin' to pay?" she asked, shocking the hell out of herself and hoping his price was higher than hers.

The man looked her from head to toe. Ra'Keeyah turned around to show him what she was working with. "I'll give you five hundred dollars," he answered quickly, his dick as hard as he could ever remember it being.

What the fuck! Ra'Keeyah thought. *Five hundred dollars? Shit, Brick can wait for that kind of money.* "Okay, come on," Ra'Keeyah moved quickly before he changed his mind. She led him into the bedroom by his tie and locked the door behind her. Ra'Keeyah put the money she had made from dancing in her overnight bag before shoving all the stuff off the bed onto the floor.

"Lie down," she commanded. Ra'Keeyah couldn't believe she was about to sleep with a white man for money. All she could do was hope it felt the same as sleeping with a black one for free. The man quickly got undressed and jumped in the king-sized bed. "No, no," Ra'Keeyah said, holding out her hand to be paid first. She almost busted out laughing when she saw the size of his package. *Do that come in adult sizes?* she wanted to ask.

The man sighed heavily before reaching over, grabbing his pants off the floor, and pulling his wallet out of his back pocket. He counted out ten fifty-dollar bills and handed them to Ra'Keeyah. She quickly counted it before sticking it in her overnight bag with the rest of her earnings.

Ra'Keeyah was nervous as she got undressed. She wasn't sure the little experience she had in sex would be worth this man's five-hundred dollars. At this point, there was no turning back, and she definitely wasn't returning his money so all she could do was pray that whatever she was about to put on him would definitely leave him satisfied.

Ra'Keeyah grabbed the bottle of St. Claire Green Tea Vodka off the dresser and took a long drink before slamming it back down. She then reached into her duffle bag and pulled out a condom, tossing it to the man. He caught it in midair, opened it, and slid it on his tiny, almost nonexistent penis.

"Come here," he said, trying to sound seductive.

Ra'Keeyah walked over to the bed and climbed on. Instantly, the man began feeling all over her. He quickly flipped her on her back. Suddenly, Ra'Keeyah had second thoughts about what she was doing. He leaned in and began aggressively kissing her on her neck.

"Whoooa, slow down," she said.

"Oh sorry," he said, embarrassed. "It's just that I've never slept with a black woman before, even though it has always been a fantasy of mine. My wife thinks I'm sick and need to get help."

"Your wife?" Ra'Keeyah was surprised.

"Yea, my wife," he mumbled, like there was nothing wrong with what he was about to do.

"Okay, let's try it again." Ra'Keeyah lay back, wanting to get this over with. *I cannot believe I'm doin' this,* she kept chanting over and over in her head.

"Okay," he replied and bent down over her. He began gently kissing her on the neck before working his way down to her breasts.

Ra'Keeyah had to close her eyes and coach herself through the entire ordeal. She wanted to scream each time his lips touched her body. All she could do was keep thinking about the five hundred dollars in her bag as Mr. White Guy sucked on her nipples. She lay there impatiently waiting on him to enter her so she could go.

"Oooooooooh," he moaned as he kissed his way back up her body. He then found Ra'Keeyah's opening and slipped his little dick inside of her. After about five minutes of moaning and groaning, he collapsed on top of Ra'Keeyah and his body began jerking.

"What the hell? You done already?" she asked, surprised and relieved, as she pushed him off of her.

"I'm sorry. It's just that, you were so wet and tight," the man said, breathing heavily.

Ra'Keeyah wanted to laugh so bad, but she knew he had to already be embarrassed about the two-minute work he'd just put in. She rolled out of the bed and grabbed her duffle bag so she could get changed.

The man climbed out of bed as well and began putting his clothes back on. "Nice doin' business with you," he looked over at Ra'Keeyah and said.

"The pleasure was all mines," she lied.

"Really?" he sounded surprised. Ra'Keeyah nodded her head. "Well, when can we do this again? I wanna go somewhere more private next time."

"Okay, just bring your wallet. Look, I would love to sit and chat, but I have to get dressed. I have somewhere to be," Ra'Keeyah said.

"That's fine. I gotta get home to my wife and kids anyways."

Ra'Keeyah turned to walk in the bathroom. "Steve," the man called out.

Ra'Keeyah turned around to face him. "Huh?" she asked, confused.

He walked over closer to Ra'Keeyah. "My name is Steve," and held out his hand for her to shake.

It hadn't dawned on Ra'Keeyah until just then that she had just slept with a man and didn't even know his name. "LisaRaye," Ra'Keeyah replied quickly while shaking his hand. She wouldn't dare give him her real name. After all, everyone says she looks like LisaRaye, so why not play the part.

"LisaRaye," Steve repeated. "That's a pretty name."

"Thanks," Ra'Keeyah replied with a smile. "Okay, well, I'll see you later, Steve."

"Can I get a kiss before I go?" he almost begged.

That's the least I can do. After all, I just made the quickest and easiest five hundred dollars of my life, she thought. "Sure."

Steve leaned in and gave Ra'Keeyah a kiss on the lips. "Thanks," he said before turning to walk away.

"No, thank you." Ra'Keeyah walked into the bathroom to get ready for round two.

After showering and getting dressed in her pink Hello Kitty shorts, a white tank with the Kitty emblem on the front, and a crisp pair of white and pink Reebok Zig Fly tennis shoes, Ra'Keeyah called a taxi. She couldn't have Brick picking her up from a hotel. She walked out into the sitting area to tell her friends she was leaving and got the shock of her life. Shayna was bent over the back of a chair getting her back blown out by one of the men, while Quiana was giving someone head. There were more men standing around watching and waiting for a turn.

"So this what be goin' on after I leave," Ra'Keeyah said, sneaking out of the hotel room. Shayna and Quiana were so engrossed in what they were doing that they never knew Ra'Keeyah was still there, making a little side money of her own. Ra'Keeyah pushed the down arrow on the elevator and waited for it to open. "Wow. I can't believe these bitches been makin' extra money behind my back." Ra'Keeyah was heated as she stepped on the elevator in disbelief. "I'ma check the shit out them foul-ass hoes!"

Once the elevator reached the first floor, Ra'Keeyah walked out, smiled at the concierge behind the desk, and went outside to wait on her taxi. She pulled the money out of her duffle bag and counted it one last time.

"Damn," she said, feeling a little bit better about her friends' betrayal. "If I woulda' known I could get five hundred dollars just for sleeping with one of these men, I woulda' been chargin' for sex a long time ago." Ra'Keeyah put her money back in her bag and waited on her taxi to arrive.

Chapter Eighteen

Once inside the taxi Ra'Keeyah phoned Brick to make sure he was at home. After confirming he was, she gave the driver the address. The cab pulled up in front of Brick's, Ra'Keeyah handed the driver a twenty-dollar bill and told him to keep the change. She then grabbed her overnight bag and exited the car. She was nervous and anxious as she walked up the walkway. She rang the doorbell and patiently waited for Brick to answer.

"What's up?" Brick asked with a smile as he opened the screen door.

"Hey," Ra'Keeyah said, dropping her bag in the foyer.

"Damn, what you tryin'a do? Move in?" he laughed, looking down at her bag.

Ra'Keeyah laughed too. "Naw, dummy. I had to get some of my clothes from over at Shayna's house," she lied.

"I don't know how y'all women be wearin' each other's clothes." Brick locked the front door before walking toward the living room with Ra'Keeyah following behind. "I can't wear another nigga's clothes, and he damn sure ain't wearin' mines. And if I do let a nigga wear 'em, he can keep 'em," Brick said sitting down on the sofa.

Ra'Keeyah kicked off her tennis shoes and sat down next to Brick. "I don't see the big deal. I mean, as long as it's my girl, I don't have a problem wit' it, but anybody else I ain't gon' be able to do it."

"Best friend, sister, brother, or cousin, I ain't lettin' nobody wear my clothes," Brick said as he looked over at Ra'Keeyah and smiled.

"What you smilin' for?"

"I'm just happy to see you, that's all," Brick admitted.

"Ahhh, ain't that sweet. Brick is happy to see me," Ra'Keeyah teased.

"Shut up," he laughed. "What you been doin' all day?" He lifted up Ra'Keeyah's tiny hand and locked his fingers with hers.

"Nothin' really. Just been sittin' over Shayna's house chillin'," she lied.

"You hungry?"

"Yea, kinda'," Ra'Keeyah answered. "I haven't eaten anything all day. That's probably why I got a slight headache. It's either that or the St. Claire Green Tea Vodka I drank earlier."

"It gotta be 'cuz you ain't ate. That St. Claire don't give you no headache. That's some top shelf shit!" Brick boasted on his favorite drink.

Ra'Keeyah rolled her eyes playfully. "Whatever. It was the St. Claire," she laughed.

"All right, don't get jacked up for talkin' about my drank," Brick laughed. "What you wanna do? Go out to eat or order in?"

"It don't matter to me," Ra'Keeyah answered.

"You like Chinese?" he asked, knowing a good spot out by the Galleria Mall.

"Yea. But I don't eat egg rolls. The cabbage don't agree wit' my stomach."

"It gives you gas?" Brick laughed and stood up from the sofa and held his hands out.

"Shut up, nigga," Ra'Keeyah said laughing and grabbing on to his strong hands so he could pull her up. She stood up and slipped her tennis shoes back on. "You got any Tylenol?" Her headache was getting worse. She didn't know if it was from the excitement of being there with Brick or from the lack of food. Whatever the pain stemmed from, Ra'Keeyah definitely needed something to ease it.

"Naw, I don't have none, but we can swing by the store and pick you up some on the way to the restaurant," he suggested, grabbing his car keys off the coffee table as they headed to the door.

"Okay, cool. What you drivin'?" she asked, walking outside.

"I don't even know. I got so many to choose from. What you feel like ridin' in? The Lex or the Camaro?" Brick hit the button on his keys to open up the three-car garage. "We can take the Explorer, the Range or the motorcycle," he smiled while bragging.

Ra'Keeyah shook her head and laughed. "Nigga, braggin' is not a good look for you."

Brick laughed too. "Let's go." He walked over to the Camaro and opened up the passenger door so Ra'Keeyah could get in.

Once again she slid in the butter-soft seats and got comfortable.

Brick got in the car and felt under his seat, put his seat belt on, and pulled out of the driveway. He changed the XM radio to an old-school rap station. Big Daddy Kane's, "I Get The Job Done" was playing. Brick turned up the volume as loud as it could go and started bobbing his head. Ra'Keeyah reached over and turned the music down.

"What? You don't like old-school music or somethin'? Or is this the way before your time?"

"Old-school music is my favorite. It's just all that bass that's bumpin' is makin' my head hurt worse."

"Oh, yea. My bad. I forgot you had a headache," Brick apologized. "We goin' to get you somethin' for your head."

Ra'Keeyah lay her head back and listened as cut after cut kept coming on. Das EXF, "They Want EFX," Poor Righteous Teachers, "Rock This Funky Joint," The Good Girls, "Your Sweetness," and MC Trouble, "Make You Mine." The music was sounding so good she almost forgot about her headache.

"What you know about this music?" Brick asked, as he drove. "I know most of these songs were out before you were even thought of!"

"All me and my daddy used to listen to is old-school music. Every Saturday we would watch *Video Soul* and some of his old recorded VCR tapes with old-music videos on them."

"Whaaat?" Brick was intrigued. "That's what's up, 'cuz me and my dad used to do the same thing."

"Yep, every Saturday," Ra'Keeyah repeated as if she was reminiscing.

"It's Funky Enough," Brick said out of nowhere.

"Huh?" Ra'Keeyah asked.

"Who sung it?"

"Let me see," Ra'Keeyah thought for a second. "It's Funky Enough" she repeated. "The D.O.C.," she said, remembering that was one of her father's favorite songs.

"Yep," Brick smiled.

"Slow Down," Ra'Keeyah asked.

Brick sucked his teeth. "That's easy."

"Well, who sung it then?"

"Brand Nubian," he answered correctly.

"Okay," Ra'Keeyah smiled.

"I got one I know you ain't gon' get," Brick smiled happily.

"You wanna bet?" Ra'Keeyah asked with confidence.

"Hell, yeah. You know I love to gamble," Brick said, stopping at a red light.

"Okay, well, what do I get if I get it right?"

Brick thought for a minute. "Okay, I'll give you a hundred dollars if you get it right."

Ra'Keeyah was excited as hell when she heard that. "Well, what do you want if I get 'em wrong?"

Brick smiled. "If you get it wrong, I want to make love to you all night long," he said, pulling off from the light. He knew he had to make the song hard so he could get between Ra'Keeyah's thick-ass thighs.

Ra'Keeyah was certain she was going to win the bet. Old-school music was her thing, so making this hundred dollars was going to almost be as easy as it was making that five hundred from Steve.

"Okay, I guess you won't be gettin' any of this tonight," she laughed.

"Whateva'. Well, since you know everything about old-school music, who sung 'Fakin' The Funk'?" Brick asked, knowing she wouldn't get it.

"Sung what?" Ra'Keeyah was dumbfounded.

"Fakin' The Funk," Brick repeated.

"Oh my goodness, I know you makin' that up 'cuz I ain't never heard of that!" she squealed. "Come on, Brick, gimme an easier one!" she begged while laughing.

Brick laughed too. "Nope, I ain't givin' you no easier one, and I didn't make it up. Just give up!"

"Naw, I don't give up. Can you at least tell me how the lyrics went?"

"Nope," Brick smiled.

"I give up then! That ain't no fair 'cuz I know that song was made way before my time," she pouted.

"So, you said give you any song and you'd guess it right," Brick laughed again.

"You right. You won fair and square. I can't believe I got it wrong," she said in disbelief.

"I can," Brick teased as he pulled up in front of Mr. Wilson's store.

Of all the stores in the world, why in the hell did we have to come to this one? Ra'Keeyah thought. "What we come here for?"

"For your Tylenol," Brick said putting the car in park. He reached under the seat, grabbed a paper bag, and opened the door. "You ain't gettin' out?" he asked noticing Ra'Keeyah hadn't budged.

"Naw, I'm cool," she stuttered, not wanting to face Mr. Wilson after their last encounter.

"You don't want *your* man to know you here wit' me?" Brick joked.

"Nigga, please, Mr. Wilson ain't none of my man," Ra'Keeyah laughed. "Just hurry up."

"Oh, I am, 'cuz I got thangs to get into," Brick winked, closed the car door and headed into the store.

Ra'Keeyah played with the radio while she waited on Brick. She looked over and almost died when she saw Marshall pulling up next to the Camaro.

"Oh shit!" Ra'Keeyah snapped. "I hope this nigga didn't see me." She sank down in the seat as low as she could go, hoping and praying that Marshall didn't notice her. After about five minutes, she peeked over the window to make sure the coast was clear. "Come on, Brick," she said aloud. As soon as she said that, Brick came walking out the door laughing. "What you laughin' at?" Ra'Keeyah asked when he got in the car.

"I was laughin' at some corny-ass nigga that came in the store talkin' all proper and shit. He gon' ask Petey if he sold *prophylactics*," Brick laughed while handing

Ra'Keeyah a pack of Tylenol and Vitaminwater. "And Petey told the nigga he didn't know what a *prophylactic* was."

"You talkin' about the nigga that just walked in there wit' that red shirt on?" Ra'Keeyah asked, checking to see if he was talking about Marshall.

"Yeah, man," Brick continued to laugh. "I ain't neva' been around so many corny-ass niggas in my life," he said, pulling off.

I wonder what that nigga was in there buyin' condoms for, Ra'Keeyah thought as Brick continued to crack on the way Marshall spoke. Her headache had just gone off the charts hearing that news. She didn't have any intentions of being with Marshall, but she still didn't appreciate him messing around while they were supposedly talking. "Hey, do you mind if we order the food and take it back to the house?" Ra'Keeyah asked Brick. "I really don't feel like bein' in no crowded-ass restaurant."

"That's cool with me," Brick replied, not really in the mood for a crowd himself. "Find the number to the Wok in my phone." He handed Ra'Keeyah his cell phone. She scrolled through his contacts until she found the number to the Wok. She saw a lot of female names while intentionally scrolling and developed a slight attitude. She dialed the number and handed Brick his phone back. He placed their order, then headed over to the restaurant to pick it up.

Brick pulled up at the restaurant and ran in to get the order. He left his cell phone lying on top of the console. Ra'Keeyah was half-tempted to look through his call log and text messages. After a few seconds of trying to resist from picking up the phone, temptation won. As soon as she picked up the phone it began to ring. It scared her so bad she accidentally dropped it on the side of her seat.

"Shit," Ra'Keeyah panicked as she struggled to get her hand in the tiny space to retrieve the phone. She moved quickly, knowing it would only be a matter of minutes before Brick would be coming out of the restaurant. "Damn," she said, breaking a nail. Ra'Keeyah opened the door, got out, and lifted the seat up. She felt around on the floor for a few seconds before she felt the phone. "Got it," she said happily before getting back into the front seat. She looked at the screen on the phone and pushed the talk button to see if she could see who the missed call was from. After pushing the button, to Ra'Keeyah's surprise, she needed a password to get into the call list. "Ain't that about a bitch," she said laying the phone back down. "All that work I put in to get the phone, and I need a damn password to look in it. That's what I get for tryin'a be nosy!" she laughed.

Brick came out of the restaurant with two big bags and got in the car. "Anybody call me?" he asked, handing Ra'Keeyah the food.

"Yeah, it rung once," she replied, setting the food on the floor between her legs.

"Who was it?" he asked, starting up the car.

"I don't know. I don't be answerin' other people's phones," Ra'Keeyah frowned.

"Whateva'," Brick smiled as he pulled out of the parking lot. "You probably was tryin'a go through my phone," he joked.

"Yeah, right. I don't do shit like that," she lied. "I don't go through nobody's stuff 'cuz I don't want nobody goin' through mines."

"Yeah, yeah," Brick said smiling as he drove home.

Ra'Keeyah loved the fact that Brick smiled so much.

After eating a variety of foods she'd never heard of and drinking Tahitian Treat, Ra'Keeyah was good and full. All she wanted to do was lie down and take a quick nap.

"I don't know 'bout you, but I'm tired," she said, looking over at Brick with weary eyes.

"Me too. Let's go take a nap," he yawned.

"I'm wit' you."

They stood up from the sofa and headed up to his bedroom. When Brick turned on the light, the first thing Ra'Keeyah noticed was he'd changed the sheets on his bed.

"I guess you didn't lie," she said, lying across the bed.

"Lie about what?" Brick grabbed the remote off the bed and turned on the forty-six-inch TV that was mounted on the wall. He turned the volume all the way down before turning off the light.

"About keepin' yo' sheets changed," she smiled.

"Brick don't lie about nothin'," he responded, climbing into bed behind Ra'Keeyah and wrapping his arm around her waist.

"Ummm-huh, we'll see," she yawned while nestling her body up against his.

"You sure will." Within a matter of minutes, the two of them were both out like the lights.

Brick woke up at four twenty-two in the morning with stomach pains from holding his urine too long. He looked over at Ra'Keeyah who was still knocked out and quietly rolled out of bed. After relieving himself, he washed his hands before quickly running the toothbrush through his mouth. Then he walked back in the room and climbed back into bed, but this time he lay facing Ra'Keeyah. He stared at her as she slept.

Damn, she's beautiful, Brick thought. "You asleep, li'l mama?" he whispered.

"Huh?" Ra'Keeyah moaned, still half-asleep.

Brick kissed her on the forehead. "Never mind, go on back to sleep."

Brick turned his back toward Ra'Keeyah and attempted to fall back asleep. A few minutes later he felt Ra'Keeyah run her fingers through his curly hair. He slowly turned around to face her. He smiled as they stared into each other's eyes. With no spoken words, Brick leaned in and kissed Ra'Keeyah on the lips. Without hesitation, she kissed him back. Brick then grabbed Ra'Keeyah and brought her in closer to him, and they kissed for what seemed like forever.

He slid his hands under Ra'Keeyah's tank top and began massaging her breast before locating the snap on the front of her bra and unfastening it. He lifted Ra'Keeyah's tank top and pulled it over her head, revealing the most perfect set of breasts he'd seen in a long time. Brick then grabbed Ra'Keeyah's shorts and panties and began pulling them down. She lifted her bottom off the bed, making it easier for him to remove them.

He stopped abruptly and got out of the bed. Ra'Keeyah thought she'd done something wrong. She lay there feeling uncomfortable as Brick stared down at her. His eyes roamed her entire body. Finally, Brick smiled and began taking off his clothes.

Ra'Keeyah watched as Brick removed his shirt, and then his pants. The light from the TV gave her a good view of the cuts in his arms and the way his manhood stood at attention, stretching the front of his boxers. *Oh my goodness, what am I gon' do wit' all that?* Ra'Keeyah thought as she lay there and watched as Brick got completely naked.

He climbed back into bed and spread Ra'Keeyah's legs with his knee before positioning himself between her thighs. Then he leaned down, and they began kiss-

ing again. Her heart beat rapidly as Brick moved his
way down her body, stopping at her breasts. Ra'Keeyah
moaned as Brick softly sucked on her nipples, one after
the other. He then placed both hands on her waist and
continued kissing his way down her flat stomach, flick-
ing her belly button ring with his tongue before continuing his journey. He kissed the inside of her thighs,
trying to catch a whiff before going all in. Pleased with
the smell, his tongue did a swan dive into Ra'Keeyah's
womanhood. Her body shook uncontrollably as she
held on to the sheets and pleaded with God. This was
the first time she'd ever experienced such intense pleasure. She was hooked, and Brick knew it.

"You okay?" he asked, coming up for air. Ra'Keeyah
nodded her head yes as her body started to settle. Brick
wiped his mouth, reached over, and pulled a condom
out of the nightstand drawer and placed it on his fully
erect pipe.

Ra'Keeyah was all too anxious to feel Brick inside of
her, but at the same time, she was nervous. She'd been
with a few guys in her time, but none was working with
a package like his.

Ra'Keeyah's body tensed when Brick lifted her legs
in the air. "Relax, li'l mama. I got you," he assured, feeling her body trembling. Brick placed the tip of his pipe
on the opening of her wet cave. "Damn, you tight," he
moaned, surprised as he tried to work his way in. After opening her up, that was all she wrote. Brick put it
down. He was a one-man band until Ra'Keeyah caught
on to his rhythm, and then their bodies played a tune of
their own. Brick and Ra'Keeyah sexed in every position
he could think of, as he schooled her along the way. He
could tell Ra'Keeyah was inexperienced, but that didn't
stop her from trying to hang.

"You thirsty?" Brick asked as they both lay in the bed trying to catch their breath.

"Very," Ra'Keeyah answered, trying to steady her breathing.

"Well, bring me somethin' back when you go down to the kitchen," Brick said, laughing before kissing Ra'Keeyah on the cheek.

"Shit, I'm tired," she said, rolling over on her stomach. "You see all the work I just put in?"

Brick rolled out of bed. "Yeah, you put in work, but not as much as me. I'ma hafta' teach you how to ride Rambo."

"I think I did a'iiiight," Ra'Keeyah smiled.

"Yeah, you did a'iiiight," Brick admitted. "You hang around me long enough and you'll know just about everything there is to know about sex."

"Is that so?" Ra'Keeyah asked, sarcastically. "So what are you, a sex guru?"

"Somethin' like that," he winked before opening the bedroom door. "What you want to drink?"

"Awwww, you really goin' to get me somethin' to drink?" Ra'Keeyah was flattered.

"Why wouldn't I?"

"I don't know," she answered. "Water is fine."

"Okay, I'll be right back," he said, walking out of the room.

Ra'Keeyah rolled over on her back and looked up at the ceiling and smiled. She was on cloud nine. She'd never had anybody put it on her like Brick just did. She refused to let any other woman have him. Brick was the total package. He had good looks, a nice personality, and most important of all, money. All the things Ra'Keeyah was looking for in a man.

She looked over at the clock and noticed it was six-eighteen. "Damn! We been sexing for almost two hours!

That's what I'm talkin' about," Ra'Keeyah smiled happily. She then realized she had less than an hour before
her mom got off work and needed to be there when she
walked through the door or else she'd be spending the
entire summer on punishment. She wasn't about to
have that. Ra'Keeyah was too embarrassed to tell Brick
she had to go home. She didn't want him to look at her
like a little girl, so she came up with an excuse for why
she had to leave.

"Here you go," Brick said walking back into the room
and handing Ra'Keeyah the opened bottle of water.

"Thanks." Ra'Keeyah took a sip before speaking.
"Um, I need to go home," she said nervous.

"Why? What's up?" he inquired.

"My mom gotta be at work by seven so I gotta babysit
my little brother," she lied.

"No problem." Brick began picking his clothes up off
the floor and putting them back on. "I betta' get you
home then before you be on punishment," he joked.

"Whatever," Ra'Keeyah laughed as she rolled out of
bed to get dressed. "Me on punishment, that's a joke,"
she said, wishfully.

After getting dressed, Brick grabbed his keys, and
the two of them headed to the car. They made plans to
go out to dinner later that day. Ra'Keeyah kept looking
at the clock as they drove, hoping he'd get her home on
time. Brick pulled up in front of her house at five minutes after seven, giving her only ten minutes to spare.

"Thank you," she smiled coyly.

"No, thank you," Brick replied.

"What you thankin' me for?" She was confused.

"For payin' yo' debt," Brick smiled.

"Oh, wow! I had forgot all about that bet," Ra'Keeyah
smiled too. "Can I let you in on a little secret?"

Brick nodded his head.

"I *let* you win," she admitted.

"Get the fuck outta here! I won that pussy fair and square," Brick laughed, sounding like a straight New Yorker. "You never even heard of the song!"

"'Fakin' The Funk' was sung by Main Source back in 1992 and was on the *White Men Can't Jump* soundtrack!" Ra'Keeyah stated with a know-it-all attitude before opening up the car door. "Nigga, what? Like I said, I *let* you win!" she laughed.

"Okay," Brick smiled impressed by her knowledge of old-school music. "You got me."

"Bye, Brick," Ra'Keeyah smiled before reaching into the backseat to grab her overnight bag.

"See you later, li'l mama," he leaned over to give Ra'Keeyah a passionate kiss good-bye. "Damn, you sho' you can't come back home wit' me?" he said, pulling back from Ra'Keeyah and pointing down at his hard pipe.

"I wish I could," Ra'Keeyah laughed and forced herself to get out of the car. As bad as she wanted to go back to Brick's for round two, she looked over at the clock on the dashboard and realized that time was ticking.

"Make sure you call me later."

"I will." She closed the car door and hurried up the walk.

Brick waited until Ra'Keeyah was safely inside the house before pulling off. Ra'Keeyah ran up the stairs to her bedroom. She threw her overnight bag into the back of her closet before getting undressed. She threw on a pair of pajamas and wrapped her head scarf around her head before jumping in the bed. About five minutes later, Ra'Keeyah heard her mother pulling up in the driveway. Her mother unlocked the front door, closed it, and made her way up the stairs. Ra'Keeyah quickly closed her eyes and pretended to be asleep. Her mom opened up her bedroom door to make sure her daughter was home, and seeing that she was, she quietly closed the door behind her and headed to her own room.

Perfect timin', Ra'Keeyah thought smiling when she heard her mother's bedroom door close. She lay in the bed thinking about Brick and how it would feel to be his main chick. She was really feeling him, and all she could do was hope and pray his feelings were the same. After a few more minutes of thinking about the man she'd already fallen in love with, Ra'Keeyah drifted off to sleep.

Brick could not get Ra'Keeyah off his mind as he drove back home. He nearly ran a stop sign thinking about how wet and tight she was when he was inside of her. He loved everything about her. The way she looked, the way she smiled, and even her fly-ass attitude turned him on. Brick thought it was cute the way she'd let him win their bet, letting him know that she wanted him just as bad as he wanted her. He could see her being the one to make him want to change his ways and settle down. If things continued going the way they were between them, it was destined to happen sooner than later.

Chapter Nineteen

Ra'Keeyah's mom had decided to let her off punishment under one condition: She had to promise to be home by curfew every night. Her mother moved her curfew up to midnight. Ra'Keeyah was okay with that; it was summer. She thought that was still too early, but her mother thought it was a reasonable time for a young lady to be in the house. Ra'Keeyah lay in the tub soaking her aching body. It had to be all the different positions Brick had her in that had her feeling this way.

"Ra'Keeyah, telephone," her mother knocked on the bathroom door and yelled. "Shit, you gon' have to get you a new cell phone! I'm tired of every time I get on the phone, somebody beepin' in for you," her mother fussed as she opened the door and handed Ra'Keeyah the phone.

Ra'Keeyah took the phone from her mother. "I'm gettin' a new one tomorrow," she said rolling her eyes. "Hello?"

"What's got your mom's panties in a bunch?" Shayna asked, laughing.

"You better keep them eyeballs under control before you find 'em on the floor," her mother snapped, and walked out of the bathroom.

"Anyways," Ra'Keeyah continued. "I don't know. You know how she gets."

"Right, how could I forget," Shayna replied sarcastically. "Anywho, what you doin' today?"

"Well, Brick is takin' me out to dinner at seven. Other than that I'm free. Why? What's up?" Ra'Keeyah asked.

"Speakin' of Brick, how did y'all night go last night?"

"It went all right," Ra'Keeyah replied nonchalantly.

"Just all right?" Shayna pried.

"Yeah, it went all right."

That answer wasn't good enough for Shayna so she tried to dig deeper. "So what did y'all do? Did y'all go out to eat, stay at the house? I mean, what?"

"You is so nosy," Ra'Keeyah laughed, knowing the suspense was killing her best friend.

"I know, right?" Shayna laughed too. "You know how I am."

"We'll talk. You know these walls have ears," Ra'Keeyah whispered.

"Just tell me, was it good, girl?" Shayna asked.

"The best," Ra'Keeyah squealed happily.

"*That's* what I'm talkin' about. Anyways, me and Quiana goin' to Starbucks and I was callin' to see if you were allowed to go."

"Hell, yeah, I'm allowed to go!" Ra'Keeyah said excited. "I haven't had a Chai Tea Latte in a long-ass time. What time we goin', and how we gettin' there?"

"Well, it's goin' on two o'clock, so Joe—"

"Ugggh," Ra'Keeyah interrupted. "One of us gotta hurry up and get a car. I can't stand him!"

"I know. I know. But shit, right now, he's our only transportation," Shayna explained.

"Yeah, you right," Ra'Keeyah replied sullenly. "What time should I be ready?"

"We'll be by to get you about three o'clock, so be ready," Shayna said.

"I'll be ready."

"Hoooolla," Shayna laughed, imitating Keyshia Cole's mom Frankie.

Ra'Keeyah laughed and hung up the phone. She finished bathing, then went into her room to get dressed. She put on pair of short khaki shorts, a tan tank top, and a pair of tan Dereon sandals. She also put on her gold hoop earrings and gold necklace. The weatherman said it was going to be a scorching ninety-one degrees; less was best. Ra'Keeyah brushed her hair up into a ponytail, applied some lip gloss, then sprayed on a few squirts of Paris Amour body spray before grabbing her new tan and brown Dolce & Gabbana bag out of the closet. She grabbed her cell phone out of her overnight bag, made sure it was turned off, and threw it in her purse along with her car charger before heading downstairs.

"Where you goin', Ra'Keeyah?" Jaylen walked out of his room and asked.

She stopped and turned around. "To Starbucks wit' Shayna and Quiana, why?"

"Can I go?"

"Naw, boy. You ain't goin' wit' me. I'll take you next time."

"You always say that!" Jaylen huffed before walking back toward his room.

"I will," Ra'Keeyah promised before continuing her way down the stairs.

"Where you bouta' go?" Ra'Keeyah's mom came out of the kitchen and asked.

"To Starbucks with Shayna and Quiana," Ra'Keeyah answered.

"Starbucks?" her mom asked surprised. "You, Shayna, and Quiana be doin' big things. I know Mr. Wilson ain't payin' you that much for you to be goin' to Starbucks, payin' ya own cell phone bill, and buyin' an expensive purse like the one on yo' arm."

Here we go, Ra'Keeyah thought. "My little two hundred dollars a week carry me a long way," she said. "I be savin' my money. And Mr. Wilson said since school is out, he's gon' have me workin' longer hours."

"That's good to know, but just know, when school starts back up, you're goin' right back down to four hours a day," she said, before going back into the kitchen.

"I know, Mom," Ra'Keeyah replied, walking out the door and taking a seat on the front porch. She rocked back and forth on the swing, waiting for Joe to pull up. As she sat there watching, a big U-haul pulled up across the street and a brand-new Suburban pulled up behind it.

"I see somebody's finally movin' into Mrs. Thomas's house," Ra'Keeyah's mom said as she stood in the doorway, startling Ra'Keeyah. She opened up the screen door, walked out on the porch, and took a seat in one of the lawn chairs. "I wonder if there's a good-lookin' man movin' over there."

"Mom," Ra'Keeyah grimaced.

"What?" she asked innocently.

They both watched as a teenage girl got out of the front seat of the Suburban with an attitude, and a few seconds later, a little boy around Jaylen's age climbed out of the back.

"I see they got kids," Ra'Keeyah said. "Now Jay-Jay gon' have somebody to play wit'."

"Yep," her mother said, barely paying her any attention. She was too busy waiting to see if a man was going to exit the vehicle. She watched in awe as a big muscular man climbed out of the driver's seat of the Suburban. "I don't see no woman so he must be a single father. Oooh, look at that body," she said getting excited.

"Mommy!" Ra'Keeyah frowned. "I don't wanna hear that!"

"What? You act like I can't look," her mother stated. "Hell, I ain't old. Momma wanna get her groove on too!"

"Oh my goodness, go in the house, Mom!" Ra'Keeyah demanded.

"Shut up, girl. I ain't thinkin' about you," her mom snapped and continued being nosy.

Ra'Keeyah and her mother watched as a tall, skinny man with his shirt tied up in the front got out of the U-haul. They watched closely as he sashayed over to the brotha with all the muscles.

"Girl, he bet' not be—he can't be! Girl, no!" Ra'Keeyah's mother stammered while tapping her on the shoulder.

"Yes, he is," Ra'Keeyah replied as the two men locked lips in broad daylight like there was nothing wrong with it. "Ewwwww," she frowned.

"What a fuckin' waste!" Ra'Keeyah's mom snapped, getting up from the chair and going in the house, letting the screen door slam behind her.

Ra'Keeyah sat on the porch cracking up over her mother's dramatics as Joe pulled up.

"I'm gone, Mom," Ra'Keeyah yelled out, grabbing her purse and heading off the porch. Her mother was so heated about what she'd just witnessed between the two men she didn't even respond.

"What you laughin' at?" Shayna asked as Ra'Keeyah got in the minivan.

"Laughin' at my mom. Man, she is crazy!" Ra'Keeyah continued laughing.

"You goin' to the block party next Saturday?" Quiana interrupted.

"What block party?" Ra'Keeyah asked.

"I snatched this flyer off the Laundromat wall last night," Shayna said, handing it to Ra'Keeyah so she could read it.

"Oh, wow, the Road Runners are havin' it," Ra'Keeyah was surprised. She wondered why Brick hadn't said anything to her about it.

"Yeah, they supposed to be supplyin' all the food, drinks, and the music. They gon' have a car show, a dance contest, and I even heard T.I. supposed to be there," Shayna said, excited about the event.

"Man, that's gon' be the biggest party of the year," Shayna said, pulling a blunt out of her purse and firing it up. "And I heard if all goes well, no drama and shit, they gon' have one every summer." Shayna passed the blunt to Joe.

"What we gon' do about dancin'?" Ra'Keeyah asked, not even sure she wanted to go to the block party since Brick hadn't mentioned it to her. Evidently he didn't want her to go either were her thoughts. "And plus, Saturday is my birthday!"

"It sure is," Shayna said. "I'm just gon' tell Calvin we got somethin' to do that night. Shit, we gon' dance about eight o'clock, and I know the block party ain't gon' start jumpin' 'til 'bout ten. We gon' go there and celebrate yo' birthday."

Who said I wanna celebrate my birthday at that dumb block party? Ra'Keeyah wanted to say, but didn't want to sound like she was whining.

"*That's* what I'm talkin' 'bout," Quiana added. "So we just gon' go in there, shake our tail feathers real quick, and wrap it up."

Joe passed the blunt back to Ra'Keeyah. She looked at the wet tip and passed it over to Quiana. As bad as she wanted to smoke, she just couldn't bring herself to put her lips on the blunt after Joe had just had taken his off of there.

"You ain't smokin'?" Quiana asked, grabbing the blunt and taking a pull.

"Naw, go on and get y'all's wigs blew back. I'm straight," Ra'Keeyah said.

Shayna turned around and smiled at Ra'Keeyah already knowing her best friend was picky about who she smoked after. It didn't matter to her or Quiana as long as they were getting high.

"Oh, before I forget," Joe said, "my sister is lookin' for three women to dance at her and her girlfriend's bachelorette party."

What the fuck? Ra'Keeyah thought. *Joe ain't the only creepy one in his family.*

"Shit, how much they gon' pay us?" Shayna asked quickly while taking the blunt from Quiana and putting the remainder of it out in the ashtray before sticking it back into her purse.

"How much you gon' charge 'em is the question," Joe said as he pulled into the plaza where Starbucks was located.

"Shit, we charge the men two-fifty a piece just for showin' up," Shayna said. "So if they willin' to pay like them, then count us in!"

Ra'Keeyah was shocked her best friend would agree to dance for a bunch of lesbians. She didn't have anything against gays; to each their own, but dancing for a bunch of women was a little too extreme for her liking.

"So when is the party?" Shayna asked, trying to get all the details in order.

"I don't know. I can't remember," Joe said, pulling up in front of Starbucks. "But I'll call my sister when she gets off work and find out."

"*That's* what's up!" Shayna replied happily. "Now don't forget." She opened the car door and got out.

"I won't," Joe replied with a smile.

Ra'Keeyah slid the door open, and she and Quiana exited the van.

"I'll call you when we ready," Shayna called over her shoulder as they made their way into the coffee shop.

"Okay," Joe replied before pulling off.

"Shit, we bouta' be paid outta the ass!" Quiana said excited as they walked up to the register.

"I know, right?" Shayna agreed. She noticed Ra'Keeyah wasn't excited over the news. "What's the matter wit' you?"

"We'll talk when we get outside on the patio." Ra'Keeyah brushed past her two friends and placed her order.

"What's her problem?" Quiana asked.

Shayna shrugged her shoulders. "I don't know."

After placing their orders, they went outside on the patio to find a nice shaded spot to sit.

"Now what's your problem?" Shayna asked, as soon as they took a seat.

"You bitches is the problem," Ra'Keeyah retorted, trying to keep her voice down so the other customers couldn't hear her. "Y'all will do damn near anything for money, won't y'all?" she frowned.

"What you talkin' about?" Shayna asked.

"Come on, Shayna, dancin' for a bunch of lesbians?"

"I don't see nothin' wrong wit' it," Quiana added her two cents.

"You wouldn't," Ra'Keeyah replied harshly.

"I mean, damn, Ra'Keeyah, you act like we gon' be fuckin' these hoes or somethin'," Shayna spat.

"That ain't the point!" Ra'Keeyah huffed. "All I'm sayin' is it's one thing we strippin' for these old white men. Now you want us to dance for a bunch of white women too? Come on. Where do our morals come in at?"

"Morals?" Shayna grimaced. "Money is money. Whether we dancin' for a bunch of white men, white women, or even a pack of white wolves, all money is green!" she responded in a raised tone before picking up her Caramel Macchiato and taking a sip.

"Yea, man," Quiana agreed.

Ra'Keeyah shot Quiana a dirty look.

"I mean, I understand if you don't wanna do it," Shayna said empathetically. "But like I said before, it ain't like we gon' be sleepin' wit' these broads."

"Shit, y'all be sleepin' wit' them white men after I leave, so what's the difference?" Ra'Keeyah spat.

Shayna nearly choked on her coffee. "What?" she asked, after clearing her throat.

"You heard me," Ra'Keeyah said, folding her arms. "Y'all bitches thought I was gone yesterday, but I wasn't. I was still in the room gettin' dressed, and when I came out, I seen you," she said pointing at Shayna, "bent over a chair, and you, nasty bitch," pointing at Quiana, "suckin' on some dick!"

"Wow!" was all Shayna could say. They had been busted.

Quiana sat back and acted as if there were an elephant in the room.

"What y'all got to say about that? I don't hear you cosigning now, Quiana," Ra'Keeyah said. "Huh man?"

"Ra'Keeyah, let me explain," Shayna started.

"I'm waitin'," Ra'Keeyah said patiently.

"Me and Quiana knew you wouldn't agree to makin' extra money sleepin' wit' these men. That's why we waited until you left before we did anything wit' 'em."

"Uh-huh. How y'all just gon' assume I wouldn't be down for makin' extra money? I like money too."

"Yeah, but you uppity," Quiana said smartly.

"Oh, wow," Ra'Keeyah sighed. "I don't know how many times I gotta tell you that hatin' is not your style. Pick somethin' else to do."

Shayna laughed at Ra'Keeyah's quip. "Yeah, you like money, but I know you."

"So y'all just think I'm some stuck-up, bourgeois-ass bitch, right?"

"Yep," Shayna and Quiana replied.

"If I was so bourgeois, how I make all this last night?" Ra'Keeyah pulled a wad of money out of her purse.

"Where the fuck you get all this money from, bitch?" Shayna squealed.

"I made it. I guess you can say I was doin' a little trickin' of my own!" Ra'Keeyah laughed.

"Hell, naw!" Shayna laughed. "When and wit' who?" she questioned, needing to know how everything went down.

"You so nosy," Ra'Keeyah laughed before telling Shayna what went down in the room between her and Steve, and then her outstanding night with Brick. Normally, she would have never discussed her sex life in front of Quiana, knowing how devious she was, but she couldn't hold it in any longer, and with Shayna continuously pressing her to find out all the juicy details, she couldn't help it. Shayna took in every word excited about her best friend's newfound happiness, while Quiana sat back and listened enviously.

After two hours of laughing and talking over coffee, the girls decided it was time to go. Shayna had made plans with Calvin, Ra'Keeyah had to get dressed for her dinner date with Brick, and Quiana had to plot about getting what her other two friends had.

Chapter Twenty

Ra'Keeyah sat on the porch swing rocking back and forth waiting on Marshall to get off work so she could call and ask him about the condoms he'd bought the other night. As much as she hated to admit it, the fact that Marshall was sleeping with someone else made her kind of jealous, even though she didn't plan on giving him none. She knew she didn't have the right to question him; she just wanted him to know that he wasn't getting anything over on her. Marshall had less than thirty minutes to clock out, and she couldn't wait. Ra'Keeyah was thinking about how she was going to come at him without giving him any idea who told her. She sat in deep thought until the little boy from across the street interrupted her.

"Hey, can I play wit' the little boy that lives here?" he asked in a Southern twang before making his way up the walk.

"Sure," Ra'Keeyah looked up and replied with a smile. "Jaylen," she called out.

A few seconds later, Jaylen ran out the front door. "What?" he answered.

"Don't be whatin' me, li'l nigga!" Ra'Keeyah snapped. "This little boy wants to play wit' you."

"I'm watchin' *Phineas and Ferb*," Jaylen replied, and was about to turn to walk away.

"Jaylen," Ra'Keeyah yelled, "stop bein' so damn rude, boy, and come out here and play wit' him!" she demanded.

"I got a remote control Monster Truck," the little boy said.

"You do?" Jaylen's eyes lit up, because he'd always wanted one.

"Yep," the little boy replied. "You want me to go get it?"

"Yeah," Jaylen said eagerly.

"Okay, I'll be right back." The little boy ran across the street and into the house.

"He talk funny," Jaylen said, waiting on the little boy to come back with the truck.

"That's 'cuz he's from down South," Ra'Keeyah laughed.

Jaylen smiled as the little boy ran back across the street with his big truck. He put it down on the ground and began making it move.

"Wow," Jaylen said walking off the porch, watching in amazement as the little boy made the truck drive backward and forward.

"Bray'yon, why you over here botherin' these folks?" the little boy's sister fussed as she made her way across the street and up the walk. "Sorry, is my li'l brother botherin' y'all?" she asked, with the exact same Southern twang as her little brother.

Ra'Keeyah watched as her homely looking neighbor walked up to the bottom of the porch step. "No, he's fine," Ra'Keeyah replied. "They just playin'."

"Are you sure? 'Cuz he can be a real pain in the butt sometimes," the girl said.

"Trust me, I know. You see, I got a little brother of my own, and he gets on my nerves all the damn time," Ra'Keeyah laughed as she watched Jaylen and Bray'yon grab the Monster Truck and run around to the back of the house.

"By the way, I'm Peighton," she said, introducing herself.

"Ra'Keeyah."

"That's a pretty name," Peighton said.

"Thanks, and yours is too," Ra'Keeyah said, smiling.

"Thanks."

"Where y'all from?" Ra'Keeyah asked.

"Birmingham, Alabama," Peighton replied.

"I knew y'all were from down South somewhere. I could tell by y'all's accents," Ra'Keeyah said.

"Accents? Y'all the ones wit' the accents," Peighton laughed.

"Why y'all move way up here from Birmingham, if you don't mind me askin'?" Ra'Keeyah pried.

"Me and my brother don't live up here. We just up here wit' our daddy for the summer. He moved from across town to over here," she explained.

"Oh, okay. Is that your dad that drives that nice-ass Suburban?" Ra'Keeyah snooped.

"Yeah, that's his faggot ass!" Peighton snapped while rolling her eyes.

"Wow," Ra'Keeyah gasped, not expecting to hear that coming from his own daughter. "That's kinda' harsh, don't you think?"

"Not really. I was bein' nice when I said that," Peighton said, shrugging her shoulders. "I coulda' said worse."

"You know, that's still your dad, no matter what he is," Ra'Keeyah preached.

"Well, how would you like it if your dad was sleepin' wit' anotha' man?" Peighton asked.

Ra'Keeyah didn't expect to be asked that question. She never had to deal with her father being gay so she couldn't relate to how Peighton was feeling. Not having an answer to the question at hand, she just left it alone.

"It sounds to me like you need to calm your nerves a little. You smoke?" Ra'Keeyah asked Peighton.

"Hell, yeah, I smoke!" Peighton replied quickly. "In order to live in the house wit' Holiday Heart and his bitch, you have to stay high off somethin'," she laughed.

Ra'Keeyah couldn't help but laugh too because her dad did put you in the mind of Ving Rhames from the movie *Holiday Heart*. He was big, cocky, and gay as ever.

"Girl, you are crazy," Ra'Keeyah said when she stopped laughing. "You can come up here and have a seat."

"What? I'm jus' keepin' it real!" Peighton walked up the steps and took a seat in one of the lawn chairs.

"I like you," Ra'Keeyah said, reaching in her purse, pulling out a blunt and a lighter. "We gon' have some fun this summer." Ra'Keeyah lit the blunt and took a long toke before passing it to Peighton.

"I need to have fun. I've been up here for two weeks and done nothin' but sit in the damn house and watch TV." Peighton took the blunt from Ra'Keeyah.

"Well, I'ma introduce you to my best friend Shayna and her cousin Quiana. And we gon' make sure you have a memorable summer," Ra'Keeyah said after she blew the smoke out.

"*That's* what up. What do y'all do around these parts for fun?" she asked, taking another pull from the blunt and passing it back to Ra'Keeyah.

Ra'Keeyah smashed the blunt out on the porch and stuck it back in her purse before answering. "Ain't shit to do, really," she said. "We basically create our own fun. They havin' a block party Saturday though. You wanna roll wit' us?"

"Is it gon' be some fine niggas there?" Peighton inquired.

"You already know!" Ra'Keeyah said, laughing.

"Hell, yeah, I'm rollin' wit' y'all then," Peighton smiled. "What's the dress code?"

"Since it's gon' be the biggest party of the year, you have to come dressed," Ra'Keeyah replied.

"Okay, I can manage that." Peighton stood up from the chair. "Well, I better get back across this street and get that kitchen cleaned before Holiday Heart gets home from work."

"You silly."

"Send Bray'yon home when you get tired of him," Peighton said on her way down the steps.

"Okay." Ra'Keeyah pulled her cell phone out of her purse and checked the time. Marshall was officially off work. She waited for Peighton to cross the street before dialing his number. She was heated when it went straight to his voice mail. "I know this nigga didn't just push the ignore button on me," Ra'Keeyah fumed, dialing his number again, only to be sent to the voice mail again. She got up from the swing and went in the house where she repeatedly dialed Marshall's number over and over, getting madder and madder each time it went to voice mail. "Fuck him!" she said before heading upstairs to her room.

Ra'Keeyah lay across her bed and tried calling Marshall one last time before giving up. "He better be lucky I got Jaylen or I would catch a cab to Burger King and spit in his face!" She was angry. Ra'Keeyah called the one person she knew could always calm her down and make her laugh.

"What it do?" Shayna answered.

"Hey, girl, what you doin'?" Ra'Keeyah asked, sounding defeated.

"Nothin', just sittin' here rollin' one," Shayna replied. "You wanna come over and blow wit' me?"

"Naw, I told my mom I had the day off, so she asked me to keep Jaylen for her."

"Oh, okay. Why you sound so down?" Shayna asked before licking the Swisher Sweet closed.

Ra'Keeyah broke the story down to Shayna about Marshall buying condoms and sending her calls to voice mail.

"Well, damn, what you want the nigga do? You ain't givin' up the nappy . . . well, at least not to him," Shayna said smartly. "You want him to sit around and wait on you to get your shit together?"

"Yeah, why wouldn't he?" Ra'Keeyah asked.

Shayna began to laugh. "You a selfish bitch!"

"I know, right?" Ra'Keeyah laughed too once she realized how she sounded. "I guess you right. I can't have it all, even though I want it all!"

"You don't need to be stressin' over that corn-muffin-ass nigga!" Shayna spat. "You got a thug in yo' life!"

"I know," Ra'Keeyah was sounding unconvinced.

"Why you say it like that?" Shayna questioned.

"I told you I was done fuckin' wit' thugs. And here my stupid ass go again settin' myself up for failure."

"Don't say that, Ra'Keeyah," Shayna protested. "I think Brick different from the rest of the niggas you used to mess around wit'. He got more polish. You'll see."

"I sure hope so. Only time will tell," she said, hopefully.

"And if he just so happens to turn out like the rest, we gon' fuck all his cars up!" Shayna laughed. "Bet?"

"Bet," Ra'Keeyah laughed too.

"Oh well, mama, Calvin is comin' to pick me up. We're goin' to Cleveland so I can find me somethin' to wear to the block party Saturday."

"Okay, well, if you see somethin' that I might like, pick it up for me."

"You know I got chu'," Shayna replied.

"Okay, talk to you later."

"Peaaaaaace!" Shayna yelled, before hanging up.

"That girl's a damn fool," Ra'Keeyah smiled, shaking her head. She rolled over on her back and stared up at the ceiling for a few seconds. She couldn't believe how Marshall was trying to play her. Ra'Keeyah couldn't help but dial his number a couple more times only for it to still go straight to his voice mail. Angry with herself for letting a nobody like Marshall get under her skin, Ra'Keeyah got up from her bed and made her way downstairs. She was determined not to dial his number again. Hell, she was the catch, not him.

Ra'Keeyah walked out on the porch, sat back down on the swing, and watched as Jaylen and his new friend played a game of freeze tag . . . and dialed Marshall's number one last time.

Chapter Twenty-one

Ra'Keeyah woke up to the sound of birds chirping outside her window. After lying still for a few minutes she decided it was time for her to get out of bed. She had a long day ahead of her. She stood up, stretched, and walked out of her bedroom. The smell of bacon tickled her nose as she made her way to the bathroom. Ra'Keeyah washed her face and brushed her teeth before heading downstairs to see what her mom and brother were up to.

"Happy Birthday!" Jaylen and their mother yelled when Ra'Keeyah walked into the kitchen.

"Thanks, y'all," she smiled happily.

"Here, this is for you," Jaylen said, shoving a card and a small box into Ra'Keeyah's face.

"What is it?" she asked, smiling.

"Open it and see," her mother said and waited.

"Oh my goodness, Mommy!" Ra'Keeyah squealed after taking the top off the box. "I've been wantin' one of these." She picked up the braided, leather Pandora bracelet with the sterling silver high-heel shoe charm dangling from it. Ra'Keeyah rushed over and gave her mom a big hug and a kiss on the cheek.

"I picked the charm out," Jaylen said proudly.

"I like it, Jay-Jay," Ra'Keeyah said, giving her a brother a hug and a kiss as well. "This is the best birthday present ever!" she said excited.

"I'm glad you like it," her mother smiled. "I worked a lot of overtime to pay for them both."

Ra'Keeyah and Jaylen took a seat at the kitchen table. She continued admiring her bracelet as her mother set a plate of food down in front of her.

"Whoa, Mom, this looks good," Ra'Keeyah said admiring the big birthday breakfast her mother had prepared. She'd made pancakes, sausage, bacon, scrambled cheese eggs, and grits.

"Thank you," her mother smiled.

Ra'Keeyah, her mother, and brother laughed and talked over breakfast until it was almost time for Ra'Keeyah to go to the hair shop.

"I'm about to go get dressed. My hair appointment is in forty-five minutes," Ra'Keeyah said, getting up from the kitchen table. "Can you drop me off?"

"Yeah, I can drop you off. What you gon' get done to it?" her mother asked as she gathered the empty dishes off the table with Ra'Keeyah's help.

"I don't know yet," Ra'Keeyah said, placing the dishes in the sink.

"You goin' to that block party I've been hearin' everybody at work talk about?" her mother asked.

"Yeah, we goin'," Ra'Keeyah answered.

"I wanna go," Jaylen said.

"Boy, the only block party you goin' to is over at Nancy's house," their mother laughed.

"Ah, man! I don't never get to go nowhere!" Jaylen huffed before walking out of the kitchen.

"I want you to be careful out there tonight," her mother said sincerely. "I got one more year to worry about you, and then you will be on your own."

"Mom, please. You gon' worry about me until I'm a hundred years old," Ra'Keeyah joked.

"You right!" her mother laughed. "You my firstborn."

"That's right!" Ra'Keeyah said before turning to walk away.

"Hey, Ra'Keeyah," her mother called out.

"Yeah, Mom?" she turned around and asked.

"I love you."

"I love you too, Mom," Ra'Keeyah responded with a smile before going to get dressed. She quickly threw on some yellow Capri sweats and a white tank top before brushing her hair up into a ponytail. Then she grabbed her cell and iPod and put them in her purse before heading back downstairs. "I'm ready, Mom," she walked into the kitchen and said.

"Okay, let's go, Jaylen," their mother said, grabbing the keys off the kitchen counter and heading out the door. Fifteen minutes later, they we pulling up in front of the hair shop.

"I'll call you when I'm ready," Ra'Keeyah said opening up the car door and getting out.

"Okay," her mother replied and waited for Ra'Keeyah to walk into the shop.

Ra'Keeyah entered the hair shop and gave the receptionist her name before walking over to the sitting area. By the number of people in the shop, she knew she was going to be there a while. As soon as she sat down and picked up an *Essence* magazine, two girls sitting across from her started whispering to each other. Ra'Keeyah was no fool; she knew they were talking about her. She wasn't on it today. All she wanted to do was get her hair done so she could celebrate her birthday.

They continued to stare as Ra'Keeyah pulled her iPod out of her purse. She stared back, making it known she wasn't the least bit intimidated by them as she put the earphones in her ears. One of the girls looked sort of familiar, but Ra'Keeyah didn't have the time or the energy to figure out where she knew her from. Their envious stares were starting to get under Ra'Keeyah's skin. Just when she removed her earphones and was about to ask the two females what they were staring at, Ra'Keeyah's hairdresser, Sha'ron, called out her name. Ra'Keeyah slowly stood up from her chair and threw her purse on her shoulder. They continued to have a stare down as Ra'Keeyah walked past them.

"What's they problem?" Sha'ron asked Ra'Keeyah as they headed over to her chair.

"I don't know. I don't even know them hoes," Ra'Keeyah replied, taking a seat.

"Who she talkin' 'bout?" Kareem, another one of the stylists, asked.

"Them two broads sittin' over there," Sha'ron pointed discreetly.

"Oh, them two hood rats," Kareem laughed. "Them my clients. One is Jazmyn. She got four kids and don't know who the daddy of none of 'em are. And the bald-headed one is Davinette. She will mess wit' anything with a pole between his legs. Word on the street is she can cook her ass off but keep a nasty house!"

"Leave it up to the homosexual in the shop to know and tell everybody's business," Tabitha, another stylist, said.

"Don't hate, 'cuz I be knowin' errrrybody's business," Kareem said. "Just don't let me start tellin' yours," he warned.

"You don't know nuttin' about me," Tabitha snapped.

"Who man was you creepin' wit' late last night?" Kareem asked and waited on an answer, along with everyone else.

"What?" Tabitha grimaced, knowing she was creeping with someone else's dude, wondering how Kareem knew about it.

"Come on, y'all play nicely. We have clients in here," Sha'ron stated.

"I can't stand you!" Tabitha mumbled.

Kareem stuck his tongue out at her before continuing on his client's hair.

"That's where I recognize her from," Ra'Keeyah said, referring to Davinette. "I met her at a restaurant. But her hair was way longer than that."

"Which one?" Sha'ron inquired.

"Davinette," Ra'Keeyah answered.

"Oh, she keeps a ton of weave in her hair," Sha'ron said. "Speakin' of hair, what are you gettin' done to yours?"

"I don't know," Ra'Keeyah answered. "What you think I should get done to it?"

Sha'ron took the ponytail holder out of Ra'Keeyah's hair and ran her fingers through it. "First off, you need a touch-up. What's the occasion today?"

"She probably just goin' to the block party like me and errrybody else in here," Kareem interjected his two cents.

"Actually, I am goin' to the block party," Ra'Keeyah said. "But today is also my birthday."

"Well, happy birthday, Ms. Thang," Kareem said, in his Wendy Williams voice.

Ra'Keeyah laughed. "Thanks."

"Well, birthday girl, we gon' have to do somethin' extra special to this hair," Sha'ron said, pulling her Design Essentials perm from under her workstation.

"*That's* what I'm talkin' about," Ra'Keeyah smiled.

After three hours of sitting in the shop laughing, talking, and listening to gossip, Sha'ron was done with Ra'Keeyah's hair. She had permed it and put straw curls that hung loosely to the middle of her back.

"Go ahead, Ms. Diva," Kareem complimented, once Sha'ron had put the finishing touches on Ra'Keeyah's hair. "You gon' have all the dudes tryin'a get on at the block party."

Davinette watched enviously from Kareem's chair.

Sha'ron handed Ra'Keeyah a handheld mirror so she could check out her hair. Pleased with what she saw, Ra'Keeyah stood up. "Thank you," she smiled while taking the slip Sha'ron handed her to take out to the receptionist.

"You're more than welcome and have a happy birthday," Sha'ron said before calling out the name of her next client.

"I like your hair," Davinette said as Ra'Keeyah walked past Kareem's chair. Ra'Keeyah didn't know if she was trying to be funny or if she was being sincere. Being raised with some morals, however, Ra'Keeyah did the right thing. "Thank you," she responded and kept it moving.

"Tell Brick he left his hat at my house the other night," Davinette called out.

Ra'Keeyah stopped and turned around. "What did you just say?" she asked, making sure she heard her right the first time.

"I said, tell Brick he left his hat at my house the other night," she repeated with a smirk.

Ra'Keeyah's heart was beating fast. She was heated but refused to let Davinette or anyone else know she was. Especially Kareem. That would only give him something else to gossip about.

"Uhhh-oh, it's about to be some hair pullin' up in here!" Kareem said, excited.

All the other clients and stylists were anticipating drama as well.

"Come on, Ra'Keeyah, she's petty," Sha'ron came from around her chair and said, touching Ra'Keeyah on the shoulder.

"I don't know if or why you're tryin'a make me think there's somethin' more than what there really is goin' on between you and Brick," Ra'Keeyah stated to Davinette. "But what you need to get through all them tracks stuck up in yo' head is I don't care! Like I told you before, me and Brick are just friends," she said and turned to walk away. "Oh, and another thing," she said, turning back around. "If Brick was my man, Kareem woulda' been right. There would be some hair pullin' up in here—yours not mines!" With that being said, Ra'Keeyah continued over to the receptionist.

"Ooooh, I guess she told you," Kareem laughed, as he continued sewing in Davinette's tracks.

"Shut up and finish my hair!" Davinette snapped, feeling salty because she just got checked.

"Well, I guess she handled that like a real playa," Sha'ron smiled before walking back over to her chair to finish up her client's hair.

Ra'Keeyah paid the receptionist and went outside to calm her nerves. She didn't know if she was mad at Brick for being over at Davinette's house or mad at herself for falling for Brick so quickly. But Ra'Keeyah was proud of how she handled Davinette. Even though she really wanted to jump on her and beat the shit out of her, she'd kept her composure. Ra'Keeyah called her mother and told her she was ready. She couldn't wait to hook up with the ladies later on because she was in much need of a drink. Today was her birthday, and she didn't intend to let nothing and nobody spoil it for her, not even Davinette.

Ra'Keeyah pulled her iPod back out of her purse, took a seat on the bench outside the salon, put in the earphones, and let the sweet sound of old-school music uplift her until her mother pulled up.

Chapter Twenty-two

Ra'Keeyah had her new theme song "Hustle Hard" bumping as she got ready. She was in love with Ace Hood because he looked a lot like Brick, without the locks. *"Same ol' shit, just a different day out here tryna get it, each and every way,"* Ra'Keeyah sang loud. *"Mama need a house, baby need some shoes—"*

"Didn't you hear me callin' you?" her mother opened her bedroom door and yelled over the music.

"Huh?" Ra'Keeyah asked walking over to the boom box, turning the volume down. "I didn't hear you."

"If you wouldna' had that bullshit turned up so loud you woulda' heard me!" her mother fussed.

"BS?" Ra'Keeyah asked. "Ace Hood don't make no BS," Ra'Keeyah laughed.

"Whatever," her mother smiled. "Anyways, that girl from across the street is here."

"Oh, Peighton, send her up, please," Ra'Keeyah said.

"Is she goin' to the block party wit' y'all?"

"Yeah, she goin'."

"That was nice of you to invite her," Ra'Keeyah's mom said. "I'll go tell her to come up." She went back downstairs and sent Peighton up.

"Hey, girl," Peighton said, walking into Ra'Keeyah's room and looking around. "Your hair is really pretty like that."

"Thanks," Ra'Keeyah replied with a smile before putting on her hoop earrings. "Why ain't you dressed yet?" she asked, looking at the clothes Peighton had on.

"I am dressed," Peighton said getting offended. She had on a pair of cutoff jean shorts, an eggshell white tank top, and some dirty K-Swiss, and her shoulder-length hair was pulled back into a ponytail.

"Where you goin' dressed like that? We ain't goin' to Ms. Millie's to pick no cotton," she joked.

Peighton didn't find the humor in Ra'Keeyah's comment. "What you mean? I don't pick no cotton," she said defensively.

"Never mind. I told you that you had to be dressed up," she reminded her, shaking her head.

"Oh sorry, I left my after five wear in Birmingham," Peighton joked.

"Ha-ha, very funny," Ra'Keeyah said. "By the looks of you, we wear about the same size."

"And?"

"And I'm about to find you somethin' to wear," Ra'Keeyah said walking over to her closet. "Shit, you can't be goin' nowhere wit' me dressed like that." Ra'Keeyah pulled out a long black-and-white with traces of pink at the bottom halter Maxi summer dress with a keyhole neck and handed it to Peighton.

"This is nice," Peighton said, taking the dress and putting it up to her body.

"I know," Ra'Keeyah said. "What yo' feet lookin' like?" she asked, while pulling out a pair of black, opened toe Dezario "Belle" wedge platform sandals with a silver buckle that she had got from Nordstroms. Peighton removed her shoes and socks. "They look a'iiiight," Ra'Keeyah laughed. "I'm about to go plug up the flat-irons, 'cuz we gotta do somethin' to that head."

"Forget you," Peighton laughed as Ra'Keeyah walked out of the room. "Why do you have all these pictures of motorcycles on your wall?" she asked Ra'Keeyah when she walked back in the room.

"Uh, 'cuz I like motorcycles," Ra'Keeyah replied sarcastically. "Come on, the flatirons should be hot."

Peighton followed her into the bathroom. She had Peighton sit on the edge of the tub while she straightened out her hair. Ra'Keeyah then applied some pink and silver eye shadow and some eyeliner to bring out the color of Peighton's eyes before handing her a brand-new tube of Mary Kay Pink Diamonds lip gloss. After Ra'Keeyah finished Peighton's hair and makeup, she looked and felt like a totally different person.

"Wow, I look so pretty," Peighton said, admiring her shoulder-length hair and made up face in the mirror. "I didn't know my hair was this long."

"If you straighten that mess out sometimes you would know how long your hair is," Ra'Keeyah joked.

"Be quiet," Peighton laughed as she continued to admire her new look.

"Okay, go in my room, get dressed, and come back in here so I can see what you look like."

"Okay," Peighton said eagerly, making her way out of the bathroom and into Ra'Keeyah's room.

Five minutes later Peighton walked back across the hall to the bathroom.

Ra'Keeyah was surprised when Peighton walked back in. She looked so pretty. She reminded Ra'Keeyah of a black Barbie doll.

"Okay, Diva," Ra'Keeyah smiled happily. "Now you ready to roll wit' me and my crew."

"I can't believe how good I look," Peighton said, still amazed by her transformation. "Can you take a picture of me?"

"Yeah, let me go get my phone, 'cuz we might not ever see you lookin' like this again," Ra'Keeyah teased.

"I got my camera wit' me," Peighton said walking back out of the bathroom to go retrieve her camera from her purse. "And I am gon' start keepin' myself up." She walked back into the bathroom and handed the camera to Ra'Keeyah.

"Only tourists walk around wit' a camera in their purse," Ra'Keeyah laughed.

"I am a tourist. I ain't from here," Peighton laughed too before posing for the camera.

Ra'Keeyah took a few more pictures of Peighton before going to her room to get dressed. She put on a dark gray, one-shoulder minidress with a Kimono sleeve and a banded bottom that fit her body in all the right places, with a pair of dark gray, five-inch pleat detailed heels. Ra'Keeyah accessorized her ensemble with a dozen silver bangles and a silver, oversized flower ring. After applying her makeup and spraying herself with some Escada S, Ra'Keeyah was dressed to kill!

"Oh my goodness!" Peighton gasped. "Girl, you look beautiful. I got to take some pictures of you 'cuz my friends back home ain't gon' believe I hung out wit' someone as pretty as you." Peighton picked up the Escada S perfume and sprayed herself with it as well.

"Aww, thanks," Ra'Keeyah said gratefully. She walked over to her closet and grabbed a black clutch for Peighton and a silver one for herself.

"Do you think my camera is gon' fit in here?" Peighton asked, taking the clutch from her hand.

Ra'Keeyah shook her head and laughed. "It should, or let's just hope it does for your sake."

Peighton laughed too taking half a dozen pictures of Ra'Keeyah before they made their way downstairs.

"Oh my goodness, look at y'all," Ra'Keeyah's mother squealed with excitement as they walked into the living room where she sat watching TV with Jaylen. "Y'all look so beautiful. Jay-Jay run and get mommy's camera out of my room. Oh wow, look at my baby." Tears of joy clouded her vision as she spoke. "You've grown into a beautiful young lady."

"Mommy, don't cry," Ra'Keeyah said, feeling herself getting emotional too. "You gon' make me ruin my makeup."

"Okay, I won't," her mother promised. "Peighton, you look like a totally different person too. Y'all look really pretty."

"Thank you," Peighton smiled.

"Here you go, Mommy," Jaylen said handing her the camera.

Ra'Keeyah and Peighton took more pictures for Ra'Keeyah's mom. Ra'Keeyah took a few with her mother and brother and more by herself before calling Shayna to let her know that they were ready.

"Well, ladies, I'm about to leave for work," Ra'Keeyah's mother said. "I want y'all to have a good and safe time at the block party."

"We will," they both said in unison.

"Happy birthday, again, Ra'Keeyah," her mother said, kissing her on the cheek.

"Thanks, Mom," she smiled.

"I want to tell you this before I leave."

Here we go wit' this same old speech, Ra'Keeyah thought.

"I'm not gon' tell you not to be out there drinkin' and gettin' high. I don't want you to do it, but I've been your age before and I know that's what y'all into," Ra'Keeyah's mother said. "I'm not proud of it, but I did it too. All I can tell you to do is be careful while you're doin' it. You understand?"

"I understand," Ra'Keeyah said, surprised, giving her mother a hug and a kiss on the cheek. Ra'Keeyah never thought in a million years that her mother would be giving her a speech like that. She was used to hearing the one about not having anyone in her house while she was gone.

"Come on, Jaylen, it's time to go," Ra'Keeyah's mother called out.

"I'm comin'," he yelled.

"Oh, Ra'Keeyah," her mother said before walking out the door.

"I know, Mom, be home before curfew."

"No, that's not what I was gon' say. I was gon' say enjoy yourselves tonight. You're only seventeen once," her mother winked and walked out the door with Jaylen in tow.

"Damn, your mom is mad cool!" Peighton exclaimed. "I wish my mom was like yours."

"Yeah, she's cool," Ra'Keeyah boasted, not knowing what caused the sudden change. "Look, I gotta tell you somethin' before we leave."

"What is it?" Peighton asked, concerned.

"Can you keep a secret?"

"Yeah, I can keep a secret," Peighton answered. "Plus, who am I gon' tell it to? You the only person I know in Ohio other than my dad," she laughed.

Ra'Keeyah studied Peighton before talking. "Okay. We're makin' a stop before we go to the block party."

"Where we goin'? To pick up some dope or somethin'?" Peighton asked curiously.

"Naw, fool," Ra'Keeyah laughed. "Me and my friends are dancers, and we have to do a show before we head over to the party. We can come back and pick you up if you don't feel comfortable goin' wit' us."

"I wanna go. I ain't never been to no strip club," Peighton said, intrigued.

"We ain't goin' to no strip club. We do our shows in a hotel suite."

"That's fine too. Can I take some pictures?" Peighton asked.

"Let me guess, for your friends back home," Ra'Keeyah laughed.

"Yeah. They not gon' believe the kinda' summer I had. But I'll have the pictures to prove it," Peighton said happily.

"I don't care, girl, as long as the pictures from the hotel don't show up on Facebook."

"I wouldn't do you like that," Peighton assured. "Shit, I don't even have a Facebook account."

Ra'Keeyah shook her head. "You need to get wit' the program. I'ma hip you to a lot of new shit this summer."

"*That's* what I'm talkin' about," Peighton smiled.

"Shit, I almost forgot my overnight bag," Ra'Keeyah said, rushing back upstairs to get it.

"What's in there?" Peighton questioned once Ra'Keeyah came back downstairs.

"Uh, nosy!" Ra'Keeyah joked. "I got my necessities in here. Condoms, perfume, FDS spray, clean panties. I got all kinds of stuff."

"I can learn a lot from you," Peighton said.

"Stick around and you will," Ra'Keeyah laughed before taking a seat on the sofa to wait for their ride.

Ten minutes later Joe pulled up in front of the house. Shayna called Ra'Keeyah to let her know they were outside. Ra'Keeyah and Peighton walked out to the minivan.

"Damn, bitch, you look like a movie star!" Shayna got out of the van and said. "Your dress is *bad!*"

"Thank you," Ra'Keeyah said, spinning around to show off her outfit. "Oh, Shayna, this Peighton, my neighbor from across the street, the one that I was tellin' you about. Peighton, Shayna," Ra'Keeyah introduced.

"Hi," Peighton spoke.

"What's up?" Shayna said. "You look nice too."

"So do you," Ra'Keeyah and Peighton both said. Shayna wore a yellow silk angel sleeve summer dress with a deep V-neck and a pair of gold cork-heeled stack sandals that wrapped around her ankles. She had on gold butterfly earrings and a oversized butterfly ring.

"Thank you," Shayna smiled.

"I feel left out," Quiana said, climbing out of the car dressed in a light blue halter dress with sequins right beneath the bust line, a pair of silver platform heels, and matching silver accessories.

"Quiana, Peighton, Peighton, Quiana," Ra'Keeyah said. "Oh, and that's Joe over there," she pointed.

"Hi," Peighton spoke to Quiana and Joe.

"Hey," they both answered.

"We all look hot tonight," Shayna bragged.

"We sho' do," Quiana agreed.

"Let take some pictures," Peighton suggested.

"You and your pictures," Ra'Keeyah laughed. "Hey, y'all, meet our own personal photographer for the night."

"That's right!" Peighton laughed too.

"Get out, Joe, and take some pictures of us," Shayna demanded.

Without hesitation, Joe got out of the minivan and did as he was told. The ladies took enough pictures to almost fill up a photo album.

"I'm ready to get this night started," Ra'Keeyah said, amped.

"Well, let's go, then," Quiana said before climbing back into the minivan with Joe and Peighton in tow.

"Let me holla' at you for a minute," Shayna said, pulling Ra'Keeyah to the side.

"What's up?" Ra'Keeyah asked.

"Do this chick know what we bouta' go do?" Shayna asked, skeptical.

"Yeah, I pulled her coattail."

"You trust her?"

"Yeah, I trust her," Ra'Keeyah answered. "If I didn't, you know she wouldn't be rollin' wit' us."

"All right, then, if you trust her, I trust her," Shayna said, still skeptical. "I know one thing. I better not see none of our pictures on Facebook."

Ra'Keeyah started cracking up laughing. "I said the same damn thang!" she said, giving Shayna a high five. "But she don't got no Facebook page."

"Oh, well, we don't got nuttin' to worry about then," Shayna laughed. "Let's get this party started," she said as she and Ra'Keeyah got into the minivan to head over to the hotel.

Chapter Twenty-three

Joe's cell phone rang on the way to the hotel. By the sound of his conversation, Ra'Keeyah could tell he was talking to his sister.

"Yeah, I talked to 'em, and they wanna know how much you gon' pay. They get paid two-fifty each from the men." After exchanging a few more words, Joe ended the call. "Janice said she'll give y'all two-fifty each as well," he said to Shayna.

"I'm wit' it," Shayna smiled.

"Me too," Quiana agreed.

"I ain't," Ra'Keeyah frowned.

"We'll talk later," Shayna said, not wanting to discuss their business in front of Peighton.

"That's fine. But my answer is still gon' be the same later," Ra'Keeyah said smartly.

Joe pulled up in front of the hotel, and the ladies gathered their belongings before exiting the minivan.

"Don't forget, Joe, we ain't gon' be here all night. I'ma call you when we ready," Shayna said.

"A'iiiight," he said before pulling off.

Like clockwork, the girls walked into the hotel lobby, Shayna got the key from the front desk, and they boarded the elevator.

"Surprise!" all the men yelled when the ladies walked in the hotel room.

"Happy Birthday," Shayna said, giving Ra'Keeyah a hug.

Ra'Keeyah smiled widely. "Is this for me?" she asked looking around the room at all the decorations, food, and drinks.

"Yep," Shayna replied. "Me and Quiana came here earlier and decorated the room, and Calvin has a friend who is a caterer, so he sent over all the food and drinks."

"Thank y'all so much," Ra'Keeyah smiled giving Shayna and Quiana a hug.

"You deserve it, girl," Shayna said sincerely.

"No problem," Quiana replied.

"I'm goin' in the room to change," Ra'Keeyah beamed.

"Me too," Quiana stated and followed behind her.

"I'm about to take some pictures, and then I'll be in there too," Peighton said. She walked over to the table, pulled out her camera, and took pictures of all the food and decorations.

"Who's the girl with the camera?" Calvin asked Shayna.

"Oh, that's my cousin Peighton," Shayna lied. "She's in town for the summer and just wanna take pictures, so don't mind her."

"How can I not? She's breathtaking," Calvin said, admiring Peighton's beauty, making Shayna jealous. "Is she dancing too?" he asked, hopeful.

"No, she's not dancin' wit' us!" Shayna snapped while rolling her eyes.

"That's too bad," Calvin said and turned to walk away.

Shayna was heated about Calvin being so interested in Peighton. Envious was something she'd never been over another female, but the way Calvin stared at Peighton had her feeling just that. Shayna walked into the bedroom with Ra'Keeyah and Quiana as they got ready.

"Let's take a birthday shot," Shayna said, needing one to calm her nerves. She pulled their outfits and her favorite St. Claire Green Tea Vodka out of her duffle bag. Quiana grabbed the cups out of the bathroom. Once she removed the plastic from the cups, Shayna poured double shots in each of them.

"Don't leave me out," Peighton said, walking in the room.

"You betta' come on then," Ra'Keeyah said, handing her a cup.

Shayna poured Peighton a double shot as well. The four ladies held their cups up in the air and each took a turn making a toast before taking their shots to the face.

"One mo' for my birthday," Ra'Keeyah said.

"*That's* what I'm talkin' about!" Quiana said, holding her cup out so Shayna could refill it.

Once Shayna refilled everyone's cup, they toasted one more time before taking their shot to the head.

"Say 'cheese,'" Peighton said, lifting her camera up. The girls posed as Peighton started snapping away.

"OK, I'm goin' to get dressed now," Shayna said heading into the bathroom.

"Me too." Ra'Keeyah followed her.

"Say 'cheese,'" Peighton said to Quiana.

Quiana stopped getting undressed and posed for the picture. "Wait until we get dressed in our outfits, and then take some pictures of us," Quiana said and continued getting ready for the show.

"Okay. Man, I can't wait to show off these pictures!" Peighton smiled happily.

Quiana shook her head. "Now I don't think these men gon' approve of you takin' their pictures because majority of 'em are married men."

"Oh, wow. I wanted more pictures," Peighton said, disappointed.

"Sneak and do it," Quiana suggested.

"Yeah, I am," Peighton smiled.

"Make sure you take a lot of 'em. We like pictures, especially Ra'Keeyah's ol' conceited ass," Quiana laughed.

"I got chu'."

"Let's get's this party started so we can blow this Popsicle stand," Ra'Keeyah said as she and Shayna walked out of the bathroom dressed in a two-piece bathing suit.

"I'm wit' you," Quiana agreed.

"Wow, y'all look hot!" Peighton said, excited. "Let me get y'all's picture."

"You ain't gay, are you?" Shayna teased.

"No, but my dad is," Peighton said innocently.

"What?" Shayna and Quiana exclaimed.

"Never mind, y'all, let's just take the picture," Ra'Keeyah said laughing. The three girls took more pictures before walking out of the room.

Peighton sat on the sideline eating off the veggie tray as the girls danced. She turned the flash off on her camera and discreetly snapped pictures. The men were so into what they were watching they never even noticed. After a quick show, the girls collected their money and freshened back up. Shayna then called Joe to let him know they were ready. Some of the men were disappointed because they were expecting to get more, but the girls promised to make it up the next week. The four girls took one more shot to the face before heading down to wait on their ride.

Traffic was bumper to bumper as Joe drove the girls to the party. They could hear the music the DJ was playing from miles away. He had to drop the girls off four blocks down because the streets were blocked off by barriers and cars were lined up everywhere so he couldn't go through to let them off any closer. They weren't the only ones walking. Some people had to park ten blocks down.

"Damn, we got a long way to walk in these heels," Quiana complained as she got out of the van.

"I know, right?" Shayna agreed. "Thanks, Joe," she said, closing the door behind her.

"You're welcome and call me when y'all ready."

"I will," Shayna said.

"My feet hurt," Ra'Keeyah complained as they walked in the middle of the street like they owned it.

"Didn't nobody tell you to wear them ten-inch heels," Shayna joked.

"Ha-ha, don't hate," Ra'Keeyah smiled.

"Shit, I ain't hatin'. I'll be over to borrow them bad boys," Shayna laughed.

"They are sharp," Quiana agreed.

"Whaaat? Quiana givin' me a compliment? You must want somethin'," Ra'Keeyah said laughing.

"I do," Quiana laughed back.

The closer they got to the party, the more excited they got. They couldn't wait to show off their outfits. They were looking fly, and they knew it!

"I wonder what Brick gon' think about your new look," Shayna looked over at Ra'Keeyah and said.

"I don't know and don't care," Ra'Keeyah said. "I'm still feelin' some kind of way from him not tellin' me about the block party."

"Maybe he forgot," Shayna said in Brick's defense.

"How do you forget to tell someone that you talk to almost every day that you hostin' one of the biggest parties of the year?" Ra'Keeyah asked. " We done been out to eat and other places, and I have been over to his house several times during the past two weeks. I just don't think he wanted me to come."

"You got a point there," Shayna laughed.

"And that bullshit Davinette said to me at the shop today still got me wonderin'," Ra'Keeyah grimaced. "If he'd stoop that low to fuck wit' a nasty bitch like her, then I'm cool on him anyway!"

"You don't even know if what Davinette said was true or not," Shayna said. "She probably was just lyin' to get you out yo' hookup."

"I don't know," Ra'Keeyah said. "If she wasn't lyin' about it, then she can have him. 'Cuz he ain't worth all the trouble."

"Well, what you gon' do when you see him?" Shayna inquired.

"Act like I don't see him," Ra'Keeyah stated, rolling her eyes. "It's my birthday, and the St. Claire Green Tea Vodka got me feelin' on point. If Brick don't want this," she said, pointing to herself, "it's a lotta other niggas out here wit' money that can get it! I'm tired of wastin' my time fuckin' wit' niggas that wanna play games."

"I feel you," both Shayna and Quiana agreed.

"Is Brick your boyfriend?" Peighton asked, butting in on their conversation.

"No, we just talkin'," Ra'Keeyah answered.

"Well, if y'all don't go together, what you so upset about?" she asked.

Shayna shook her head. "You don't got no boyfriend in Birmingham, do you?" she asked.

"Actually, I do," Peighton answered.

"Wow, that's surprisin'," Shayna laughed, trying to get under Peighton's skin. "I bet you still a virgin, ain't you?"

"Shayna!" Ra'Keeyah called. "That ain't none of yo' business."

"Shit, I'm just askin'," she said.

"Actually, I'm not," Peighton responded. "Just 'cuz I ain't out in the streets fuckin' everything that moves you think I'm a virgin! My mom raised a lady. I'm classy not trashy," Peighton said with an attitude and continued walking.

Shayna was speechless, along with Ra'Keeyah and Quiana. This was the first time they'd ever witnessed Shayna get checked without a comeback.

"Hey, they playin' my song," Ra'Keeyah yelled, trying to lighten the mood. She started dancing in the middle of the street.

"This the cut," Quiana laughed and started dancing with her.

"Who is this?" Peighton asked, bobbing her head to the beat.

"Who is this?" Ra'Keeyah repeated, not believing Peighton didn't know whose song was playing.

"Girl, this Ace Hood," Ra'Keeyah answered.

"You just like him 'cuz he looks like Brick," Shayna laughed, letting Ra'Keeyah know that she wasn't upset about getting checked.

"You know it," Ra'Keeyah laughed too, giving Shayna a high five.

When the girls finally made it to the party, people were everywhere. The smell of barbeque teased their taste buds as they maneuvered through the crowd.

"Damn, that barbeque smells good," Shayna said.

"I know. Let's go find it," Ra'Keeyah suggested.

"Let's roll," Quiana stated as they looked for a food stand. "There it is," she said, pointing.

"Hey, baby, what's yo' name," a dude walking with a group of his friends asked, pulling Ra'Keeyah by the arm.

"Get up off of me, nigga!" Ra'Keeyah snapped, snatching her arm away.

"Stuck-up bitch," the dude retorted as he and his friends laughed.

"Oh, she gotta' be stuck-up 'cuz she don't wanna be bothered wit' yo' dusty ass?" Shayna grimaced.

"Who is this, yo' bitch?" the dude asked Ra'Keeyah.

"I would have a better chance of gettin' wit' her than you would," Shayna retorted.

Ra'Keeyah, Shayna, and Peighton started laughing along with the dude's group of friends.

"Fuck you, bitch!" he spat angrily, heated because he'd just got checked in front of his boys.

"You don't got enough money to fuck none of the girls in my crew," Shayna continued, snapping.

"Hey, is there a problem over here?" Bob T walked his 240-pound solid frame over to the girls and asked.

"What's up, Bob T?" Shayna spoke. "This ol' dust ball givin' me and my girls problems," she said.

So this is who Brick be talkin' about, Ra'Keeyah thought. *Damn, he huge!*

"Hey, man, you fuckin' wit' my li'l sista and her girls?" Bob T frowned.

"Naw, man," the dude lied.

"Yes, he was. He was callin' us bitches and hoes," Shayna smirked while stretching the truth just a little.

"I'm gon' need you to apologize to them," Bob T demanded.

"Man, I ain't even say nuttin' to them," the dude pleaded, not wanting to apologize in front of his boys.

"So you sayin' my sista lyin'?" Bob T asked.

"Naw, I ain't sayin' that."

"I ain't gon' tell you no mo' to apologize to them."

The dude sized Bob T up, knowing he couldn't take him and didn't want to be embarrassed a third time in front of his boys. "My bad, y'all," he said.

"That ain't good enough. Tell 'em you sorry," Bob T said.

"Come on, man, I apologized," dude whined.

Bob T gave dude a look to let him know he meant business.

"I'm sorry," dude said softly.

"That's more like it. Now get outta here, chump," Bob T laughed. "Y'all all right now?" he asked the girls. The dude's friends clowned him as they walked away.

"We cool," Shayna smiled.

Peighton was turned on by the way Bob T handled that dude. She's never had anyone take up for her before. Even though the dude wasn't really talking to her, she was a part of the group.

"Introduce me to yo' friends," Bob T said, while checking out all the ladies.

"This Key-Key, Peighton, and my cousin Quiana," Shayna introduced.

"Key-Key, huh?" Bob T asked with a sly grin. "You got a man, Key-Key?"

"You don't wanna talk to her," Shayna interjected.

"Why not?" Bob T asked. "She of age, ain't she?"

"Yeah, but it's more to it than just that," Shayna said, not wanting to tell Ra'Keeyah's and Brick's business.

"You can't speak for yourself?" Bob T asked Ra'Keeyah.

"Yeah, I can," Ra'Keeyah answered.

"So do you got a man?" Bob T asked again.

"Somethin' like that."

"You love him?" Bob T questioned.

"I mean, I wouldn't say I love him yet 'cuz we just started talkin'," she answered. "Let's just say I'm content."

"You faithful?"

Damn, this Rick Ross-lookin' ass nigga sho' ask a lot of questions, Ra'Keeyah thought. "Yeah," she answered.

"You can't knock a nigga for tryin'," Bob T smiled. "I'll tell you what. Yo' nigga lucky as fuck," he said, checking Ra'Keeyah out from head to toe.

"Thanks," Ra'Keeyah replied bashfully.

"What y'all bouta' get into?" Bob T asked Shayna.

"Bouta' go over here and get us some barbeque," she replied.

"Come on, I got y'all," he said leading the ladies over to the food. "Order what y'all want."

Peighton couldn't keep her eyes off this big, black, muscle-bound dude standing before her. Bob T caught her staring a few times, but Peighton played it off like she was looking behind him.

After the girls placed their orders, Bob T paid for their food and told them he'd catch up with them later.

"He was nice," Peighton said, before taking a bite of her pulled pork sandwich.

"Yeah, Bob T is cool as fuck," Shayna replied.

"What we gon' do next?" Quiana asked.

"I heard them say the car show is about to start," Shayna said, taking a sip of her lemonade.

"*That's* what's up," Ra'Keeyah said. "Let's head that way when we done eatin'."

"I'm game," Shayna replied.

"Me too," both Peighton and Quiana said.

"Eh, man, I just saw one of the finest bitches I done seen in a long time. She can't be from around here," Bob T said to Brick as they got ready to judge the wet T-shirt contest. "She got a nigga, tho."

Brick laughed. "That ain't neva' stopped you befo'e."

"I know, man. I'ma shoot my shot when I run into her again."

"Go for it," Brick replied while checking out a group of females that was walking by. "Hey, y'all gon' get in the wet T-shirt contest?" Brick called out to the ladies.

The group of girls realized Brick was talking to them and stopped. "What time it start?" one of the girls asked as she and her friends walked over to Brick and Bob T.

"In about ten minutes," Brick replied. "Y'all gon' get in it?"

"Who judgin' it?" she asked.

"I am," Brick answered.

"What do I get if I win?" she asked, before biting down on her bottom lip.

"What you want?" Brick asked.

"What you got to offer?"

"I got a lot to offer," Brick smiled.

"You think I can win?" the girl asked, looking at Brick seductively.

"I think you got a good chance," he said looking down at her breasts.

"There she go, man," Bob T said, excited.

"Who?" Brick asked, never taking his eyes off the fine shorty standing in front of him.

"That fine-ass bitch I was talkin' about," he said pointing as Ra'Keeyah and her girls walked by. "I'm bouta' get at her, dog."

Ra'Keeyah spotted the group of girls surrounding Brick and Bob T from a mile away. So she and her girls intentionally walked past, ignoring them as they strutted by. Ra'Keeyah wanted Brick to think she wasn't pressed, even though deep down she wanted to cry.

"Where?" Brick said finally looking up.

"Right there in the dark gray dress," Bob T said, pointing again.

"Ra'Keeyah?" Brick asked, surprised.

"They told me her name was Key-Key."

"That's me, dog," Brick said, walking away from the group of groupies and over to Ra'Keeyah and her girls.

"Damn, nigga, you lucky," Bob T called out as Brick headed over to them.

"No, he didn't," the girl Brick was talking to frowned.

"What's up, ladies?" Brick smiled widely.

"What's up?" Shayna, Quiana, and Peighton said.

"What's up wit' you, li'l mama?" Brick asked, admiring Ra'Keeyah's new look.

"Nothin'," she replied nonchalantly.

"You look good as fuck!" Brick smiled. He'd always thought Ra'Keeyah was pretty, but seeing her all dressed up put her beauty on a whole 'nother level.

"Thanks," she replied, uncaringly.

"You all right?" he asked, concerned.

"Yeah, I'm all right. Are you?" she asked smartly.

Sensing Ra'Keeyah didn't want to be bothered with him, Brick decided to leave. "Okay, you ladies enjoy the rest of your evenin'. I'm bouta' go judge this wet T-shirt contest," he said, turning to walk away, trying to act like he wasn't pressed about Ra'Keeyah blowing him off.

Hearing Brick was about to go judge a bunch of bitches in wet T-shirts crushed Ra'Keeyah's heart in a million pieces, but she refused to let it show.

Shayna knew her best friend was hurt. "Come on, let's go have some fun," she said, grabbing Ra'Keeyah by the arm.

The girls walked around and looked at all the different booths they had set up, collecting a lot of phone numbers and souvenirs along the way. Dudes were trying to holla' at them all night. They were the flyest chicks at the party, and they knew it! They were really enjoying themselves, keeping Ra'Keeyah's mind off Brick. They even stopped at a booth and had a caricature drawn of themselves. Other than a bunch of chicks flirting with Brick and him judging a wet T-shirt contest, the night was going by smoothly with no drama, just the way Ra'Keeyah liked it.

Peighton had never had this much fun in her life. She was already looking forward to coming to Ohio next summer. She took enough pictures to last her a lifetime as they walked around.

"I got too much shit in this purse," Peighton said. "My camera won't even fit in it now," she laughed.

"I don't have no room either," Ra'Keeyah said.

"I'll hold it," Quiana replied quickly, taking it and putting it in her purse.

"Thanks," Peighton said.

"Hey, Ra'Keeyah," a familiar voice called out.

Ra'Keeyah turned around. "What's up, Marshall?" she asked.

"Nothing," he replied.

"We goin' over here to look at them purses," Shayna said to Ra'Keeyah, wanting to give her and Marshall some privacy.

"How come you ain't been answerin' the phone when I call you?" Ra'Keeyah started in.

"Ra'Keeyah, I work two jobs now. You know I'm trying to get ready for college. I've been so busy," he said. "I haven't had time to do anything other than work."

"You sho' had time to be at the store buyin' condoms," Ra'Keeyah spat.

"Who told you that?" Marshall grimaced.

"Never mind who told me. Who was you buyin' 'em for?" Ra'Keeyah asked putting her hands on her hips, wanting to know.

"If you must know, I was buying them for my brother, Ra'Keeyah."

"Ummm-huh," she said.

"For real I was. I wouldn't lie to you, Ra'Keeyah," Marshall said, convincing her that he was telling the truth.

"I guess I believe you," she smiled.

Marshall grabbed Ra'Keeyah's hands and held them in his. "For real I was. Hell, the old man that sold them to me didn't even know what they were at first," Marshall laughed.

"Well, I betta' get back over here wit' my girls," Ra'Keeyah said. "Call me," she smiled.

"I will," he smiled back, kissing the back of both of her hands before letting them go. "And by the way, you look beautiful tonight."

"Uhh-oh, Brick on his way over to Ra'Keeyah and Marshall," Shayna said quickly, heading over to her best friend with Peighton and Quiana behind her.

"Thanks," Ra'Keeyah said sincerely before turning to walk away.

Brick got stopped by the same girl he was talking to earlier as Ra'Keeyah met up with her girls.

"That was close," Shayna said.

"What was?" Ra'Keeyah asked, clueless.

"Brick was on his way over to you and Marshall, but got stopped by that hood rat he over there talkin' to," Shayna said, pointing with her head.

Ra'Keeyah turned and looked over in Brick's direction. "Shit, I don't know what he was comin' over to me for," she said. "He betta' keep talkin' to all them bitches that been up in his face all night and leave me the fuck alone!"

"Here he come," Peighton warned.

"So?" Ra'Keeyah snapped.

"Let me holla' at you, li'l mama," Brick walked up and said.

"About what?" Ra'Keeyah grimaced. "Keep hollerin' at them bitches you been talkin' to."

"Man, fuck them broads. I don't want them hoes," Brick frowned. "They too easy for me."

"I can't tell. Every time I turn around they all up in yo' face," Ra'Keeyah argued.

"And? So that don't mean I want 'em," he snapped.

"Whatever, Brick. Do you," Ra'Keeyah said, fed up.

"Brick always gon' do Brick, 'cuz that's how Brick rock," he said with a cocky attitude. "I can fuck any ho out here I want. I choose not to 'cuz I ain't cut like that no mo'," Brick yelled loudly.

"Whatever," she said, waving him off.

"Hey, y'all, do y'all got a ride home?" Brick asked Ra'Keeyah's friends, ignoring what she was talking about.

"Not yet," Shayna answered.

"Hey, Bob T," Brick called out to his boy.

"'Sup, man?"

"What you bouta' do?"

"The party almost over so me and Malcolm bouta' ride and smoke somethin'," Bob T answered.

"Y'all smoke?" Brick asked Ra'Keeyah's friends.

"Hell, yeah!" Shayna quickly answered for everyone.

"Do me a favor and take these beautiful ladies home for me," Brick said. "And make sure they smoke good before you drop 'em off," Brick winked.

"I got chu', my nigga," Bob T said, giving Brick dap.

"See you, girl," Shayna said, giving Ra'Keeyah a hug.

"I ain't goin' wit' him. I'm goin' wit' y'all," Ra'Keeyah said.

"No, she not. She's comin' wit' me," Brick said, pulling her over to him. "We'll talk to y'all later."

Ra'Keeyah was turned on by the way Brick took charge. "You kidnappin' me?" she asked, jokingly.

"Yep."

"I'll holla' at y'all tomorrow," Ra'Keeyah said to her friends. It didn't take much to convince her to leave with Brick.

"No, she won't," Brick said. "She gon' be too tired."

"No, I'm not," Ra'Keeyah laughed. "Take care of my girls," she said to Bob T.

"I got chu', shorty," he said as they all went their separate ways.

Brick wrapped his arm around Ra'Keeyah's shoulder and pulled her close to him. They got mean-mugged by males and females alike as they walked to his car. Ra'Keeyah didn't care; she knew they were all jealous because of who she was leaving with and vice versa. Brick was happy it didn't take much to convince Ra'Keeyah to leave with him. But if he had to beg and plead, he refused to leave the party without her. No matter how many chicks he came in contact with, Brick knew Ra'Keeyah had his best interest at heart. He didn't know what challenges life was about to throw his way, but as long as he had Ra'Keeyah he didn't even care.

Chapter Twenty-four

Ra'Keeyah lay in Brick's bed sore and completely exhausted after a night of raw and uncut lovemaking.

"This was the best birthday ever," she smiled at Brick as they lay face to face.

"Wait, yesterday was your birthday?"

"Yep," she answered.

"Word? Well, how come you didn't tell me?"

Ra'Keeyah shrugged her shoulders. "I don't know. Probably the same reason you didn't tell me about the block party," she said smartly.

"I didn't think I had to tell you about it. You was there, wasn't you? Somebody told you," he said.

"It wasn't you. You probably didn't want me to come. That's why you didn't mention it to me."

"Get the fuck outta' here," he laughed. "I thought everybody knew about it. It was all on the radio and everything."

"I don't listen to the radio," she said.

"Whateva', man. Like I said, you came. Anyways, what you want for you birthday?"

"I don't know. Get me what you think I should have."

"You don't know? You ain't nothin' like the average woman," Brick laughed. "Anybody else woulda' been ramblin' off a whole list of shit to me."

"You know, what I really want is another charm for the Pandora bracelet my mom got me."

"Where's the bracelet?"

"In my purse." Ra'Keeyah rolled over and grabbed the bracelet out of her purse and showed it to Brick. "My mom started me out with this high-heel charm. Jaylen picked it out," she laughed.

"What's the whole concept behind these bracelets?" Brick inquired.

"I just like 'em 'cuz you can collect different charms."

"Well, why is there only one charm on here?"

"Shit, some of these charms be costin' like three and four hundred dollars," Ra'Keeyah answered. "That's why I only have one charm."

"Okay, well, I'll get you one to add on here," Brick said, handing back Ra'Keeyah her bracelet. "What kind of charm you want?"

"I don't know. You pick out what you want me to have."

"Okay, now when I come back wit' somethin' crazy, I don't wanna hear your mouth," Brick laughed.

"I won't. I'm not ungrateful," Ra'Keeyah said.

"Okay. You want anything else?"

"Ummm-huh," she answered.

"What?"

"This," Ra'Keeyah said, grabbing his manhood and gently began stroking it.

Brick instantly got hard. "It's all yours," he smiled, while reaching over on the nightstand, grabbing a condom and opening it up. "Now you know if you want this dick you gotta' take me too," he said, sliding the condom on his fully erect pipe.

"What you mean? I do want you too," Ra'Keeyah said spreading her legs as Brick rolled over on top of her.

"No, I mean *really* want me," he said, sliding his fishing pole into Ra'Keeyah's lake.

"I do, Brick. I *really* want you," Ra'Keeyah panted. "Can I have you all to myself?"

Brick nodded his head yes.

"Promise me," Ra'Keeyah said, working her hips just like Brick liked it.

"I promise you," he said, before switching his love-making into overdrive.

After half an hour of sexing, all Brick wanted to do was go back to sleep. But he couldn't because he had too much to do.

"So, does that mean we're officially a couple?" Ra'Kee-yah asked out of nowhere as she lay looking up at the ceiling.

Brick rolled over and got out of bed. "Yep. So tell all them ho-ass niggas you be talkin' to that you belong to Brick now," he said walking over to his closet to find something to wear.

"Why you always talkin' in third person?" Ra'Keeyah sat up and laughed.

"That's what Brick do," he said, pulling out a pair of Artful Dodger jeans and a matching T-shirt. "Did you hear me?"

"I heard you. But I don't be talkin' to no ho-ass nig-gas," Ra'Keeyah said.

"Whateva', betta' let 'em know," Brick warned, be-fore grabbing some boxers and heading into the bath-room to take a shower.

It was official, she and Brick were a couple. Be-ing with a man that made her feel the way Brick did, Ra'Keeyah couldn't have been any happier. She lay back and smiled.

After showering and getting dressed, Brick dropped Ra'Keeyah off at home and told her he would be back to get her in a few hours. He wanted to take her to a nice restaurant to celebrate her birthday.

"Hey, Ms. Ra'Keeyah," Peighton yelled from her front porch as Ra'Keeyah made her way up the walk.

Ra'Keeyah stopped and turned around. "Hey, Peighton," she smiled.

"Come here," Peighton said, waving Ra'Keeyah over to her.

"Lawd, I wonder what this child want," Ra'Keeyah said as she walked across the street. "What's up?"

"How was your night last night?" Peighton asked when Ra'Keeyah walked up on the bottom step.

"It was good," Ra'Keeyah smiled, as she quickly re-played bits and pieces of her night spent with Brick.

"That's good," Peighton said happily. "I know you're probably tired, but I wanted to know if you could call Quiana and tell her I forgot to get my camera from her last night. I wanna go get my pictures developed."

"I'll call her and tell her," Ra'Keeyah said. "Did you have fun last night?"

"I had a ball!" Peighton said excited. "I wanna thank you and you're friends for inviting me to kick it wit' y'all."

"No problem," Ra'Keeyah smiled, happy that Peighton enjoyed herself. "All right, girl, I'll talk to you later. I gotta go get ready."

"Where you goin'?"

"Brick takin' me out to lunch for my birthday."

"I hope you don't take this the wrong way, but Brick is fine!" Peighton said. "They don't make 'em like that where I'm from. At least not in my neighborhood."

Ra'Keeyah didn't know if she should be offended by Peighton's comment or take it as a compliment. This time she took it as a compliment, but if it happened again, she might not be so understanding. Ra'Keeyah made a mental note to keep a close eye on Peighton around Brick.

"Thanks," she said reluctantly before turning to walk away.

"Don't forget to call Quiana for me."

"I won't," Ra'Keeyah called over her shoulder and continued on her way. She attempted to fix her clothes and hair before going in the house. She didn't want to look as if she had a wild night, even though she did. "Mornin', Momma," she said, walking into the house, surprised to see her mother was still up after working a double shift.

"Mornin'," her mother said. "Did you have a good time last night?"

"I had fun," Ra'Keeyah smiled. "I ran into Marshall last night at the block party. He told me he work two jobs now."

"That's good," her mother said before heading toward the stairs. "Oh, I seen Quiana at Walgreens this morning. I stopped there on my way home from work."

I hope this hatin'-ass bitch didn't say nothin' about me bein' wit' Brick. "You did?" Ra'Keeyah asked nervously.

"Yeah. She told me that you and Shayna were still at the house asleep. She got in the car wit' some white man."

"It mighta' been Joe," Ra'Keeyah replied, relieved Quiana hadn't opened her mouth about who she was with last night.

"Naw, I know Joe. It was some other white man. Anyways, I'm about to go lie down before I go get Jaylen. I'm tired," her mother said and started up the stairs.

"Okay. Oh, Mom," Ra'Keeyah called out.

Her mother stopped and turned around. "Yeah?"

"Today is Marshall's only day off, and he want to take me out to lunch for my birthday. Is that okay?"

"Sure. That's nice of him," her mother said smiling before continuing up to her room.

"I wonder what Quiana was doin' at Walgreens wit'a white man early this mornin'," Ra'Keeyah said, dialing her number and having her call go straight to voice mail. "Ain't no tellin'." She left Quiana a voice mail about Peighton's camera and went into the kitchen to get herself a bottle of water. She brushed her thoughts to the side. There were more important things to think about, like what she was going to wear to lunch. Now that she was Brick's main line, she had to step her dress game all the way up and make sure she kept herself presentable at all times. Ra'Keeyah finished off her bottle of water before going up to her room.

As Ra'Keeyah rambled through her closet she couldn't get Brick off her mind. It made her smile knowing the dude that all the females went bananas over was actually hers. Even though she'd never had a problem getting any man she wanted, Ra'Keeyah just never imagined herself with a guy like Brick.

After a couple hours of going back and forth about what to wear, Ra'Keeyah finally decided on a short, light blue, banded bottom tunic with a silver chain belt. She snuck into her mother's room and borrowed two of her oversized silver necklaces and bangles that went well with her outfit and a pair of silver sandals that she had bought for her mom. She hadn't even had a chance to wear them yet. Ra'Keeyah then showered, spruced up her falling curls, and went outside on the front porch. She watched as Peighton walked off her front porch. The way she nervously glanced around it looked as if she was sneaking. Peighton was dressed differently from what Ra'Keeyah was used to seeing her in. Her hair was still neatly pressed, and from afar, it looked like she had makeup on.

"Where you bouta' go?" Ra'Keeyah called out.

"To the store," Peighton said nervously.

"You want me to walk wit' you?" Ra'Keeyah asked, knowing Peighton was up to something. She was too nervous acting.

"Naw, I'm cool. I can walk by myself," Peighton quickly answered.

"Ummm-huh," Ra'Keeyah smirked. "Don't do nothin' I wouldn't do," she hollered out.

"I won't," Peighton said, checking her watch. "I'll be over later," she said walking away before Ra'Keeyah could respond.

"Whatever," Ra'Keeyah replied, but Peighton was already halfway down the street. "That hefah is up to somethin'. She betta' be glad I'm leavin' or I'd follow her ass to see what it is," Ra'Keeyah said aloud.

She dug in her purse, pulled out her ringing cell phone, and checked the caller ID. A smile crept across her face when she saw Brick's name on the screen.

"Hello?" she answered, smiling.

"You ready, li'l mama?" Brick asked.

"Been ready," she answered.

"Where yo' mom at?" he asked, not wanting to get her into trouble.

"She went over to my aunt's house to get my li'l brother."

"Okay, well, I'm right down the street. I'll be there in about three minutes."

"Okay," Ra'Keeyah smiled happily before hanging up the phone and waiting on her chocolate prince to arrive.

Brick pulled up in front of the house in the Range Rover. Ra'Keeyah could tell he'd just left the car wash by the way the truck sparkled. She walked off the porch and headed to the truck. She could see herself clearly in the freshly waxed paint.

"What's up, li'l mama?" he asked when Ra'Keeyah got in the truck before leaning over for a kiss. "You look nice."

"Thanks," she replied, before meeting his lips with hers.

"I missed you," he smiled.

"Dang, you just dropped me off a few hours ago," she said, playing the hard role, knowing she missed him too, but didn't want him to know it.

"Don't act like you didn't miss me, nigga," Brick laughed as he pulled away from the curb.

"I did," Ra'Keeyah admitted. "Just a little bit, though," she joked.

"Whateva'," Brick laughed. "You hungry?"

"I'm starvin'."

"Good 'cuz we bouta' go throw down at the best restaurant in town."

"I don't care where we go. Just feed me," Ra'Keeyah said.

"I got somethin' you can eat," Brick said with a sly grin.

"I can eat that for dessert," she smirked, catching on to what Brick was insinuating.

"That's what I'm talkin' about," Brick smiled before finding a nice mellow jazz radio station. He then sat back in the butter-soft leather seats and enjoyed the ride to the restaurant with his new girl by his side.

Chapter Twenty-five

Brick pulled in the driveway of a well maintained, ranch-style house and turned the engine off.

"This don't look like a restaurant to me," Ra'Keeyah said.

Brick smiled as he opened his door. "It's not a restaurant. It's my momma's house," he said, getting out of the truck.

"Your mom's house?" Ra'Keeyah asked confused. "What we doin' over here?"

"I told you we was goin' to the best restaurant in town."

"Nigga, if I woulda' known we was comin' to yo' momma's house, I would of at least put on somethin' more presentable," Ra'Keeyah fussed. "I wonder what she gon' have to say about the outfit I'm wearin'?"

"Don't worry. You look good, li'l mama," Brick smiled.

"Yeah, to you. But yo' mom is probably gon' think I look like a tramp or somethin'!"

"Yeah, probably," he joked.

"Brick, it ain't funny," Ra'Keeyah whined. "I don't want your mom to look at me like that."

Brick shook his head and laughed. "Stop overreactin', li'l mama. You don't have nothin' to worry about. My mom is not into judgin' people."

"Yeah, not until she sees how I'm dressed," Ra'Keeyah said, reluctantly opening up the passenger-side door and getting out. "Ooooh, I'ma get you for this," she threatened Brick.

"You can pay me back later on," he smiled as they walked to the front door.

"Shut up," Ra'Keeyah smiled back as Brick put the key into the lock.

"Ma, where you at?" Brick called out as he and Ra'Keeyah entered the house.

The aroma from the food Brick's mother was cooking had Ra'Keeyah ready to eat.

"I'm in the kitchen," Pauline yelled back. "Here I come." She wiped her hands on her apron before exiting the kitchen.

Ra'Keeyah instantly recognized Brick's mom as the owner of the Road Runners diner they'd gone to when they first met.

"Hey, baby," Pauline said, kissing Brick on the cheek.

"Hey, Ma, you remember Ra'Keeyah, don't you?" Brick asked.

"Yes, I remember her. How ya' been, baby?"

"Good," Ra'Keeyah replied with a smile.

"Y'all have a seat and get comfortable. The food is almost ready," Pauline said, leading them to the living room. "That's a pretty outfit you have on."

"Thanks," Ra'Keeyah replied, relieved.

"I got one just like it, but it's a different color."

"Okay," Ra'Keeyah said, surprised.

"Let me go check on the corn bread. I don't want it to burn up," Pauline said, excusing herself from the living room.

"How come you didn't tell me your mom was the owner of the Road Runners diner?" Ra'Keeyah asked Brick as soon as Pauline left the room.

Brick laughed. "I thought I did," he joked.

"Whatever! You just wanted me to think you had pull at the restaurant," Ra'Keeyah laughed.

"You got me," Brick admitted. "But don't get it twisted; Brick got pull!"

"Lunch is ready," Pauline said, carrying a glass dish toward the dining room.

Brick got up from the sofa and went and gave Pauline a hand carrying the food. After they got all the food on the table, Brick called Ra'Keeyah to eat.

"Well, I hope y'all enjoy the meal. I'm bouta' go to work."

"All right, Ma," Brick said, giving Pauline a kiss on the cheek.

"Nice seein' you again," Ra'Keeyah said.

"You too," Pauline smiled before walking out of the dining room.

"Would you like me to fix your plate?" Brick asked Ra'Keeyah.

"Please."

Brick put a piece of fried chicken, some collard greens, sweet potatoes, macaroni and cheese, and hot water corn bread on Ra'Keeyah's plate before setting it down in front of her. He then fixed his own plate. They bowed their heads in prayer before going all in.

After they finished the deliciously prepared meal, Ra'Keeyah and Brick put the food away before cleaning up the kitchen.

"Your mom can throw down in the kitchen," Ra'Keeyah said as they made their way to the living room. "I might need to send her a thank-you card for that meal," she laughed, taking a seat on the sofa.

"Yeah, she can cook. Ever since I can remember she has always had a passion for cooking. Every holiday we would have at least thirty to forty people at the house," Brick reminisced as he sat down behind Ra'Keeyah. "That's why when the opportunity came open for her to buy that restaurant, I bought it for her. I'm tryin' to talk her into openin' up anotha' one too."

"That was nice of you," Ra'Keeyah smiled before leaning back on Brick's chest.

Brick wrapped his arms around Ra'Keeyah's body and held her. "I didn't do it to be nice. I did it because that's the woman that took care of me," Brick said.

"You know, by the way you speak of your mother, you would have never thought you used to have some type of animosity toward her," Ra'Keeyah said. "And you don't look nothin' like your mom either. You musta' got your color from your father, 'cuz your mom is light as hell."

Brick laughed. He didn't know if he was ready to tell Ra'Keeyah his background or not, but the vibes she gave when he was around her made him feel he could trust her.

"Pauline is not my real mother," Brick said.

"Oh, sorry," Ra'Keeyah said, embarrassed.

"It's okay," he assured. "Pauline took me in when I was nine. She watched me grow up wit' nothin'. I had no decent place to lay my head at night, no clean clothes to wear, and no food on the table," Brick said, reliving his past.

"Wow," Ra'Keeyah said, not thinking his life could get any worse than him having to witness his mother working in a strip club. The painful look on Brick's face told Ra'Keeyah that he needed to get this off his chest so he continued on with his story. "My biological mother was smoked out, and my father was doin' a life bid on Riker's Island for murder," Brick continued. "I had nowhere else to turn but to the streets," he said, as if he was justifying why he sold drugs. "I was out there on the streets sellin' drugs at eight years old. That's how I met Pauline."

Ra'Keeyah was amazed at Brick's story. It brought tears to her eyes. She couldn't fathom the idea of a little boy Jaylen's age out on the street selling drugs.

"Food wasn't the only thing Pauline was good at cookin'," Brick laughed. "She used to cook dope for all the neighborhood dope boys. She was named one of the best!"

"Whaaat?" Ra'Keeyah asked, shocked.

"The lady I used to go to at first was beatin' me out my dope. So I went to Pauline's house wit' my OG, which was her baby brother, and he had her cook my dope for me. I can still remember the look she gave me when she found out the dope was mines," Brick laughed.

"I bet," Ra'Keeyah smiled and waited to hear the rest of Brick's story.

"Pauline couldn't believe a boy the same age as her youngest son was out in the streets sellin' dope. She made her brother promise her that he would always make sure I'm straight, and he did until somebody smoked him," Brick said, shaking his head. "He's the one that gave me the nickname, Brick, 'cuz by the age of twelve I was sellin' straight bricks."

"That's sad," Ra'Keeyah said.

"I know, man. Roger was a good dude," Brick said. "After that, Pauline took me under her wing and looked out for me. She made sure I ate every day, she held my money for me, and didn't touch it. And she gave me a comfortable bed to sleep in every night, just so I wouldn't have to sleep at the trap house. That's just *one* of the reasons why I owe this woman my life. She can get anything from me," he stressed.

"I don't blame you," Ra'Keeyah agreed. "How many kids do Pauline got altogether?"

"She had two," he answered. "But they both got killed."

"Oh wow," Ra'Keeyah said apologetically. "What happened to 'em?" Ra'Keeyah asked carefully, hoping Brick didn't think she was trying to be nosy, but showing concern.

Brick sat quietly for a brief minute as if he was con-
templating on whether he should share with Ra'Keeyah
what happened to his brothers.

"Never mind, you don't have to tell me," Ra'Keeyah
replied, sensing his hesitation.

"Naw, it's just that sometimes it hard to talk about
it. The NYPD shot and killed my oldest brother, Ryan,"
Brick continued, recollecting the night the police
knocked on Pauline's door with the news. "It was a case
of mistaken identity." Brick's voice cracked as he spoke.
"Ryan was in college; he didn't drink, smoke, or bother
nobody. He had a baby on the way. He didn't deserve
to die, not like he did. Brick shook his head in disbelief.
"They shot him twelve times. They said they thought
he was reachin' for a gun when they pulled him over,
thinkin' he was somebody else. All he was doin' was
reachin' for his cell phone 'cuz it was Momma callin' to
let him know that his baby mama had went into labor."

"Damn, that's messed up," Ra'Keeyah said sympathetically.

"Who you tellin'?" Brick agreed, fighting back tears.
"His baby momma was givin' birth the same time he
was dyin' on the operating table. Ryan Jr. was born at
11:45 P.M., and Ryan Sr. was pronounced dead at 11:59
P.M. One minute before midnight. Pauline got paid a lot
of money, but it still didn't replace the loss of her son."

"Wow! So his son was born on the same day he died,"
Ra'Keeyah said, shocked.

"You know the old folks say every time someone
dies, a baby is born in their place. Pauline is one of the
strongest women I know. Losing two sons in the same
year and still managed to hold her life together," Brick
said.

Ra'Keeyah wanted to ask what happened to her other son, but didn't want to come off as tacky. So she waited to see if he would tell her.

Brick really didn't want to tell Ra'Keeyah the story about Caleb either, but he knew he had too. He had so much hurt and pain built up in him since the death of his best friend, and he knew it was time to let it go before he ended up hurting someone. What better time to do it than now, and with someone whom he trusted.

"Her youngest son, Caleb, was my best friend. We did everything together. I mean, everything," Brick smiled, reminiscing about some of the good times he had with his boy. "If I fought, he fought. If I went to juvenile, he was right there wit' me. That was my nigga!"

Ra'Keeyah smiled because Caleb reminded her of Shayna.

Brick's smile slowly faded. "I still blame myself for his death." Brick got real quiet and stared at the wall as if he was in deep thought. "This story I'm about to tell you, I've never shared wit' anyone. I trust you enough to know that you will never speak on it again."

Ra'Keeyah was giddy behind Brick saying he trusted her, recalling him saying Pauline was the only person in the world he trusted wholeheartedly. But she wasn't sure if she was ready to hear what was about to come out of Brick's mouth. Ra'Keeyah hoped she would still be able to look at Brick the same if he revealed to her that he'd done something horrific.

"I can trust you, right?"

"Yeah, you can trust me," Ra'Keeyah said, feeling bad because she hadn't been completely honest with Brick about her lifestyle.

"This nigga name Bam used to run wit' us. He was a li'l ol' dusty-ass nigga," Brick chuckled, remembering how homely he used to look. "We felt sorry for the li'l nigga so we cleaned him up. You know, taught him how to dress and shit so he could get pussy. He kept beggin' for me to put him on. I shoulda' listened to my first mind, 'cuz I kept tellin' the nigga no."

"My momma always taught me to listen to that first voice in yo' head," Ra'Keeyah interrupted.

"I should have," Brick agreed. "I put the nigga on, and true enough, he was gettin' paper, but he would trick all his money off wit' all the neighborhood rats. After he paid me what he owed me, the nigga was broke. Anyways, the nigga got robbed one night and came to the speakeasy cryin' and shit, snot runnin' all down his nose, wantin' me and Caleb to get his money back from some niggas over in Long Island. I guess he was over there trickin' wit' one of they hoes or somethin', and the bitch set his dumb ass up to get robbed."

"He got caught wit' his pants down," Ra'Keeyah laughed.

"Yeah, literally," Brick laughed too. "Anyways, we get suited and booted to go over to Long Island. We pull up behind the Shacks, that's a project on Parkside, and cut the engine off. Caleb kept tryin'a tell me to wait, but I was like, let's gon' and get it over wit' so I can get back to the dice game."

"You really are addicted to gamblin', huh?"

Brick smiled and kept talking. "We get over there, find the niggas that robbed him, and lit up the Shacks! People was screamin' and runnin'. We heard kids cryin' and shit." Hearing that made Ra'Keeyah cringe. "Luckily, no kids got hurt," Brick clarified, seeing the look on Ra'Keeyah's face. "Caleb ran all the way back to the car and didn't even know he'd been hit twice in the chest. He didn't have his vest on. He'd given his to me, 'cuz I let my nigga Draco D borrow mines." Brick dropped his head in his hands and vigorously shook his head.

Ra'Keeyah sat still. She was afraid to make a move just in case Brick had a flashback of that night.

After a few silent minutes, Brick lifted his head and continued talking. "Two of the niggas got killed, and Caleb died two weeks later from complications. One day he was up laughin' and talkin', and then the next he was in a coma." Ra'Keeyah's heart went out to Brick when she saw tears welling up in his eyes. "We got away wit' it. But I guess Bam couldn't help himself, 'cuz he got to braggin' to niggas about what went down that night. A few days later, the cops come pickin' me up from my girl's house and took me in for questionin'. I got out eleven hours later. They tried to break me, but I'm unbreakable."

"Damn. Eleven hours?" Ra'Keeyah asked.

"Eleven hours," Brick repeated. "When I got out, I sent word to Bam about them pickin' me up. I didn't go myself 'cuz I knew they was watchin' me. So this bitch-ass nigga Bam sends word back that I don't got nothin' to worry about 'cuz he ain't gon' say nothin' either. A few days later, they pick this ho-ass nigga up, and they said he was up there singin' like New Edition. He told 'em everything. Even down to Caleb givin' me his vest to wear."

"You gotta be jokin'," Ra'Keeyah said, shaking her head.

"They arrested me at the hospital while I was up there visitin' Caleb. They charged me wit' murder," Brick said. "I was devastated 'cuz Pauline wouldn't speak to me and my attorney kept tellin' me she was gon' testify against me. He said she blamed me for the way Caleb turned out."

"Dang," Ra'Keeyah said.

"Bam got on the stand and pointed me out as the shooter. He blamed everything on me. They gave him six months. He did three and shocked out," Brick said, angry. "They tried to give me life without parole. The only thing that saved me was when Pauline got on the stand. Instead of testifyin' against me, she testified in my favor. She told the court that her son admitted to her before he went into a coma that he was the one who did the shootin'. Caleb even made a statement to the police that he was the one who killed them two dudes. They tried to withhold the evidence until Pauline brought up Caleb's statement. Come to find out, she wouldn't talk to me 'cuz she didn't want them to think me and her concocted the story together."

"Wow, that was dirty," Ra'Keeyah stated. "So did Caleb really make a statement?"

Brick nodded his head yes. "He wasn't the one that killed them niggas, though. He had a .357, and I had a 9 mm. They found 9 mm bullets in both of their bodies. Bam had a punk-ass .22 that he took outta his momma's closet. I don't know what he thought he was gon' do wit' that against all that heat them niggas had." Brick got quiet again. "Even on his deathbed, Caleb was a true friend."

"He sure was," Ra'Keeyah agreed. "Well, where's Bam at now?"

"Somebody told me his dumb ass caught a murder case up here in Ohio. He cool, though. They say he got him a boy in there and settin' up COs and inmates left and right."

"Wow. So he was a snitch on the streets, and now he's one in the penitentiary?"

"What you expect? Snitchin' is in the nigga blood."

"That's sad," Ra'Keeyah said, shaking her head. "That had to be devastating to Pauline to lose both of her sons in the same year."

"Yep. That's why she clings to me like she does. I'm all she got left, for real," Brick said. "Not meanin' to bring my ex-girl Piper up, but she couldn't understand my relationship wit' Pauline. It was like she was jealous of her or somethin'."

"Whaaat? Why?" Ra'Keeyah asked, confused.

"Because anytime Pauline called me, I was at her beck and call," Brick said, hoping Ra'Keeyah would be the understanding person he needed her to be. "I tried to explain to Piper without tellin' her the whole story that I owe Pauline my life. She saved me for real."

"Wow, I can't believe she could be so inconsiderate of your relationship with Pauline," Ra'Keeyah grimaced. "She *is* your mother, so to speak."

"I just hope you gon' be able to deal wit' the fact that every time my momma call me or need me that I'm gon' be right there for her until the day she die," Brick said, hopeful.

"I would be less of woman if I didn't support you havin' your mother's back at all times," Ra'Keeyah said. "What give me the right to bitch or complain because you're doin' somethin' for your mom? I can see if you was doin' the shit for another woman," Ra'Keeyah fussed, hoping her speech was getting her brownie points with Brick.

"I tried to tell Piper the same damn thing!" Brick said, glad that he and Ra'Keeyah were on the same page when it came to Pauline. "She couldn't get that through her head for nothin' in the world. I'm glad you understand, li'l mama, where I'm comin' from." Brick's feelings grew even stronger for Ra'Keeyah.

"I have somethin' for you," Brick said reaching on the side of the sofa and grabbing a Purse Snickety bag and handing it to Ra'Keeyah. "Happy Birthday."

A huge smile came across Ra'Keeyah's face as she reached in the bag and pulled out a medium-sized box. She took the top off and was surprised when she saw the box full of Pandora charms for her bracelet.

"Oh my goodness," she squealed happily. "Look at all these charms," she said, picking them up one by one and examining them. Brick had bought Ra'Keeyah twenty-four different color-coordinated charms to fill up the bracelet her mother had gotten her for her birthday. She was ecstatic when she picked up the fourteen karat gold pink murano glass charm. She'd seen that one in the catalog and it ran at least $270. She leaned in and passionately kissed Brick to show him how much she appreciated her birthday gift. "Thank you," she smiled.

"You're welcome." Brick was happy that Ra'Keeyah liked her present. Pauline did a good job at picking out all the different charms. Brick hated shopping for women; that's why he always sent Pauline out to do it, and he hasn't had one complaint yet.

After spending hours talking to Brick, Ra'Keeyah looked at him in a whole new light. Here was a man that had been through so many trials and tribulations at a young age and still managed to come out on top. Brick was somewhat of a hero in Ra'Keeyah's eyes and underneath all the muscles and the hard-core attitude there was a soft side that only Ra'Keeyah had been privileged enough to witness.

Chapter Twenty-six

Over the next few weeks, Ra'Keeyah and Brick had been spending all of their free time together, enjoying each other's company. Brick learned that Ra'Keeyah always wanted to learn how to fish, so he took her up to the lake, rented a pontoon boat, and showed her how. After a few unsuccessful attempts of trying to catch a fish, Ra'Keeyah finally caught herself a tiny bluegill. She was so excited about her first catch, she asked Brick to take her to a taxidermist so she could display her fish over his fireplace. After he laughed and talked about how tiny her fish was, Ra'Keeyah threw it back in the water and tried for something bigger.

Ra'Keeyah had even been spending a lot of time with Pauline, trying to get a feel for her. She remembered her mother once saying that the best way to a man's heart is through his stomach, but that was back in the olden days. Ra'Keeyah was no dummy; she knew the best way to a man's heart nowadays was through his mama. They went shopping together, out to lunch, and Pauline even taught her how to make Brick's favorite meal, lasagna. What drew Ra'Keeyah even closer to Pauline was when she told her that if she ever needed anything, don't hesitate to call her.

It seemed like forever since the last time Ra'Keeyah had hung out with her girls, and it was long overdue. Brick had business to take care of so Ra'Keeyah called up Shayna and invited her and Quiana to Starbucks to catch up on the latest. Ra'Keeyah asked Peighton if she wanted to tag along as well, but she declined, saying she had to go somewhere with her dad. Peighton had been acting real suspicious for a while now, and Ra'Keeyah didn't know why.

Oh, well, she'll be all right, Ra'Keeyah thought as she got dressed and waited for Joe to come pick her up.

"I can't believe your mom hate drug dealers that much that you have to tell her you're goin' out wit' Marshall," Shayna laughed before sipping on her Caramel Frappuccino. "And she be fallin' for it," she continued laughing.

"Haven't your mom figured out by now that you too old for her to be tellin' you who you can and cannot fuck wit'?" Quiana asked. "I'm jus' sayin'."

"For real," Shayna agreed. "I wish my mom would!"

"Your mom is mad hard on you, man," Quiana added.

"Y'all bitches lucky! Y'all moms talk that punishment shit, but don't go through wit' it. When my mom say I'm on punishment, that's what she mean," Ra'Keeyah complained.

Shayna thought for a brief second before speaking. "We ain't really lucky. Your mom ain't really hard on you. She just love and care about you, that's all," Shayna said, slightly jealous of the love Ra'Keeyah's mother showed her.

"Girl, y'all moms love y'all too. They just got a funny way of showin' it," Ra'Keeyah said.

"Real funny," Shayna replied sarcastically.

"Ain't no way my mom can love me," Quiana said, shaking her head in disgust. "I've known that ever since I was a little girl. I've just learned how to accept it." Shayna shot Quiana an "I wish you would" look. Ra'Keeyah noticed the look but didn't pay it much attention.

"Whatever, man," Ra'Keeyah laughed. "How you figure that? 'Cuz she didn't get you the Cabbage Patch you wanted one Christmas or the latest Barbie?" Ra'Keeyah joked.

"I wish that's all it was," Quiana said sullenly.

"Anyways, girl, what you and Brick been up to?" Shayna said, changing the subject.

Ra'Keeyah smiled widely. "Girl, I love me some *him!* He is everything I want in a man. He treats me like a queen. I don't want for nothin' when I'm wit' him. Me and his mom even get along good," Ra'Keeyah boasted. "I enjoy every minute we spend together."

"Well, is *he* the reason why you bailed out on us for the past two weeks?" Quiana asked smartly.

"Quiana!" Shayna warned. "Our girl is happily in love. You should be happy for her."

"I am," Quiana said sarcastically.

"And to answer your question, yes, *he* is the reason why I haven't danced in two weeks. We been spendin' so much time together," Ra'Keeyah smiled. "I'ma be there Saturday, though, just so I can keep my stash stacked, even though Brick keepa bitch papered up!"

"Girl, even if you can't make it, me and Quiana can hold it down until you decide to come back."

"You know, I really been thinkin' about givin' up dancin', bein' that Brick hate strippers and is dead set against ever bein' wit' one," Ra'Keeyah said. "I don't wanna mess this relationship up."

"So you just gon' give up on us? We all supposed to be in this together. You done got a nigga and done got new on us!" Quiana grimaced.

"I didn't get new! I'm just tryin'a respect his wishes, that's all," Ra'Keeyah argued.

"Damn, Quiana, her nigga don't want her dancin'. Why you so mad?" Shayna asked.

"Damn, she gon' mess our money up!"

"How am I gon' mess y'all money up? Them men come to see all of us, not just me," Ra'Keeyah said.

"You just don't get it!" Quiana snapped before standing up and walking away.

Ra'Keeyah and Shayna were both shocked by Quiana's reaction.

"What just happened?" Ra'Keeyah asked Shayna.

"I don't know, dog," Shayna laughed. "All I know is Quiana really been trippin' lately. I don't know what's got into her."

"I don't know either. Maybe she need some dick!" Ra'Keeyah laughed.

"Maybe," Shayna laughed too. Then her facial expression turned serious. "I think Calvin is messin' around on me," she said out of nowhere.

"Well, he is married, you know," Ra'Keeyah teased.

"I know that," Shayna smiled. "No, but I really think he's messin' wit' somebody other than me and his wife."

"Why you say that?"

"He's been actin' funny lately too. Maybe it's in the water," Shayna said, seriously.

"It gotta be," Ra'Keeyah agreed. "'Cuz Peighton's ass been actin' different too. She been MIA a lot lately. Every time I try to call her or invite her to kick it wit' us, she either don't answer her phone or say she got somethin' to do."

"Maybe he's messin' around wit' Peighton. Did you see how he was droolin' all over her when we took her to the hotel wit' us?" Shayna asked, jumping to conclusions.

"Yeah, he was checkin' her out pretty tough. Even when we were dancin' he wasn't payin' attention to us; he was too busy over at the food table whisperin' in Peighton's ear," Ra'Keeyah pointed out.

"I don't see her bein' that scandalous, though," Shayna said, giving Peighton the benefit of doubt.

"Me either, but you never know," Ra'Keeyah replied.

"I know one thing; I need you to keep your eye on her for me. If you even think you see Calvin over there pickin' her up, call me," Shayna said.

"I got chu'," Ra'Keeyah assured before sipping on her lukewarm Chai tea.

Ra'Keeyah and Shayna watched as Quiana hung up her cell phone and made her way back over to their table.

"You okay now?" Shayna asked when Quiana sat down.

"Yeah, I'm fine. I know I overreacted a little," Quiana admitted.

"A little? I thought you were gon' start turnin' over tables," Ra'Keeyah joked.

"Me too," Shayna laughed.

"Naw. It wasn't that serious. And plus, in the end, everything will work out in my favor anyway," Quiana said confidently.

"What you mean by that?" Ra'Keeyah asked with raised eyebrows.

"I'm wit' Ra'Keeyah. What the fuck you mean by that?" Shayna snapped.

"Oh my goodness. What the fuck is wrong wit' y'all?" Quiana laughed. "Only thing I meant was I'm gon continue to keep gettin' my money no matter what. Damn! Stop readin' so much into shit!"

"Oh. I just wanted to make sure. Shit, especially the way everybody flippin' gangsta'," Shayna stated.

Ra'Keeyah was convinced that Quiana's statement meant more than what she said it did. She just didn't say anything. Knowing about some of the scandalous acts she'd pulled in the past, Shayna should have realized it too. Shayna could sleep to her cousin if she wanted to, but Ra'Keeyah made up in her mind that she wasn't about to let her guard down around Quiana ever again. One thing she did pay attention to her mother saying is "A jealous person is a dangerous person." And Quiana deviously wore jealousy like a badge of honor.

Chapter Twenty-seven

Peighton saw Ra'Keeyah sitting on the porch and decided to walk over and visit for a while. It had been well over a month since they'd last talked and had only seen each other in passing. Peighton had less than a week before she went back home to Birmingham and thought it would nice to catch up as well as come clean about why she'd been avoiding her.

"What you doin'?" Peighton asked, walking up on Ra'Keeyah's porch and taking a seat in one of the lawn chairs.

"Nothin'. Just enjoyin' this warm weather," she responded with a smile. Ra'Keeyah was kind of glad that Peighton came over to keep her company. It had been awhile since they'd sat and chatted with each other. "So, what you been up to?" Ra'Keeyah asked.

"Nothin' really," she replied, nonchalantly.

"I see you still been keepin' your hair done and dressin' nice," Ra'Keeyah complimented.

"Yeah. I think it was about time for me to start lookin' and dressin' like a young lady."

"Did Quiana ever bring your camera?"

"Yeah, she brought it the same day you called her."

Both girls were silent as they watched traffic move up and down the street. Ra'Keeyah was trying to feel Peighton out, and Peighton was trying to figure out how to break the news. Ra'Keeyah could wait no longer and broke the silence first.

"Why when I see you, you be movin' fast, like you up to somethin'?" Ra'Keeyah asked, cutting to the chase.

"Look, Ra'Keeyah, I'm just gon' be honest and come right out and tell you, 'cuz I like you," Peighton said, piquing Ra'Keeyah's curiosity. "And I hope you don't be mad at me after I tell you what I've been doin'."

Peighton had Ra'Keeyah's heart beating fast. She was really ready to hear what Peighton had to tell her.

"I've been messin' around wit' Bob T behind your back," Peighton said quickly.

"Bob T?" Ra'Keeyah asked, confused.

"Please don't be mad, Ra'Keeyah. I know I was wrong for doin' that to you. But after he dropped Shayna and Malcolm off at his house and Quiana off at home, I was the last one in the truck. He kept complimentin' me on my looks. And we got to talkin' and one thing led to another," Peighton rambled.

"Wait a minute," Ra'Keeyah said, interrupting her. "How was you messin' around wit' Bob T behind my back? He ain't none of my dude."

"I know, but he did try to holla' at you first."

"So what? It ain't like I was tryin' to holla' back. I'm wit' who I wanna be wit'," Ra'Keeyah stated.

"So that means you're not mad at me then?" Peighton asked, relieved.

"Girl, please, I'm happy for you. All this time you been sneakin' around wit' Bob T, thinkin' I would be mad 'cuz he tried to holla' at me first." Ra'Keeyah shook her head and smiled. "Girl, we coulda' been goin' on double dates together."

"I know, right?" Peighton smiled apologetically. "Maybe when I come back next summer, we can all do somethin' together."

"How do you know we'll all still be messin' around next summer? You gon' put roots on him?" Ra'Keeyah busted out laughing.

"Fuck you! Everybody down South don't practice voodoo," Peighton laughed too.

"I know they don't. Well, I guess I can call Shayna and let her know it ain't Calvin you messin' around wit'," Ra'Keeyah laughed.

"Calvin? Why she think I was messin' wit' him?"

"I don't know. She thinks he's messin' around wit' somebody other than her."

"Well, please believe, it ain't me. I don't do white. I'm not racist. I just like my men black. Like Bob T," Peighton smiled.

"I'm wit' you on that," Ra'Keeyah said giving Peighton a high five. "Wait a minute. Did you say Bob T dropped Shayna and Malcolm off at his house?" Ra'Keeyah asked just to make sure she heard right the first time.

"Yep. We all rode around and smoked a blunt, went to Steak and Shake, and then he dropped everybody off. Well, we dropped them off," Peighton laughed.

"Sounds to me like you had a good night."

"The best. We've been spendin' a lot of time together too. I really like him," Peighton giggled.

"Well, like I said before, I'm happy for you," Ra'Kee-yah smiled. The two women looked across the street as Peighton's dad, brother, and significant other came out of the house. Ra'Keeyah waved as they made their way off the porch.

"Oh, they must be ready to go," Peighton said, standing up from the chair. "My dad is takin' me and my brother school shoppin' today."

"Oh, okay. Well, come over later."

"Shit, is you gon' be at home? You be wit' Brick more than I be wit' Bob T," Peighton laughed.

"Brick went outta town, so I'ma be here," Ra'Keeyah laughed too.

"Okay, well, I'll be over when we get back," Peighton said, making her way down the steps.

"I'll be here." Ra'Keeyah watched as Peighton walked across the street and got in her father's SUV before calling Shayna.

"What it do?" Shayna answered.

"Bitch, how come you didn't tell me about you and Malcolm?" Ra'Keeyah started in.

"What you talkin' about? I thought I told you," Shayna laughed.

"You know you ain't told me shit," Ra'Keeyah laughed as she continued to fuss. "I had to hear it from Peighton."

"Damn, she talks too much."

"At least she told me. My best friend shoulda' been the one tellin' me."

"I coulda' swore I told you. Oh, I know what happened," Shayna remembered.

"What happened?"

"I was gon' tell you the day we went to Starbucks, but Quiana got to trippin' and it slipped my mind."

"Ummm-huh," Ra'Keeyah said, jokingly.

"I'm for real, Key-Key. Now you know I don't keep nothin' from you."

"I know, girl, but funky-breath Malcolm? He don't got it all. He kinda' crazy," Ra'Keeyah said.

Shayna started cracking up laughing. "I know, right? He does act a little spaced out at times, and his breath smells like he just got finished eatin' a shit sandwich every time he comes to pick me up."

"I bet it do," Ra'Keeyah laughed. "Remember, he was all dirty lookin' in school?"

"Yep. But he hooked up wit' Brick and 'nem, and they cleaned his dusty ass up," Shayna said.

"Brick known for cleanin' niggas up," Ra'Keeyah said, thinking back on the story Brick told her about Bam.

"Money can make almost anybody look good," Shayna said.

"Well, Malcolm need to take some of that money he makin' and go get that shit pumped outta his stomach," Ra'Keeyah laughed.

"I know, man, 'cuz that smell be seepin' outta his pores," Shayna joked.

"You a fool," Ra'Keeyah continued laughing. "I don't see how you can fuck him!" she grimaced.

"I ain't never slept wit' him. I let him think he gon' get some. And as long as he keep gettin' my hair and nails done, buyin' me clothes and shoes, I'm gon' let him continue to think he gon' get some," Shayna laughed.

"Girl, you betta' stop playin' wit' that crazy-ass nigga like that, knowing he ain't wrapped too tight."

"Girl, please, he used to bitches doin' him like that. Every chick he get wit' don't do nothin' but use his dumb ass. And as long as he continue to give me what I want, I will be doin' the same," Shayna stated.

"Okay, don't say I didn't warn you."

"I got this, girl. You know how I get down," Shayna cut her off not wanting to hear what her best friend had to say.

"I know. I just wanna make sure you be all right, that's all."

"I know. Anyway, are you still gon' dance Saturday?"

"I doubt it," Ra'Keeyah said. "Then again, I might. I'll call you and let you know Friday night."

"Quiana gon' fuck you up for not showin' up," Shayna teased.

"Girl, please, I'll beat the fuck outta Quiana."

"Okay, mama. Well, let's get together before then," Shayna suggested. "I'm about to call Malcolm and have him take me to get somethin' to eat. You wanna roll wit' us?"

"I'm straight. Just call me later on."

"Peace out," Shayna said before hanging up.

Ra'Keeyah shook her head and laughed. She knew Shayna was good at getting what she wanted from dudes, but playing Malcolm just didn't sit well with her. Ra'Keeyah closed her eyes and said a quick prayer for her best friend's protection before going in the house.

Chapter Twenty-eight

"I wish you could live here wit' me," Brick said, as he and Ra'Keeyah lay cuddling after making love. "I hate when you have to go home."

Ra'Keeyah smiled at the thought. "I wish I could too, but you know my momma ain't havin' that!"

"She ain't gon' be able to say nothin' when you turn eighteen."

"I know, man, I can't wait either. You think we still gon' be together when I turn eighteen?" Ra'Keeyah asked.

"Now why would you ask me some shit like that?"

"I was just wonderin'."

"Hell, yeah, we gon' be together when you turn eighteen. Shit, we gon' be together when you turn a hundred and eighteen," Brick joked.

"We gon' be too old to do anything," Ra'Keeyah laughed.

"Shit, I'ma be hittin' this ass until I'm two hundred and eighteen," he smiled.

"Whatever," Ra'Keeyah smiled back. Her facial expression became serious as she stared at Brick.

"What's on yo' mind?" he asked.

"Nothin' really. I was just thinkin' about somethin' that happened a couple months ago."

"What is it?" Brick inquired.

Ra'Keeyah hesitated, not really knowing if she wanted the truth or if she would be able to handle the truth. "I got into it wit' Davinette on my birthday 'cuz she told me to tell you that you left your hat at her house."

"What?" Brick grimaced.

"I was at the shop gettin' my hair done, and Davinette told me to tell you that you left your hat at her house," Ra'Keeyah repeated. "Now I don't know if she was tryin'a get under my skin or if she was bein' for real."

"Man, that broad lyin'," Brick said in a raised tone. "I ain't been over to her house!"

"Calm down, baby. That's why I didn't wanna say nothin' 'cuz I knew you would get mad."

"I ain't mad at you. I'm mad 'cuz the broad is lyin' on me. And me leavin' my hat over there. Oh, wait a minute," Brick said, remembering. "I did go over to her house."

"Come again?" Ra'Keeyah asked.

"My mom let the broad use a pan to make lasagna in, and she asked me to go over there and pick it up for her. Her son kept beggin' me to wear my hat while Davinette looked for the pan. So I put it on his head, and when he finally gave it back, it had jelly or somethin' on it. So I told the li'l nigga he could keep the hat," Brick said.

Ra'Keeyah shook her head in disbelief. "Wow. And she tried to make me think there was more to it than what it was."

"I told you before, man, she crazy as hell! And for the record, don't wait so long to tell me nothin' else. If you wanna know somethin' about Brick don't be afraid to ask."

"I see you talkin' in third person again," Ra'Keeyah laughed. "And if I wanna know anything else, I won't hesitate to ask."

"That's my baby," Brick said, leaning over to kiss Ra'Keeyah. "You ready to go?" he asked, rolling out of bed.

"You puttin' me out now?" Ra'Keeyah asked, offended.

"Naw. You said you had to be home by four 'cuz your mom was gettin' off early to take you and Jaylen school shoppin'."

"Oh, right. I forgot all about that." Ra'Keeyah climbed out of bed and started getting dressed.

"Get yo' mind right," Brick said, walking to the bathroom to pee.

His cell phone began to vibrate. Ra'Keeyah wanted badly to pick it up and check the caller ID, but she didn't, fearing he might catch her snooping. Instead, she told Brick his phone was ringing.

"Answer it," he yelled while washing his hands.

Feeling honored, Ra'Keeyah answered the phone. "Hello?" she said proudly.

"Hello, may I speak to Brick, please?" a female asked.

Ra'Keeyah could feel her heart pounding all the way up in her throat. "May I ask who's callin'?" she asked with a slight attitude.

"Tammy."

"Who is it?" Brick yelled from the bathroom.

"Somebody name Tammy," Ra'Keeyah huffed.

"Oh, bring me the phone," Brick stuck his hand out the bathroom door and yelled.

Ra'Keeyah walked over and shoved the phone into his hand before continuing to put on her clothes. She listened as Brick laughed and joked with the chick on the phone. Ra'Keeyah was on fire.

"How dare that nigga talk to another bitch while I'm here," she said, gathering her belongings. Ra'Keeyah finished getting all of her things and took a seat on the edge of the bed waiting for Brick to come out of the bathroom.

"What's that look for?" Brick walked out of the bathroom still smiling, noticing the mug on Ra'Keeyah's face.

"What look?"

"That stank-face look," he said, slipping his clothes back on.

"You trippin'. Get yo' mind right," Ra'Keeyah forced a smile before grabbing her things and heading down the stairs.

Ra'Keeyah sat quietly the entire way home while Brick rambled on about any and everything. The entire ride home Ra'Keeyah argued back and forth with herself about asking Brick who this Tammy chick was. She didn't want to seem like she was insecure so she kept her mouth closed.

"Call me when you get back," Brick said, pulling up in front of Ra'Keeyah's house.

"I will," she said, opening the door.

"What? I don't get no kiss?"

"Oh yeah," she said, leaning over.

"Naw, I'm straight," Brick said, putting his hand up in front of her mouth.

"Okay," Ra'Keeyah said, getting out of the car.

"Hey," Brick called out.

"Yeah?" Ra'Keeyah got back in the car.

"Didn't we just have this talk? I told you if you wanna know somethin' to ask. Tammy is my cousin, knucklehead."

"I didn't ask you nothin' about who you was on the phone wit'," Ra'Keeyah said smartly.

"You didn't have to. Your actions showed it. I don't have shit to hide from you. If I did, I wouldna' had you answer my damn phone."

Ra'Keeyah knew Brick had a point and was embarrassed by her actions. She didn't know what to say.

"I'm sorry," was all she could say.

"Don't let it happen again." Brick reached in his pocket, pulled out a wad of money, and counted out five one-hundred-dollar bills. "Here," he said, handing Ra'Keeyah the money.

"What's this for?" she asked, taking it.

"It's to help get you school shit."

Help out wit' my school shit? This way more than my mom spends on me and Jaylen put together, Ra'Keeyah thought.

"I'm proud of you. I like a woman who's doin' somethin' other than sittin' around relyin' on a man to take care of them."

"Thank you," Ra'Keeyah smiled.

"Buy my li'l dude somethin' too."

"I will."

"You better. I'ma ask him if you bought him somethin'."

"Whatever. I'm always buyin' him somethin'."

"All right, call me later," Brick said.

"Okay." Ra'Keeyah leaned over to give Brick a kiss.

"Don't even try it," he said, blocking her lips again. "You on punishment."

"Punishment?" Ra'Keeyah laughed. "You got me bent, you betta' give me a kiss," she said, pushing Brick's hand down.

"All right, you better go on. The warden gon' pull up and see me sittin' here," Brick joked.

"Ha-ha, very funny," Ra'Keeyah laughed, before getting out of the car.

"I love you," Brick said.

Ra'Keeyah could have sworn Brick just told her he loved her, or maybe her ears were playing tricks on her.

"What you just say?" she asked just to make sure.

"I said I love you," he smiled.

Ra'Keeyah's heart fluttered. "I love you too," she was proud to say.

"I know," Brick smiled, then winked before pulling off.

Ra'Keeyah put the money in her purse before going in the house to shower. She dreaded going school shopping with her mom. Year after year it was the same thing: her mother fussing about how tight her jeans are or how much her shoes cost. It never failed. But this year, Ra'Keeyah didn't have to worry about any of that because this time she had her own money!

After getting dressed, Ra'Keeyah went outside and sat on the porch to wait for her mother to arrive. She glanced across the street. It was weird not seeing Peighton sitting on the front porch or sneaking off to be with Bob T. It had only been a couple days since she went back to Birmingham, but Ra'Keeyah missed her already. She was sad to see her go, but Ra'Keeyah knew she'd be back next summer.

She smiled as her mother and little brother pulled up in the driveway. She grabbed her purse and headed to the car.

"What's up?" Ra'Keeyah spoke when she got in.

"Hey," her mother spoke back as she put the car in reverse and drove off. "Did you talk to Mr. Wilson today like I asked you to?"

"Yeah, I talked to him and told him that he gotta' cut my hours back down since school is bouta' start," Ra'Keeyah lied.

"Did he have a problem wit' it?" her mother asked.

"Naw. He said it's fine."

"Good, 'cuz even though I hate goin' in Mr. Wilson's store unless I just absolutely have to, I will go down there and give him a piece of my mind!"

Ra'Keeyah shook her head and laughed. *You so tough*, she wanted to say. She pulled her iPod out of her purse and put the headphones on. Then she pushed PLAY and listened to music until they pulled up at the mall.

After a few hours of shopping and picking out the clothes she wanted this year, Ra'Keeyah, her mother, and brother decided to go to the food court in the mall to get something to eat.

"Can I go over there and play in the balls, Mommy?" Jaylen asked.

"Are you finished wit' your food?"

"Yeah," he replied, nodding his head.

"Go ahead. You can go play. But stay where I can see you."

"Okay," he smiled before hopping up from the table and running over to the play area.

"I can't believe I had to get that boy size eight," Ra'Keeyah's mom said as she watched her growing son run off. "You wanna talk?"

"About what?"

"About anything. You know this is the first time me and you have been alone together in a long time. I just thought maybe we could talk about some things," her mother said.

"Like what?" Ra'Keeyah asked.

"Let's talk about Marshall."

"What about him?"

"What college is he goin' to? When does he leave for school? Where is his second job?" her mother asked trying to make general conversation.

"I don't know the answer to any of those questions," Ra'Keeyah said not wanting to talk about Marshall at all, but wishing she could share her feelings about Brick with her mom.

"What do y'all talk about when y'all together?" her mother asked, confused.

"We talk about a lot of stuff."

Ra'Keeyah's mother stared at her like she was trying to read her. "Are y'all havin' sex?" her mother blurted out.

"Heck, naw!" Ra'Keeyah grimaced. "What made you ask me somethin' like that?"

"You're always wit' him. And if y'all not really talkin' much y'all gotta be doin' somethin'."

"Ma, just 'cuz I don't know what school he's goin' to or when he leaves for college or what his second job is doesn't mean we're havin' sex," Ra'Keeyah stated, while rolling her eyes.

"I just wanna make sure. Just in case I need to take you to the Planned Parenthood and get you on the pill. I don't want you to be a teenage mother like I was."

"You don't hafta' worry about that, Mom. I don't plan on havin' kids no time soon," Ra'Keeyah assured her mother.

A huge smile swept across Ra'Keeyah's mom's face. Ra'Keeyah turned around to see what her mother was smiling at. Her heart instantly jumped into her throat.

"Speakin' of the devil," her mother said as Marshall walked toward them.

Oh my goodness! What the fuck is he doin' here? Ra'Keeyah panicked.

"Hello, Ms. Jackson and Ra'Keeyah," Marshall said, bending down giving them a hug.

"Well, hello, Marshall. Me and Ra'Keeyah was just talkin' about you."

"I hope in a good way," he joked.

"It was," her mother laughed. "Won't you join us?"

"No, I'm sure he's way too busy to just be sittin' here wit' us doin' nothin'," Ra'Keeyah said quickly.

Ra'Keeyah's mother and Marshall looked at her like she was crazy.

"Actually, I do have to work tonight. I just came out here to pick up a new pair of work shoes," Marshall said.

"Okay. Well, I never get to see you when you be co-min' to pick Ra'Keeyah up. I already be gone to work when you get there." Marshall had a confused look on his face as Ra'Keeyah's mom continued. "Next time y'all go out, try to come a little earlier. I would like to know about your college plans."

"Okay . . ." Marshall answered slowly.

"Ra'Keeyah told me things are gettin' kinda' serious between you two," her mother smiled widely.

Marshall looked over at Ra'Keeyah. "Oh, she did?" he asked. "Wow, I'm glad she let *you* know."

"Okay, Mom, I'm sure Marshall has to get goin'," Ra'Keeyah said nervously. The last thing she needed was for Marshall to bust her out.

"So, when is the next time we're goin' out?" Marshall toyed with Ra'Keeyah.

"You said tomorrow night, remember?" Ra'Keeyah lied. She and Brick had made plans to go see the new *Twilight* movie.

"Oh yeah. Silly me. How could I have forgotten that?" Marshall asked.

"I don't know," Ra'Keeyah let out a nervous chuckle.

"Okay, well, if it's not too late, come in and holla' at me," her mother said.

"Oh, it won't be late. I'm off tomorrow, so I'll be over early," Marshall smiled.

"Okay. Well, I'm not gon' hold you. See you tomor-row," her mother said.

"See y'all later," Marshall said before walking away.

"Y'all make a cute couple," her mother beamed.

"Yeah, we do, don't we?" Ra'Keeyah said unenthused, wanting to go find a rock and crawl up under it.

Chapter Twenty-nine

Ra'Keeyah had been anticipating seeing Brick all day. He had to run out of town but promised Ra'Keeyah he would be back in time to take her to the movies. It was getting harder for Ra'Keeyah to leave each time she had to come home. She wished there was a way she could move in with him permanently. The only way she could think of offhand was over her mother's dead body.

Ra'Keeyah was in the bathroom flat ironing her hair when her mother came in and dropped the bomb on her.

"You didn't hear your phone ringin'?" her mother stood in the doorway and asked.

"No. It's in my room," Ra'Keeyah replied before picking up the comb.

"Oh. Well, Marshall just called and said he's almost here so be ready."

"For what?" Ra'Keeyah grimaced.

"To take you to dinner and a movie, duh!" her mother replied before walking away.

Ra'Keeyah was heated. She didn't think Marshall was really going to try to take her out. She hadn't been anywhere with him in a long time and planned on keeping it that way.

"Oh, I can't stand him!" she huffed before slamming the comb down and going into her room to finish getting dressed. "I shoulda' known this nigga was gon' pull this slick shit!" Ra'Keeyah didn't know what she was going to do. She'd just received a text from Brick stating he was looking forward to tonight. She needed to find an excuse for Marshall and quick.

"Ra'Keeyah, Marshall here," her mother yelled up to her.

"Damn!" she snapped angrily. "I don't wanna go nowhere wit' this goofy-ass nigga!" Ra'Keeyah ranted as she snatched her purse off the bed.

Her mother was standing at the doorway talking to Marshall about college with her back turned as Ra'Keeyah headed down the stairs. She looked over at Marshall who stood in front of her mother and frowned. In return, he greeted her with a huge smile.

"You look nice," Marshall said.

Ra'Keeyah's mother turned around. "You sure do," she smiled.

Ra'Keeyah forced a fake smile and said, "Thank you. Now let's go," she said with authority and stormed out the front door.

"Well, it was nice talkin' to you, Ms. Jackson. My princess is in such a hurry," Marshall laughed.

"Okay. And good luck at Morris Brown College."

"Thank you." Marshall headed out to the car and got in. "What's eating you?" he looked over at Ra'Keeyah and asked.

"I got shit to do tonight! I thought you were just playin' about comin' over here!" Ra'Keeyah snapped. "You got problems!"

"You the one lying to your mother talking about you be out with me and how serious we're getting," Marshall snapped. "And you say *I* got problems?" He started the car and backed out of the driveway.

"Look, the only way my mom will let me out late is if she thinks I'm wit' you, okay?" Ra'Keeyah admitted.

"So you've been using me, and I didn't know any-thing about it," Marshall shook his head. "So who do you really be with?" he asked, not knowing if he really wanted to know the answer. He stared straight-ahead as he drove, not wanting Ra'Keeyah to see the pain in his eyes.

Ra'Keeyah hesitated. She didn't know if she should tell Marshall who she was really going out with. Know-ing the kind of guy he was, she knew his feelings would be crushed.

"Being that you were using me for a scapegoat, the least you could do is tell me the truth," he said, stop-ping at a red light.

Even though Ra'Keeyah hated to admit it, Marshall was right. He did deserve the truth. "I be wit' Brick," she answered.

"Brick, huh?" he asked rhetorically. "So that's who told you about me buying them prophylactics, isn't it?" he looked over at Ra'Keeyah and asked.

Ra'Keeyah didn't answer.

"Isn't it?" Marshall yelled.

"Yeah, that's who told me," she admitted.

"I know because I remember seeing him in the store the day I went and got them condoms for my brother."

"Marshall, look, I never meant to—" Ra'Keeyah started.

"Let me ask you this, then. All those times you told me you were sick or on punishment, you were lying, weren't you? Just so you could go out with Brick?" Marshall asked, cutting her off.

The look in Marshall's eyes kept Ra'Keeyah from tell-ing him the truth. "No. That's not true. I was sick or on punishment. You know how my mom is," she pleaded.

"I don't believe you," Marshall said as he began to speed.

"Marshall, you really need to slow down," Ra'Keeyah begged. "And where are we goin'?"

"Are you afraid?"

"Actually, I am," she answered.

"Are you be afraid when Brick be driving fast in his Camaro?"

"Whatever, Marshall," she said, pretending not to be fazed.

"Well, I'll tell you what. Since you've been using me, I'm about to use you. We are about to go out to dinner and to the movies. So whatever plans you had, you better cancel them!" Marshall said as he continued to drive to the outskirts of town.

"It's okay. We can go eat and to the movies. I'll just reschedule my plans for tomorrow."

About twenty-five minutes later, Marshall pulled the car over and put it in park.

"What are you doin'?" Ra'Keeyah asked, confused.

"Do you actually think I'm gon' to spend my hard earned cash on takin' you out to eat and to the movies? And I know I'm not the person you want to be with right now. What type of fool do you actually think I am?" Marshall frowned. "My whole intentions were on takin' yo' ass way out in the country and puttin' you out my car. But you ain't worth my energy or no more of my gas!" he snapped.

Ra'Keeyah wondered what had happened to all the proper language she was used to hearing coming out of Marshall's mouth.

"You cute and all and got a bad-ass body, but you ain't all that! I done seen and had better! Now get the fuck outta my car!" he snapped.

Ra'Keeyah's mouth flew open. She was shocked. She had never heard Marshall speak this way before.

"How am I supposed to get home, Marshall?" Ra'Kee-yah asked.

"What you askin' me for? I don't give a fuck how you get home. You betta' click the heels of them sandals you got on. And the next time I see your mom, I'm gon' tell her the truth about who you really be wit'! Ain't no more usin' me!"

"You a real live asshole!" Ra'Keeyah snapped as she opened the door.

"And you a real live, lyin'-ass stuck-up bitch!" Marshall retorted. "Now hurry up and get out. I got some pussy to go get."

Ra'Keeyah couldn't believe the way Marshall was acting. She grabbed her purse and stepped out of the car. Before she could say anything else, he sped off with the door still open, leaving her in the middle of nowhere.

"What the fuck just happened?" Ra'Keeyah asked herself as she looked around. "I can't believe this corny-ass nigga just put me outta his car."

Ra'Keeyah wasn't familiar with the neighborhood she was in so she needed to get out of there and fast. She contemplated calling her mom, but quickly changed her mind, knowing she would have a lot of explaining to do. She wanted to call Brick, but didn't feel like answering questions from him either. So the only other choice she had was to call a taxi. Ra'Keeyah pulled out her cell and tried dialing the taxi number but could get no signal.

"What the fuck am I gon' do?" she asked herself and started walking, checking her phone for a signal every step of the way. What seemed like two hours later, but in reality was only thirty minutes, Ra'Keeyah arrived at a gas station. "Do y'all have a phone I can use?" she asked a big burly white guy with a big bushy beard and lightning bolt tattoos on the side of his neck.

"Out there," he said, pointing to a payphone.

"The payphone? I didn't even know they still had those around," she joked lightly, but the guy didn't crack a smile.

She dug in her purse for some change but came up empty-handed. "Do you have change for a twenty?" she asked the guy.

"We don't give out change. You gotta buy somethin'," he said sternly.

Ra'Keeyah rolled her eyes before picking up a pack of Big Red gum.

"You have to spend at least a dollar."

"Wow," Ra'Keeyah replied before grabbing a bag of plain Jones chips and laying them on the counter along with the gum.

After the store clerk rang up Ra'Keeyah's items, she handed him a twenty-dollar bill. When he dropped her change in her hand all she had was four pennies, plus nineteen dollars.

"I still don't have enough to use the payphone. I need change for a dollar now."

"Read the sign," he said pointing. "We don't give out change."

What the fuck! Ra'Keeyah thought. She was on fire. She wanted to go off on the store clerk and would have if this store was in her neck of the woods. Ra'Keeyah walked over to the cooler and grabbed two Coca-Colas that were on sale two for $2.50. She then walked up to the register and handed him a five-dollar bill, knowing he would have to give her two quarters in change. The clerk rang up the items and handed her $2.43 back. "I'm supposed to get $2.50 back," she said to the clerk.

"Tax," he stated.

By this time Ra'Keeyah wanted to wring this guy's neck, and if he wasn't so big, she would have tried to.

She let out a deep sigh and looked down at the floor. Lying by her foot was a dime. Ra'Keeyah smiled and picked it up and walked toward the door.

"Have a good night," the store clerk called out as Ra'Keeyah walked out the door.

"Fuck you," Ra'Keeyah mumbled as she headed over to the payphone. "Out of order? Out of fuckin' order?" she repeated the words on the sign that hung from the payphone. "What the fuck?" Ra'Keeyah was furious as she headed back toward the store. She noticed the sinister grin on the clerk's face as she walked through the door. "Is there another payphone around here anywhere?" she asked in a raised tone.

"'Bout five miles up the road," he smirked.

"What the fuck? Five miles up the damn road?" Ra'Kee-yah screamed as tears clouded her vision and she stood in the middle of the store yelling. "You knew the damn phone was broke when you sent me out there."

"I'm gonna have to ask you to leave, miss," the clerk said.

"If you would let me use the damn phone I can get outta this hick-ass town!" Ra'Keeyah yelled as tears of anger streamed down her face.

"Is there a problem in here? I heard all the yelling and screaming from outside," a highway patrol officer walked through the door and asked.

"Yeah, Stevie, this broad here is flippin' out 'cuz the payphone is broke. I think she needs to be admitted to the psych ward for an evaluation or somethin'," the store clerk smiled.

"Ain't shit wrong wit' me. All I'm tryin'a do is get the hell outta this town. I kept askin' him for change for the payphone, and he wouldn't give it to me. When I finally got change, I went out to the payphone, and it's out of order. Oh just forget it!" Ra'Keeyah yelled before burying her face in the palms of her hand and crying like a baby.

Customers were standing around watching in astonishment as Ra'Keeyah boohooed.

The officer placed his hand on Ra'Keeyah's shoulder. "Calm down, ma'am. Here, wipe your face," he said, handing Ra'Keeyah a handkerchief.

Ra'Keeyah took the handkerchief and wiped the snot and tears away. "Thank you. I know I must look ridiculous standing here cryin'," she said looking up at the officer, recognizing the face. "Steve?" she asked, shocked.

"LisaRaye?" he asked with a smile.

"Yeah," she smiled back. Ra'Keeyah was relieved to see a familiar face.

"What are you doin' way out here?" he asked.

"It's a long story. But can you please get me outta here?"

"Where do you know this broad from?" the clerk grimaced.

"Let's just say she's an old friend," Steve smiled before escorting Ra'Keeyah out of the store. "I haven't see you in a while. I've been going to the parties, hoping to see you there, but you never show up."

"I know. My mom started a new job, and I have to keep my little brother for her on Saturdays now. That's why I haven't been showin' up," Ra'Keeyah lied.

"Well, let me know the next time you wanna make some money," Steve said, opening up the back door to his cruiser so Ra'Keeyah could get in.

Ra'Keeyah couldn't pass up the chance to make another easy five hundred dollars. "I'll be there Saturday," she said, climbing in the backseat of the car.

"Great! I'll see you there," Steve smiled as he climbed into the cruiser. "Where to?"

Ra'Keeyah gave Steve directions to Shayna's house before attempting to get comfortable in the tiny backseat. She stared out the window as Steve rambled on about how much he enjoyed having sex with her and couldn't wait until Saturday. Ra'Keeyah still couldn't believe the man who had paid her five hundred dollars to sleep with her was a state highway patrol officer.

After dropping her off, Ra'Keeyah couldn't wait to tell Shayna how her day had gone. She gave Shayna a blow-by-blow description. At the end of her story, Shayna was ready to hunt Marshall down and stomp a mud hole in his ass. After convincing her best friend he wasn't worth it, Ra'Keeyah and Shayna smoked a blunt to calm their nerves, then laughed and talked until Brick came and picked her up.

Chapter Thirty

As Ra'Keeyah sat on her bed putting on lotion she began thinking about her life with Brick and how happy he made her. She knew she had to be sprung because she felt bad lying to him and saying she had to babysit Jaylen. Ra'Keeyah knew she couldn't keep goin' on like that so she made up her mind that tonight would be her last night dancing, at least for a while. She knew Shayna would understand, but it would take a lot of convincing, which she wasn't about to do, for Quiana to.

Ra'Keeyah had less than a month before Marshall was to leave for college, so she didn't know who or what she was going to use for an excuse to spend time with Brick after that. She would just wait when the time came to deal with it. Right now, all she wanted to do was live in the moment.

"What you mean Calvin didn't rent the suite tonight?" Ra'Keeyah asked as she walked into Shayna's house.

Ra'Keeyah instantly became disgusted when she walked in. She had seen it messy before, but nothing quite like this. People were everywhere. Some were laid on the sofa as if they lived there, while another guy sat in the old, dirty recliner half-asleep and scratching the skin off his arm. He looked just like her daddy did after he'd finished sticking his "insulin needle," as he used to call it, into his arm. Beer cans and cigarette butts decorated the chipped coffee table, and the smell of ass reeked throughout the front room. Ra'Keeyah knew she couldn't have been the only one in the house to bear witness to the smell. She was amazed at how Shayna and Quiana continued talking like living this way was normal.

"So where we supposed to dance at then?" Quiana asked, stepping over a pizza box on the floor.

"Calm down, y'all. Let's go talk in my room." Shayna led her girls out of the midst of all dope fiends and drunks and into her bedroom. "Okay, Calvin's nephew, Richard, said we can use his condo to dance," Shayna replied once she closed her room door. "So everything is under control."

"That's cool. Shit, wherever we dance at we still makin' money," Quiana smiled while taking a seat on Shayna's bed.

Ra'Keeyah shoved over a pile of clothes before taking a seat next to Quiana. "What's the catch?" she asked, knowing there had to be one.

"The catch to what?" Shayna replied, walking into the middle of her bedroom floor, kicking dirty clothes and shoes along the way.

"You need to clean your room," Ra'Keeyah said, looking around at the clutter that was everywhere. Shayna had boxes upon boxes of new shoes and new clothes with the tags still on them all over the bed, floor, and some even managed to make it to the closet. Blunt casings and wrappers were all over the dresser and floor. The room was a total disaster area. "This don't make sense," she laughed.

"Clean up for what? You seen the rest of the house, right? So why should one room be clean when all the rest of 'em fucked up?" Shayna asked.

"You got a point there, but anyway, like I was sayin', what's the catch to us dancin' at Richard's condo?" Ra'Keeyah asked.

"You always readin' too much into shit!" Quiana frowned.

"Shut up!" Ra'Keeyah spat.

Shayna hesitated before speaking. "Well, Richard said he wouldn't have a problem wit' us usin' his condo if him and a couple of his buddies were allowed to come watch."

"Okay, well, that's more money for us," Ra'Keeyah said, trying to go out with a bang, being that tonight was her last night dancing for a while.

"See?" Quiana smiled.

"For free," Shayna added quickly.

"You got me fucked up!" Ra'Keeyah and Quiana both snapped simultaneously.

"Why not? I don't see nothin' wrong wit' his nephew and friends watchin' for free," Shayna said.

"For one, I'm already out here degradin' myself for these old perverted-ass men, but at least I'm gettin' paid for it. Do you actually think I'm gon' belittle myself for *free?* And you only think it's okay 'cuz it's Calvin's nephew!" Ra'Keeyah replied with an attitude.

"I'm wit' y'all on that, Ra'Keeyah. You be the main one talkin' about makin' money and make these men pay for this or that, and now that Calvin's nephew and friends wanna join in for free, you game?" Quiana frowned. "I ain't wit' that!"

"Quiana, please, you been degradin' yourself for free as long as I can remember," Shayna snapped, and then turned her attention back to Ra'Keeyah.

Quiana had had enough of Shayna's fly-ass mouth to last her a lifetime. Shayna had been talking crazy to her ever since she could remember and she'd always let it slide, but not today; enough was enough!

"Hold up! And while I've been degradin' myself, what the fuck do you think you been doin?" You been a fuckin' ho ever since I can remember! And you always wanna talk down to me like you better than some-damn-body. Bitch, we one and the same," Quiana snapped.

"Shut up talkin' to me, Quiana! And I am betta' than you, and a whole lotta otha' mutha'fuckas too," Shayna said, waving her cousin off.

"You kill me! You always tryin'a play the little Ms. Innocent role. You ain't innocent, Shayna," Quiana grimaced.

"Come on, y'all, we need to stay focused here," Ra'Keeyah said, trying to be the mediator.

"No, let the bitch talk. It seems like that's all she ever wanna do anyway," Shayna spat.

"You don't want me to start talkin'," Quiana warned.

"Do you," Shayna replied and waited for Quiana to open her mouth so she could go up in it like a dentist. "Anyways, Ra'Keeyah, this bitch gets on my nerves. Ever since I can remember, all this worthless-ass ho have done was talk stupid!"

"Worthless? Bitch, you the one worthless!" Quiana jumped up and said.

"Come on, y'all, damn. Y'all always arguin'. Can't we all just get along?" Ra'Keeyah joked.

"I ain't thinkin' about Quiana," Shayna said.

"And Quiana ain't thinkin' about you either," Quiana said, rolling her eyes.

"When we was little, she used to pee in the bed and lay in it, and I think that done somethin' to her brain," Shayna laughed.

Ra'Keeyah laughed too. "You a fool."

"You always tellin' Ra'Keeyah about shit I used to do. I bet you ain't never told her about none of the shit you used to do, have you?" Quiana asked, tauntingly.

"Shut up talkin' to me, and I ain't gon' tell you no more," Shayna said in a more serious tone.

"Naw, I ain't shuttin' up this time. My fuckin' mouth been closed long enough." Tears filled Quiana's eyes as she began talking, letting Ra'Keeyah know things were about to get serious, maybe a little too serious. "I bet you ain't never told Ra'Keeyah how yo' momma used to make you have sex wit' niggas just so she could get high, have you? Or how many dicks she made you suck for a lousy-ass twenty-dolla' rock."

Ra'Keeyah's eyes bucked, and her mouth nearly hit the floor. She was confused. She thought they were playing like they normally did, but what just came out of Quiana's mouth told her otherwise.

"Tell Ra'Keeyah how many tricks you had to turn for yo' momma 'cuz you was way prettier than her, and the dope boys didn't wanna touch her." The way Quiana stared at Shayna when she spoke was cold and antagonizing.

"Oh my goodness! Y'all come on, don't do this. Let's just get dressed so we can go make this money," Ra'Keeyah begged frantically, seeing things were about to get way out of hand.

Shayna stood in the middle of her bedroom floor looking at Quiana like she had just lost her damn mind. She couldn't believe the words coming out of her mouth. Tears formed in her eyes as her own cousin continued to bring up her ugly past. She didn't know if the tears were from betrayal or from the harsh childhood she had to endure. Shayna wanted to pounce on Quiana and beat her to a bloody pulp to make her shut up, but something wouldn't let her move. She was stuck in one spot frozen in the middle of her bedroom while her cousin continued adding fuel to the fire.

"I bet you never even told Ra'Keeyah why Joe, or should I call him you and yo' momma's boyfriend, or the father of the baby yo' momma made you have an abortion wit', jump at yo' every beck and call, have you? 'Cuz he's afraid that you might turn him in to the police for molestin' you since you was twelve. But do you think her momma gave a fuck? Naw, she didn't. As long as Joe continued to feed her crack habit, everything was cool," Quiana smirked.

"Enough! I don't wanna hear no more! Stop tellin' all these lies," Ra'Keeyah yelled. She couldn't understand why Shayna was standing in the middle of her bedroom crying while Quiana was making up all these accusations about her.

"Lyin'? If I was lyin' I wouldn't be standin' here reliving our past while this bitch for the first time in her life standing here with her mouth closed! It wasn't only her mother who made her do those things. I had to do them too," Quiana cried angrily.

Ra'Keeyah realized Quiana's bottled up words that were rushing out were more of a relief to get them off of her chest than words to hurt Shayna because she too had been forced to endure the same horrendous acts as her cousin.

There was an awkward silence in the room. No one made a move. Ra'Keeyah looked at Shayna, and then over at Quiana. Her heart went out to both of the girls. Ra'Keeyah could always sense that they had a dark and mysterious past; she just never realized how dark and mysterious it was until now. And she thought she had a hard life. Listening to Quiana rehash their past made Ra'Keeyah's love for her mother even stronger, and she promised herself as soon as she got home she was going to wrap her arms around her mother and tell her how much she loved and appreciated her.

Shayna wiped her tears away, only to have more follow. She looked over at Quiana as if she was trying to find the right words to say, but nothing came out. She then looked over at Ra'Keeyah and shook her head in disbelief. She couldn't believe her own flesh and blood had revealed dark secrets they'd sworn they take to their graves, like it was nothing.

After a few more minutes of silence, Shayna cleared her throat. "Bitch, I hope you catch AIDS and die a slow, miserable death." With that being said, she walked out of her bedroom, leaving Ra'Keeyah shocked and Quiana relieved.

Chapter Thirty-one

Over the next several weeks, Shayna was MIA and Ra'Keeyah was starting to worry. She wasn't returning any phone calls or text messages, and she hadn't been to school. Every time Ra'Keeyah went by the house, someone would always come to the door and say she's not home. She decided to ask Quiana if she had seen her, but Quiana hadn't been an easy one to catch up with either. Ra'Keeyah had only caught glimpses of her in the hallway during fourth period while they were switching classes. Mr. Ephraim, Ra'Keeyah's fourth-period English teacher, was handing out after-school detentions like government cheese, so there was no way she could be late showing up to his class.

Ra'Keeyah sat at their favorite lunch table hoping to catch Quiana. She didn't just want to find out where Shayna was, but also wanted to know what had possessed Quiana to air their dirty laundry out like she had. They knew Ra'Keeyah well enough to know she'd never utter a word of their business to anyone. It was the principle of why she'd played her own flesh and blood that way. Ra'Keeyah was just about to get up from the lunchroom table when she saw Quiana making her way down the stairs. Quiana acted like she didn't see Ra'Keeyah and continued walking to the food line.

"Oh, so this bitch gon' act like I'm invisible," Ra'Keeyah said, getting up from the table and walking over to get in line as well. "Quiana," she called out.

"'Sup?" she turned around and asked.

"You didn't see me sittin' over at the table?"

"Yeah, I saw you. What you want me to do? Run over there and give you a hug?" Quiana asked smartly.

Ra'Keeyah closed her eyes and took a deep breath. "You talk to Shayna?"

"Naw, that's yo' best friend. You ain't talked to her? You know she don't fuck wit' me."

"Can you blame her for not fuckin' wit' you?" Ra'Keeyah asked.

"You know, I really don't give a fuck! I ain't pressed. I got sicka' her always tellin' mutha'fuckas about what I used to do; now she see how that shit feels. Fuck her!" Quiana spat.

"Wow! Man, y'all family," Ra'Keeyah said, surprised.

"Fuck family. That bitch can't say nothin' else to me in life. Now if you'll excuse me, I'm bouta' get somethin' to eat," Quiana said, walking away from Ra'Keeyah.

Ra'Keeyah was left speechless. She was so used to Shayna and Quiana falling out, then making up the same day. She could tell by the sound in Quiana's voice that this time there was no making up.

Shayna was heavy on Ra'Keeyah's mind all day, and all she could do was hope and pray that she was okay. She couldn't concentrate on any of her classes and wanted the school day to hurry up and end. As soon as the bell rang, Ra'Keeyah quickly gathered her books and headed for the door.

"Ms. Jackson," Mrs. Sanchez, her Spanish teacher, called out.

Ra'Keeyah sighed before turning around. "Yeah?" she huffed.

"I would like to speak with you for a minute, por favor."

Ra'Keeyah walked over to the desk and stood. Mrs. Sanchez pulled out the test they'd taken at the beginning of class and handed it to Ra'Keeyah. Ra'Keeyah took the test and looked at her grade.

"Okay, I got an F. I didn't study," she admitted, throwing her hands up.

"I could tell your mind was preoccupied with something else while you were taking this test," Mrs. Sanchez said, laying the paper back down on her desk. "Is everything okay at home?"

Ra'Keeyah wanted to crack up laughing. *Why is that the first thing people ask?* "Yeah, everything's cool at my house. I just got a lot on my mind today, that's all."

"Well, if you need to speak with a counselor, let me know and I can set that up for you."

"A counselor?" Ra'Keeyah grimaced.

"I just want you to know that we're here to help our students who are dealing with certain kinds of issues," Mrs. Sanchez smiled.

"Okay, I'll be able to sleep better at night knowin' that you're here for me," Ra'Keeyah said sarcastically. "Can I go now? My ride is outside waitin' on me."

"You may be excused."

Ra'Keeyah turned and quickly exited the classroom. She couldn't wait to see Brick's smiling face. As she exited the school doors, like clockwork, Brick was sitting out front waiting on her with one or two groupies, as she called them, all on his jock. Ra'Keeyah wasn't the least bit bothered by it, because they recognized what it was when she stepped on the scene. She smiled widely as she headed to the truck. Her smile slowly faded when she noticed Quiana leaning inside the driver-side window skinning and grinning all up in Brick's face.

Brick was so engrossed in the conversation he was holding he didn't even notice Ra'Keeyah standing at the passenger-side door. "Uh-huh," Ra'Keeyah said, clearing her throat.

"Oh, what's up, li'l mama?" Brick turned his attention toward Ra'Keeyah and smiled.

"I guess I better let you go," Quiana smirked. Brick was so happy to see his girl he didn't even respond.

"What she want?" Ra'Keeyah asked getting in and buckling her seat belt.

"Nothin' really. Just talkin' about the block party and how much fun y'all had," he replied.

"Well, I don't want you talkin' to her," Ra'Keeyah said.

"What's wrong wit' her? I thought that was yo' girl?" Brick asked.

"Can you just do that for me, please?" Ra'Keeyah asked, not wanting to go into any details.

"Whateva' you say," Brick smiled before pulling off. "You hungry?" he looked over at Ra'Keeyah and asked.

"I'm starvin'. What we eatin'?"

"I gotta' taste for some breakfast. I want some pancakes, sausage, and eggs," Brick said.

"Let's go to the Cracker Barrel then."

"Cracker Barrel it is," Brick said hitting the expressway.

After Brick dropped Ra'Keeyah off at home, she went to her room and lay across her bed. She tried calling Shayna once again and after getting no response, sent her a text asking her to call. Ra'Keeyah didn't know what else to do. All she could do was sit back and wait for Shayna to contact her.

As she lay across her bed doing her homework, her mother stuck her head into her room. "Shayna, downstairs," she said.

Ra'Keeyah sat straight up. "She is?" She put on her house slippers and quickly headed downstairs. A huge burden was lifted off Ra'Keeyah's chest once she laid eyes on her best friend.

"Hey, mama," Shayna smiled.

"Girl, I'm gon' kill you. Had me all worried about you and shit," Ra'Keeyah fussed.

"Hi, Shayna," Jaylen said, walking into the living room.

"What's up, Jay-Jay," Shayna smiled. "He gettin' so big."

"Who you tellin'?" Ra'Keeyah agreed. "Let's go outside on the porch."

The two best friends walked out on the porch. Ra'Kee-yah noticed Joe sitting out front in the car and instantly got heated. The thought of what he'd done to her best friend when she was younger had her wanting to throw an alley red through his windshield. Shayna sat down on the swing, and Ra'Keeyah sat down next to her. For the first few minutes they both were silent. Shayna was trying to collect the right words to say while Ra'Keeyah was trying to calm her attitude.

"How come you ain't been returnin' no texts or calls?" Ra'Keeyah finally asked.

"I didn't wanna face you 'cuz I didn't know what to say," Shayna admitted.

"About what?"

"My past and all the shit Quiana told you. I didn't want you to look at me differently. Like I'm some kind of freak." Tears formed in her eyes. "I don't want things to change between us."

Tears formed in Ra'Keeyah's eyes as well. "Shayna, we've been friends since the second grade, and I've never judged you, so I wouldn't start now. I don't look at you no different. You're still my best friend; you're still Shayna to me, and I still love you the same. Matter of fact, I love you even more, knowin' all the shit you went through and still survived."

"Oh, wow, you sound like a homo," Shayna laughed through tears.

"I know, right?" Ra'Keeyah laughed too as the tears flowed.

"No, but for real, I love you too. And I'm glad to have you as my best friend," Shayna said, leaning over and giving Ra'Keeyah a hug.

"I'm glad to have you as my best friend too. But I tell you what. You bet' not ever have me worried about yo' ass like that no more," Ra'Keeyah smiled.

"I won't," Shayna laughed.

"Promise me," Ra'Keeyah demanded.

"I promise, girl," Shayna said while laughing. She stood up from the swing. "I better get goin'. Joe waitin' on me."

"Ummph," Ra'Keeyah grunted.

"Ra'Keeyah?" Shayna warned.

"Okay, okay," Ra'Keeyah threw her hands up as if she was surrendering.

"I'll call you tomorrow," Shayna said, walking off the porch.

"You better," Ra'Keeyah threatened.

"I will."

"Hey, Ra'Keeyah," Joe hollered out the window.

Ra'Keeyah ate crow and quickly threw her hand up for the sake of her best friend.

Ra'Keeyah watched as Shayna climbed into Joe's minivan. She had so many unanswered questions as she watched them pull off. Ra'Keeyah couldn't understand how Shayna could deal with Joe after all he'd done to her. Or why her mother had never pressed charges on him and still continued to keep him around. She decided these weren't questions you'd asked someone. She was just grateful her best friend was okay.

Chapter Thirty-two

Ra'Keeyah was in her room getting ready for the romantic night Brick had planned for them when her mother rushed into her room.

"Ra'Keeyah, I need you to keep Jaylen for me. Nancy had a heart attack, and I need to go up to the hospital before I go to work," her mother said quickly.

Of all the nights for Aunt Nancy to have a damn heart attack, Ra'Keeyah thought. As much as she wanted to tell her mother no, she agreed, not that she would have had much of a choice anyway.

"Call me and let me know how she's doin'," Ra'Keeyah said disappointed.

"I will, and tell Marshall I'm sorry," her mother said while rushing down the stairs and out the door.

Ra'Keeyah sat on the edge of her bed. She had really been looking forward to the full night of pampering Brick had planned. They were going to start out with a nice romantic dinner, then take a nice bubble bath together before he gave her a much-needed massage, and then, of course, end the night with passionate lovemaking. Now her night would consist of eating pizza, watching Nickelodeon and the Disney Channel, and reading tons of Dr. Seuss books.

Ra'Keeyah called Brick and broke the news to him. Like always, he came up with a solution. He suggested Ra'Keeyah bring Jaylen along and they all have fun together. Instead of a romantic dinner, they would take

Jaylen to Chuck E. Cheese and bowling, and then, since Jaylen loved video games, they could end the night playing the PlayStation 3.

Pleased with the plans, Ra'Keeyah changed into something more comfortable.

"Jaylen," she called out while tying up her tennis shoes.

"What?" he hollered from his room.

"Find you somethin' decent to wear. We bouta' go."

Jaylen ran out of his room and stood in his sister's doorway. "Where we goin'?"

"It's a surprise," she said.

"I don't like surprises," Jaylen replied.

"Okay, I'll tell you, but you gotta' promise you won't tell Mommy."

"I promise," he said quickly.

"I mean it, Jaylen. If you tell her you will never go anywhere wit' me again," Ra'Keeyah warned.

"I said I wasn't gon' tell Mommy. Did I tell her any of our other secrets?" he asked smartly.

Ra'Keeyah thought for a brief second. "You right. Well, we're goin' to Chuck E. Cheese and bowlin' wit' Brick," Ra'Keeyah said.

"We are?" Jaylen asked with big eyes.

"Yep," she smiled seeing the happy look on her brother's face. "Now go get ready."

Jaylen ran out of his sister's room as fast as he could and back into his own. He put on the best-looking outfit in his closet before hurrying back into Ra'Keeyah's room. "I'm ready," he said.

"That was quick," she laughed.

"When is he comin'?"

"He's on his way. Come on, let's go wait on him," Ra'Keeyah said, grabbing her cell phone and turning it off. She tossed it in her purse not wanting any interruptions tonight. She then headed downstairs with Jaylen following behind her.

As soon as Ra'Keeyah and Jaylen walked outside on the porch to sit and wait for Brick, he pulled up in front of the house and got out. He walked around to the passenger's side of the car and opened the door.

"Whoooa, look at that car! I seen one of those on TV," Jaylen said excited.

Ra'Keeyah shook her head and smiled as they made their way down the walk.

"Hey, li'l man," Brick smiled, as he lifted up the front seat so Jaylen could get in the back.

"'Sup?" Jaylen replied, trying to sound cool.

"What's up, li'l mama?" Brick smiled before leaning in giving Ra'Keeyah a kiss.

"Ewwwww, y'all nasty," Jaylen giggled.

"Shut up, boy," Ra'Keeyah said, laughing. Brick laughed as well.

He walked back around to the driver's side of the car and got in. "You got yo' seat belt on?" he looked back at Jaylen and asked.

"Yep," he answered happily.

"All right, well, let's go have some fun," Brick said pulling off.

Brick laughed and joked with Jaylen the entire ride to Chuck E. Cheese, and once they got there, they played all the games together. Brick was acting like a big kid. He was enjoying the games more than Jaylen. Ra'Keeyah laughed when Jaylen and Brick had an eating contest, seeing who could eat the most slices of pizza. Of course, Brick's greedy butt won. Ra'Keeyah didn't mind that they weren't paying her any attention. She enjoyed watching Brick spend time with Jaylen, since that his father had never taken the time to do so. Watching Brick interact with Jaylen made Ra'Keeyah

think of how good of a father he'd be to his own child, if
or when he decided to have one.

After spending two hours at the bowling alley letting
Jaylen win, they decided to go back to Brick's house
and play a game. Jaylen and Brick played the PS3 while
Ra'Keeyah sat back and watched. She had never seen
her brother this happy before. Seeing him smile made
her smile. She was tired of listening to all the yelling
and screaming they were doing so she decided to go
upstairs and lie on Brick's bed, and before too long, she
drifted off to sleep.

Brick kicked off his tennis shoes and removed his
shirt before lying in the bed beside Ra'Keeyah. He
looked over at her and smiled. Brick couldn't resist
waking her up by planting a loud, sloppy, wet kiss on
her cheek.

"Stop it, boy," she giggled. "Where's Jaylen?"

"Downstairs asleep on the couch," Brick answered
before wrapping his arms around her.

"On that white leather couch?"

"He ain't gon' hurt it. And if he do, I'll buy a new
one."

"Thanks, Brick," Ra'Keeyah said sincerely.

"Thanks for what?" Brick asked, confused.

"For takin' the time to play wit' Jaylen. He needed
that. I have never seen my brother so happy before,"
Ra'Keeyah said.

"Man, I love that li'l nigga. He funny and very outspoken," Brick laughed.

"Who you tellin'?" Ra'Keeyah laughed too.

"He said his birthday is comin' up. I'ma buy him a
PlayStation 3. He said he got an older Xbox, but I can
tell he like the PlayStation better."

"Oh, wow. He'll love that."

"I'm gon' start spendin' more time wit' him. He's my
new best friend," Brick smiled.

"That's what's up," Ra'Keeyah said happily.

"Now that I'm finished playin' wit' your brotha, it's time for me to play wit' you," he said, kissing Ra'Keeyah on the lips.

"How do you know I wanna play wit' you?" she joked.

Brick reached down, unzipped his pants, and pulled his manhood out. "You might not wanna play wit' me, but I know you can't resist playin' wit' Rufus."

Ra'Keeyah eyed the rock-hard piece of meat Brick held in his hand. "You right. I can't," she said, rolling over on top of Brick and kissing him. She sat up and stared down at him. They looked into each other's eyes for what seemed like an eternity, as if they were trying to search each other's souls.

"Get up," Brick finally said.

Ra'Keeyah rolled over on her back and removed her clothes while Brick stood and did the same. He climbed back into bed and kissed her. She spread her legs and waited for Brick to grab a condom, but he never did. Instead, he entered her throbbing walls bare. Ra'Keeyah couldn't believe it, and neither could he. Being inside of Ra'Keeyah without protection solidified the way he felt about her. He was in love and wasn't afraid to admit it. Feeling Ra'Keeyah's wetness on his manhood was the most real feeling Brick had experienced in a long time, making him cum a little too quick.

"I'm sorry," Brick said, embarrassed.

"It's okay. I know I got that good shit!" Ra'Keeyah bragged.

"Whateva', man," Brick laughed, before rolling over on his back.

Ra'Keeyah looked over at the clock. "I guess you better get me and Jaylen home before Cruella De Vil gets off work," she laughed.

"Man, I wish you didn't have to go," he said, cuddling up against Ra'Keeyah for a few seconds before getting out of bed to get dressed.

"Who you tellin'?" Ra'Keeyah replied, climbing out of bed to get dressed as well.

Ra'Keeyah and Brick got dressed and headed downstairs. They both smiled at Jaylen who was still knocked out on the sofa, holding the toy gun he'd got with all the tickets he won at Chuck E. Cheese.

"You gon' have to wake him up, 'cuz I can't carry his big butt," Ra'Keeyah looked over at Brick and said.

"That's 'cuz you weak," he said, bending down and picking Jaylen up off the sofa. Jaylen was still asleep when Brick laid him in the backseat. "He musta' really been tired."

"I'm sure he was. All that playin' y'all did," Ra'Keeyah laughed.

"I really enjoyed myself," Brick said walking around to the driver's side of the car.

"I can tell," she laughed before getting in the car.

Brick turned on Ra'Keeyah's street, and she just knew her eyes had to have been playing tricks on her. She swore she saw a woman standing in front of her house with trash bags in front her and puffing on a cigarette that looked exactly like her mother.

"Fuck!" Ra'Keeyah snapped.

"Is that yo' mutha, man?" Brick asked, surprised.

"Yes. This ain't gon' be good. Jaylen, wake up," Ra'Keeyah said nervously as her heart pounded.

"Huh?" he asked, rubbing his eyes.

"You want me to pull up in front of the house?" Brick asked Ra'Keeyah.

"Yeah, no, I don't know. You might as well," she stammered, wanting to go ahead and get it over with.

Brick was nervous like he was the one in trouble as he pulled up in front of the house. "Hey, li'l mama, she look mad as hell," Brick said as if Ra'Keeyah didn't notice the scowl on her face.

"I know. Here we go," Ra'Keeyah said, taking a deep breath before opening up the car door and getting out. She lifted up the backseat and let Jaylen out.

"Hey, Mommy, look what I got," Jaylen said, showing her his gun.

"That's nice, now go on in the house," she said, never taking her eyes off Ra'Keeyah.

Ra'Keeyah watched as Jaylen ran up the walk and into the house, wishing she could do the same, but she knew better than that.

"I'll call you later," Ra'Keeyah said to Brick.

Brick was speechless. He didn't know if he should say okay or just pull off without saying anything.

Ra'Keeyah's mother bent down and looked in the car at Brick and said, "Hold on a minute, she gon' need a ride."

"A ride where, Mommy?" Ra'Keeyah asked.

"The fuck away from *my* house. Where the fuck you been, Ra'Keeyah?"

"I took Jaylen to Chuck E. Cheese and bowlin'," Ra'Keeyah said, hoping her mother would give her a pass, being that she did something with her little brother.

"I thought you were supposed to go somewhere wit' Marshall?" her mother asked, busting her out.

"I was, but—"

"Quit lyin'," her mother said cutting her off. "I called Marshall's phone for you since you wouldn't answer yours. I felt bad 'cuz I was keepin' you from your date with him. I was callin' to tell you to drop your brother off over at Nancy's 'cuz they sent her home. She ain't have no damn heart attack; she had gas built up in her chest! When I talked to him he told me everything."

"Let me explain, Mommy," Ra'Keeyah said.

"Explain what? That you a big-ass liar?"

"No."

"No, what? So you tellin' me that every time you left you was leavin' wit' Marshall and not this drug dealer," her mother said pointing over at Brick.

"Wow," Brick said loudly, making Ra'Keeyah and her mother look back him.

"And you had my fuckin' son around this nigga?" her mother asked angrily.

Ra'Keeyah knew her mother was heated because she never heard her use the "N" word before.

"I been standin' out here for about two hours. My first thought was to kick yo' mutha'fuckin' ass when you got home, but after smokin' a half a pack of ciga-rettes I calmed down and I changed my mind. I'm just gon' put yo' ass outta my house."

"Where I'ma go?" Ra'Keeyah asked frantically, as tears filled her eyes.

"I don't give a fuck where you go. You wanna act grown? Yo' grown ass can figure out where you gon' live," her mother snapped.

"Mommy, don't do this to me," Ra'Keeyah begged.

"Do what to you, Ra'Keeyah? Raise you right, take care of you like I'm supposed to. Feed you, put clothes on your back and a roof over your head. What have I done wrong?" her mother asked, as tears filled her eyes too.

"Mommy, I don't have nowhere to go," Ra'Keeyah said as tears rolled down her cheeks.

"Go live wit' Brick. Shit, you spend all yo' damn time wit' him. He should let you move in wit' him," her mother said smartly.

"Mommy, please," Ra'Keeyah begged.

It broke her mother's heart to hear her daughter beg. She no longer saw a seventeen-year-old young lady standing in front of her, but a seventeen-year-old child that wanted to live the fast life, with no clue about where it was going to take her.

"I don't know what to tell you, Ra'Keeyah. Here is most of yo' shit. You can come back later on when I'm home and get the rest," her mother said, pointing down at the four trash bags.

Ra'Keeyah quickly thought about the money she had stashed in her closet but decided to get it when she came to pick up the rest of her belongings. She looked at her mother with sorrowful eyes, only to have her mother turn her head as if she could have cared less. In reality, it tore her mother to pieces to see her baby girl in pain.

"Can you give me a ride?" she turned around and asked Brick.

Brick popped the trunk and got out of the car. Ra'Keeyah's mom watched as he grabbed two of the trash bags and put them in the trunk and put the other two in the backseat. *Damn, he fine*, she thought, but wouldn't have dared let her daughter know.

"I don't know what you cryin' for, Ra'Keeyah. You chose to sneak around wit' this nigga. I told you time and time again that I don't want you around no drug dealers. You know how I feel about 'em. You made yo' bed, so lie in it. This is what you wanted, ain't it?" her mother fussed, loudly.

"No," Ra'Keeyah sniffed.

"Yes, it is. If it wasn't, you woulda' listened to me."

"Come on, li'l mama," Brick said.

Ra'Keeyah just stood there and waited for Ashton Kutcher to jump out of the bushes and tell her she'd just been punk'd, but that never happened. When reality set in that her mother wasn't playing, Ra'Keeyah got in the car.

"She's yo' responsibility now," she looked over at Brick and said before turning to walk away.

"Where Key-Key goin'?" Jaylen asked when his mom reached the front porch.

"I don't know, baby," she said as tears streamed down her face before making her way up to her bedroom.

Brick shook his head before pulling off. He couldn't believe what had just transpired and took full responsibility. He felt so bad for Ra'Keeyah as she sat in the passenger's seat with tears steadily falling. He knew that even though she looked and acted grown, she was still a kid trying to do grown women things.

Brick looked over at Ra'Keeyah. "Your mom was right. You my responsibility now, and I'ma take care of you," he promised.

Ra'Keeyah looked over at Brick. "Okay," she said softly.

Brick pulled up at his house and popped the trunk. He handed Ra'Keeyah the house keys before grabbing the bags. She walked in the house, kicked off her shoes, and headed straight upstairs to Brick's bedroom and lay across the bed.

Brick carried all of the bags into the house and up to his room. He walked in and looked over at Ra'Keeyah. "You hungry?" he asked.

Ra'Keeyah shook her head yes, even though she wasn't. She just wanted to be alone.

"All right. I'm bouta' go to my mom's house to drop somethin' off and then swing by Bob Evans on the way home," he said, bending down giving her a kiss.

"All right," she replied before Brick walked out of the room.

Ra'Keeyah grabbed the comforter and covered herself up. She still couldn't believe she was homeless. What if Brick got tired of her and wanted her to leave? What if their relationship went downhill now that they lived together? Not wanting to think about the "what-ifs" anymore, Ra'Keeyah waited until the front door closed and cried like a baby.

Chapter Thirty-three

Brick walked into Pauline's house and instantly got hungry. He could smell food cooking in the kitchen.

"Momma," he called out.

"I'm in the kitchen, Brice."

Brick walked into the kitchen with a huge smile on his face.

"Hey, baby," Pauline spoke.

"Hey, Ma," he said walking over, kissing her on the cheek. "What you cookin'?"

"I'm tryin' out this new recipe for this honey glazed chicken. Here, try some," she said, cutting a piece of the tender bird and feeding it to Brick.

"Ummm, this is bangin'. It's so juicy," he said, helping himself to another piece.

"You think so?" she asked, smiling.

"Hell, yeah. When you puttin' it on the menu?" he asked with his mouth full of chicken.

"I was thinkin' about waitin' until next week."

"Oh, okay. I can't wait," he said, taking a seat at the kitchen table.

"What brings you over so early? You thought I was cookin' breakfast, didn't you?" Pauline joked.

"Naw. I just needed to get away from the house and let Ra'Keeyah be by herself for a minute. I can tell she didn't really wanna cry in front of me. Plus I needed to drop this money off to you," Brick replied, handing her two wads of money that were both wrapped in rubber bands.

Pauline wiped her hands on her apron, took the money, and sat down at the table across from Brick. "What's wrong wit' Ra'Keeyah?" she asked, concerned, as she placed the money in her apron pocket.

"Her mom put her out this mornin'."

"Whaaaat?" Pauline asked, surprised.

"Yeah, Ma. We pulled up to the house, and she was standin' out front wit' Ra'Keeyah's shit in trash bags. Goin' ham on her. Then she started talkin' shit about me," he replied.

"What she say about you?" Pauline asked, eyebrows raised.

"She all out in the street yellin' about me bein' a drug dealer and shit."

"And what did you say after she said that?" Pauline inquired.

"I didn't open my mouth. I just let her talk shit. Don't get me wrong. I wanted to cuss her ass out, but I didn't," he said.

"You did the right thing, son," Pauline said, nodding her head in approval.

"I just feel that it's mainly my fault she got put out. If it wasn't for me always wantin' to spend time wit' her, she wouldna' got in trouble," Brick said, feeling guilty.

"Well, Brice. It's not all your fault. You have to put some of the blame on Ra'Keeyah as well. She do got a mind of her own. You didn't put no gun in her mouth to make her stay, did you?"

"It wasn't a gun I put in her mouth to make her stay," Brick joked.

"Boy, you nasty," Pauline cracked up laughing.

"I'm just playin'," he laughed too.

Pauline's demeanor became serious again. "Well, what you gon' do? I mean, how do you think its gon' work out wit' her livin' wit' you? You hurried up and sent Piper back home, not sayin' you didn't do the right thing," Pauline slid in.

"Ra'Keeyah ain't nothin' like Piper. They cut from two totally different cloths. Piper stuck up and bourgeois as hell. I can't stand her fucked up attitude. Ra'Keeyah ain't shit like that. She so down-to-earth. I can be myself when I'm around her. She keeps a smile on my face. I really can't see myself livin' without her," Brick said.

Pauline smiled at her son. "So in other words, what you tellin' me is Ra'Keeyah is the one?"

"She's the one, Ma," Brick smiled widely.

"Wow, my baby is finally in love. Now that you found your future wife, do you think I can get some grandbabies now?" Pauline asked.

"You pushin' it," he laughed.

"I just thought I'd try. Well, I'm about to get ready to head to work," Pauline said standing up. "Tell Ra'Keeyah I said hello and to keep her head up. She's definitely in good hands."

"Thanks, Ma," Brick smiled. "And I'll tell her." He stood from the table and gave his mother a kiss on the cheek. "See you later."

"Okay," Pauline said as Brick walked out of the kitchen and headed out the front door.

When Brick got in the car his cell phone began to ring. He looked at the name on the screen before answering it. "What's up, nigga?"

"'Sup, man?" Bob T asked.

"Chillin'. On my way to get me and my girl somethin' to eat before I go back to the crib."

"Oh, word?" Bob T replied. "You know this chick have nerve enough to call me the otha' day and told me she was pregnant."

"Who?" Brick asked as his other line beeped. He looked at the screen and saw Pauline's name. "Hey, man, let me call you back. This my mom callin' me."

"Oh, aiiiight. Don't forget," Bob T said.

"I won't," Brick said before clicking over. "'Sup, Ma?"

"You didn't give me no amount," she said, referring to the money Brick gave her.

"Oh, I sure didn't. Twenty," he replied.

"Okay, just wanted to make sure."

"A'iiiight, Ma, love you," Brick said.

"Love you too," Pauline replied before hanging up.

Brick dialed Bob T's number to find out which one of his chicks had he gotten knocked up this time, but it went straight to voice mail. With six kids and five baby mommas, you think he would have learned by now to stay strapped.

Brick stopped by Bob Evans on his way home and picked Ra'Keeyah and himself up something to eat. Once at the house, he headed straight upstairs with the food, wanting it to still be hot when she ate. Brick walked into his room and looked down at Ra'Keeyah who was sleeping like a baby. He laid the tray of food on the nightstand before walking to his dresser, tripping over one of the trash bag of clothes. Brick couldn't stand clutter so he went over to his closet and opened the double doors, trying to find room for Ra'Keeyah's clothes. Seeing that there was none, Brick started grabbing clothes he hadn't worn in months and some of the ones he hadn't wore at all and moved them to the closet in the guest room. After making space, he started neatly hanging up Ra'Keeyah's clothes in his closet. He then cleared out one of his drawers and made room for the few pairs of panties and bras that her mom had put in one of the trash bags. She only had a couple pairs of shoes so he stacked them neatly next to his. Once he got all of Ra'Keeyah's things organized, Brick grabbed his food and went downstairs to make some important phone calls.

After a two-hour nap, Ra'Keeyah woke up and looked around the room. Brick had left the closet doors open intentionally so the first thing she would see when she woke up were her clothes hanging neatly in there on her own side of the closet. Ra'Keeyah smiled, rolled over, and grabbed her cell phone out of her purse. She tried to turn it on but the battery was dead and her charger was still plugged up at her mom's house. She climbed out of bed and walked to the bathroom, where she looked in the mirror. Her eyes were puffy and red from all the crying she had done. She grabbed a washcloth and washed her face before heading downstairs. She could hear Brick's voice coming from the kitchen so she headed in there.

"Hey, li'l mama," he took the phone away from his ear and said.

"Hey," she smiled and sat down at the table.

"Hey, Frank, let me call you back," Brick said. After ending his call, Brick looked over at Ra'Keeyah. "You hungry?"

"No," she said, shaking her head.

"I left your food upstairs on the nightstand. So whenever you feel like eatin', it's there."

"Okay. Do you have a charger that can fit my phone? Mine is at home. I mean at my mom's house," she quickly corrected herself.

"Let me see," he said taking her phone and trying to stick his charger into her phone. "It'll fit, but it's not chargin'. Get dressed and we'll go get you a new charger. You gon' need some underclothes too, 'cuz yo' mutha didn't put that many in yo' bags."

"Okay. And thanks for hangin' up my stuff," Ra'Kee-yah said, getting up from the table.

"You're welcome," Brick said walking over to her and wrapping his arms around her waist. "I finally got you where I want you. Here wit' me," he said, before biting down on his bottom lip.

"You sure this is what you want?" Ra'Keeyah asked.

"I'm positive. I wouldn't have it no otha' way," Brick said earnestly.

"Okay, we'll see six months from now if you're feelin' the same way," Ra'Keeyah laughed.

"You'll see," Brick said, letting go of her.

"I'm goin' to get in the shower," she said.

"You just tellin' me or are you invitin' me?" he asked with a smile.

"I'm invitin' you."

"Let's roll then."

Brick led Ra'Keeyah out of the kitchen and upstairs to the bathroom. He turned on the shower and grabbed two towels before getting undressed and stepping in. Ra'Keeyah removed her clothes and stepped in as well. Brick grabbed her and pulled her close to him and kissed her lovingly before turning her around. Ra'Keeyah lifted her wet hair with her hands while Brick planted soft kisses on the nape of her neck. She placed her hands on the tile walls and bent over while Brick slowly entered her from behind. Ra'Keeyah pushed back on his thick love muscle as Brick stroked long and deep. Their bodies were in sync with each thrust. Not being able to hold on any longer, Brick busted a good one. Once he pulled himself together, he grabbed a washcloth and the shower gel and lathered it. With no spoken words, Brick ran the washcloth across Ra'Keeyah's body, hoping to wash away all her pain and insecurities of thinking he didn't want her there right down the drain.

Chapter Thirty-four

It had been well over a month since Ra'Keeyah had been put out of her mother's house, and to be honest, she didn't miss it at all. Only thing she truly missed was seeing Jaylen, but she made sure she called him every day when he went over to Nancy's house. Other than that, she was living the good life. Brick did what he promised; he took care of her in every way possible. Shopping sprees, keeping her hair and nails done, spending quality time with her along with putting money in her pocket—what more could she ask for? Ra'Keeyah took care of Brick's needs as well.

She cooked dinner when they didn't feel like going out to eat; she took his clothes to the cleaners; kept the entire house clean; and gave him sex on a regular. So fair exchange ain't no robbery. Ra'Keeyah had even started driving the Range to school, but that was short-lived once someone carved the word *bitch* on the passenger-side door. After that, Ra'Keeyah decided to give school a break for a minute. Brick didn't approve of her leaving school, and the only way he agreed was if she promised him to take online classes. Ra'Keeyah did just that. She signed up to take computer classes instead of sitting in a classroom. School was no longer fun for her, and she felt all alone now that both Shayna and Quiana had dropped out as well.

Ra'Keeyah was sitting at the kitchen table on the new laptop Brick had bought her doing her homework when his cell phone began to ring. When no one answered the call, the phone began ringing again. Brick was upstairs in the shower, so Ra'Keeyah got up to see who was desperately blowing up her man's phone. She picked up the phone, looked at the screen, and saw Piper's name, and instantly got an attitude. Ra'Keeyah thought about going upstairs and going off on him about Piper calling his phone. She wanted to know why he still had her number programmed in his phone. Her mother always told her if you think your man is doing wrong, don't jump to conclusions right away; just sit back and take notes. One thing for sure and two for certain; by laying low and keeping an eye on things, if Brick was doing anything behind her back, he was sure to slip up.

Brick strolled into the kitchen dressed nicely and smelling good. He walked over to Ra'Keeyah and kissed her on the neck. "I'll be back, li'l mama," he said, grabbing his phone off the counter and checking it for missed calls.

Ra'Keeyah sat back and watched his reaction.

"Was my phone ringin'?"

Nigga, you see them missed calls from Piper, Ra'Keeyah wanted to say but kept it cool. "Yeah, it rang a few times. I started to answer it, but I didn't know if you wanted me to or not," she smirked.

"You could have," he said, before placing his phone in his pocket.

Oh, don't worry, next time I will, she thought. "Aren't you gon' call the person back that kept blowin' your phone up?" Ra'Keeyah asked on the sly.

"I will when I get in the car," Brick replied.

His response had Ra'Keeyah's blood boiling.

"Now gimme a kiss and wish me luck. Joelle and Aamaad throwin' a dice game tonight."

Ra'Keeyah cut her eyes at Brick. "Good luck," she said sarcastically before walking out of the kitchen.

"What's wrong wit' you?" Brick walked out of the kitchen behind Ra'Keeyah and asked.

"Nothin'," she replied on her way up the stairs.

"Well, how come you didn't give me a kiss like I asked you to?" he frowned.

Ask Piper for a kiss, she thought. "I don't know," she stopped and shrugged her shoulders.

"What you bouta' do while I'm gone?" he asked, picking up his car keys.

"I don't know. Probably call Shayna and see what she gon' get into."

"I like Shayna and all, and I know she's yo' girl, but she be doin' a little too much for me," Brick said.

"Don't go there," Ra'Keeyah warned. "Shayna has been my best friend since the second grade. And I ain't lettin' nothin' and *nobody* come between that."

"I ain't tryin'a come between that. I'm jus' sayin' she out there, and I don't want nobody thinkin' my woman is out there too," Brick explained.

"Yeah, okay," Ra'Keeyah said, waving him off before continuing up the stairs.

"Ra'Keeyah," Brick called out.

Ra'Keeyah stopped and turned around. "What?" she snapped.

"What the fuck is yo' problem?" he asked.

"I don't have no problem."

"Whateva', man. I'm not about to argue wit' you. You tryin'a make me mad so I can lose all my damn money tonight. You know I can't concentrate when I'm upset," Brick said, opening the front door.

"You the one arguin'. Bye," Ra'Keeyah said before continuing her way up the stairs.

Brick was about to comment, but he knew there was no winning when it came to arguing with a female. So instead, he shook his head and continued out the door. Once inside the car, Brick called Joelle to let him know not to start the dice game until he got there.

Ra'Keeyah stood in the bedroom window, peeking out of the side of the blind down at Brick to see if he was smart enough to at least wait until he got around the corner to call Piper back. He wasn't. Her heart sank as she watched him talk on the phone. She continued to watch as he backed out of the driveway and pulled off. Ra'Keeyah walked over to the nightstand, grabbed her cell phone, and called Shayna.

"What it do?" Shayna asked.

"What you gon' get into tonight?"

"I don't know, man. I need to get chocolate wasted. Calvin been playin' me real shady like here lately," Shayna ranted.

Here Ra'Keeyah thought she was calling Shayna to vent, but turns out she had problems of her own to worry about.

"Well, I think we should get dressed and go out and enjoy ourselves. I'm havin' man problems myself," Ra'Keeyah suggested.

"What's wrong?" Shayna asked, concerned.

"We'll talk when we meet up. Right now, all I wanna do is get dressed and get the hell outta here!"

"Well me and Joe will be to get you in about an hour."

The thought of Joe made Ra'Keeyah angry. "I'm straight. How about I come pick you up in about an hour," she said.

"What we ridin' in? You ain't wide enough for me to get on yo' back," Shayna joked.

"Shut up, fool. We ridin' in the Range," Ra'Keeyah laughed.

"Shit, my girl got her own set of keys to the Range. You doin' big thangs over there," Shayna replied.

Ra'Keeyah laughed. "I'm doin' all right over here," she bragged. "Anyways, get dressed. I'll be there shortly."

"A'iiiight," Shayna replied before hanging up and going to find her something to wear.

After showering and getting all dolled up in her "fuck 'em" dress and her five-inch stilettos, Ra'Keeyah was ready to hit the scene. She couldn't wait to go pick up her girl. Playing house with Brick the past couple of months kept her from doing a lot of the things she and Shayna used to do. Tonight, Ra'Keeyah was going to let her hair down and enjoy herself. She quickly grabbed her keys, set the house alarm, and headed out to the truck.

Ra'Keeyah pulled up in front of Shayna's house and blew the horn. Shayna rushed out the front door and down the walk.

"I see you, girl," she smiled as she opened up the truck door.

"You silly," Ra'Keeyah blushed.

"Girl, this truck is nice," Shayna said, checking out the plushed out interior.

"Thanks," Ra'Keeyah smiled as she pulled off. "What we gon' do tonight?"

"I don't know. You called me and asked me to go out. I thought you had somethin' in mind," Shayna said.

"Shit, I haven't been out in so long. What's poppin' on Saturdays?"

"I heard club Low Key be jumpin'," Shayna said.

"Yeah, but you gotta have an ID to get up in there. My cousin Tracie said they don't be playin' about lettin' all them young folks in. When they say ID, that's what they mean. It ain't like the Second Level and the rest of them hole-in-the-wall joints where any young girl wit' a short skirt can get up in there."

"Child, please. I can get us in the White House if I needed to," Shayna teased.

"I'm tryin' to tell you they not gon' let us in," Ra'Kee-yah stressed.

"You just handle the drivin' and let me handle the ID situation," Shayna replied.

"Okay," Ra'Keeyah said, giving in and heading to the club. "You heard from Quiana?"

"Nope. Joe told me she been goin' to Columbus to dance for some nigga name Jamal and his friends. He also said she snortin' that shit too."

"Wow. She still gettin' that money, I see," Ra'Keeyah laughed.

"Yeah, I ain't mad at her about that. I just hope her naïve ass be careful. Even though we beefin', I still don't wanna see nothin' happen to her," Shayna said.

"She learned from a pro, so she should be all right," Ra'Keeyah assured.

"Yeah, you right. Speakin' of gettin' money, do you still wanna dance for Calvin and his boys maybe once or twice a month?"

Ra'Keeyah thought for a brief second before answering. Even though Brick kept money in her pockets, making a little extra of her own wouldn't hurt. They could dance on the days that Brick made his runs out of town so it would make it almost impossible for him to find out.

"I'm game," Ra'Keeyah said pulling up in the crowded parking lot of the club. She couldn't find a parking space anywhere so she circled around a few times until someone finally pulled out.

"I hope we don't get shamed when we go up to the door," Ra'Keeyah said hesitantly getting out of the truck.

"Girl, please, trust. We are not about to get embarrassed. Have I ever let you down before?" Shayna said before applying some lip gloss to her lips and making sure her hair was intact.

"Naw."

"Well, I ain't gon' start tonight." Shayna got out of the truck and pulled her already short skirt up a little bit higher before walking toward the club. "Hey, ain't that Brick's Camaro parked over there," she said pointing.

"Where?" Ra'Keeyah inquired with an attitude.

"Right there," Shayna said walking toward the car with Ra'Keeyah close behind.

"It sho' is. That bitch-ass nigga told me he was goin' to a dice game! He didn't have to lie," Ra'Keeyah fumed.

"Well, what you expect? He's a fuckin' man, and that's what they do—lie!" Shayna replied as they crossed the busy street.

Ra'Keeyah was beyond mad as they walked up to the door.

"Here we go," Shayna replied as they bypassed the other people standing in line and walked straight up to the bouncer.

Wow, we bouta' get embarrassed, Ra'Keeyah thought as she walked a little ways behind her girl.

"IDs, please," the big muscular bouncer said, never looking up from the clipboard he held in his hand.

"I accidentally left it at home," Shayna replied.

"No ID, no gettin' in," the bouncer looked up and stated.

Ra'Keeyah was just about to turn and look for a hole to crawl in.

"Harry?" Shayna asked.

"Shayna, is that you?"

"Yeah, it's me," she smiled widely.

"Come here, girl, and gimme a hug," Harry said, wrapping his strong arms around her body.

"Oh my goodness, Harry, it's been a long time. When you come home?"

"I know. You done grew up," he said, checking out her fully developed body. "I've been home goin' on a year now. I done cleaned my life up, bought me a house and a nice car. I'm doin' real good."

"Ol' Harry," Shayna smiled happily. "I'm glad to hear you doin' all right. I wish I could say the same about my momma."

"Don't tell me Honey is still on that stuff? Last I heard, she was messin' wit' some white man," Harry frowned.

"Well, I ain't gon' tell you. And yeah, she got herself a snowflake," Shayna laughed.

"Wow. I used to love me some Honey," Harry said shaking his head.

"Come on, hurry up," somebody yelled from the crowd.

"Shut the fuck up before I won't let nobody else in," Harry barked fiercely.

"Well, let me let you get back to work," Shayna said. "Is it cool for me and my girl to go in?"

"Yeah. And tell 'em at the bar that you my daughter and you and yo' girl can drink for free," he said.

"That's what's up!" Shayna smiled as she and Ra'Keeyah walked past him.

"Hey," Harry called out.

"Huh?"

"Tell yo' momma I asked about her and would like to see her," Harry winked.

"I got chu'," Shayna smiled back and continued into the club.

"ID," Harry said to the next person in line.

"See, I told you I was gon' get us in. Now maybe next time you'll have a little more faith in yo' girl."

"I will," Ra'Keeyah laughed. "Where do you know Harry from? You know every-damn-body."

"He used to be my momma's boyfriend back in the day. Word is, he the one got her hooked on crack," Shayna mused for a brief second before continuing. "Even though he was smokin', he took care of me and my momma until he lost his job. After that, he didn't care about nothin' but gettin' high. He was strung out so bad he tried to rob Kmart at gunpoint. He did 'bout ten years for it. You heard him say he just got out almost a year ago."

"Wow, that's crazy," Ra'Keeyah said, shaking her head. "So you gon' tell your mom he wanna see her, even though she's wit' Joe?"

"Hell, yeah, I'ma tell her. Fuck Joe. Maybe Harry can help her get off that shit like he did," she replied.

"I feel you."

"Anyways, enough about crackheads and ex-boy-friends and shit. Let's head over to the bar," Shayna said as she maneuvered her way through the crowd.

"I feel you on that too," Ra'Keeyah laughed as she followed her best friend.

Ra'Keeyah tried her best to have fun. She drank, laughed, danced, and got hit on by so many different men. But it was hard for her to keep her mind off Brick. She'd searched the entire club looking for him, but he was nowhere to be found. At the end of the night, she and Shayna sat scrunched down in the truck and waited to see who was going to get into his car.

"Who is it?" Ra'Keeyah whispered as they watched some guy and his chick walk toward the car and get in.

"I don't know," Shayna whispered back.

"Me either. I never seen 'em before."

"Why we whisperin'?" Shayna laughed.

"I don't know. It must be the vodka," Ra'Keeyah cracked up laughing.

"It must be," Shayna cracked up too. "Let's follow 'em."

"Yeah," Ra'Keeyah said excited. She sat up and started the truck. When Brick's Camaro pulled out of the parking lot she waited a few seconds, and then pulled out behind them. She stayed two car lengths behind, not wanting to make it obvious they were playing detective. Fifteen minutes later, the car pulled up in a drive two blocks from where Ra'Keeyah's mom stayed. Ra'Keeyah parked a few houses down and watched as the dude and the chick got out and disappeared into the house.

"Who live here?" Shayna looked over at Ra'Keeyah and asked.

Ra'Keeyah shrugged her shoulders. "I don't know. Let's sit here for a minute and see if they come back out." The two friends sat in the truck for an hour straight staking out the house like two real-live cops. Ra'Keeyah's heart ached as she watched a couple other dudes pull up at the house with three females.

"You think Brick is really in that house?" Shayna finally asked.

"His car is here. Where else could he be?" she answered, hurt.

"They must be about to kick it," Shayna said as they watched more females pull up and get out of the car laughing and talking with bottles of liquor in hand.

"Brick's ass probably up in there all hugged up wit' some bitch! I should go kick the door in and whoop him and the ho!" Ra'Keeyah snapped, knowing she couldn't beat Brick up even if Shayna helped her.

"Let's do it," Shayna said, game for it. "You beat up Brick, and I'll maul the bitch or vice versa!"

Shayna and Ra'Keeyah looked at each other and busted out laughing. "We sound like some damn fools! How we gon' just run up in somebody's house we don't even know and start fightin'?"

"I know, right?" Shayna agreed. "We just drunk and trippin'. Let's go home."

"I'm wit' you. Let's get out of here. I'm tired," Ra'Kee-yah said starting up the truck and pulling off. She drove in silence. She was disappointed in herself. How could she dare think Brick was any different than any other dude she'd ever messed around with? She was mad at herself for putting him on a pedestal when he deserved to be in the mud with the rest of the snakes she'd dealt with in the past.

"You okay?" Shayna asked, noticing Ra'Keeyah was in deep thought.

"Yeah, I'm all right. I'm just feelin' some kinda' way about puttin' all my trust in Brick, and he done turned out to be a dog just like all the rest," Ra'Keeyah said, upset.

"Don't get mad when I say this and don't think I'm hatin' 'cuz you know hatin' ain't in my blood."

Ra'Keeyah braced herself for what was about to come out of Shayna's mouth. She knew how outspoken she was and respected her for speaking the truth, even if it did hurt.

"What did you really expect? Brick is like the Denzel Washington of the hood. You know all these hoes be throwin' pussy his way. A nigga only gon' turn it down for so long until he find that one that they really wanna fuck and whoop, then there it is. Before you know it, yo' nigga rollin' around in the bed wit' somebody else," Shayna explained.

Ra'Keeyah didn't want to admit it, but she knew what Shayna was saying was the truth. She did have the hood's most wanted. But she was his woman and wanted to be his one and only.

"Well, what am I supposed to do?" Ra'Keeyah asked desperately.

"Truthfully, you accepted the role of bein' Brick's *main* bitch. So you can either deal wit' it or push the fuck on. The choice is yours! But if you gon' stay wit' him and play wifey, all I can tell you is you betta' play the part well and make him wanna come back each and every time. There ain't no room for half-steppin'," Shayna stated.

Ra'Keeyah sat back and listened as Shayna spit knowledge and truth her way. Shayna was very precocious, and it wasn't that she wanted to be. She was forced to be.

"Do you love him?" Shayna asked already knowing the answer but wanted to be all the way sure.

"Very much. You know I've never felt this way about anybody else. He makes me so happy," Ra'Keeyah admitted as tears formed.

"Well, I suggest you stay wit' his ass and take the nigga up top. Get all you can get from him and y'all can still love each other along the way. 'Cuz I know you don't wanna take a chance on leavin' somebody you really love for another nigga that nine times outta ten gon' do the exact same thing."

"Naw, I don't," Ra'Keeyah responded sullenly as she pulled up in front of Shayna's house.

"Always remember there's a lot of responsibility that come along wit' bein' a nigga's bottom bitch. Nobody said it would be easy. If you thought it would be, then you was heavily mistaken, baby girl," Shayna replied, opening the truck door.

Ra'Keeyah sighed heavily. "Thanks, Shayna," she said wholeheartedly.

"You don't have to thank me. That's what friends are for. I'd be fake and dead-ass wrong for sugarcoatin' the truth. You know me betta' than that. I'ma tell you like it is, 'cuz nobody ever told me. I had to find out on my own. I don't want you to make the same mistakes I made. You my girl, and I love you," Shayna smiled.

"I love you too," Ra'Keeyah smiled back.

"Call me if you need to talk. Think about what I said, but don't go tradin' yo' Beamer in for a Honda," Shayna winked as she got out and closed the truck door before heading up the walk.

Ra'Keeyah waited for Shayna to get in the house before pulling off. She thought about everything Shayna had said on her way home and knew she was going to have to step her game up. There was no way she was going to let another female take her place like she'd taken Piper's, not without a fight. Ra'Keeyah turned on their street and her heart sank when she noticed Brick still hadn't made it home. She pulled up, got out, took off her heels, and headed up the walk. Ra'Keeyah wanted to cry, but refused to. She unlocked the front door and went in. She threw her shoes off to the side, reset the alarm, and headed upstairs. When she walked into the room, to her surprise, Brick was lying in the bed in nothing but his boxers watching TV.

"What's up, li'l mama? Where you been?" he looked over and asked.

Ra'Keeyah was surprised to see him at home. She wanted to do a backflip before yelling at the top of her lungs.

"I went out wit' Shayna for a little while. Then we stopped and got somethin' to eat, and then I came home," Ra'Keeyah lied. "What you doin' home?" she asked, acting as if she didn't care if he was there or not. "I thought you were goin' to a dice game?"

"I did go to a dice game, but I couldn't concentrate. All I kept thinkin' about was the little argument we had. I lost like fifteen hundred and came on home."

Ra'Keeyah felt stupid thinking about how she and Shayna had followed Brick's car, hoping to catch him in the wrong, staked out somebody's house, and plotted to kick the door in—and the entire time Brick was home in bed waiting on her arrival.

"Well, where's your car at? It's not in the driveway," Ra'Keeyah pried.

"Oh, I let my nigga Flossy use it. He was creepin' wit' some chick and didn't want his broad to find out, so I had him drop me off and let him do his thang," Brick said before changing the channel.

"Oh, so that's how y'all do it when y'all wanna cheat?" Ra'Keeyah asked as she began getting undressed, tossing her clothes in the hamper.

"Not me. Shit, if I wanted to cheat I would use my own car," Brick laughed.

"Ummm-huh?" Ra'Keeyah smirked as she stood completely naked. She removed her jewelry and laid it on the dresser before making her way over to the bed.

Brick's manhood started to pulsate as he looked over at his woman's banging body. "I'm serious, but I don't have no reason to cheat. I got everything I need right here," Brick said as Ra'Keeyah climbed into bed and mounted him.

"Is that so?" she asked with a seductive look.

Brick nodded his head yes as Rufus stood at full attention.

"And we gon' keep it that way, right?" Ra'Keeyah asked before leaning down and kissing Brick on the lips. He nodded his head yes again as she kissed her way down his chest to his washboard abs, stopping once she reached Rufus. She pulled him out of his cubbyhole and began planting soft kisses all around him, before placing him inside of her warm mouth. The entire time she pleasured her man, she replayed Shayna's conversation in her head over and over again. The part about making him wanna come back each and every time stuck out the most. Soon, Ra'Keeyah had Brick begging for mercy. His body was bucking while he moaned loudly as she worked her magic. Making love for the next hour, Ra'Keeyah was pleased with the work she'd put in. She wasn't leaving any room for another chick to slide up in her space.

Chapter Thirty-five

The months passed by rather quickly. Ra'Keeyah stood staring out the window as the snow fell to the ground, covering it like a clean, white sheet. Christmas was right around the corner, her favorite holiday of them all. This year would be different, though. It wouldn't be as special as the rest. There would be no decorating the Christmas tree as a family. She and Brick had decorated theirs, but it wasn't the same. No snowball fights between her and Jaylen, no staying up late watching the marathon of *A Christmas Story* with her mother and brother to see who could recite the words the best. There would be no baking cookies and fudge with her mother and Aunt Nancy as the Temptations's Christmas CD played loudly and the little kids ran around the house yelling and screaming. The thought of not spending Christmas with her mother and brother had Ra'Keeyah feeling down.

"What's on yo' mind, li'l mama?" Brick asked, walking up behind Ra'Keeyah, wrapping his arms around her waist.

"Nothin' really. Just thinkin', that's all," she said, closing the curtains and walking over to the sofa, taking a seat.

Brick could sense not being able to spend the holidays with her mother and little brother was really eating Ra'Keeyah up. He wished there was something he could do to cheer her up. He had tried getting her to call her mother, but she refused, saying if her mother wanted to talk to her, then she would call her. Brick knew of no other way to cheer his lady up other than giving her money to shop. That always put a smile on Ra'Keeyah's face.

"You finish your Christmas shoppin' yet?" Brick asked.

"I haven't even started. Haven't been in the mood to shop," Ra'Keeyah replied.

Brick walked over and placed his hand on Ra'Keeyah's forehead. "You don't feel like you got a temperature," he joked.

"Move, boy," Ra'Keeyah laughed as she playfully slapped Brick's hand away from her. "I'm not sick."

"Shit, you sure? I never met a woman who wasn't in the mood to shop. Especially when they usin' somebody else's money," Brick laughed as he made his way to the kitchen.

Ra'Keeyah did need to go out and get Jaylen and Shayna something for Christmas. She also needed to shop for Brick and Pauline. She'd spoken with Peighton a few times and knew she'd be in town for Christmas, so she could pick her up a thing or two as well. Ra'Keeyah got up from the sofa and walked toward the kitchen.

"Okay, I changed my mind," she announced, walking into the kitchen as Brick sat at the table counting money.

"I figured you would," he smiled and pointed to a stack of money he'd set aside, knowing Ra'Keeyah would reconsider going shopping.

"You know me well," she smiled back, grabbing the stack of money off the table. "What you want for Christmas?"

"I already got what I want," he winked and continued counting his money.

"*That's* what I'm talkin' about," she beamed as she headed out of the kitchen and upstairs to change her pants because the ones she was wearing were feeling a little snug. She took half of the three thousand dollars that Brick had given her and put it with the rest of her stash.

Ra'Keeyah had really been stacking her ends. She'd taken all the money she made from dancing with Shayna when Brick was out of town and half the allowance he would give her and put it in a shoebox in the back of the closet. Her mother had always told her not to carry all of her eggs in the same basket. She'd never really understood what she'd meant by that, but now that she was a little older and not under her mother's roof anymore, she fully understood the meaning. Not trying to burn bread, but if or when things took a turn for the worse in their relationship, Ra'Keeyah wanted to be financially prepared for whatever came her way. She'd witnessed way too many females messing around with drug dealers and instead of stacking their paper, they spent it on shopping sprees, getting their hair and nails done, and trying to live like the Kardashians.

Ra'Keeyah and Brick were getting ready for the extravagant Christmas dinner Pauline was preparing, and afterward, they were heading to the UAW hall for the Christmas party the Road Runners were having. Brick invited Bob T over since all his family lived in New York. Peighton was in town so Bob T asked if he could bring her. Ra'Keeyah thought that was a great idea, since she hadn't seen her friend since the summer. She also wanted to know what the big surprise was Peighton had for her.

Ra'Keeyah dressed in a long sleeved, black, zip-up-the-front jumpsuit, with a deep V-neckline and studded belt. She slid into a pair of black, studded booties to accentuate her outfit before checking herself out in the mirror. Ra'Keeyah wasn't feeling the way the outfit was fitting so tightly on her body. She thought the suit made her look wide at the bottom. She hoped nobody else would notice.

"Damn," Brick snapped as he walked into the bedroom.

"What? I look fat, don't I? I'm about to change," she panicked.

"Naw, you don't look fat," Brick laughed.

"Yes, I do. Then why you laughin'?" Ra'Keeyah asked.

"No, you don't. I said damn 'cuz you look good as hell in that outfit," Brick complimented.

"Are you sure? 'Cuz I think this outfit makes my hips and butt look too big," Ra'Keeyah complained.

"That's a good thang. Honestly, you are gettin' a little thicker, but that's only because I'm hittin' that ass right," he bragged.

"Whatever," Ra'Keeyah laughed as she continued checking herself out in the mirror.

"You know you ain't neva' had anotha' nigga hit that ass like me," Brick smiled.

"I gotta give it to you, you do know how to make a sista feel good," Ra'Keeyah admitted.

"I do, don't I?" Brick asked before kissing her on the lips. Ra'Keeyah closed her eyes and rolled her head back as Brick planted soft kisses all over her neck. He then palmed her backside with both of his hands as he began kissing her lips again.

"Come on, baby, Pauline waiting on us," Ra'Keeyah panted heavily, feeling the huge bulge in the front of Brick's pants.

"You right. But later on tonight, that ass is mines," he said, pulling himself together.

"I can't wait," Ra'Keeyah smiled happily. She grabbed her duffle coat out of the closet and followed Brick downstairs.

"You got everybody's presents?" he asked.

"Yep. I already loaded 'em in the truck. Can we drop Jaylen's and my mom's off first?"

"Okay, that's fine." Brick grabbed his car keys, locked the front door, and headed to the truck with Ra'Keeyah right behind him.

Ra'Keeyah was nervous as they pulled up in front of her mother's house. She didn't know what to expect being this was the first time she'd been back since her mother had put her out. She didn't know whether her mother would welcome her with open arms or with an open palm to the face. She had so many different emotions going on as they sat parked with the truck still running.

"You a'iiiight?" Brick asked, sensing her nervousness.

Ra'Keeyah let out a nervous chuckle. "Not really."

"You want me to go in wit' you?" Brick asked.

"Would you?"

"You know I got cha' back. And plus, I might need to pull her up off yo' ass," Brick joked as he opened up the truck door and got out.

"Whatever," Ra'Keeyah laughed, getting out of the truck and waiting as Brick grabbed the big, fifty-gallon trash bag out of the trunk that was filled to the top with presents.

Ra'Keeyah's knees felt like they were about to buckle right from under her as they walked up on her mother's front porch. She hesitated before ringing the doorbell.

"Mommy, somebody's at the door," Ra'Keeyah heard Jaylen yell.

Ra'Keeyah looked over at Brick and smiled.

A few seconds later her mother opened the front door. She was surprised to see Ra'Keeyah and Brick standing there. She was more happy than anything and stared in disbelief, and Ra'Keeyah did the same. No words were exchanged in the brief staring match.

"Key-Key," Jaylen squealed happily as he walked up behind his mother to see who was at the door.

Finally her mother opened the screen door. "Come on in," she said, stepping aside.

Ra'Keeyah and Brick walked into the house. He set the heavy bag down in the foyer.

"How you doin'?" Brick spoke.

"Fine," Ra'Keeyah's mother replied dryly.

Jaylen wrapped his arms around his sister's waist and nearly squeezed the life out of her.

"Man, you gettin' tall," Ra'Keeyah smiled at her growing brother.

"Hi, Brick," Jaylen spoke once he let go of Ra'Keeyah.

"'Sup, li'l man?" Brick replied, giving him some dap.

Ra'Keeyah avoided eye contact with her mother as much as possible, fearing if she looked at her for too long, she would break out in tears.

"I told the Santa Claus at the mall that all I wanted for Christmas was for my sister to come home . . . oh, and a PlayStation 3," Jaylen said.

A lump formed in Ra'Keeyah's throat as she fought back the tears. Jaylen's comment touched Brick as well.

"What's in the bag?" Jaylen questioned.

"Well, Santa came by my house and dropped this stuff off for you," Ra'Keeyah replied quickly to keep the tears from falling.

"Oh, boy. Can I open 'em, Mom? Please, please," Jaylen begged.

Ra'Keeyah and Jaylen looked at their mother and waited for confirmation. She wanted to tell Jaylen no, because she wasn't too keen on them buying her son presents with drug money. But the anxious look on his face wouldn't let her.

"Go ahead," she smiled.

Ra'Keeyah had gone all-out for her brother. She'd bought him a PlayStation 3 with just about all the latest games, the new LeBron James tennis shoes, a pair of Tims, clothes, underclothes, WWF wrestlers, and a bunch of other things she thought he'd enjoy.

"Oh my goodness, a PlayStation 3! I can't believe I got one. Look, Mommy," Jaylen screamed happily.

"I see," she smiled. "Tell your sister thank you for all your gifts."

"Thanks, Ra'Keeyah," Jaylen jumped up from the floor and yelled before giving her a hug.

"Don't forget to thank Brick too," Ra'Keeyah said. After all, it was his money that had bought everything.

"Thank you, Brick," Jaylen said, hugging him too.

"No problem," Brick smiled down at Jaylen and said.

"Can you help me hook my game up?" Jaylen asked Brick.

"If it's all right wit' yo' mutha."

"Go ahead, 'cuz I don't know how," their mother replied.

"Yesssss," Jaylen cheered carrying his game into the living room so Brick could hook it up.

Ra'Keeyah and her mother bent down and started cleaning up the mess Jaylen had made. Jaylen was overjoyed with all the presents he'd gotten. Their mother had wanted desperately to buy him a PS3 for Christmas, but her budget wouldn't allow her to. She was glad her baby girl had come through and made this the best Christmas Jaylen has ever had, even if it was with drug money.

"Here you go," Ra'Keeyah said handing her mother two presents that said "Mom" on the tags. Her mother eyed the big engagement ring Brick had bought her for Christmas. To avoid an argument she didn't say anything about it.

"Girl, you didn't hafta' get me nothin'. All that stuff you bought for Jaylen . . ."

"It was nothin'," Ra'Keeyah smiled.

Ra'Keeyah watched as her mother unwrapped the pair of Isotoner slippers that she was in dire need of and then the sterling silver, black-and-white diamond bracelet. The look on her face let Ra'Keeyah know her mother was pleased.

"This is beautiful, but it must of cost an arm and a leg," her mother replied while eyeing the expensive piece of jewelry.

"It was nothin'. You deserve it. You work too hard not to have nice things," Ra'Keeyah replied.

"Thank you," Ra'Keeyah's mother said before hugging her.

"You're welcome."

"We got you somethin' too," her mother said.

"You did?" Ra'Keeyah asked surprised.

"Jaylen, bring yo' sister her present from under the tree," their mother called out.

"Awwww, Mom, I'm playin' the game," Jaylen huffed.

"Boy, you betta' bring me that damn present before I come in there," she warned.

Jaylen ran in the foyer, handed Ra'Keeyah her present, and dashed back into the living room to continue playing the game.

Ra'Keeyah quickly unwrapped the tiny box. Inside lay another Pandora charm for the bracelet her mother had gotten her for her birthday.

"Thanks," Ra'Keeyah smiled, picking up the gold bear charm and admiring it.

"Now you have two charms," her mother smiled.

"Yep," Ra'Keeyah lied, not having the heart to tell her mother that Brick had already filled up her bracelet with charms.

"Take yo' coat off and stay a while," her mother suggested.

Just as Ra'Keeyah was about to remove her coat, Brick walked into the foyer. "We better get goin'. Mom just called and said dinner is almost done."

"Oh, y'all goin' over to his mother's house for Christmas dinner?" her mother asked, instantly getting jealous.

"Yeah," Ra'Keeyah answered, not really wanting to.

"Awwww, why y'all gotta leave already?" Jaylen whined.

"Well, ask Mommy if you can come over tomorrow since we're on Christmas break," Ra'Keeyah said.

"Mommy, can I go over to Key-Key's house tomorrow?" Jaylen asked.

"Naw. You good right where you at," their mother said snottily.

Ra'Keeyah rolled her eyes and shook her head. "You ready?" she asked Brick, sensing her mother's instant attitude.

"Yeah," he replied, sensing it as well.

"See y'all later," Ra'Keeyah said before giving her brother a tight hug and a kiss on the cheek.

"Ewwwww," Jaylen laughed as he wiped away at his face before running off to finish his game.

Brick and Ra'Keeyah laughed too.

"I'm goin' to warm up the truck," Brick said excusing himself, wanting to leave Ra'Keeyah and her mother alone.

"Okay."

Brick threw his hand up to Ra'Keeyah's mother before walking out the front door.

Ra'Keeyah and her mother stood in the foyer and stared at each other for a brief moment, not knowing the right words to say.

"Well, I better get goin'," Ra'Keeyah said nervously.

"Okay. Take care of yourself," her mother said, walking her to the door.

Ra'Keeyah turned around and hugged her mother before quickly walking out the door.

"Ra'Keeyah," her mother called out.

"Yea?" she turned around and answered.

"Make him wear protection at all times. You ain't ready for no babies. You're just a baby yourself," her mother said.

"What are you talkin' about, Mom? We not havin' sex," Ra'Keeyah lied.

"Just do what I said, please," her mother replied before closing the door.

Ra'Keeyah knew she looked like the liar her mother accused her of being. Her mother was no fool. She knew there was no way her daughter was living in a house with a man and wasn't giving it up to him. How could she hide it? The spreading of her hips and ass told it all. Ra'Keeyah stood looking at the door long after her mother had closed it. She stood there hoping her mother would open it up and tell her that everything was going to be okay between them. Realizing that wasn't going to happen, she slowly walked off the porch, made her way to the truck, and got in.

Chapter Thirty-six

Brick and Ra'Keeyah pulled up in front of Pauline's house and got out. They were both surprised to see that Bob T and Peighton had already arrived.

"That's a nice truck," Ra'Keeyah said, admiring the new, fully loaded Silverado.

"Yeah, I like it too," Brick said, grabbing the remaining presents out of the back of the truck. "But that nigga shoulda' got a minivan."

"A minivan for what?" Ra'Keeyah laughed as they headed up the walk.

"For all them damn kids." Brick stuck his key in the lock and turned it.

"How many kids he got?" Ra'Keeyah inquired.

"Six that I know of and one on the way," he said, opening the door.

"Damn," Ra'Keeyah snapped.

"I know, right?" Brick laughed as they headed into the house.

"Merry Christmas!" Pauline said with a huge smile as Brick and Ra'Keeyah walked into the living room where everyone sat talking. She gave both of them a hug and a kiss on the cheek.

"Merry Christmas!" Ra'Keeyah and Brick said simultaneously.

Peighton had a huge smile on her face as she struggled to get off the sofa. "Merry Christmas, girl," she said, walking over toward Ra'Keeyah with her belly poking out.

Ra'Keeyah's eyes got real big and her mouth flew open. "You pregnant?" she asked, shocked.

"Surprise!" Peighton said with a huge smile on her face.

"Oh my goodness! Who you pregnant by?" Ra'Keeyah asked without thinking first.

"It better be me," Bob T intervened.

"Oh, duh," Ra'Keeyah said, realizing she had asked a dumb question.

"Trust me, it's yours," Peighton laughed.

"All them times I done talked to you on the phone, how come you didn't tell me you were pregnant?" Ra'Keeyah put her hands on her hips and asked.

"I told you I had a surprise for you," Peighton laughed.

"Yeah, but I never woulda' thought you were pregnant," Ra'Keeyah said, still blown away by the news.

"Yep, five months."

"Look at you, you all belly. You ain't gainin' weight nowhere else," Ra'Keeyah said, removing her coat.

"Damn, I wish I could say the same for you," Peighton said, checking out how thick Ra'Keeyah had gotten. "What you been eatin'? Whatever it is, I need some!"

"That ain't only eatin' that got them hips and ass lookin' like that," Brick smirked. "That's all that work a nigga be puttin' in!" Brick and Bob T busted out laughing while giving each other dap.

"Whatever, nigga," Ra'Keeyah said before taking a seat on the sofa. "Am I fat, Bob T?"

"Hell, naw. You thick as hell," he responded with a big smile.

"Ummm, you said that wit' a little *too* much enthusiasm," Peighton joked before taking her seat back on the sofa.

"I'm wit' you on that, Peighton," Brick laughed.

"Nobody said you was fat, girl. You're just gettin' a little thicker at the bottom. You got them childbearin' hips," Pauline added before walking toward the kitchen.

"Girl, you far from fat. Fat is when you got stomach hangin' over the top of yo' pants and dinner rolls hangin' from your back," Peighton laughed.

Brick walked up behind his woman and wrapped his arms around her. "You strapped in all the right places, baby. Don't let nobody tell you no different. Ain't that right, Bob T?"

Bob T looked over at Peighton and smiled. "I plead the Fifth."

"You better plead the Fifth," Peighton teased.

"Okay, okay, enough already. Are we gon' make this entire day all about my thunder thighs and donkey butt?" Ra'Keeyah asked, pretending to have an attitude.

"I need you two big, strong fellas to help me get the food from the kitchen to the dining room," Pauline stuck her head out of the kitchen and said.

"Yeah, it's time to eat!" Bob T said, excited.

"That's all you think about is eatin'," Brick joked as they walked into the kitchen to give Pauline a hand.

Ra'Keeyah looked over at Peighton and smiled.

"What you smilin' for?" Peighton asked.

"I'm just happy to see you, and I still can't believe you got a baby inside of you."

"Trust me, I can't believe it either," Peighton said, rubbing her round belly.

"What did your mom and dad say? What did you do when you found out? How does it feel to have somethin' movin' inside of you? I got so many questions I wanna ask," Ra'Keeyah rambled.

"Well, trust me, I will be in town long enough to answer all of 'em."

"How long you here for?"

"Probably until my daughter turns eighteen," Peighton replied.

"Huh?"

"You heard right. When my mom found out I was pregnant she said I couldn't stay in her house. She said she could barely feed me and my brother, let alone a baby. So she called Bob T and my dad, cussed them out, and told them she was shippin' me to Ohio. Surprisingly, they both said okay," Peighton said.

"Wow, our moms must be long lost sisters," Ra'Keeyah said.

"Ain't no tellin'."

"Well, I guess you won't be wearin' the Aéropostale outfits I got you for Christmas no time soon," Ra'Keeyah laughed.

"Nope. But it won't take me long after I have the baby to get in 'em."

"It's time to eat, y'all," Bob T announced as he walked into the living room to help Peighton get up off the sofa.

They all headed to the dining room and sat at the table that was decorated with festive flowers and a deliciously prepared meal. Ra'Keeyah had never seen so much food at one time in her life. She was used to the normal turkey, potato salad, greens, and dressing for Christmas. But Pauline outdid herself this time. She had the normal Christmas meal, plus meat loaf, pasta salad, cube steak, and rice, along with a bunch of other foods Ra'Keeyah wasn't used to eating on holidays. They all bowed their heads while Pauline said grace. After the chorus of amens, they dug into the food like a bunch of hungry hostages, laughing and talking the entire time.

Once everyone was full, they were too tired to do anything else. Everyone helped Pauline put the food away before kicking back in the living room.

"I don't feel like goin' to this Christmas party now," Brick said, rubbing his bulging stomach.

"I was thinkin' the same thing. All I wanna do is go home and go straight to bed," Ra'Keeyah said, feeling like a stuffed pig.

"How is the president of the Road Runners not gon' show up at the party?" Pauline looked over at Brick and asked.

"They can manage without me," Brick looked up and said.

"We need to go to this party so we can dance off some of these pounds we just gained," Pauline laughed.

"Y'all have fun," Ra'Keeyah said, leaning over and kissing Brick on the cheek.

"You goin' to," he laughed.

"Well, let me go pee before we go anywhere," Ra'Keeyah said, getting up from the sofa.

"Don't be in there blowin' my mom's spot up," Brick joked.

"I'll try not to," Ra'Keeyah scrunched up her nose and made her way down the long hall toward the bathroom.

"Somebody's phone is ringin'," Pauline said.

"It ain't mines," Brick said.

"Mines either," Peighton and Bob T replied.

"It's Ra'Keeyah's 'cuz the ringin' is comin' from her coat," Pauline said.

"I'll tell you what, that was some of the best carrot cake I've ever tasted in my life," Peighton complimented.

"Thank you. Make sure you take some home and share it wit' your dad," Pauline smiled.

"I sure will," Peighton agreed.

"Hey, baby, your phone was ringin'," Brick said when Ra'Keeyah walked back into the living room.

"Oh, okay," she replied before walking over and retrieving her phone out of her coat pocket. Ra'Keeyah checked the caller ID and saw it was Shayna who had called. Just when she was getting ready to call her back, her phone began ringing again.

"'Sup? Oh my goodness, what's the matter?" Ra'Keeyah panicked as her best friend screamed words she could barely make out into the phone receiver. "I can't understand you, Shayna; slow down."

Brick, Pauline, Bob T, and Peighton all stopped talking and got real quiet.

"Shayna, where are you? Please, stop cryin' and tell me what's wrong," Ra'Keeyah begged.

Brick stood up and walked over to comfort his girl.

"I'll be there as soon as I can," Ra'Keeyah said before pushing the END button on her phone.

"Is everything okay wit' Shayna?" Brick asked, concerned.

"I really don't know. I couldn't make out all she was sayin'. She was cryin' and slurrin' her words, talkin' about she really messed up this time and somethin' about Quiana." Ra'Keeyah didn't know what was wrong with her best friend, but she sure was about to find out and fast. "Brick, I need to go check on Shayna." Tears began to fill Ra'Keeyah's lids.

"It's cool, li'l mama, go check on yo' girl. Take the truck and I'll ride to the party wit' Momma. I'll just catch up wit' you back at the house."

"Thank you, baby." Ra'Keeyah quickly grabbed her coat and put it on.

"Call me if you need me. And be careful," Brick said, giving Ra'Keeyah a kiss on the lips.

"I will. Sorry I can't go to the party wit' y'all," Ra'Kee-yah said, giving Pauline and Peighton a hug.

"That's fine, call me later," Peighton said.

"Yeah, go take care of yo' friend," Pauline added.

"I will," Ra'Keeyah responded before heading out the door.

Ra'Keeyah was a nervous wreck the entire drive to the Holiday Inn. She knew whatever was wrong with Shayna had to be bad, because she'd never heard her girl cry before, at least not like that. Ra'Keeyah pulled up in the hotel's parking lot, jumped out of the car, and rushed inside the hotel. She hurried over to the elevator and waited impatiently for the doors to open. Once they did, she walked in and pushed the number eight. It seemed like it took forever for the elevator to reach its destination. When it did, she ran over to room 806 and tapped lightly on the door.

"Shayna, it's me, Ra'Keeyah. Let me in."

A few seconds later, Shayna opened the door looking a hot mess and reeking of vodka. Ra'Keeyah was at a loss for words. She'd never seen her best friend look this bad before. Her eyes were red and puffy from all the crying she had done. Her hair looked as if it was matted to her head on one side, and the clothes she had on looked as if they were at least two sizes too big. Not to mention the hotel room was a mess.

"Shayna, what's goin' on?" Ra'Keeyah walked into the room and asked, shutting the door behind her.

Shayna walked over to the bed and sat down, closed her eyes, and threw her head back as if she was trying to collect her thoughts. Finally, she opened her eyes and sighed heavily. "My life is so fucked up," she said as tears began to fall from her eyes.

"What happened?" Ra'Keeyah walked over and took a seat on the bed next to Shayna.

"I don't even know where to start. All I know is I don't wanna go on livin'," Shayna sobbed.

"Don't talk like that, Shayna. Just tell me what happened," Ra'Keeyah pleaded, soothingly.

Shayna wiped her tears away with the back of her hands before speaking. "I called Calvin today to see where my Christmas presents were at. And he told me that he couldn't see me anymore because his wife found out about us."

"Whaaaaat? Who told her?" Shayna asked, shocked.

"His wife got on the phone and told me I better leave Calvin alone or she'd destroy every man we danced for, including her husband. She threatened to call their wives, their jobs, and even go to the newspaper if I didn't stop messin' wit' him."

"Do you believe she would do that?"

"Yeah, 'cuz I could hear it in her voice. Plus, I don't wanna take any chances. She knew my name, my real age, where I lived. She knew about all the shoppin' sprees, about all times I went to their house; she broke everything down to me," Shayna said in disbelief as the tears continued to flow.

"Wow," Ra'Keeyah said, shaking her head.

"My first thought was one of Calvin's friends told, but then she told me she'd hired a private investigator. Then she went on to tell me that me and my cousin, Quiana, wasn't the only young, black girls that her husband was messin' around wit'. She said there were plenty more."

"So he was fuckin' Quiana too?" Ra'Keeyah asked, just to make sure she heard her right.

"Yes, he was fuckin' her too."

"That bitch is foul. I wanna kill that ho," Ra'Keeyah snapped angrily.

"Don't bother. She's already dyin'. And it's all my fault," she said before bursting into tears again.

"What you do?" Ra'Keeyah asked, confused.

"Oh my God, my God, my God. It's all my fault," Shayna bawled.

"Shayna, please talk to me," Ra'Keeyah said, getting teary eyed as she watched for the first time her best friend cry her heart out.

"I burnt bread on my cousin," she cried.

"I don't understand."

"Oh my goodness, it hurts; it hurts so bad," Shayna wailed without elaborating.

Ra'Keeyah was starting to get frustrated because she was trying to piece together everything Shayna was telling her, but it wasn't making much sense. She rubbed her best friend's back and waited on her to calm down so she could get the full story.

"My mom told Joe that Quiana was HIV positive and she won't go get no help," Shayna finally said.

Ra'Keeyah couldn't believe that someone she'd gone to school with, used to kick it with, ran the streets with, and smoke blunts with, was HIV positive. She'd always heard about other people having the disease, like Eazy-E, Liberace, Rock Hudson, the dad off of the *Brady Bunch*, and even Craig the dope fiend, but not someone she was so close to. Ra'Keeyah didn't know whether to be mad at Quiana for being so careless or feel sorry for her.

"So how is it your fault?"

"Remember when I told her I hope she catch AIDS and die a slow, miserable death?" Shayna sobbed.

"It's not your fault. We all say things we don't mean in the heat of the moment. Who woulda' thought somethin' like that would come to pass?" Ra'Keeyah explained.

"I know, but I said it, and it happened," Shayna cried.

"Look, Shayna, you warned Quiana about makin' a nigga use protection so many times. She chose to have unprotected sex. Her catchin' this disease has nothin' to do wit' you. You did your part by tryin' to instill the fact that you can't just be sleepin' around wit' all these nasty niggas without usin' somethin'. She thought just 'cuz a nigga looked clean that his dick was clean. You tried to tell her it didn't work like that. Even if a nigga is cleaner than the bill of health, you still make the nigga strap up, especially if he ain't yo' man!"

"I know, but—"

"But nothin'," Ra'Keeyah said, cutting her off. "You did what you were supposed to do. You tried to help her in every way possible! Quiana was the only one who could have prevented this from happenin'."

"If I wouldna' got mad at her, maybe I coulda' saved her from catchin' that shit," Shayna said.

"How could you have saved her? She didn't wanna be saved. No matter how you look at it, like I said, she made her own choice, Shayna. It's not your fault, so stop thinkin' that it is," Ra'Keeyah pleaded.

Normally the shoe was on the other foot. Shayna would be the one doing all the schooling. But every now and then, even the teacher needed to be taught a lesson.

Shayna sat and tried to soak up everything Ra'Keeyah was saying to her. On one hand, she knew what she was saying was true. She had looked out for Quiana their entire lives and tried her best to keep her off the path of destruction. But on the other hand, she still felt that it was her fault, because even though they were only a couple months apart, Quiana always looked up to her not only as a cousin, but as a mother figure as well, and she felt she had let her down.

Ra'Keeyah was quiet as Shayna sat in deep thought. She hoped what she'd said was sinking in. The last thing she needed was for Shayna to walk around for the rest of her life feeling responsible for the bad choices Quiana had made. It was bad enough she'd went this long.

After a moment of silence, Ra'Keeyah's phone rang. She took it out of her pocket, looked at the caller ID, walked to the middle of the room, and answered it.

"Hello?"

"You okay?" Brick yelled over the loud music.

"I can't hear you," Ra'Keeyah yelled back.

"I said are you okay?" he repeated.

"Yeah, I'm cool," she answered.

"Is Shayna cool?"

"Yeah, she doin' better."

"What time you goin' home?" Brick asked.

"Shortly."

"Okay, I love you and see you when I get there."

"Love you too," Ra'Keeyah replied before hanging up. She walked back over and took a seat on the bed.

"You can go home if you want to. I know you have more important things to do than to sit here wit' me," Shayna sniffed.

"I'm cool. I don't have anything better to do than to sit here wit' my girl," Ra'Keeyah smiled.

"Thanks," Shayna said, giving Ra'Keeyah a hug.

"Don't thank me. That's what friends are for, remember?" she smiled, hitting Shayna with her own words.

"Okay." Shayna smiled for the first time that night. "You glowin'," Shayna said, looking at her.

"Brick has that affect on me," Ra'Keeyah teased.

"Either that, or yo' ass pregnant," Shayna laughed.

"Bitch, please, ain't no babies comin' up outta this here."

"You sure, 'cuz you sho' gettin' a little wide?"

"Don't you start that shit too," Ra'Keeyah laughed.

"You look good, girl," Shayna said.

"I know," Ra'Keeyah teased before sticking out her tongue.

The two girls talked until after 2:00 A.M. They laughed and reminisced about any and everything they could think of. Ra'Keeyah was glad her girl was feeling better. She made her promise to call the next morning so they could make plans to go out to lunch. Shayna was hesitant at first until Ra'Keeyah said she'd keep bugging her until she agreed, so she accepted.

"All right, girl, I'm bouta' go home. Now you sure you're all right?" Ra'Keeyah asked.

"Yeah, I'm cool. I'm bouta' take a shower, do something to my head, and take my ass to sleep."

"You *need* to take a shower," Ra'Keeyah joked.

"Whatever," Shayna laughed back.

"And stop worryin' about Quiana. She gon' be all right," Ra'Keeyah assured.

"Okay," Shayna responded, hopeful.

"I'll see you tomorrow, right?" Ra'Keeyah asked, standing up from the bed.

Shayna nodded her head yes. She stood up from the bed as well and walked Ra'Keeyah to the door. "I love you, girl," Shayna said hugging Ra'Keeyah as tight as she could.

"Dang, you hugged me like you ain't gon' see me no more," Ra'Keeyah joked.

"You silly," Shayna laughed.

"Love you too, girl," Ra'Keeyah said, opening up the door. She walked out into the hallway and pushed the DOWN button on the elevator. Shayna waved good-bye as the doors opened.

"Get a pregnancy test," Shayna yelled as Ra'Keeyah stepped on the elevator.

"Yeah, right," Ra'Keeyah laughed as the doors closed shut. "Folks better leave my hips and ass alone. Shit, I look good," she said to her reflection in the stainless steel elevator walls.

Shayna walked back into her room and looked around. She had made a huge mess and decided to clean it up. She'd been in the room for two days, and it looked like she'd been there for two weeks. After she got everything nice and tidy, she grabbed the complimentary notepad and pen from the drawer; then she sat down at the desk and began writing. After she finished, she went down to the front desk, asked for a stamped envelope, and filled it out. She put her note in the envelope, sealed it, and walked it outside to the mailbox that stood in front of the hotel. After accomplishing that, she went back to her room, where she showered, changed clothes, applied some makeup, and fixed her hair.

"Now I look like the old Shayna," she said, smiling at her reflection. Pleased with her makeover, Shayna reached into her purse, grabbed a bottle of pills, and opened them up. She was in pain and wanted it to go away. She poured half the pills in her hand before reaching over and grabbing her glass of St. Claire Green Tea Vodka that sat on the nightstand. She tossed the pills in her mouth and washed them down with her drink. Afterward, Shayna lay down in the bed and thought long and hard about her life, the good and the bad, before crying herself to sleep.

Chapter Thirty-seven

Ra'Keeyah pulled up in the driveway and got out. She hit the alarm to the truck before making her way up the walk. She yawned as she stuck her key in the lock. She was tired, and all she wanted to do was go straight to bed. Deep down she hoped Brick wasn't home so she could go straight to sleep without any interruptions. She opened the door and typed the code into the alarm before making her way upstairs. She walked into the bedroom and immediately knew something was wrong by the look on Brick's face.

"Hey, baby," she spoke, just in case it was her he was mad at.

Brick didn't speak back. Instead he mugged her like she was the scum of the earth.

"What's the matter wit' you?" Ra'Keeyah asked, trying to remember if she'd done anything wrong. Coming up blank, she started taking off her shoes.

"You might wanna leave them on," Brick said.

"What I do now?" Ra'Keeyah grimaced.

"Here. Somebody left this on the doorstep," he said throwing a nicely wrapped gift box at her.

Ra'Keeyah tried to catch the box, but it hit the floor, causing its contents to spill out. She bent down and picked up one of the pictures. Her heart jumped into her throat when she noticed it was a picture of her, Shayna, and Quiana stripping for Calvin and his friends on her birthday. Ra'Keeyah was speechless. She'd been caught.

That dirty bitch, Ra'Keeyah thought. She knew exactly who placed those pictures on Brick's doorstep. She planned on handling that at a later time. Right now, she had to try to save her relationship.

"Cat gotcha' tongue?" Brick asked.

"Brick, let me explain," Ra'Keeyah said, trying to come up with a quick lie, but her mind wasn't working fast enough.

"I'm waitin'," he frowned.

"I'm sorry," was all Ra'Keeyah could think to say, hoping that would be enough.

"You *sorry* is all you could come up wit'?" Brick asked.

"I don't know what else to tell you."

"Tell me why a mutha'fucka put a gift wrapped box of pictures of my girl strippin' for a bunch of white men on my front porch? That's what I want you to tell me," Brick snapped.

"Brick, I don't know why she would play me like that. Maybe 'cuz her life is fucked up, she want mines to be fucked up too," Ra'Keeyah said.

"She who?" Brick grimaced.

"Quiana." Her mind quickly flashed back to when Quiana had held Peighton's camera for her, and then *conveniently* forgot to give it back. She also remembered her mom mentioning she saw Quiana at Walgreens the day after the photos were taken. Ra'Keeyah couldn't prove it but she knew Quiana was behind these pictures popping up.

"Why would Quiana do some ill shit like that to you? I thought she was yo' girl?"

"We ain't never been girls. I just dealt wit' her on the strength of Shayna," Ra'Keeyah replied.

"I can't tell. Y'all mutha'fuckas all hugged up and shit in them pictures. Anyways, y'all relationship is irrelevant to me. Only thing I wanna know about is why my girl been hidin' the fact that she's a stripper?" Brick stated.

"Brick, I'm not now, nor have I ever been a stripper. I was a dancer," Ra'Keeyah said.

"Man, miss me wit' that shit!" Brick marched over and picked the pictures up off the floor. "Here you go givin' a mutha'fucka a lap dance, here go one of you shakin' yo' ass, here go one of some mutha'fuckas puttin' money in a G-string that I've never seen you in befo'e," Brick argued as he tossed the pictures at her like a Frisbee. "So if you ain't no stripper, what the fuck are you? A ho? They the same thing!"

"Hell, naw, I ain't no ho," Ra'Keeyah snapped, getting offended that Brick would think of her as such.

"I can't believe you been playin' me all this time. How long you been strippin', Ra'Keeyah?" Brick asked, outdone.

Ra'Keeyah was nervous as hell. She didn't want to lose Brick, not over this. She didn't know whether to tell the truth or make something up, but lying had gotten her nowhere in the past. So for the first time in a long time, Ra'Keeyah decided to woman up and lay all her cards out on the table; well, maybe not *all* but half the deck for the man she loved. She had high hopes of them getting past this and moving on with their lives.

"I've been doin' it since March or April. I'm not really sure," Ra'Keeyah answered truthfully.

"And how long have you known that I despise strippers?"

Ra'Keeyah rolled her eyes into the top of her head, wondering what Brick was getting at by asking all these irrelevant questions. "For a minute, I guess," she answered.

"Since the very first fuckin' time I brought you to my house is the correct answer," Brick barked, making Ra'Keeyah jump. "You didn't even take my feelin's into consideration."

"Yes, I did, Brick. That's why I stopped dancin'."

"What made you go out and do some nasty shit like that in the first place?" he asked, disgusted.

"I did it because I needed the money, that's why! My mom was over there strugglin', tryin'a take care of me and Jaylen, plus maintain the house. So I thought if I made my own money it would take some of the stress off of her." The thought of her mom working her fingers to the bones just to provide for her and Jaylen brought tears to her eyes.

"A fuckin' stripper, though? You coulda' done somethin' otha' than that," Brick shook his head in disbelief.

"Like what? Get a job at Burger King or McDonald's? I tried that already," she lied, hoping it would help her with the case she was trying to plead.

"Wow, Ra'Keeyah a fuckin' stripper, though?" he repeated. Every time he thought about his girl being a stripper, it brought back memories of the childhood he'd tried to forget.

" Look, Brick, I did it. I'm not proud of it. But I can't go back and change it. If I could I would."

"So when did you stop? Or should I ask *have* you stopped?"

"I haven't did it since my birthday," Ra'Keeyah lied again, being her birthday pictures was his only proof.

"Wow," Brick said, shaking his head.

"I don't know what else to say."

"Did you fuck any of these cats?" Brick asked, not knowing if he really wanted to know the answer to that question.

"No, Brick. I didn't fuck any of 'em. I danced for 'em, that's all," Ra'Keeyah replied quickly, hoping that would help him forgive her for deceiving him.

Brick was silent for a brief moment as if he was trying to collect his thoughts. The wait was killing Ra'Keeyah. She wished he would just hurry up and say what he needed to say and get it over with.

"The fucked up thing about the whole situation is, I asked you was you a stripper and you told me no. You lied to me," Brick finally said.

"I only lied to you 'cuz I liked you and wanted to be wit' you, and I know that woulda' never happened if I'd told you the truth. And you know it," Ra'Keeyah said honestly.

"You right, but you shoulda' let me make that decision on my own insteada' lettin' me find out by somebody leavin' a fuckin' present on my doorstep," he argued.

"Yeah, it was fucked up how you found out about it. I shoulda' been woman enough to tell you outta my own mouth. Again, I'm sorry."

Brick stared at Ra'Keeyah and couldn't believe the one girl he fell in love with turned out to be something he hated most. He took into consideration her reasoning behind shaking her ass for cash and wanted to wrap his arms around her and tell her he understood, but he couldn't. No reason was good enough back when his biological mother was doing it, and no reason was good enough now.

"So where do we go from here?" Ra'Keeyah finally had enough nerve to ask.

Brick closed his eyes and shook his head. "I don't know about you, but I'm about to go to bed. Before you leave, get all yo' shit, put my keys on the dresser, oh, and my ring, and lock up behind you."

Ra'Keeyah was stunned. She couldn't believe it was over between her and Brick—just like that. Just this morning they were the perfect couple. How did it take a turn for the worse so quickly?

"Where am I gon' go?"

"I don't know," Brick said while getting dressed for bed.

"Brick, I know I fucked up, but please don't leave me over something so dumb," Ra'Keeyah pleaded.

"Oh, I ain't leavin', *you* are," he said, as he climbed in his big, comfortable bed.

"Brick, I know I fucked up, and I'm sorry," she replied sincerely, as tears streamed down her face.

Brick turned his back toward Ra'Keeyah. It was eating him up to see her cry.

"Bye, Ra'Keeyah. I'm done talkin'. Get yo' shit and go on."

"I don't have nowhere to go," she said.

"Take some of the money you made strippin' and go get you a hotel room," he said harshly.

Ra'Keeyah realized there was no getting through to Brick. She changed into a pair of sweatpants, a thick sweatshirt, and threw on her Ugg boots, and began packing her things. She didn't know where she was going or how she was going to get there. She grabbed her duffle bag and only threw a couple items in it. She figured that Brick was mad right now, so she would leave for the night, and hopefully, they would talk things out in the morning.

Brick lay in the bed pretending to be asleep. He listened as Ra'Keeyah gathered her things. He wanted to get up, tell her to stop packing, and come to bed, but his pride wouldn't let him. He loved Ra'Keeyah with all his heart, but she'd hurt him, just like his mother had done. If he could cut all ties with the woman who gave birth to him, cutting ties with Ra'Keeyah would be a walk in the park . . . he hoped.

After Ra'Keeyah had finished packing her clothes, she grabbed her cell phone and her savings out of the shoe box and stuck it in the inside pocket of her duffle bag. Then she walked over and stood by the bed. She removed the house key and the truck key from her key ring and laid them on the nightstand before taking off the big rock and laying it next to the keys. Taking off the ring hurt more than anything. She then reached over and touched Brick's arm.

"I'm gone," she said.

Brick didn't respond. He continued to lay there and play possum.

Ra'Keeyah shook her head and headed downstairs. She put on her warm winter coat along with her hat and gloves and bundled up real good. Then she looked around the living room, threw her duffle bag on her shoulders, and walked out the door with no destination in mind, locking it behind her.

When Brick heard the front door close, it felt like his heart had just been ripped out of his chest. He rolled over and got out of bed. He looked down at the nightstand where his keys and the ring he'd bought for his future wife lay. He picked the ring up, walked over to his dresser, and put it back in the box it came in before climbing back into bed. He grabbed the pillow Ra'Keeyah slept on, put it up to his nose before hugging it tight, and for the first time in years, he cried.

The wind was tearing through Ra'Keeyah's coat as she maneuvered through the bitter predawn chilled air. It was after four in the morning, and she had nowhere to go. She couldn't go to her mother's house, not wanting to hear "I tried to tell you." She even thought about going to the hotel to crash in the room with

Shayna, but it was way too far to walk. So she decided to head to the only other place she would be welcomed at. Ra'Keeyah picked up her pace and headed over to Pauline's. Ra'Keeyah had been so upset that it never dawned on her to use her cell phone to call a taxi. She was relieved to have made it to Pauline's front door after a thirty-minute walk in the cold weather. Her nose was runny, her hands and feet were numb, and they felt like they might be frostbitten. As soon as she was about to ring the doorbell, Pauline opened the door.

"I've been waitin' on you," Pauline smiled and welcomed Ra'Keeyah in with open arms.

Chapter Thirty-eight

It was late in the afternoon when Ra'Keeyah finally woke up. She grabbed her cell phone off the nightstand and checked it for missed calls from Brick. When she saw there were none, she laid the phone back down and climbed out of bed. She looked around Pauline's guest bedroom and shook her head. Ra'Keeyah couldn't wait to call Shayna and tell her what had gone down between her and Brick and to see if she had any advice on how to get her man back. But first, she had to shower and get dressed. She grabbed her outfit out of her duffle bag and headed out into the hallway where she heard Pauline in the kitchen rattling pots and pans as she headed into the bathroom.

"Man, I feel a lot better," Ra'Keeyah said walking out of the bathroom fully dressed. Now she headed toward the kitchen, hoping Pauline had cooked something because she was starving.

"Good afternoon," Pauline smiled when Ra'Keeyah walked in.

"Good afternoon," Ra'Keeyah spoke back before taking a seat at the table.

"You missed breakfast. You want some lunch?" Pauline asked.

"Yes, please. I'm so hungry I feel sick in my stomach."

Pauline began preparing Ra'Keeyah a plate of leftovers from Christmas dinner before placing it in the microwave.

"Thanks for lettin' me stay here last night," Ra'Keeyah said.

"No problem. Brice called me and told me you'd probably come over here, being I don't live too far away from him," Pauline said, taking the plate out of the microwave and setting it down in front of Ra'Keeyah.

"This was the closest place. It was too cold to walk anywhere else," Ra'Keeyah admitted before sticking a piece of turkey in her mouth.

"Why didn't you just catch a cab?" Pauline asked.

"I don't know. I guess I wasn't thinkin' at the time. Usin' my phone was the last thing on my mind."

"Ra'Keeyah, I usually don't get in my son's business," Pauline started.

Those are the exact words mothers say right before they get into their kids' business, Ra'Keeyah thought.

"I know whatever y'all argued about last night really must of hurt him, 'cuz I could hear it in his voice when he called me. And whatever it is y'all goin' through, all I can do is hope and pray that y'all can work it out."

"He didn't tell you why he put me out in the middle of the night, in a blizzard?" Ra'Keeyah asked, finishing off her sweet potatoes.

"Nope, and I didn't ask. Only thing he told me was to watch out for you 'cuz you left walkin'. He was worried about you walkin' alone that time of mornin'."

I couldn't tell, or else he woulda' gave me a ride, Ra'Keeyah wanted to say.

"Whatever y'all's disagreement was about, I'm quite sure it's resolvable," she smiled.

"I don't think so, Miss Pauline. Brick was pretty mad."

"You know, Brice has had that same feisty attitude since he was a little boy. And once he calms down and thinks about what he did, he'll be ready to talk," Pauline smiled.

"I sure hope so. 'Cuz I really love your son, Miss Pauline," Ra'Keeyah said, finishing off her plate of food.

"I know you do, and he loves you too."

"Can I ask you a question, Miss Pauline?"

"Sure, go ahead."

"Why don't you ever call Brick by his nickname like everyone else?"

"Well, baby, because Brice's nickname represent somethin' I'm against now. I don't approve of what Brice does. But he's grown and I have no control over it. But I do have control over what name I call him. I've never called him Brick, and I never will. His momma named him Brice, and that's what I'm gon' call him," Pauline explained.

"I was just wonderin'," Ra'Keeyah smiled.

"No problem."

"No disrespect to your cookin', Miss Pauline, but I'm startin' to feel sick. I think I ate too fast," Ra'Keeyah said, grabbing her stomach.

"You did put a hurtin' on that plate," Pauline laughed.

"I did, didn't I?" Ra'Keeyah laughed too.

"Go on back in the room and lie down for a minute and see if that make you feel any better. I'll bring you a glass of soda water in there in a few," Pauline said.

"Okay." Ra'Keeyah got out from the table and walked out of the kitchen. She grabbed a candy cane off the tree on her way back to the guest room. She could remember her mother always sucking on peppermints for medicinal purposes. She walked into the room, checked her phone again, disappointed that she only had three missed calls all from her mother. She decided she would call her back later. Ra'Keeyah turned her ringer off and lay across the bed. Before long, she had drifted back off to sleep.

Ra'Keeyah woke up to the sound of people talking in the living room. She was excited to hear Brick's voice, hoping he had come to take her back home with him. But the other voices she couldn't make out. As crazy as it may seem, it sounded like her mother's voice. Ra'Keeyah quickly climbed out of the bed and tried to get herself together. She wanted to look presentable when Brick laid eyes on her.

"Ra'Keeyah, can you come in here for a minute?" Pauline called out, once she realized Ra'Keeyah was up and moving.

"Here I come," she replied before smoothing down her hair. She walked out of the room and down the hall. She was shocked to see Brick, her mother, and Joe all in the same room. The looks on their faces told her that something bad had happened.

"Yes, Miss Pauline?" Ra'Keeyah asked slowly while looking over at Brick for answers.

"Sweetie, I need you to sit down," Pauline said.

Ra'Keeyah took a seat on the sofa next to Brick. He scooted over and wrapped his arm around her shoulder.

"Can somebody tell me what's goin' on, please?" Ra'Keeyah asked nervously.

"Baby, they found Shayna's body this mornin' at the Holiday Inn," her mother said.

Ra'Keeyah knew that she was still a little groggy from her nap and all, but she could have sworn her mother just said that they found Shayna's *body* at the Holiday Inn. "Say that again," Ra'Keeyah asked.

"Shayna overdosed on drugs, Ra'Keeyah," Joe stepped in and said.

"Shayna don't do no damn drugs," Ra'Keeyah stood up and vouched for her girl.

"Baby, they found a bottle of prescription pills by the bed," her mother said.

"Prescription drugs? Shayna didn't take pills," Ra'Keeyah frowned.

"She was on nefazodone," Joe admitted.

"On what?" Ra'Keeyah asked.

"An antidepressant medication," he replied.

"Shayna ain't depressed. What hospital is she in? I wanna go see her so I can ask her what the fuck she takin' an antidepressant for!" Ra'Keeyah demanded.

"Baby, Shayna is gone," her mother said carefully.

"Gone? Gone where?" Ra'Keeyah asked, looking around the room at everybody. "I know you ain't talkin' about dead?"

Ra'Keeyah's mother slowly nodded her head yes.

"Yeah, right, y'all playin'," Ra'Keeyah said as tears filled her eyes.

"It's all on the news, li'l mama."

"Oh my God, noooooooo," Ra'Keeyah screamed.

Brick stood up, pulled Ra'Keeyah into his chest, and wrapped his arms around her. She cried like a newborn baby as the news of her best friend's death began to set in.

"Why?" she moaned.

Pauline, Joe, and Ra'Keeyah's mother all cried too as they watched Brick try to soothe Ra'Keeyah. Brick even shed a few tears as he tried to rock her pain away.

She quickly turned her anger toward Joe. "It's all yo' fuckin' fault that she was depressed," Ra'Keeyah yelled. "If it wasn't for you, she'd still be here."

Brick, Pauline, and Ra'Keeyah's mother grabbed her, trying to calm her down, but it was no use. Ra'Keeyah was madder than a raging bull. "Y'all get the fuck off of me!" Ra'Keeyah screamed, snatching away from everybody as she made her way out of the living room.

"Ra'Keeyah," her mother called out, but it was no use. She had disappeared into the bathroom.

"I'll go talk to her," Brick said, making his way out of the living room and down the hall.

"Yeah, go do that," Pauline suggested, wiping away her tears.

"Ra'Keeyah," Brick called out as he tapped lightly on the bathroom door. When she didn't answer, he opened up the door and walked in. She was sitting on the floor with her arms wrapped around the rim of the toilet. "You okay?"

She shook her head no before throwing up everything she had in her stomach, and then some.

Brick grabbed a washcloth out of the linen closet, wet it, and wiped her mouth.

"Come on," he said helping her off the floor and into the guest bedroom where she lay across the bed and continued crying. Brick didn't know the right words to say to ease her pain . . . if there were any. All he could do was lay behind her, wrap his arm around her waist, and let her mourn.

It had been two days since the death of her best friend, and Ra'Keeyah had yet to get out of bed, other than to use the bathroom. Brick tried getting her to eat something and even tried getting her out of the house, but she wouldn't budge. All she wanted to do was lie in the bed with the blinds closed and cry. She wasn't taking or returning anyone's phone calls; she just wanted to be left alone.

By day three, Pauline couldn't take it anymore. "Get up, Ra'Keeyah," Pauline barged into her guest bedroom with her cleaning bucket and demanded. She started opening up blinds to let sun shine in and even cracked the window to let some of the funk seep out.

"Where am I goin'?" Ra'Keeyah asked, still half-asleep.

"The first place you goin' is to the shower. Then I'm takin' you over to your mother's house 'cuz your little brother has been blowin' up your phone; he's worried about you," Pauline said.

"Jaylen," Ra'Keeyah smiled halfheartedly.

"Yes, Jaylen," Pauline replied, snatching blankets and pillows off the bed so they could be washed.

Ra'Keeyah eased out of bed and instantly got light-headed. She grabbed her head and sat back down on the bed.

"That's because you ain't ate in three days," Pauline said. "You go on and get in the shower, and I'll go fix you somethin' to eat."

"Do I have to?" Ra'Keeyah asked.

"Yes, you have to," Pauline said sternly.

"Okay," Ra'Keeyah said, standing up again. She grabbed the robe Brick had brought over with the rest of her clothes and headed to the bathroom.

As soon as Pauline heard the shower turn on, she stripped the sheets off Ra'Keeyah's bed, grabbed the Lysol out her cleaning bucket, and sprayed the bed down. She then put clean linens and blankets on the bed before going to fix Ra'Keeyah something to eat.

After showering and eating a decent meal, Ra'Keeyah felt a little better, even though the food she ate came right back up. Pauline dropped her off over at her mother's and told her to call her when she was ready to come back home.

Ra'Keeyah's mother came out to the car to thank Pauline for dropping Ra'Keeyah off. Ra'Keeyah waved good-bye to Pauline and headed into the house.

"It's no problem. Shit, she needed to get outta the house. She just wastin' away lyin' in that damn bed, and I know her tear ducts gotta be dry," Pauline said.

"I know. I wish there was somethin' I could do to make her feel better."

"There is," Pauline said.

"And what would that be, might I ask?"

"Pray for her. It sho' helped me when I lost my two boys," Pauline responded.

"I sure will and thanks again," Ra'Keeyah's mother smiled and closed the car door.

Ra'Keeyah played with Jaylen for a few minutes before walking upstairs to her old bedroom. It was still in the same condition she had left it in. She walked over to the closet to make sure her stash was still in place. Seeing that it was, she took a seat on the bed and smiled as she looked at the motorcycle pictures on the wall.

"You okay?" her mother stuck her head in the door and asked, before walking in and taking a seat in the bed.

"I don't know. Some days I think I am, and other days I don't know," Ra'Keeyah admitted.

Ra'Keeyah's mother placed her hand on top of Ra'Keeyah's. "You will be 'cuz God gon' see you through, and I'll be prayin' for you."

Ra'Keeyah looked at her mother like she was crazy. She had never really heard her mom mention God unless she was using His name in vain, let alone praying for someone. "Are you okay, Mom?"

"Yep. I'm just fine. I think we should find a church to join," her mother suggested.

"Okay, whatever you say," Ra'Keeyah replied sarcastically.

"Well, I'ma give you a minute to yourself. I'll be in my room if you need me," she said standing up.

"Thanks, Mom," Ra'Keeyah smiled.

"Anytime, baby," she smiled back before exiting the room.

Ra'Keeyah sat on her bed and just looked around the room as if she were in a foreign place. She glanced over at her dresser and noticed a letter sitting behind her bottle of Juicy Couture. She walked over and picked the letter up that was addressed to her.

Who would be writin' me, she thought as she tore open the envelope. When she read the first line of the letter her eyes instantly welled up with tears. "Jaylen," Ra'Keeyah called out.

A few seconds later, Jaylen ran into his sister's room. "Huh?" he answered.

"When did this letter come?" she questioned.

"Ummm, the other day. Mommy had to use the bathroom real bad so she told me to get the mail, and this one had your name on it so I brought it up here and put it on your dresser," he replied with a long, drawn out explanation.

"Okay, thanks," Ra'Keeyah replied.

"You welcome," he smiled and skipped out of his sister's room.

Ra'Keeyah sat back on the bed and continued reading her letter.

LisaRaye,

I know, I know, don't call you that 'cuz Lisa-Raye don't got nothin' on Ra'Keeyah Jaz'mire Jackson (smile). I just wanted to make you smile in your time of mourning. You are mourning over me, right? Anyways, first and foremost, I want to say sorry for puttin' you through this. I know we're supposed to get money together until we turn eighty years old, but, Ra'Keeyah, I couldn't go on livin' my life pretendin' I wasn't hurtin' on the inside. The hell I went through because of my mom and because I wasn't strong enough to say "no" even as I got older has always made me feel dirty inside. All the fancy clothes, shoppin' sprees, and dancin' for money could never erase my real feelin's, only put them at bay for a little while. But when I would come down off my high, I would feel even lower than I did.

No one ever looked at me and liked me for me except for you, and I loved you for that. Even when Quiana put me on blast, you didn't judge me; you embraced me. Every time I slept with a man for money, it was like relivin' my past over and over, and I could never get the feelin' of not bein' good enough out of my mind.

Remember when you tried to warn me about Malcolm? Well, I didn't listen and karma finally caught up to me. I could never bring myself to tell you he raped me, especially not after everything else you had learned about me. Malcolm rapin' me was the final straw for me, sis. There is a difference when you're young and made to do vile and disgustin' acts by the ones who are supposed to love and protect you. You don't fully realize this isn't right. Then when you get older, you choose to do these same acts for money because this is all you know and this is how you can feel in control. But then that false sense of control is taken away by someone, and what do you have left? Nothing.

Key-Key, I realized the way I treated and spoke to Quiana was wrong. I tried to separate myself from the reality that we both had been forced to live the same life. She needed me more than anyone, and in my heart I know I failed her, and when I failed her I failed myself as well. Key-Key, make it right with your mom. You were never cut from the same cloth as us, and I always wished

*I had the relationship you and your moms have.
You gon' need her now more than ever.*

*Ra'Keeyah, when you think of me please don't
be sad. I want you to smile and know that your
girl is finally at peace. So continue gettin' your
money the best way you know how and live yo'
life to the fullest. Don't let nobody keep you from
doin' that, not even Brick's sexy ass. Yeah, I called
him sexy. You can't do nothin' to me 'cuz I'm dead
. . . You supposed to be laughin'.*

*Oh, before I forget, I went by your mom's one
day to see how she was doin' after she put you
out. I told her I had to use the bathroom and I
stashed my life savings in your blue Members
Only jacket, the one I always hated. I woulda
left it at my mom's house, but they wouldn't do
nothin' but smoke it up. I left it to you 'cuz I know
you gon' put it to good use. Oh well, sis, I'm bouta'
rest in paradise. Just know I will always be wit'
you in spirit, and that I love you more than life
itself, obviously . . . (smile). And please do me a
favor. Get yo' ass a pregnancy test 'cuz yo' hips
are gettin' a little wide . . . (smile)*

Ra'Keeyah was bawling as she folded up the letter,
placing it back into the envelope. She wasn't only crying because her best friend was gone, but also because
she was pain and worry free. Ra'Keeyah wiped her
tears away, stood up from the bed, and walked over to
the dresser, placing the letter in her top drawer. Then
she went over to the closet, dug way in the back, and
grabbed her Member's Only jacket and checked the
pockets, pulling out two stacks of money. Ra'Keeyah
hurried over to her bed and began counting it. She was
beyond ecstatic to find Shayna had left her over thirty-
eight thousand dollars.

"Where the fuck she get this kinda' money from?" Ra'Keeyah shook her head and smiled. "That damn girl." She peeled off ten stacks and walked across the hall to her mother's room. She would have given her more if it wasn't for the fact that she'd put her out. With the money she had at Pauline's, and the stash she had in the closet on top of the money Shayna had left her, Ra'Keeyah would be financially set for a while. She tapped lightly on her mother's bedroom door.

"Come in," her mother called out.

Ra'Keeyah walked into her mother's room and smiled.

"What you smilin' for?" her mother asked.

"At Shayna," she replied.

Her mother looked at her like her daughter had lost her mind.

"You wouldn't understand," Ra'Keeyah said, walking over to her mother's bed and laying the money down in front of her.

Her mother sat up and picked up the money. "Where did you get all this money from?" she asked, shocked.

"Don't ask no questions. Just go out and buy yourself somethin' nice before you pay any bills," Ra'Keeyah replied.

"I do need a new purse. I seen this purse at Macy's that I wanted but couldn't afford," her mother said, excited.

"Well, you got enough money to buy a thousand purses. Enjoy yourself, Mommy, life is too short not to." With that being said, Ra'Keeyah turned and walked away. She stopped in the doorway and turned back around. "Mom, I love you, and I'm sorry for all that I put you through. I spent all my life blamin' you for my shortcomings and my have-nots, but actually, I had everything a girl could ask for. I had a mother's love, and that's more important than anything you can buy at the mall," Ra'Keeyah said sincerely.

Ra'Keeyah's mother was touched by the words her daughter had just expressed to her. Tears rolled down her cheeks as she climbed out of bed. She walked over to her daughter and wrapped her arms around her and hugged her for what seemed like eternity.

"I love you too," her mother said, as the tears steadily flowed.

"Can you drop me back off over at Pauline's, please? The majority of my dress clothes are over there, and I need to get my outfit ready for Shayna's funeral tomorrow."

"I sure will," her mother said, wiping away the remainder of her tears.

Ra'Keeyah walked back across the hall and into her bedroom. She stuck her money back into its hiding place before heading downstairs.

"Can you come back and play the game wit' me tomorrow?" Jaylen asked his big sister as they made their way to the car.

"I would love to come over here and beat you at the game," Ra'Keeyah smiled.

"I'm good, so you betta' get some practice," Jaylen laughed.

"Whatever," Ra'Keeyah laughed too, waving her brother off as they got in the car.

That day Ra'Keeyah discovered that even in death, Shayna still had a huge impact on her life and was forever grateful to have had her as a best friend. Ra'Keeyah knew that eventually she would make new friends, but no one could ever take the place of her girl Shayna.

Chapter Thirty-nine

Ra'Keeyah woke up with a dry mouth and feeling sick to her stomach. She thought about the last line in Shayna's letter as she headed to the bathroom to shower. For shits and giggles, she decided after the funeral she would go get a pregnancy test for Shayna's sake. Ra'Keeyah got dressed in an all-black tweed pantsuit with silver buttons going down the front. She accessorized with a couple of silver pieces, not wanting to overdo it. She slicked her growing hair back into a neat ponytail before going into the living room to wait for Brick's arrival.

Brick walked through Pauline's door dressed like a million bucks and smelling good enough to eat. He sported a charcoal gray, Sean Jean, double-breasted suit with a light gray shirt. He wore a pair of charcoal and light gray ostrich dress shoes with an ostrich belt to match.

The entire time Ra'Keeyah had been messing around with Brick she'd never seen him look this good before. She'd actually never seen him dressed up. His presence had her turned on.

"You ready?" he asked.

"Yep."

Even though Brick and Ra'Keeyah weren't together, she was glad he'd offered to go to the funeral with her for moral support.

"You look nice," Brick said, as they headed to the Explorer.

"Thank you," Ra'Keeyah replied before opening the truck door and climbing in.

Brick and Ra'Keeyah played it safe with small talk on the way to the funeral home, not wanting to strike up an argument. They tried to be cordial when they were in each other's presence, but Brick was still mad at Ra'Keeyah for lying to him, and she really didn't have much to say to him either since he had the audacity to put her out in the middle of the night. So to avoid conflict, they tried to stay out of each other's way.

Brick pulled in the crowded funeral home lot and found a parking space. He could tell Ra'Keeyah was nervous by the way she kept pulling on her suit jacket.

"You okay?" he looked over and asked.

"Yeah, I guess," she replied before opening the door and getting out.

The two of them walked into the funeral home. Brick hated funerals almost as much as he did strippers. He took a seat next to Ra'Keeyah's mother while Ra'Keeyah walked up to the casket to see her best friend one last time. Ra'Keeyah laid her hand on top of Shayna's and smiled, knowing she'd be pleased with the way she looked. Before Ra'Keeyah left Shayna's side, she leaned in close. "I'm goin' to get that pregnancy test when I leave here," she whispered in Shayna's ear. Ra'Keeyah kissed Shayna on the forehead before making her way to her seat.

Ra'Keeyah maintained her composure during the funeral better than she thought she would have. She shed a few tears, but not many, only because she knew Shayna was in a better place. Ra'Keeyah watched as Shayna's mother put on an award-winning performance. She was hootin' and hollerin' all over the casket, knowing she didn't give a damn about her daughter for real. Ra'Keeyah was waiting on someone to walk over to her and hand her an Oscar. Brick held Ra'Keeyah's hand through the entire funeral which gave her a feeling of comfort.

After leaving the cemetery, everyone met back at the funeral home for the repast. Brick found himself a seat while Ra'Keeyah walked around and mingled with some of Shayna's family. He watched as Quiana walked toward Ra'Keeyah and Shayna's mom. He didn't want any fights breaking out so he hurried over to Ra'Keeyah.

"Hey, Auntie," Quiana said as she walked in between Ra'Keeyah and Shayna's mom. She looked over at Ra'Keeyah and smirked.

Ra'Keeyah knew this wasn't the time or the place to go off about the foul shit Quiana had done to her and Shayna, but her blood was boiling. She couldn't contain herself. Just when she was about to blow her top, Brick walked up behind her and wrapped his arms around her tense body.

"You okay, li'l mama?" he asked, before kissing her on the cheek. Brick didn't like how Quiana had played her hand, so he didn't want to give her the satisfaction of thinking she came in between his relationship with Ra'Keeyah.

"Yeah, I'm good, baby," Ra'Keeyah responded with a smile, catching on to what Brick was doing.

"I found us some seats over there next to your mother," he said, grabbing her hand.

"Okay. I'll check on you later," Ra'Keeyah said to Shayna's mother, knowing after today she'd never speak to her again.

"See you ladies later," Brick replied with a smile before walking away with Ra'Keeyah.

"Ol' bitch," Quiana mumbled as Ra'Keeyah walked away.

Ra'Keeyah stopped and tried to turn around, but Brick's grip tightened on her hand as he pulled her away.

"You heard her call me a bitch, and you gon' pull me away?" Ra'Keeyah stated angrily.

"Ra'Keeyah, this is not the time or the place to be gettin' in no altercations. You'll see her on the streets," he explained.

Ra'Keeyah knew Brick was right. This wasn't the time or the place.

"I'm ready to go," Ra'Keeyah huffed.

"Are you sure?"

"Hell, yeah. I can't be around these fake-ass folks any longer." Ra'Keeyah frowned as she looked around the room at all the people who had turned their backs on her girl when she needed them the most, and it literally made her want to vomit.

"Let's go then."

Ra'Keeyah put Shayna's obituary in her purse before walking over and giving her mother a hug. "I'll be over later on to play the game wit' Jay-Jay," she said.

"Y'all leavin' already?" her mother asked.

"Yeah, Mom, I gotta go," Ra'Keeyah said, feeling disgusted.

"What's the matter?"

"We'll talk later," Ra'Keeyah replied, wanting to get away from there as fast as she could. She and Brick exited the funeral home.

"Can you run me by the drugstore?" Ra'Keeyah asked Brick.

"Yeah, I can. What you gettin'?"

"I need to pick up a few things," she replied before getting in the truck.

"A'iiight," Brick replied as they pulled out of the funeral home parking lot.

As soon as Brick pulled up at the drugstore Ra'Keeyah quickly hopped out. "I'll be right back," she said, closing the door behind her.

"I'll be right here," Brick said, but she had already walked away.

Ra'Keeyah walked into the drugstore and asked the clerk behind the counter what aisle they kept the pregnancy tests in.

"Aisle twelve," the clerk replied.

Ra'Keeyah hurried down aisle twelve and grabbed a test kit. On her way back up to the counter she grabbed a big pack of toilet paper and paper towels for Pauline. Really, she wanted to hide the pregnancy test in between the two. She paid for her stuff and hurried back out to the truck.

"That was quick," Brick said upon Ra'Keeyah's return.

"How long you think it take to get some toilet paper and paper towels?" she asked smartly.

"Normally, for a woman, at least three to four hours," he smirked.

"Whatever," Ra'Keeyah laughed as Brick pulled off.

Later that evening Ra'Keeyah was in the room packing her overnight bag. She'd made plans to spend the night with Jaylen so they could play the game like she'd promised. Ra'Keeyah wrapped her pregnancy test in one of her T-shirts before placing it in the bottom of her bag.

"Where you goin'?" Brick walked in the room and asked, startling Ra'Keeyah.

"My, aren't we nosy?" she joked.

"I was just wonderin'."

"Naw, I'm just playin'. I'm goin' over to my mom's to spend the night wit' Jaylen."

"*That's* what's up! Did my mom happen to tell you what time she gettin' off work?" Brick asked.

"No, why?" Ra'Keeyah asked as she continued packing.

"I just need to talk to her, that's all."

Ra'Keeyah could sense the urgency in Brick's voice.

"You okay? You can talk to me, that is, unless you still hate me," Ra'Keeyah said sincerely.

"I don't hate you, li'l mama. I was just hurt and mad, that's all," he admitted.

"That's good to know," Ra'Keeyah smiled.

There was an awkward silence in the room as Ra'Keeyah zipped up her duffle bag.

"Peggy called me last night," Brick said out of nowhere.

"Who?" Ra'Keeyah asked, not knowing who he was talking about.

"Peggy, my real mom," he answered.

"Oh, she did?" Ra'Keeyah asked, surprised.

"Yeah, man. She said she ran into Piper a couple months ago at the mall and tried callin' me a few times from her phone, but I didn't answer. I remember seeing Piper's name on my phone the same night of Joelle's dice game, but I never called her back," Brick said.

Ra'Keeyah remembered the exact night, but could have sworn Brick had called Piper back once he'd gotten in the car.

"I didn't even know who she was at first. I started to hang up when I realized who she was, but somethin' told me to just hear what she had to say."

"What she say?" Ra'Keeyah asked carefully.

"She got cancer and the doctors gave her two months to live," Brick replied as tears formed in his eyes. "She just called me to tell me she love me and she's sorry for everything she took me through." Brick couldn't help himself; he broke down.

Ra'Keeyah walked over and wrapped her arms around Brick. She became his strength in his time of need.

"Oh, wow, I can't believe I'm cryin' like this," Brick chuckled lightly as he wiped his face.

"It's okay to cry sometimes," Ra'Keeyah assured him. "Everybody reaches their breakin' point at least once in their life."

"I fucked up, Ra'Keeyah. I let all this time pass by without tryin' to fix things wit' my mutha, and now it's too late. I spent all them years mad at her, and for what? 'Cuz I was too stubborn to realize everything she'd done, she done it for me. But I pushed her away, right in the arms of a crack pipe."

"It's never too late to repair a broken relationship, Brick. What's wrong wit' startin' over now?"

"She only got two months to live, if that," he replied, shaking his head.

"It don't matter if she got two hours to live. You make those the best two hours of y'all's life together. Brick, I know what it feels like to lose a parent. I would give anything to be able to see my daddy again. Your mom is still here. Take advantage of that," Ra'Keeyah said.

Brick was touched by Ra'Keeyah's words. "Wow, li'l mama, you kinda' deep. I see why I fell in love wit' you," he smiled.

"I learned from the best," she responded, referring to Shayna.

"I'm bouta' go call Peggy and tell her I'll be up to see her and my little brother this weekend," Brick said, feeling like a weight had just been lifted off his chest.

"You got a brother?" she asked.

"Yeah, his name is André. He's ten years old," Brick said proudly.

"Well, when he comes down to visit, you can always take him over to Mom's house and let him and Jaylen play together," Ra'Keeyah suggested.

"True dat," Brick replied.

"When you get time, can you drop me off over my mom's house?" Ra'Keeyah asked.

"Yeah, I will. I been yo' personal taxi all day. I'm bouta' start chargin'," Brick joked as he grabbed Ra'Keeyah's overnight bag and carried it to the car for her.

"I will pay you . . . no attention," she laughed too while she waited for Brick to unlock the truck doors.

"You can't help but pay all dis' some attention," Brick laughed while flexing his pecs.

"Whatever, nigga," Ra'Keeyah laughed, getting in.

Brick talked the entire ride. He told Ra'Keeyah about all the things he planned to do for Peggy and André when he got to New York. He needed to make up for lost time. The first thing he wanted to do was take his little brother shopping and buy him all the latest gear with shoes to match, so he could be just like his big brother. He planned on sending Peggy and some of her friends on an all-expense paid trip to a day spa to be pampered. Brick planned on doing a lot in so little time, but left up to him, he'd get it all accomplished. He went on and on about his plans until he pulled up in front of Ra'Keeyah's mother's house.

"Thank you," Ra'Keeyah said.

"No, thank you, li'l mama," Brick smiled gratefully.

"You been there for me so many times, Brick, it was such an honor to return the favor," Ra'Keeyah replied sincerely. She opened the truck door and got out.

"Ra'Keeyah," Brick called out.

"Huh?"

"Do you remember when you said that it's never too late to fix a broken relationship?"

"Yeah, I remember sayin' it," she said wanting to smile, already knowing where this was headed.

"Well, is it too late to fix ours?"

"Are you askin' me to be yo' girl again?" Ra'Keeyah toyed.

"Yea, I'm askin' you," Brick laughed.

"I don't know. I can't say yes right now, but I'm definitely not sayin' no," she stressed.

"Well, can you gimme yo' answer over a nice romantic dinner?"

"No, but I can give you my answer over a nice diamond tennis bracelet," she beamed.

"You drive a hard bargain, but I got chu'," he winked.

"Well, then, I got chu' too," she winked back before grabbing her overnight bag out of the backseat and heading up the walk.

Brick shook his head and smiled. "Damn, I love that girl," he said pulling off.

Ra'Keeyah carried her overnight bag up to her room and set it on the bed before removing Shayna's obituary from her purse. She smiled at the picture and hung it up on her mirror before walking over to the bed and taking a seat. Soon, Ra'Keeyah lay back and stared up at the ceiling. The thought of her and Brick getting back together was the best feeling ever.

"I thought we was gon' play the game," Jaylen barged in and said.

Ra'Keeyah sat up and smiled. "We are. Gimme a minute, okay?"

"Okay," Jaylen said before running back downstairs to set the game up.

"We orderin' pizza for dinner. You hungry?" Ra'Keeyah's mother stuck her head in the door and asked.

"I'm starvin'!"

"I'm goin' downstairs to make a salad to go wit' the pizza. Do you need anything?" her mother asked.

"No. Just tell Jaylen I'm bouta' change into my pj's, and then I'll be down there to whoop his tail on the game," Ra'Keeyah smiled.

"Okay," her mother responded before disappearing down the stairs.

Ra'Keeyah unzipped her overnight bag, grabbed a pair of lounging pants, and put them on. She reached back in the bag and pulled out a T-shirt, and as she did that, the pregnancy test fell out on the bed. She picked it up and looked at Shayna's obituary. "I'm about to take this for yo' ass so you can shut up," she smiled. She quickly read the directions which said she could use it any time of the day.

She removed the test from the box and hurried across the hall into the bathroom. She peed on the stick, flushed the toilet, and anxiously waited on the results. She hadn't had her period yet this month, but she was blaming it all on stress. She hadn't been having any symptoms, like cravings and morning sickness other than the few times she waited too long to eat. Ra'Keeyah was just taking this test to appease her best friend's assumptions, not because she thought there might be a possibility that she could be pregnant. Ra'Keeyah watched as one line appeared, and then another quickly followed. Not sure what that meant, she picked up the instructions to see.

"God, this can't be right," Ra'Keeyah said nervously as she read and reread the directions over and over. It took her a minute, but Ra'Keeyah finally accepted the fact the results of the test were positive. *What am I gon' do? How am I gon' tell my mom? What is she gon' think of me? Is she gon' say I told you so? Is she gon' be disappointed in me? What is Brick gon' say, 'cuz he don't want no kids?* Ra'Keeyah panicked as all these thoughts ran through her mind while pacing back and forth in the bathroom.

She walked back across the hall to her bedroom and went over to Shayna's obituary. "Damn, girl, you told me I was pregnant. How did you know?" she asked as if Shayna were going to answer her back. Tears filled Ra'Keeyah's eyes as she continued holding a conversation with her girl's picture. "I'm so scared I don't know what to do. Why did you have to die? I need you so much right now," Ra'Keeyah cried. "I guess this is what you meant in your letter 'I'm gon' need my mom now more than ever.' I need to go tell her." Ra'Keeyah turned and headed toward the door, but stopped and turned back around. "Thanks," she said wiping her tears away, before heading downstairs to tell her mother the news.

Ra'Keeyah knew telling her mother was the right thing to do; she just hoped everything worked out in her favor. She walked into the kitchen where her mother stood cutting up tomatoes for the salad. Ra'Keeyah was apprehensive to tell her mother about the pregnancy while she held a sharp knife. But she took her chances and decided to tell her anyway.

"Mom," Ra'Keeyah said.

"Yeah, baby?" she replied while tossing the tomatoes into the salad bowl.

"Can I talk to you for a minute?"

"Sure, what about?" her mother asked, wiping her hands on her apron.

Ra'Keeyah sat down at the kitchen table and just broke down crying. Her mother walked over and wrapped her arms around her daughter. "You pregnant, ain't you?" she asked, hoping the answer would be no, but her mother's intuition told her otherwise.

"Yes," she bawled.

"My goodness, Ra'Keeyah, I tried to tell you to make that nigga wear protection," her mother said, hurt.

"I know, Mommy. I'm sorry, I'm so sorry," Ra'Keeyah cried in her mother's arms.

"What's wrong wit' Key-Key?" Jaylen ran in the kitchen and asked, concerned.

"Go on back in the livin' room and play yo' game. Yo' sister will be all right," their mother yelled.

Jaylen hesitated a brief second, trying to make sure his sister was okay.

"I said go on now," their mother yelled.

Jaylen scurried out of the kitchen and back to his game.

"How many months?" her mother asked.

"I don't know. I just found out a few minutes ago," Ra'Keeyah said, wiping her tears away, only to have more follow.

Her mother had to sit down after news like that. She wanted to tell her daughter, "I told you so," but didn't want to push her further away than she already had. "Okay, let's see," her mother said, trying to get her thoughts together. "So Brick or Pauline don't know anything about this then?"

Ra'Keeyah shook her head no.

"So what you gon' do, baby?"

"I don't know. Have an abortion, I guess," Ra'Keeyah said slowly.

"The hell you are! I didn't have no abortion wit' you, and I ain't lettin' you have one either. I was seventeen when I got pregnant too, and I'ma tell you like yo' grandma told me, may God rest her soul, 'If you fuck for 'em, you gon' fend for 'em.' You not takin' the easy way out, so get prepared for motherhood," her mother snapped.

"But Brick don't want no kids, Mommy," Ra'Keeyah said.

"Brick tellin' a damn lie. If he didn't want no kids, then he woulda' never went up in you without protection, knowin' there could be a strong chance of you gettin' pregnant. So I don't wanna hear that 'Brick don't want no kids' shit. Brick gon' take care of this one, or he gon' hafta answer to me," her mother fussed.

Ra'Keeyah had never heard her mom talk like this before, so it was kind of funny. She didn't know if she was angry or just trying to get her point across.

"The first thing we gon' do is make you a doctor's appointment Monday mornin'. I'm gon' take you over to Pauline's to get yo' stuff 'cuz I want you here wit' me, at least until after you have the baby. You gon' get signed back up for school so you can get your education. I refuse to let you turn out like me; I want you to be better so you can get you a good job and not have to struggle to raise your child if the baby's daddy decides to turn his back on you."

Ra'Keeyah didn't see Brick as being the type of man that would turn his back on his child, but you never know. Movie stars and athletes are always in the news for not supporting their children.

"Let's get one last thing straight. I will keep the baby for you when you need to do somethin' important like go to school or work or when I want to. Don't think just 'cuz y'all live here that you got a built-in babysitter," her mother said.

"I got chu', Ma," Ra'Keeyah smiled. "So does this mean you're not mad at me for gettin' pregnant?"

"Mad, no, a little disappointed, yes, but I'll get over it," her mother smiled.

"I love you, Grandma," Ra'Keeyah laughed, wrapping her arms around her mother and giving her a hug.

"Girl, I'm too young and too fine to be a grandma. The baby gon' hafta' call me nanny or somethin' like that," her mother laughed too, hugging her back.

Ra'Keeyah was relieved to know that her mother had her back and was going to be there for her at all costs. The hardest part was over; now, the only challenge she had left to face was Brick. No matter what the outcome of telling him the news about the baby would be, she knew she had the right person in her corner. Watching her mother struggle and work her fingers to the bone in order to care for her and Jaylen all by herself gave Ra'Keeyah a new perspective of strong, single, independent women everywhere. So she figured as long as she had her mother standing by her, nothing else really mattered.

Chapter Forty

Almost one year later . . .

"Do you got everything in the diaper bag?" Brick looked over at Ra'Keeyah and asked as he grabbed Brice Jr. out of his crib, kissing him on his chubby cheek.

"Yeah, I got everything. Why wouldn't I?" she asked as she scrambled around the bedroom looking for her psychology book.

"You remember last time you forgot the diapers?" Brick reminded.

"Shut up, nigga. You ain't gon' never let me live that down, are you?" Ra'Keeyah laughed.

"Why would I?" he laughed too.

"Have you seen my psych book?"

"Last place I seen you wit' it was in the kitchen studyin' and breast-feedin' BJ."

"Oh yeah, that's right." She whizzed by Brick, but not before stopping to kiss BJ on the cheek.

"Tell Mommy to get off you," Brick said to his son in a funny voice.

Ra'Keeyah shot down the stairs to the kitchen and grabbed her psych book off the table. "André, turn that game off and finish gettin' ready for school," she yelled into the living room before heading back up to the bedroom.

"Okay, so what all you gotta do today?" Ra'Keeyah asked as she stuffed her books into her book bag.

"Well, after I drop BJ off at your mom's, I gotta meet the contractor over at Momma's otha' restaurant and talk to him about a few things. Then I have to go by the house to see if they got the hardwood floors down in the kitchen yet," Brick said.

"When is the house gon' be ready?" Ra'Keeyah asked anxiously.

"Hopefully before the snow hits the ground. I would like to celebrate Christmas with our families in our new house," Brick said, laying the baby back down in his crib.

"That would be excitin' to have everybody at *our* house for Christmas," Ra'Keeyah said, stressing *our*. Even though Ra'Keeyah had only given Brick twenty thousand toward the purchase of a two-hundred-thousand-dollar home, she still considered it half hers since her name would be on the lease too, making it almost impossible for her to be put out a third time.

"You ain't gon' neva' let me live that down, are you?"

"Why would I?" Ra'Keeyah laughed.

"Too bad Peggy can't be wit' us for the holidays," Brick said, sounding down.

"She'll be there wit' us in spirit and in our hearts," Ra'Keeyah replied.

"You gon' make a great psychologist. You gon' be able to save a lot of our young, troubled youths 'cuz you know just the right words to say," Brick complimented.

"Thank you," Ra'Keeyah said, before planting a kiss on her man's lips.

"Oh, don't forget, you gotta be at the Men's Wearhouse by three," Ra'Keeyah said, pulling her hair back into a ponytail.

"Damn, I forgot about that."

"You betta' be there 'cuz Bob T ain't gon' have no understandin' if his best man don't show up to get fitted for his tux," Ra'Keeyah said, slipping on her shoes.

"Now you know we next, right?" Brick smiled.

"You think you can handle bein' married to Ra'Keeyah Jaz'mire Jackson?" she asked, playfully.

"It'll be a piece of cake," Brick laughed.

"I'm happy for my girl, Peighton. Speakin' of which, I picked up some clothes for Bianca the other day. My goddaughter is gettin' so big," Ra'Keeyah smiled.

"Just like her daddy," Brick laughed.

"You know you ain't right," Ra'Keeyah laughed too.

"The newspaper's here," André said, running into the room and handing it to Ra'Keeyah.

"You eat breakfast?" Brick asked.

"Yes," he replied before hurrying back down to finish his game.

"It don't never have shit in it anyways. I don't know why you don't cancel the subscription," Ra'Keeyah complained.

"You signed up for it," Brick said before walking over to put BJ's coat on.

"Let me see what's goin' on in the world today," Ra'Keeyah said while unrolling the newspaper.

WOMAN FOUND BEATEN TO DEATH was plastered on the front page. Ra'Keeyah was curious to see if she knew who the person was found dead behind the same hotel that she, Shayna, and Quiana had made all their money at.

"Oh my goodness!" Ra'Keeyah gasped as she began reading the article.

"What's the matter, li'l mama?" Brick asked concerned.

Malcolm Benton was apprehended and charged with the murder of eighteen-year-old Quiana Monay Parker. She was found beaten to death behind the Holiday Inn. Witnesses report seeing Mr. Benton continuously beat his victim with a blunt object while yelling, "You gave me that shit!" According to police reports, Miss Parker was wanted on charges of having sex with at least a dozen men and not disclosing the fact that she was HIV positive. If convicted, she would have been facing life in prison. When initially brought in for questioning, Detective Horsley asked Mr. Benton the reason behind the vicious beating/murder of his victim. Without showing remorse, he simply stated:

"Everybody ain't to be tricked!"

ORDER FORM
URBAN BOOKS, LLC
78 E. Industry Ct
Deer Park, NY 11729

Name: (please print):_____

Address: _____

City/State: _____

Zip: _____

QTY	TITLES	PRICE
	16 On The Block	$14.95
	A Girl From Flint	$14.95
	A Pimp's Life	$14.95
	Baltimore Chronicles	$14.95
	Baltimore Chronicles 2	$14.95
	Betrayal	$14.95
	Black Diamond	$14.95
	Black Diamond 2	$14.95
	Black Friday	$14.95
	Both Sides Of The Fence	$14.95
	Both Sides Of The Fence 2	$14.95
	California Connection	$14.95

Shipping and handling-add $3.50 for 1st book, then $1.75 for each additional book.

Please send a check payable to:

Urban Books, LLC

Please allow 4-6 weeks for delivery

ORDER FORM
URBAN BOOKS, LLC
78 E. Industry Ct
Deer Park, NY 11729

Name: (please print): _____

Address: _____

City/State: _____

Zip: _____

QTY	TITLES	PRICE
	California Connection 2	$14.95
	Cheesecake And Teardrops	$14.95
	Congratulations	$14.95
	Crazy In Love	$14.95
	Cyber Case	$14.95
	Denim Diaries	$14.95
	Diary Of A Mad First Lady	$14.95
	Diary Of A Stalker	$14.95
	Diary Of A Street Diva	$14.95
	Diary Of A Young Girl	$14.95
	Dirty Money	$14.95
	Dirty To The Grave	$14.95

Shipping and handling-add $3.50 for 1st book, then $1.75 for each additional book.
Please send a check payable to:
Urban Books, LLC
Please allow 4-6 weeks for delivery

ORDER FORM
URBAN BOOKS, LLC
78 E. Industry Ct
Deer Park, NY 11729

Name: (please print):_____

Address: _____

City/State: _____

Zip: _____

QTY	TITLES	PRICE
	Gunz And Roses	$14.95
	Happily Ever Now	$14.95
	Hell Has No Fury	$14.95
	Hush	$14.95
	If It Isn't love	$14.95
	Kiss Kiss Bang Bang	$14.95
	Last Breath	$14.95
	Little Black Girl Lost	$14.95
	Little Black Girl Lost 2	$14.95
	Little Black Girl Lost 3	$14.95
	Little Black Girl Lost 4	$14.95
	Little Black Girl Lost 5	$14.95

Shipping and handling-add $3.50 for 1st book, then $1.75 for each additional book.
Please send a check payable to:
Urban Books, LLC
Please allow 4-6 weeks for delivery

ORDER FORM
URBAN BOOKS, LLC
78 E. Industry Ct
Deer Park, NY 11729

Name:(please print):_____

Address: _____

City/State: _____

Zip: _____

QTY	TITLES	PRICE
	Loving Dasia	$14.95
	Material Girl	$14.95
	Moth To A Flame	$14.95
	Mr. High Maintenance	$14.95
	My Little Secret	$14.95
	Naughty	$14.95
	Naughty 2	$14.95
	Naughty 3	$14.95
	Queen Bee	$14.95
	Say It Ain't So	$14.95
	Snapped	$14.95
	Snow White	$14.95

Shipping and handling-add $3.50 for 1st book, then $1.75 for each additional book.

Please send a check payable to:

Urban Books, LLC

Please allow 4-6 weeks for delivery